Prince of the Blood

Also by Raymond E. Feist

MAGICIAN
SILVERTHORN
A DARKNESS AT SETHANON
FAERIE TALE

Raymond E. Feist
PRINCE OF THE BLOOD

A FOUNDATION BOOK

Doubleday

NEW YORK   LONDON   TORONTO   SYDNEY   AUCKLAND

A FOUNDATION BOOK
PUBLISHED BY DOUBLEDAY
a division of Bantam Doubleday Dell Publishing Group, Inc.
666 Fifth Avenue, New York, New York 10103

FOUNDATION, DOUBLEDAY, and the portrayal of the letter F
are trademarks of Doubleday, a division of Bantam Doubleday
Dell Publishing Group, Inc.

*All of the characters in this book are fictitious,
and any resemblance to actual persons, living or dead
is purely coincidental.*

MAP BY JACKIE AHER
BOOK DESIGN BY BEVERLEY GALLEGOS

Library of Congress Cataloging-in-Publication Data applied for
ISBN 0-385-23624-7
Copyright © 1989 by Raymond E. Feist
ALL RIGHTS RESERVED
PRINTED IN THE UNITED STATES OF AMERICA
AUGUST 1989
FIRST EDITION
BG

This book is dedicated with love to my wife,

Kathlyn Starbuck,

who makes everything make sense

ACKNOWLEDGMENTS

As is usual, I am deeply indebted to the talents of other people in finishing a project like *Prince of the Blood*. So, I would like to publicly thank the following people:

April Abrams, for giving me what she had of Kesh and letting me bend it beyond recognizable shape.

Pat LoBrutto, my editor, for putting up with one type of madness after another.

Janny Wurts, for letting me take care of one problem before giving me another, and for taking such good care of our horse.

Stephen Abrams and Jon Everson, for thinking up the entire mess in the first place.

The other "fathers and mothers" of Midkemia, for letting me play in their world again.

Peter Schneider, for his "usual" duty above and beyond.

All the fine people at Bantam Doubleday Dell who work so hard at making things work.

Jonathan Matson, my agent and friend, for keeping me pointed north when I need to be and for letting me run amok when I need to.

And, most of all, Kathy, my wife, who is mentioned somewhere else in this work for making everything around me work.

Without the goodwill and loving care of the above people, none of this would be possible.

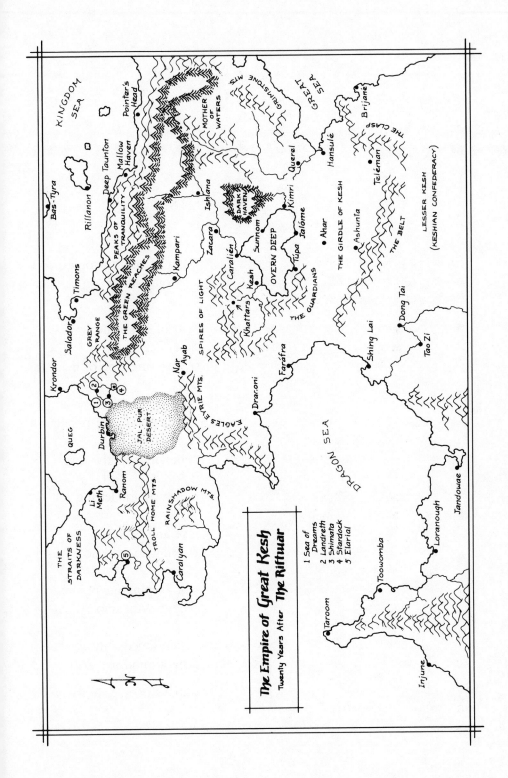

The Empire of Great Kesh

Twenty Years After The Riftwar

1 Sea of Dreams
2 Landreth
3 Shimata
4 Stardock
5 Elarial

Prince of the Blood

Chapter One
Homecoming

The inn was quiet.

Walls darkened with years of fireplace soot drank in the lantern light, reflecting dim illumination. The dying fire in the hearth offered scant warmth and, from the demeanor of those who chose to sit before it, less cheer. In contrast to mood of most establishments of its ilk, this inn was nearly somber. In murky corners, men spoke in hushed tones, discussing things best not overheard by the uninvolved. A grunt of agreement to a whispered proposal or a bitter laugh from a woman of negotiable virtue were the only sounds to intrude upon the silence. The majority of the denizens of the inn called the Sleeping Dockman were closely watching the game.

The game was *pokiir,* common to the Empire of Great Kesh to the south and now replacing *lin-lan* and *pashawa* as the gambler's choice in the inns and taverns of the Western Realm of the Kingdom. One player held his five cards before him, his eyes narrowed in concentration. An off-duty soldier, he kept alert for any sign of trouble in the room, and trouble was rapidly approaching. He made a display of studying his cards, while discreetly inspecting the five men who played at the table with him.

The first two on his left were rough men. Both were sunburned and the hands holding their cards were heavily callused; faded linen shirts and cotton trousers hung loosely on lank but muscular frames. Neither wore boots or even sandals, barefoot despite the cool night air, a certain sign they were sailors waiting for a new berth. Usually such men quickly lost their pay and were bound again for sea, but

1

from the way they had bet all night, the soldier was certain they were working for the man who sat to the soldier's right.

That man sat patiently, waiting to see if the soldier would match his bet or fold his cards, forfeiting his chance to buy up to three new cards. The soldier had seen his sort many times before: a rich merchant's son, or a younger son of a minor noble, with too much time on his hands and too little sense. He was fashionably attired in the latest rage among the young men of Krondor, a short pair of breeches tucked into hose, allowing the pants legs above the calf to balloon out. A simple white shirt was embroidered with pearls and semiprecious stones, and the jacket was the new cutaway design, a rather garish yellow, with white and silver brocade at the wrists and collar. He was a typical dandy. And from the look of the Rodezian slamanca hanging from the loose baldric across his shoulder, a dangerous man. It was a sword only used by a master or someone seeking a quick death—in the hands of an expert it was a fearsome weapon; in the hands of the inexperienced it was suicide.

The man had probably lost large sums of money before and now sought to recoup his previous losses by cheating at cards. One or the other of the sailors would win an occasional hand, but the soldier was certain this was planned to keep suspicion from falling upon the young dandy. The soldier sighed, as if troubled by what choice to make. The other two players waited patiently for him to make his play.

They were twin brothers, tall—two inches over six feet he judged—and fit in appearance. Both came to the table armed with rapiers, again the choice of experts or fools. Since Prince Arutha had come to the throne of Krondor twenty years before, rapiers had become the choice of men who wore weapons as a consideration of fashion rather than survival. But these two didn't look the type to sport weapons as decorative baubles. They were dressed as common mercenaries, just in from caravan duty from the look of them. Dust still clung to tunic and leather vest, while their red-brown hair was lightly matted. Both needed a shave. Yet while their clothing was common and dirty, there was nothing that looked neglected about their armor or arms; they might not pause to bathe after weeks on a caravan, but they would take an hour to oil their leather and polish their steel. They looked genuine in their part, save for a feeling of vague familiarity which caused the soldier slight discomfort: both spoke with none of the rough speech common to mercenaries, but rather with the educated crispness of those used to spending their days in court, not fighting bandits. And they were young, little more than boys.

The brothers had commenced the game with glee, ordering tankard after tankard of ale, letting losses delight them as much as wins, but now that the stakes of the game were rising, they had become somber. They glanced at each other from time to time, and the soldier was certain they shared silent communication the way twins often did.

The soldier shook his head. "Not me." He threw down his cards, one of them flipping completely over for an instant before it came to rest upon the table. "I've got duty in an hour; I'd best be back to the barracks."

What he really knew was that trouble was imminent and if he were still around when it arrived, he'd never make muster. And the duty sergeant was a man not given to receiving excuses kindly.

Now the dandy's eyes turned to the first of the two brothers. "Play?"

As the soldier reached the door of the inn, he took note of two men standing quietly in the corner. They stood in great cloaks, faces obscured slightly by the shadows of their hoods, despite the night being warm. Both made a show of quietly watching the game, but they were taking in every detail of the inn. They also looked familiar to the soldier, but he couldn't place them. And there was something about the way they stood, as if ready to leap to action, that reaffirmed the soldier's determination to reach the city barracks early. He opened the door to the inn and stepped through, closing it behind.

The man closest to the door turned to his companion, his face only partially illuminated by the light from the lantern above. "You'd better get outside. It's about to break loose."

His companion nodded. In the twenty years they'd been friends, he had learned never to second guess his companion's ability to sense trouble in the city. He quickly stepped through the door after the soldier.

At the table, the betting reached the first of the two brothers. He made a face, as if perplexed by the play of the cards. The dandy said, "Are you staying or folding?"

"Well," answered the young man, "this is something of a poser." He looked at his brother. "Erland, I would have sworn an oath to Astalon the Judge that I saw a Blue Lady flip when that soldier tossed in his hand."

"Why," answered his twin with a twisted smile, "does that pose a problem, Borric?"

"Because I also have a Blue Lady in my hand."

Men began to back away from the table as the tone of conversation shifted. Discussion of what cards one held was not the norm. "I still see no problem," observed Erland, "as there are two Blue Ladies in the deck."

With a malicious grin, Borric said, "But you see, our friend over here," he indicated the dandy, "also has a Blue Lady tucked just not quite far enough back in his sleeve."

Instantly the room erupted into motion as men put as much distance as possible between the combatants and themselves. Borric leaped from his seat, gripping the edge of the table and overturning it, forcing the dandy and his two henchmen back. Erland had his rapier and a long dirk out as the dandy drew his slamanca.

One of the two sailors lost his footing and fell forward. As he tried to rise, he found his chin met by the toe of Borric's boot. He collapsed into a heap at the young mercenary's feet. The dandy leaped forward, executing a vicious cut at Erland's head. Erland deftly parried with his dirk and returned a vicious thrust his opponent barely dodged.

Both men knew they faced an opponent worthy of wariness. The innkeeper was circling the room, armed with a large cudgel, threatening anyone who sought to enlarge the fray. As he neared the door, the man in the hood stepped out with startling speed and gripped his wrist. He spoke briefly, and the innkeeper's face drained of color. The proprietor briskly nodded once and quickly slipped out the door.

Borric disposed of the second sailor with little trouble and turned to discover Erland in a close struggle with the dandy. "Erland! Could you use a hand?"

Erland shouted, "I think not. Besides, you always say I need the practice."

"True," answered his brother with a grin. "But don't let him kill you. I'd have to avenge you."

The dandy tried a combination attack, a high, low, then high series of chops, and Erland was forced to back away. In the night the sound of whistles could be heard.

"Erland," said Borric.

The hard-pressed younger twin said, "What?" as he dodged another masterfully executed combination attack.

"The watch is coming. You'd better kill him quickly."

4

"I'm trying," said Erland, "but this fellow isn't being very cooperative." As he spoke, his boot heel struck a pool of spilled ale and he lost his footing. Suddenly he was falling backward, his defense gone.

Borric was moving as the dandy lunged at his brother. Erland twisted upon the floor, but the dandy's sword struck his side. Hot pain erupted along his ribs. And at the same instant the man had opened his left side to a counter thrust. Sitting upon the floor, Erland thrust upward with his rapier, catching the man in the stomach. The dandy stiffened and gasped as a red stain began to spread upon his yellow tunic. Then Borric struck him from behind, using the hilt of his sword to render the man unconscious.

From outside the sound of rushing men could be heard, and Borric said, "We'd best get clear of this mess," as he gave his brother a hand up. "Father's going to be upset enough with us as it is without brawling—"

Wincing from his injury, Erland interrupted, "You didn't have to hit him. I think I would have killed him in another moment."

"Or he you. And I'd not want to face Father had I let that happen. Besides, you really wouldn't have killed him; you just don't have the instinct. You'd have tried to disarm him or something equally noble," Borric observed, catching his breath in a gasp, ". . . and stupid. Now, let's see about getting out of here."

Erland gripped his wounded side as they headed toward the door. Several town toughs, seeing blood upon Erland's side, moved to block the twin's exit. Borric and Erland both leveled their sword points at the band of men. Borric said, "Keep your guard up a moment," picked up a chair, and threw it through the large bay window facing the boulevard. Glass and leading showered the street, and before the tinkle of shards upon stone had stopped, both brothers were leaping through what remained of the window. Erland stumbled and Borric had to grip his arm to keep him from falling.

As they straightened, they took in the fact that they were looking at horses. Two of the more bold thugs jumped through the window after the twins, and Borric smashed one in the side of the head with his sword hilt, while the other man pulled up short as three crossbows were leveled at him. Arrayed before the door was the small company of ten burly and heavily armed town watchmen commonly known as the Riot Squad. But what had the half-dozen denizens of the Sleeping Dockman standing in open-mouth amazement, was the sight of the thirty horsemen behind the Riot Squad. They wore the tabards of Krondor and the badge of the Prince of Krondor's own

Royal Household Guards. From within the inn someone overcame his stupefication and shouted, "Royal Guardsmen!" and a general evacuation through the rear door of the tavern began, while the gaping faces at the window vanished.

The two brothers regarded the mounted men, all armed and ready in case trouble came. At their head rode a man well known to the two young mercenaries.

"Ah . . . good evening, my lord," said Borric, a smile slowly spreading across his face. The leader of the Riot Squad, seeing no one else in sight, moved to take custody of the two young men.

The leader of the Royal Guard waved him off. "This doesn't concern you, watchman. You and your men may go." The watch commander bowed slightly and led his men back to their barracks in the heart of the Poor Quarter.

Erland winced a bit as he said, "Baron Locklear, what a pleasure."

Baron Locklear, Knight-Marshal of Krondor, smiled an unamused smile. "I'm certain." Despite his rank, he looked barely a year or two older than the boys, though he was nearly sixteen years their senior. He had curly blond hair and large blue eyes, which were presently narrowed as he watched the twins in obvious disapproval.

Borric said, "And I expect that means that Baron James—"

Locklear pointed. "Is standing behind you."

Both brothers turned to see the man in the great cloak framed in the doorway. He threw back his hood to reveal a face still somewhat youthful despite his thirty-seven years of age, his curly brown hair slightly dusted with grey. It was a face the brothers knew as well as any, for he had been one of their teachers since boyhood, and more, one of their closest friends. He regarded the two brothers with ill-disguised disapproval and said, "Your father ordered you *directly* home. I had reports of your whereabouts from the time you left Highcastle until you passed through the city gates . . . two days ago!"

The twins tried to hide their pleasure at being able to lose their royal escorts, but they failed. "Ignore for a moment the fact your father and mother had a formal court convened to welcome you home. Forget they stood waiting for *three hours!* Never mind your father's insisting that Baron Locklear and I comb the entire city for two days seeking you out." He studied the two young men, "But I trust you'll remember all those little details when your father has words with you after court tomorrow."

Two horses were brought forward and a soldier deferentially held out the reins to each brother. Seeing the blood along Erland's side, a Lieutenant of the Guard moved his horse nearby and said in mock sympathy, "Does His Highness require help?"

Erland negotiated the stirrup and heaved himself into the saddle without aid. In irritated tones, he answered, "Only when I see Father, Cousin Willy, and I don't think you can do much for me then."

Lieutenant William nodded and in unsympathetic tones, he whispered, "He did say come home at once, Erland."

Erland nodded in resignation. "We just wanted to relax for a day or two before—"

William couldn't resist laughing at his cousins' predicament. He had often seen them bring disaster down upon themselves and he never could understand their appetite for such punishment. He said, "Maybe you could run for the border. I could get very stupid following you."

Erland shook his head. "I think I'll wish I had taken your offer, after tomorrow morning's court."

William laughed again. "Come along, this dressing down won't be much worse than a dozen you've already had."

Baron James, Chancellor of Krondor and first assistant to the Duke of Krondor, quickly mounted his own horse. "To the palace," he ordered, and the company turned to escort the twin princes, Borric and Erland, to the palace.

Arutha, Prince of Krondor, Knight-Marshal of the Western Realm, and Royal Heir to the throne of the Kingdom of the Isles, sat quietly attentive to the business of the court being conducted before him. A slender man in his youth, he had not gained the bulk commonly associated with middle age, but rather had become harder, more angular in features, losing what little softening effects youth had given his lanky appearance. His hair was still dark, though enough grey had come with the twenty years of ruling Krondor and the West to speckle it. His reflexes had slowed only slightly over the years, and he was still counted one of the finest swordsmen in the Kingdom, though he rarely had reason to exercise his skill with the rapier. His dark brown eyes were narrowed in concentration, a gaze that seemed to miss nothing, in the opinion of many who served the Prince. Thoughtful, even brooding at times, Arutha was a brilliant military leader. He had rightfully won his reputation during the nine years of the Riftwar—which had ended the year before the twins' birth—after taking command of the garrison at Crydee, his family's castle, when only a few months older than his sons were now.

He was counted a hard but fair ruler, quick to dispense justice when the crime warranted, though often given to acts of leniency at the request of his wife, the Princess Anita. And that relationship more than anything typified the administration of the Western Realm: hard, logical, evenhanded justice, tempered with mercy. While few openly sang Arutha's praises, he was well respected and honored, and his wife was beloved by her subjects.

Anita sat quietly upon her throne, her green eyes looking off into space. Her royal manner masked her concern for her sons from all but those who knew her most intimately. That her husband had ordered the boys brought to the great hall for morning court, rather than to their parents' private quarters last night, showed more than anything else his displeasure. Anita forced herself to be attentive to the speech being given by a member of the Guild of Weavers; it was her duty also to show those coming before her husband's court the consideration of listening to every petition or request. The other members of the royal family were not normally required at morning court, but since the twins had returned from their service upon the border at Highcastle, it had become a family gathering.

Princess Elena stood at her mother's side. She looked a fair compromise between her parents, having red-brown hair and fair skin from her mother but her father's dark and intelligent eyes. Those who knew the royal family well often observed that if Borric and Erland resembled their uncle, the King, then Elena resembled her aunt, the Baroness Carline of Salador. And Arutha had observed on more than one occasion she had Carline's renowned temper.

Prince Nicholas, Arutha and Anita's youngest child, had avoided the need to stand next to his sister, by hiding from his father's sight. He stood behind his mother's throne, beyond his father's gaze, on the first step off the dais. The door to the royal apartments was hidden from the eyes of those in the hall, down three steps, where, in years past, all four children had played the game of huddling on the first step, listening to their father conduct court, enjoying the delicious feeling of eavesdropping. Nicky waited for the arrival of his two brothers.

Anita glanced about with that sudden sense mothers have that one of their children is somewhere he shouldn't be. She spied Nicholas waiting down by the door, and motioned him to stand close. Nicky had idolized Borric and Erland, despite them having little time for the boy and constantly teasing him. They just couldn't find much in common with their youngest sibling, since he was twelve years younger.

Prince Nicholas hobbled up the three broad steps and moved to his mother's side and, as it had every day since his birth, Anita's heart broke. The boy had a deformed foot, and neither surgeon's ministrations nor priest's spell had any effect, save to enable him to walk. Unwilling to hold up the deformed baby to public scrutiny, Arutha had ignored custom and refused to show the boy at the Presentation, the holiday in honor of a royal child's first public appearance, a tradition that may have died with Nicholas's birth.

Nicky turned when he heard the door open, and Erland peered through. The youngest Prince grinned at his brothers as they gingerly slipped through the door. Nicky scrambled down the three steps with his canted gate to intercept them, and gave each a hug. Erland visibly winced and Borric bestowed an absent pat on the shoulder.

Nicky followed the twins as they slowly mounted the stairs behind the thrones, coming to stand behind their sister. She glanced over her shoulder long enough to stick out her tongue and cross her eyes, causing all three brothers to force themselves not to laugh. They knew no one else in court could see her fleeting pantomime. The twins had a long history of tormenting their little sister, who gave back as good as she got. She would think nothing of embarrassing them in the King's own court.

Arutha, sensing some exchange between his children, glanced over and gifted his four offspring with a quick frown, enough to silence any potential mirth. His gaze lingered on his elder sons and showed his anger in full measure, though only those close to him would recognize it as such. Then his attention was back upon the matter before the court. A minor noble was being advanced into a new office, and while the four royal children might not find it worthy of much dignity, the man would count this among one of the high points of his life. Arutha had tried to impress such awareness upon them over the years but continuously failed.

Overseeing the Prince's court was Lord Gardan, Duke of Krondor. The old soldier had served with Arutha, and his father before him, thirty years and more. His dark skin stood in stark contrast to his beard, almost white in color, but he still had the alert eyes of one whose mind had lost none of its edge and a ready smile for the royal children. A commoner by birth, Gardan had risen on his ability, and despite an often expressed desire to retire and return to his home in Far Crydee, he had remained in Arutha's service, first as Sergeant in the garrison at Crydee, then Captain of the Prince's Royal Household, then Knight-Marshal of Krondor. When the previous Duke of Krondor, Lord Volney, had died unexpectedly after seven years' loyal service in his office, Arutha had awarded the office to Gardan. Despite the old soldier's protestations of not being suited to the nobility, he had proven an able administrator as well as a gifted soldier.

Gardan finished intoning the man's new rank and privileges and Arutha proferred a terribly oversized parchment with ribbons and seals embossed upon it. The man took his award of office and retired to the crowd, to the hushed congratulations of others in court.

Gardan nodded to the Master of Ceremonies, Jerome by name, and the thin man brought himself to his full height. Once a boyhood rival of Baron James, the office suited Jerome's self-important nature. He was, by all accounts, a thorough bore and his preoccupation with trivia made him a natural for the post. His love of detail manifested itself in the exquisite stitching of his cloak of office and the pointed chin beard he spent hours in trimming. In pompous tones, he spoke: "If it pleases Your Highness, His Excellency, Lord Torum Sie, Ambassador from the Royal court of Great Kesh."

The Ambassador, who had been standing off to one side, conferring with his advisors, approached the dais and bowed. By his attire, it was clear he was of the true Keshian people, for his head was shaved. His scarlet coat was cut away, revealing a pair of yellow pantaloons and white slippers. His chest was bare in the Keshian fashion, a large golden torque of office decorating his neck. Each item of clothing was delicately finished in almost imperceptible needlework, with tiny jewels and pearls decorating each seam. The effect was as if he was bathed in shimmering sparkles as he moved. He was easily the most splendid figure in court.

"Highness," he said, his speech tinged by a slight singsong accent. "Our Mistress, Lakeisha, She Who Is Kesh, inquires as to the health of Their Highnesses."

"Convey our warmest regards to the Empress," responded Arutha, "and tell her we are well."

"With pleasure," the Ambassador answered. "Now, I must beg of His Highness an answer to the invitation sent by my mistress. The seventy-fifth anniversary of Her Magnificent's birth is an event of unsurpassed joy to the Empire. We will host a Jubilee that will be celebrated for two months. Will Your Highnesses be joining us?"

Already the King had sent his apologies, as had the ruler of every neighboring sovereignty from Queg to the Eastern Kingdoms. While there had been peace between the Empire and her neighbors for an unusually long time—eleven years since the last major border clash—no ruler was foolish enough to come within the borders of the most feared nation upon Midkemia. Those rejections were considered proper. The invitation to the Prince and Princess of Krondor was another matter.

The Western Realm of the Kingdom of the Isles was almost a nation unto itself, with the responsibility for rulership given to the Prince of Krondor. Only the broadest policy came from the King's court in Rillanon. And it was Arutha, as often as not, who had been the one to deal with Kesh's Ambassadors, for the majority of potential conflict between Kesh and the Kingdom were along the Western Realm's southern border.

Arutha looked at his wife, and then the Ambassador. "We regret that the press of official duty prevents us from undertaking so long a journey, Your Excellency."

The Ambassador's expression didn't change, but a slight hardening around the eyes indicated the Keshian considered the rejection close to an insult. "That is regrettable, Highness. My mistress did so consider your presence vital—should I say a gesture of friendship and goodwill."

The odd comment was not lost upon Arutha. He nodded. "Still, we would consider ourselves remiss in our friendship and goodwill to our neighbors in the south if we did not send one who could represent the Royal House of Isles." The Ambassador's eyes at once fixed upon the twins. "Prince Borric, Heir Presumptive to the Throne of Isles, shall be our representative at the Empress's Jubilee, my lord." Borric, suddenly the focus of scrutiny, found himself standing more erect, and felt an unexpected need to tug at his tunic. "And his brother, Prince Erland, will accompany him."

Borric and Erland exchanged startled glances. "Kesh!" Erland whispered, astonishment barely contained.

The Keshian Ambassador inclined his head toward the Princes a moment in appreciation. "A fitting gesture of respect and friendship, Highness. My mistress will be pleased."

Arutha's gaze swept the room, and for an instant fixed upon a man at the rear of the room, then continued on. As the Keshian Ambassador withdrew, Arutha rose from his throne and said, "We have much business before us this day; court will resume tommorow at the tenth hour of the watch." He offered his hand to his wife, who took it as she stood. Escorting the Princess from the dais, he whispered to Borric, "You and your brother: in my chambers in five minutes." All four royal children bowed formally as their father and mother passed, then fell into procession behind them.

Borric glanced at Erland and found his own curiosity mirrored in the face of his twin. The twins waited until they were out of the hall and Erland turned and grabbed Elena, spinning her roughly around in a bear hug. Borric gave her a solid whack on the backside, despite the softening effect of the folds of fabric of her gown. "Beasts!" she exclaimed. Then she hugged each in turn. "I hate to say this, but I am glad to see you back. Things have been dreadfully dull since you left."

Borric grinned. "Not as I hear it, little sister."

Erland put his arm around his brother's neck and whispered in mock conspiracy, "It has come to my attention that two of the Prince's squires were caught brawling a month ago, and the reason seems to be which would escort our sister to the Festival of Banapis."

Elena fixed both brothers with a narrow gaze. "I had nothing to do with those idiots brawling." Then she brightened. "Besides, I spent the day with Baron Lowery's son, Thom."

Both brothers laughed. "Which is also what we heard," said Borric. "Your reputation is reaching even to the Border Barons, little sister! And you not yet sixteen!"

Elena hiked up her skirts and swept past her brothers. "Well, I'm almost the age Mother was when she first met Father, and speaking of Father, if you don't get to his study, he'll roast your livers for breakfast." She reached a point a dozen paces away, swirled in a flurry of silks, and again stuck her tongue out at her brothers.

Both laughed, then Erland noticed Nicky standing close by. "Well, then, what have we here?"

Borric made a show of glancing around, above Nicky's head. "What do you mean? I see nothing."

Nicky's expression turned to one of distress. "Borric!" he said, almost whining.

Borric glanced down. "Why, it's . . ." He turned to his brother. "What is it?"

Erland slowly walked around Nicky. "I'm not sure. It's too small to be a goblin, yet too big to be a monkey—save perhaps a very tall monkey."

"Not broad enough in the shoulders to be a dwarf, and too finely tailored to be a beggar boy—"

Nicky's face clouded over. Tears began to form in his eyes. "You promised!" he said, his voice catching in his throat. He looked up at his brothers as they stood grinning down at him, then with tears upon his cheeks he kicked Borric in the shins, turned, and fled, his half-limping, rolling gate not slowing him as he scampered down the hall, the sound of his sobs following after.

Borric rubbed at the barked shin. "Ow. The boy can kick." He looked at Erland. "Promised?"

Erland rolled his eyes heavenward. "Not to tease him anymore." He heaved a sigh. "Another round of lectures. He's sure to run to Mother and she'll speak to Father and . . ."

Borric winced. "And we'll get another round of lectures."

Then as one they said, "Father!" and hurried toward Arutha's private quarters. The guard stationed at the door, seeing the approaching brothers, opened the doors for them.

Once inside, the twins found their father seated in his favorite chair, an old thing of wood and leather, but which he preferred to any of the dozen others in the large conference hall. Standing slightly to his left were Barons James and Locklear. Arutha said, "Come in, you two."

The twins came to stand before their father, Erland moving with a slight awkwardness, as his injured side had stiffened overnight. "Something wrong?" asked Arutha.

Both sons smiled weakly. Their father missed little. Borric said, "He tried a beat and counterlunge when he should have parried in six. The fellow got inside his guard."

Arutha's voice was cold. "Brawling again. I should have expected it, as Baron James obviously did." To James he said, "Anyone killed?"

James said, "No, but it was a bit close with the son of one of the city's more influential shippers."

Arutha's anger surfaced as he slowly rose from his chair. A man able to hold emotions in check, the sight of such a display was rare, and for those who knew him well, unwelcome. He came to stand before the twins and for a moment appeared on the verge of striking them. He stared into the eyes of each. He bit off each word as he sought to regain control. "What can you two possibly have been thinking of?"

Erland said, "It was self-defense, Father. The man was trying to skewer me."

Borric chimed in, "The man was cheating. He had an extra Blue Lady up his sleeve."

Arutha almost spit as he said, "I don't care if he had an extra deck up his sleeve. You aren't common soldiers, damn it! You are *my* sons!"

Arutha walked around them, as if inspecting horses or reviewing his guard. Both boys endured the close perusal, knowing their father's mood brooked no insolence.

At last he threw up his hands in a gesture of resignation and said, "These aren't my sons." He walked past the twins to stand next to the two Barons. "They've got to be Lyam's," he said, invoking the King's name. Arutha's brother had been known for his temper and brawling as a youth. "Somehow Anita married me, but bore the King's ruffian brats." James could only nod in agreement. "It must be some divine plan I don't understand."

Returning his attention to his boys, he said, "If your grandfather still lived, he'd have you over a barrel, a leather strap in his hand, no matter your size or age. You've acted like children, once again, and should be treated like children."

His voice rose as he walked back before them, "I sent *orders* for you two to come home *at once!* But do you obey? No! Instead of coming straight away to the palace, you vanish into the Poor Quarter. Two days later, Baron James finds you brawling in a tavern." He paused, then in a near shout, he exclaimed, "You could have been killed!"

Borric began to quip, "Only if that parry—"

"Enough!" cried Arutha, his temper frayed beyond his ability to control it. He gripped Borric's tunic and pulled his son forward, off-balance. "You will not end this with a joke and smile! You have defied me for the last time." He punctuated this with a shove that sent Borric half-stumbling into his brother. Arutha's manner showed he had no patience for the flippancies from his son he usually ignored. "I didn't call you back because the court missed your peculiar sort of chaos. I think that another year or two on the border might have settled you down a bit, but I have no alternative. You have princely duties and you are needed *now!*"

Borric and Erland exchanged glances. Arutha's moods were old business to them, and they had endured his anger—which was usually justified—before, but this time something serious was occurring. Borric said, "We're sorry, Father. We didn't realize it was a matter of duty that called us home."

"Because you are not expected to *realize* anything, you are expected to obey!" shot back their father. Obviously out of patience with the entire exchange, he said, "I am done with you for now. I must compose myself for the business of dealing in private with the Keshian Ambassador this afternoon. Baron James will continue this conversation on my behalf!" At the door, he paused, and said to James, "Whatever you need do, do! But I want these miscreants impressed with the gravity of things when I speak to them this afternoon." He closed the door without waiting for a response.

James and Locklear moved to either side of the young Princes, and James said, "If Your Highnesses would be so kind as to follow us."

Borric and Erland both glanced at their life-long tutors and "uncles" and then at each other. Both had an inkling of what was to come. Their father had never laid strap nor hand upon any of his children, to the profound relief of his wife, but that still didn't prevent regular bouts of "fighting practice," when the boys were unruly, which was most of the time.

Waiting outside, Lieutenant William quietly fell into step with the twins and the Barons as they moved down the hall. He hurried to open the door, which led to Prince Arutha's gymnasium, a large room where the royal family could practice their skills with sword, dagger, or hand-to-hand combat.

Baron James led the procession down the hall. At the door to the gymnasium, William again moved to open the door, for while he was second cousin to the twins, he was still merely a soldier in the company of nobles. Borric entered the room first, followed by Erland and James, with Locklear and William behind.

Inside the room, Borric nimbly turned and walked backwards, his hands raised in a boxers pose, as he said, "We're a lot older and bigger, now, Uncle Jimmy. And you're not going to sucker punch me behind the ear like you did last time."

Erland leaned to the left, clutching his side in exaggeration and suddenly developed a limp. "And faster, too, Uncle Locky." Without warning, he threw an elbow at Locklear's head. The Baron, a seasoned soldier of almost twenty years, dodged aside, allowing Erland to overbalance. He then turned him in a circle by hauling on one arm, and pushed him into the center of the gymnasium.

The two Barons stood away as both brothers stood poised for a fight, fists upraised. With a wry grin, James raised his hands palms out and said, "Oh, you're too young and fast for us, all right." The tone of sarcasm was not lost on the boys. "But as *we* have to be clear headed over the next few days, we thought we'd forego the pleasure

15

of seeing how far you've come in the last two years." He hiked his thumb behind him, indicating a far corner. "Personally, that is."

Two soldiers, stripped to breeches only, stood in the corner. Each had massive arms crossed over impressively muscled chests. Baron James waved for them to approach. As they did, the boys glanced at one another.

The two men moved with the fluid motion of a thoroughbred war horse, supple, but with power waiting. Each looked as if he was carved from stone, and Borric whispered, "They're not human!" Erland grinned, for both men had large jaws, suggesting the protruding mandible of mountain trolls.

"These gentlemen are from your Uncle Lyam's garrison," said Locklear. "We had a demonstration of the Royal Fist-Boxing Champions last week and asked them to stay with us a few extra days." The two men began to move away from each other, circling the boys in opposite direction.

Jimmy said, "The blond-haired fellow is Sergeant Obregon, from the Rodez garrison—"

Locklear injected, "He's champion of all men under two hundred pounds—ah, Erland should be your student, Obregon; his side is injured. Be gentle with him."

"—and the other," continued Jimmy, "is Sergeant Palmer, from Bas-Tyra."

Borric's eyes narrowed as he studied the approaching soldier. "Let me guess: he's the champion of all men over two hundred pounds."

"Yes," said Baron James, with an evil smile.

Instantly, Borric's field of vision was filled by an oncoming fist. He quickly tried to move away from it, but abruptly discovered another had found the side of his head. Then he was considering who painted the frescos on the ceiling of the room his father had converted to a gymnasium. He really should ask someone.

Shaking his head as he slowly sat up, he could hear James saying, "Your Father wanted us to impress upon you the importance of what you face tomorrow."

"And what might that be," said Borric, allowing Sergeant Palmer to help him to his feet. But the Sergeant didn't release Borric's right hand, but rather held it tightly as he brought his own right hand hard up into Borric's stomach. Lieutenant William visibly winced as Borric's breath exploded from his lungs and his eyes crossed as he sank to the floor once more. Erland began warily moving away from the other fist-boxer, who now was stalking him across the floor.

16

"If it has escaped your notice, your uncle the King has sired only daughters since young Prince Randolph died."

Borric waved off the offered hand of Sergeant Palmer and said, "Thanks. I'll get up by myself." As he came to one knee, he said, "I hardly dwell on the fact of our cousin's death, but I'm aware of it." Then as he started to stand, he drove a vicious blow into Sergeant Palmer's stomach.

The older, harder fighter stood rock steady, forced himself to take a breath, then smiled in appreciation and said, "That was a good one, Highness."

Borric's eyes rolled heavenward. "Thank you." Then another fist filled his vision and once more he considered the wonderful craftsmanship displayed upon the ceiling. Why hadn't he ever taken the opportunity to notice it before? he mused to himself.

Erland attempted to keep distance between himself and the approaching Sergeant Obregon. Suddenly, the young man was not backing up, but striking out with a flurry of blows. The Sergeant, rather than back away, raised his arms before his face and let the younger man strike his arms and shoulders. "Our uncle's lack of an heir is a fact not unknown to us, Uncle Jimmy," observed Erland as his own arms began to tire while he futilely pounded upon the muscular sergeant. Abruptly, the Sergeant stepped inside Erland's reach, and drove another blow into the youngster's side. Erland's face drained of color and his eyes crossed, then unfocused.

Seeing the reaction, Sergeant Obregon said, "Pardon, Highness, I'd meant to strike the uninjured side."

Erland's voice was a bare whisper as he gasped, "How very kind of you."

Borric shook his head to clear his thoughts, then quickly rolled backwards and came to his feet, ready to fight. "So then, there's a point to this iteration on our family's lack of a Royal Prince?"

"Actually, so," agreed James. "With no male issue, the Prince of Krondor still is Heir."

Erland's voice returned in a strangled gasp. "The Prince of Krondor is always Royal Heir."

"And your father is Prince of Krondor," interjected Locklear.

With a clever feint with his left, Borric drove his right into the jaw of Sergeant Palmer and momentarily staggered the older man. Another blow to the body and the boxer was retreating. Borric grew confident and stepped in to deliver a finishing blow, and abruptly the world turned upside down.

Borric's vision turned yellow then red for a long while, and while he hung in space, the floor came up to strike him in the back of the head. Then blackness crowded in at the edge of his vision and he saw a ring of faces looking down a deep well at him. They seemed friendly faces, and he thought he might know who they were, but he didn't feel any need to worry on it, as he was so very comfortable sinking into the cool, dark of the well. Staring past the faces, he absently wondered if any of them might know who the artists of the frescos above might be.

As his eyes rolled up into his head, William poured a small bucket of water on Borric's face. The elder twin came back to consciousness sputtering and spitting water.

Baron James was upon one knee and helped the Prince sit upright. "Are you still with me?"

Borric shook his head and his eyes focused. "I think so," he managed to gasp.

"Good. For if your father is still Heir to the throne, you royal infant," he slapped Borric on the back of the head to emphasize what came next, "then you are *still* Heir Presumptive."

Borric turned to study James's face. The point of James's message was still lost on the young Prince. "So?"

"So, ninny, as it is unlikely that our good King, your uncle, will father any sons at this stage in his life—given the Queen's age—should Arutha survive him, he will then be King." Reaching out to aid Borric to his feet, he added, "And as the Goddess of Luck would have it"—he slapped Borric playfully on the side of the face—"you almost certainly will outlive your father, which means that someday after, you shall be King."

"May heaven forfend," interjected Locklear.

Borric looked around the room. The two Sergeants had stepped back, as the pretense of a boxing lesson was forgotten. "King?"

"Yes, you stone-crowned dolt," said Locklear. "If we're still alive, we'll have to kneel before you and pretend you know what you're doing."

"So," continued James, "your father has decided that it's time for you to stop behaving like the spoiled child of a rich cattle merchant and start acting like a future King of Isles."

Erland came to stand beside his brother, leaning upon him slightly. "So why not just simply"—he winced as he moved the wrong way, straining his reinjured side—"tell us what's going on?"

James said, "I convinced your father the lesson needed to be . . .

18

emphasized." He studied the two Princes. "You've been educated, taught by the best instructors your father could employ. You speak . . . what . . . six, seven languages? You can do sums and calculate, like engineers at a siege. You can discourse on the teachings of the ancients. You have music and painting skills, and you know the etiquette of the court. You are skilled swordsmen and"—he glanced at the two boxers—"somewhat gifted students of fisticuffs." He stepped away. "But in nineteen years since your birth you've never given a single sign that you're anything other than spoiled, self-indulgent children. Not Princes of the realm!" His voice rose and his tone turned angry. "And when we're done with you, you'll be acting the role of a Crown Prince instead of a spoiled child."

Borric stood crestfallen. "Spoiled child?"

Erland grinned at his brother's discomfort. "Well, that's it, then, isn't it? Borric shall have to mend his ways, and you and Father will be happy—"

James's wicked grin turned on Erland. "As will you, my lovely! For if this child of foolish nature should go and get his throat cut by the angry husband of a Keshian court lady, it's you who'll wear the con-Doin crown in Rillanon someday. And should he not, you'll still be Heir until the unlikely event of your brother becoming a father. Even then, you'll most likely end up a duke somewhere." Letting his voice drop a bit, he said, "So both of you begin to learn your office."

Borric said, "Yes, I know. First thing tomorrow. Come, let's get some rest—" Borric looked down and discovered a restraining hand upon his chest.

"Not so fast," said James. "You haven't finished your lesson."

"Ah, Uncle Jimmy—" began Erland.

"You've made your point—" said Borric, anger in his voice.

"I think not," answered the Baron. "You're still a pair of rude sods." Turning to the two Sergeants, he said, "If you please, continue."

Baron James signaled for Locklear to accompany him as he quickly left the two young Princes readying themselves for a professionally administered beating. As the two nobles left the court, James motioned to Lieutenant William. "When they've had enough, get them to their quarters. Let them rest and see they eat, then insure that they are up and ready to see His Highness by midafternoon."

William saluted and turned to watch as both Princes tumbled to the canvas mat again. He shook his head. This wasn't going to be a pretty sight.

Chapter Two
Accusation

The boy cried out.

Borric and Erland watched from the window of their parents' private chamber as Swordmaster Sheldon pressed his attack on young Prince Nicholas. The boy shouted again in eager excitement as he executed a clever parry and counterthrust. The Swordmaster retreated.

Borric scratched at his cheek as he observed, "The boy can scamper about, for certain." The angry bruise from the morning's boxing practice was darkening.

Erland agreed. "He's inherited Father's skills with a blade. And he manages to do right well despite his bad leg."

Borric and Erland both turned as the door opened and their mother entered. Anita waved her ladies in waiting to the far corner of the room, where they commenced to discuss quietly whichever current piece of gossip was judged most interesting. The Princess of Krondor came to stand between her sons and peered through the window as a joyous Nicholas was lured into an overbalanced extension and found himself suddenly disarmed.

"No, Nicky! You should have seen it coming," shouted Erland, though the glass window prevented his words from reaching his younger brother.

Anita laughed. "He tries so hard."

Borric shrugged as they turned away. "Still, he does well enough for a boy. Not much worse than when we were his age."

Erland agreed. "The monkey—"

Suddenly his mother turned on him and slapped him hard across the face. Instantly, the women in the other corner of the room ceased their whispers and stared in wide-eyed amazement at their Princess. Borric looked at his brother whose astonishment matched his own. Not once in the nineteen years of their lives had their mother raised a hand to either boy. Erland was more stunned by the act than any pain from the slap. Anita's green eyes revealed a mixture of anger and regret. "Never talk that way about your brother again." Her tone left no room for argument. "You have mocked him and caused him more pain than all the unkind whispers among the nobles together. He is a good boy and he loves you, and all you have for him is ridicule and torment. Your first day back in the palace and within five minutes of speaking with you he was in tears again.

"Arutha was right. I've let you go unpunished for your trespasses too long." She turned as if to leave.

Borric, seeking to rescue his brother and himself from the embarrassment of the moment said, "Ah, Mother. You did send for us? Was there something else you wanted to discuss?"

Anita said, "I didn't send for you."

"I did."

The boys turned to see their father standing quietly at the small door that opened between his study and the family room, as Anita called his part of the royal apartment. The brothers glanced at one another and knew their father had been observing long enough to have witnessed the exchange between mother and sons.

After a long silence, Arutha said, "If you'll excuse us, I would have a private word with my sons."

Anita nodded and indicated to her ladies they should come with her. Quickly the room emptied, leaving Arutha with his sons. When the door was closed, Arutha said, "Are you all right?"

Erland made a display of stiff muscles and said, "Well, enough, Father, given the 'instructions' we received this morning." He indicated his tender side was not further injured.

Arutha frowned and shook his head slightly. "I asked Jimmy not to tell me what he had in mind." He smiled a crooked smile. "I just requested he somehow impress upon you that there are serious consequences to not doing what is required of you."

Erland nodded. Borric said, "Well, it is not entirely unexpected. You did order us directly home and we did stop to play a bit before coming to the palace."

"Play . . ." Arutha said, his eyes searching his eldest son's face. ". . . I'm afraid there will be little time for play in the future."

He motioned for the boys to approach and they came to him. He turned back into his study and they followed as he moved past his large writing table. Behind it was a special alcove, hidden by a clever locked stone, which he opened. He withdrew a parchment bearing the royal family crest and handed it to Borric. "Read the third paragraph."

Borric read and his eyes widened. "This is sad news, indeed."

Erland said, "What is it?"

"A message from Lyam," Arutha said.

Borric handed it to his brother. "The royal chirurgeons and priests are certain the Queen will have no more children. There will not be a Royal Heir in Rillanon."

Arutha moved to a door at the back of the royal chambers and said, "Come with me."

He opened the door and moved up a flight of stairs. His sons followed quickly after, and soon all three stood on the top of an old tower, near the center of the royal palace, overlooking the city of Krondor. Arutha spoke without looking to see if his sons had followed.

"When I was about your age, I used to stand upon the parapets of the barbican of my father's castle. I would look down over the town of Crydee and the harbor beyond. Such a small place, but so large in my memory."

He glanced at Borric and Erland. "Your grandfather did much the same when he was a boy, or so our old Swordmaster, Fannon, once told me." Arutha spent a moment lost in memory. "I was about your age when command of the garrison fell to me, boys." Both sons had heard tales of the Riftwar and their father's part in it, but this wasn't the same sort of old stories they had heard swapped by their father and their uncle, Laurie, or Admiral Trask over dinner.

Arutha turned and sat in one of the merlons and said, "I never wanted to be Prince of Krondor, Borric." Erland moved to sit in the merlon next to his father, as he sensed that Arutha's words were more for his older brother than himself. They had both heard often enough that their father had no wish to rule. "When I was a boy," Arutha continued, "I had no larger desire than to serve as a soldier, perhaps with the border lords."

"It wasn't until I met the old Baron Highcastle that I realized that boyhood dreams are often with us as adults. They are difficult to be shed of, and yet, to see things as they really are, we must lose that child's eye view of things."

He scanned the horizon. Their father had always been a direct man, given to direct speech and never at a loss for words to express himself. But he was obviously having difficulty saying what was on his mind. "Borric, when you were much younger, what did you think your life would be like now?"

Borric glanced over at Erland, then back at his father. A light breeze sprang up and his thick, ill-cut mane of reddish brown hair blew about his face. "I never gave it much thought, Father."

Arutha sighed. "I think I have made a terrible mistake in the manner in which you were raised. When you were both very tiny you were very mischievous and upon one occasion upset me—it was a little thing, a spilled inkwell, but a long parchment was ruined and a scribe's work for a day was lost. I swatted you upon the bottom, Borric." The elder brother grinned at the image. Arutha did not return the grin. "Anita made me promise that day that never again would I touch either one of you in anger. By doing so, I think I have coddled you and ill-prepared you for the lives you will lead."

Erland couldn't help feeling embarrassed. They'd been scolded often enough over the years, but rarely punished and, before this morning, never physically.

Arutha nodded. "You and I have little in common in the manner in which we were raised. Your uncle the King felt our father's leather belt on more than one occasion when he was caught. I only took one beating as a boy. I quickly learned that when Father gave an order, he *expected* it to be obeyed without question." Arutha sighed, and in that sound both boys heard uncertainty from their father for the first time in their lives. "We all assumed Prince Randolph would be King someday. When he drowned, we assumed Lyam would have another son. Even as daughters came and the prospects for a Royal Heir in Rillanon lessened with the years, we just never considered that someday you"—he put his finger on Borric's chest—"would be ruler of the nation."

He looked over at his other son and in an uncharacteristic gesture, reached out and placed his hand over Erland's. "I am not given to speaking of strong feelings, but you are my sons and I love you both, though you try my patience to distraction."

Both sons were suddenly uncomfortable with this atypical revelation. They loved their father but, like him, were discomforted by any

23

attempt to expresses such feelings openly. "We understand," was all Borric could manage.

Looking Borric directly in the eyes, he said, "Do you? Do you really? Then understand that from this day forth you are no longer my sons alone, Borric. You are both now sons to the Kingdom. Each of you is a Prince of the Blood Royal. You are to be King someday, Borric. Wrap your mind around that fact, for it is so, and nothing this side of death will change that. And from this day on a father's love of his son will no longer shield you from life's harshness. To be a king is to hold men's lives by a thread. A thoughtless gesture will end those lives as certainly as if you had chosen to tear the threads."

To Erland, he said, "Twins pose a serious threat to peace in our Kingdom, for should old rivalries surface, you'll find some claiming the birth order was reversed, some who will raise your cause without your consent, as an excuse to make war upon old foes.

"You both have heard the story, of the First King Borric and how he was forced to slay his own brother, Jon the Pretender. And you have also heard, often enough, of how I stood with the King and our brother Martin in the hall of our ancestors, before the Congress of Lords, each of them with a just claim to the crown. By Martin's signal act of nobility, Lyam wears his crown and no blood was shed." He held his thumb and forefinger a scant fraction of an inch apart. "Yet we were but this far from civil war that day."

Borric said, "Father, why are you telling us this?"

Arutha stood, sighed, and put his hand upon his eldest son's shoulder. "Because your boyhood is at an end, Borric. You are no longer the son of the Prince of Krondor. For I have decided that should I survive my brother, I will renounce my own claim upon the crown in favor of yours." Borric began to protest, but Arutha cut him off. "Lyam is a vigorous man. I may be an old one when he dies, if I don't precede him. It is best if there is not a short rule between Lyam's and your own. You will be the next King of Isles."

Glancing at Erland, he said, "And you will always stand in your brother's shadow. You will forever be one step from the throne, yet never permitted to sit upon it. You will always be sought out for favor and position, but never your own; you will be seen as a stepping-stone to your brother. Can you accept such a fate?"

Erland shrugged. "It doesn't seem too grave a fate, Father. I shall have estates and title, and responsibilities enough, I am certain."

"More, for you need stand with Borric in all things, even when you disagree with him in private. You will never have a public mind that

24

you may call your own. It must be so. I cannot stress this enough. Never once in the future can you publicly oppose the King's will." Moving a short way off, he turned and regarded them both. "You have never known anything but peace in our Kingdom. The raids along the border are trivial things."

Erland said, "Not to those of us who fought those raiders! Men died, Father."

Arutha said, "I speak of nations now, and dynasties, and the fate of generations. Yes, men died, so that this nation and its people may live in peace.

"But there was a time when war was always with us, when border skirmishes with Great Kesh were a monthly occurrence and when Quegan galleys took our ships at their leisure, and when invaders from the Tsurani world held part of your grandfather's lands—for nine years!

"You will be asked to give up many things, my sons. You will be asked to marry women who will most likely be strangers to you. You will be asked to relinquish many of the privileges lesser men know: the ability to enter a tavern and drink with strangers, to pick up and travel to another city, to marry for love and watch your children grow without fear of their being used for others' designs." Gazing out over the city, he added, "To sit at day's end with your wife and discuss the small matters of your life, to be at ease."

Borric said, "I think I understand." His voice was subdued.

Erland only nodded.

Arutha said, "Good, for in a week you leave for Great Kesh, and from this moment forward you *are* the Kingdom's future." He moved toward the stairs that led down into the palace and halted at them. "I wish I could spare you this, but I can't." Then he was gone.

Both boys sat quietly for a time, then as one turned to look out over the harbor. The afternoon sun beat down, yet the breeze from the Bitter Sea was cooling. In the harbor below, boats moved as punts and barges carried cargo and passengers back and forth between the docks and great sailing ships anchored in the bay. In the distance white dots signaled approaching ships, traders from the Far Coast, the Kingdom of Queg, the Free Cities of Yabon, or the Empire of Great Kesh.

Then Borric's face relaxed as a smile spread. "Kesh!"

Erland laughed. "Yes, to the heart of Great Kesh!"

Both shared the laughter at the prospect of new cities and people, and travel to a land considered exotic and mysterious. And their father's words vanished upon the wind to the east.

Some institutions linger for centuries, while others pass quickly. Some arrive quietly, others with fanfare. In years past it was considered a general practice to give apprentices and other servants the latter half of the sixth day of the week for themselves. Now the practice had come to include a general closing of businesses on sixthday at noon, with seventhday generally held to be a day of devotions and meditations.

But within the last twenty years another "tradition" had arisen. From the first sixthday following the winter equinox, boys and young men, apprentices and servants, commoner and noble, began preparing. For upon the holiday of First Thaw, held six optimistic weeks after the equinox, often despite inclement weather, football season commenced.

Once called barrel ball, the game had been played for as long as boys had kicked balls of rags into barrels. Twenty years before, the young Prince Arutha had instructed his Master of Ceremonies to draw up a standard set of rules for the game, more for the protection of his young squires and apprentices, for then the game was rough in the extreme. Now the game had been institutionalized in the minds of the populace; come spring, football returned.

On all levels, from boys playing in open fields up to a City League, with teams fielded by guilds, trading associations, or rich nobles eager to be patrons, players could be seen racing up and down attempting to kick a ball into a net.

The crowd shouted its approval as the Blues' swiftest forward broke away from the pack with the ball, speeding toward the open goal net. The Reds' goalkeeper hunkered down, ready to leap between ball and net. With a clever feint, the Blues' player caused the Reds to overbalance, then shot it past him on his off side. The goalkeeper stood with hands on hips, evidencing disgust at himself while the Blues' players mobbed the scorer.

"Ah, he should have seen it coming," commented Locklear. "It was so obvious. I could see it up here."

James laughed. "Then why don't you go down and play for him?"

Borric and Erland shared in James's laughter. "Certainly, Uncle Locky. We've heard a hundred times how you and Uncle Jimmy invented this game."

Locklear shook his head. "It was nothing like this." He glanced about the field at the stands erected by an enterprising merchant years before, stands that had been expanded upon and enlarged until as many as four thousand citizens could crowd together to watch a match. "We used to have a barrel at each end and you couldn't stand before the mouth. This net business and goalkeepers and all the other rules your father devised . . ."

Borric and Erland finished for him in unison, ". . . It's not sport anymore."

Locklear said, "That's the truth—"

Erland inserted, "Not enough bloodshed!"

"No broken arms! No gouged eyes!" laughed Borric.

James said, "Well, that's for the better. There was one time—"

Both brothers grimaced as one, for they knew they were about to hear the story of the time Locklear was hit from behind by a piece of farrier's steel an apprentice boy had concealed in his shirt. This would lead, then, to a debate between the two Barons on the general value of rules and which rules enhanced the game and which impeded.

But the lack of further comment from James caused Borric to turn. James had his eyes focused not on the game below which was drawing to a close, but upon a man down near the end of the row upon which the Baron sat, one row behind the Princes. Rank and a well-placed bribe had given the sons of the Prince of Krondor two of the best seats for the match, at the mid-field line halfway up the stands.

James said, "Locky, is it cold?"

Wiping perspiration from his brow, Locklear said, "You're joking, right? It's a month after midsummer and I'm roasting."

Hiking his thumb toward the end of the row, James said, "Then why does our friend over there feel the need to wear such a heavy robe?"

Locklear glanced past his companion and noticed a man sitting at the end of the bench, muffled in a large robe. "A priest perhaps?"

"I know of no order that has members with an interest in football." James glanced away as the man turned toward him. "Watch him over my shoulder, but not as if you're listening to everything I'm saying. What's he doing?"

"Nothing presently." Then a horn was blown, signaling the end of the match. The Blues, a team sponsored by the Millers Guild and the Worshipful Association of Iron Mongers, had defeated the Reds, a team sponsored by a group of nobles. As such sponsorship was well-known among those in attendance, the result of the match met with general approval.

As the crowd began to depart, the man in the robe stood. Locklear's eyes widened as he said, "He's taking something out of his sleeve."

James whirled about in time to see the man raise a tube to his lips and point it in the direction of the Princes. Without hesitation, James pushed hard, knocking the two young men into the row below. A strangled gasp sounded from a man standing just beyond where Erland had been, and the man raised a hand to his neck. It was a gesture never finished, for as his fingers neared the dart protruding from his throat, he collapsed.

Locklear was only an instant behind James to react. As James and the twins went sprawling below, accompanied by angry shouts as spectators were knocked about, Locklear had his sword out and was leaping toward the robed and cowled figure. "Guards!" he shouted, as an honor guard was stationed just below the viewing stands.

The sounds of boots pounding upon wooden stairs answered his call almost instantly as soldiers of the Prince raced to intercept the fleeing figure. With little concern for bruises caused, the guardsmen roughly shoved innocent onlookers out of their way. With the silent understanding mobs possess, suddenly everyone knew that something was wrong in the viewing stands. While those nearby scampered to get away, those in other parts of the field turned to observe the cause of such turmoil.

Seeing guardsmen mere yards away, with only a few confused citizens blocking their approach, the robed man put one hand upon the rail of the stairs and vaulted over the side, falling a full dozen feet to the earth below. A heavy thud and an exclamation of pain could be heard by Locklear as he reached the railing.

Sprawled upon the ground, two stunned commoners sat inspecting the unmoving form that lay next to them. One man pushed himself back without standing while the other crawled. Locklear vaulted over the rail and landed upon his feet, sword point leveled at the robed figure. The form upon the ground stirred, then leaped at the young Baron.

Almost taken by surprise, Locklear let the man get inside his guard. The robed man had his arms around Locklear's waist as he drove him back into the supports of the viewing stand.

Locklear's breath burst from his lungs as he struck the heavy wooden beams, but he managed to strike the man behind the ear with his sword hilt. The man staggered away, obviously intent upon escape rather than combat, but the shouting voices heralded the approach of more guardsmen. Turning, the man struck out at Locklear, who was struggling to regain his breath, and his fist found Locklear's ear.

Pain and confusion overwhelmed Locklear as the assailant rushed into the darkness under the viewing stands. The Baron shook his head to clear it, then turned and hurried after.

In the sudden darkness under the stands, the man could be hiding anywhere. "In here!" Locklear yelled, in reply to an inquiring shout, and within seconds a half-dozen guardsmen were standing behind him. "Spread out and be alert."

The men did as they were bidden and slowly advanced beneath the viewing stands. The men closest to the front were forced to stoop, as the lowest risers of the stands were but four feet off the ground. One soldier walked along, poking his sword into the gloom, against the fugitive having crawled under the frontmost stands to hide. Above them the sounds of citizens leaving the stands filled the gloom with a thunderous clatter of sandals and boots upon wood, but after a few minutes, the noise diminished.

Then the sounds of struggle came from before them. Locklear and his men hurried forward. In the dark, two figures held a third. Without seeing who was whom, Locklear drove his shoulder into the nearest body, knocking everyone to the ground. More guards piled on top of the fray, until at last the struggle at the bottom of the mass was ended by sheer weight. Then the guards were quickly unpiling and the combatants were pulled up. Locklear grinned as he saw that one of them was James and the other Borric. Looking down, he could see the still form of the man in robes. "Drag him out into the light," he ordered the guards. To James he said, "Is he dead?"

"Not unless you broke his neck jumping on him that way. You damn near broke mine."

"Where's Erland?" asked Locklear.

"Here," came an answering voice in the gloom. "I was covering the other side of the fray in case he got past these two," he indicated James and Borric.

"Nursing your precious side, you mean," shot back Borric with a grin.

Erland shrugged. "Maybe."

They all followed the guards, who were carrying the still form of the assailant, and when they were in the afternoon sunlight again, discovered a cordon had been thrown up by other guards.

Locklear bent over. "Let's see what we have here." He pulled back the hood and a face stared blankly up at the sky. "He's dead."

James was instantly on his knees, forcing open the man's mouth. He sniffed and said, "Poisoned himself."

"Who is he?" said Borric.

"And why was he trying to kill you, Uncle Jimmy?" said Erland.

"Not me, you idiot," snapped James. He pointed at Borric. "He was trying to kill your brother."

A guard approached. "My Lord, the man struck by the dart is dead. He died within seconds of his wounding."

Borric forced himself to a nervous grin. "Why would anyone wish to kill me?"

Erland joined in the strained humor. "An angry husband?"

James said, "Not you, Borric conDoin." He glanced around the crowd, as if seeking other assassins. "Someone tried to kill the future King of Isles."

Locklear opened the man's robe, revealing a black tunic. "James, look here."

Baron James peered down at the dead man. His skin was dark, even darker than Gardan's, marking him as Keshian by ancestry, but those of Keshian ancestry were common in this part of the Kingdom. There were brown- and black-skinned people in every strata of Krondorian society. But this man wore odd clothing, a tunic of expensive black silk and soft slippers unlike anything the young Princes had seen before.

James inspected the dead man's hands, and noticed a ring set with a dark gem, then looked for a necklace and found none. "What are you doing?"

"Old habits," was all Jimmy would answer. "He's no Nighthawk," he observed, mentioning the legendary Guild of Assassins. "But this may be worse."

"How?" asked Locklear, remembering all too well when the Nighthawks had sought to kill Arutha twenty years before.

"He's Keshian."

Locklear leaned down and inspected the ring. Ashen-faced, he stood. "Worse. He's a member of the Royal House of Kesh."

The room was silent. Those who sat in the circle of chairs moved slightly, as discomfort over the attempt upon Borric manifested itself in the creaks of leather and wood, the rustle of cloth, and the clink of jewelry.

Duke Gardan rubbed at the bridge of his nose. "It's preposterous. What would Kesh gain in killing a member of your family? Does the Empress wish war?"

Erland chimed in. "She's worked as hard as anyone to preserve the peace, or at least all the reports say that. Why would she want Borric dead? Who—"

Borric interrupted his brother. "Whoever wants war between the Kingdom and the Empire."

Locklear nodded. "It's such a shallow lie; so transparent an attempt that it is not believable."

"Yet . . ." Arutha mused aloud, "what if that assassin was chosen to fail? A dupe. What if I am supposed to withhold my envoy, keep my sons at home with me."

Gardan nodded. "Thereby insulting the Royal House of Kesh."

James, who leaned against the wall behind Arutha said, "We've managed a fair job already by dispatching a member of the Empress's house. He was a very distant cousin, true, but a cousin, nevertheless."

Gardan returned to rubbing the bridge of his nose, a gesture of frustration more than fatigue. "And what was I supposed to say to the Keshian Ambassador? 'Oh, we've found this young fellow, who seems to be a member of your Royal House. We had no idea he was in Krondor. And we're sorry to tell you he's dead. Oh, by the way, he tried to murder Prince Borric.'"

Arutha leaned back in his chair, his fingers forming a tent before his face, absently flexing in a gesture that all in the room had come to recognize over the years. He glanced at last at James.

"We could dump the body," offered the young Baron.

Gardan said, "I beg your pardon?"

James stretched. "Take the body down to the bay and toss it in."

Erland grinned. "Rough treatment for a member of the Royal House of Kesh, wouldn't you say?"

Arutha said, "Why?"

James moved to sit on the edge of Arutha's desk, as the Prince over the years had come to conduct very informal sessions with close advisors and family. "He's not officially a guest in the city. We aren't supposed to know he's here. No one is supposed to know. The only Keshians who will know he's here are those who know *why* he's here. And I doubt any of them will inquire as to his well-being. He's now the forgotten man, unless we call attention to his whereabouts."

Dryly, Borric added, "And his condition."

"We can claim he tried to kill Borric," James acknowledged, "but all we have is a Keshian corpse, a blowgun, and some poisoned darts."

"And a dead merchant," added Gardan.

"Dead merchants are a frequent enough commodity on any given day in the Western Realm, my Lord Duke," observed James. "I say we strip him of his ring and toss him into the bay. Let the Keshians who sent him wonder for a while."

Arutha said nothing for a while, then gave one affirmative nod. James indicated with a jerk of his head that Locklear should use Royal Guardsmen for the job, and the other young Baron slipped through the door. After a short conference with Lieutenant William outside, Locklear returned to his seat.

Arutha sighed. Looking at James, he said, "Kesh. What else?"

James shrugged. "Hints, rumors. Their new Ambassador is . . . an odd choice. He's what they call a 'trueblood,' but not of the Royal House—the assassin would have been a more logical choice. The Ambassador is a purely political appointment. It's rumored that he may actually have stronger influence in Kesh's court than many with royal blood. I can't find any obvious reason why he should be given such an honor—save as a compromise, to appease some faction in court."

Arutha nodded. "While none of this makes apparent sense, still, we must play according to the rules of such games." He was silent for a while, and no one spoke as the Prince gathered his thoughts. "Send word to our people in Kesh. I want our agents hard at work before my sons arrive. If someone seeks to suck us into war with Kesh, striking at the King's nephews would be a logical choice. You will accompany the Princes to Kesh. There is no one I trust more to swim through these murky waters."

Baron Locklear said, "Highness?"

Looking at the other young Baron, Arutha said, "You will accompany Baron James, as Master of Ceremonies, Chief of Protocol, and the rest of that idiocy. The Imperial Court is dominated by women. We will at last find a use for that infamous Locklear charm. Instruct Captain Valdis he will act in your place as Knight-Marshal. And have Cousin William take over the Household Guard as acting Captain." Arutha drummed his fingers on the table. "I want you," he said to James, "shed of any office and protocol on this journey. Your only title will be 'tutor.' You must be free to come and go as you need."

James had come to understand Arutha's moods as well as any outside his family. A mind as complex and deep as the Prince's was like a chess master's; Arutha was planning every conceivable outcome as many moves in advance as possible.

James motioned the boys and Locklear to come outside with him, and once all four were in the hall, he said, "We leave early in the morning."

Borric said, "We're not due to leave for another three days."

James said, "Officially. If your Keshian friend has compatriots about, I would prefer they not know our plans." He glanced at Locklear. "A small mounted troop, twenty guards, dressed as mercenaries. Fast horses, and send word to Shamata we're going to need fresh mounts and stores enough for two hundred escorts."

Locklear said, "We'll be arriving in Shamata at the same time as any message and two hundred—"

James cut him off. "We're not going to Shamata. We want them to think we'll travel in state to Shamata. We're going to Stardock."

Chapter Three
Stardock

Dust swirled.

Twenty-four riders moved at a steady pace along the edge of the Great Star Lake. A week and a half of hard riding had taken them southward from Krondor, to Landreth on the north coast of the Sea of Dreams. Then, from where it entered the sea, the Star River led them further southward, the rugged mountains of the Grey Range always in sight as they entered the lush Vale of Dreams. Years of border wars between the Kingdom and the Empire had seen this rich farming land changing hands many times. Those who lived in this part of the world spoke the languages of the Southern Kingdom and the Northern Empire with equal fluency. And the sight of fourteen armed mercenaries evoked no notice. Many armed bands of men rode the vale.

At the midpoint of the river, near a small waterfall, they forded the currents, making for the south shore. Upon reaching the headwaters of the Star River, the Great Star Lake, they turned to track the shore-line southward, seeking that point closest to the island dominating the center of the lake, Stardock. There they would find the ferry that provided passage from the shore to the island.

Along the banks of the shore they passed tiny fishing and farming villages, often no more than an extended family, little groups of huts and cottages, but all looking prosperous and well tended. The community of magicians upon Stardock had grown over the years, and now other communities had developed to meet the demands for food of those upon the island.

Borric urged his horse forward, as they rounded a small promontory of land, bringing them their first clear view of the large building upon the island. It nearly shone in the orange light of the sunset, while the advancing night behind turned the distant sky violet and grey. "Gods and demons, Uncle Jimmy, look at the size of that place!"

James nodded. "I had heard they were building a massive center for learning, but the tales never did it justice."

Locklear said, "Duke Gardan visited here many years ago. He told me they had laid a huge foundation for the building . . . but this is larger than anything I've seen."

Glancing at the falling light, James said, "If we hurry, we'll make the island within the next two hours. I'd rather a warm meal and clean bed than another night on the trail." Setting heels to his horse's sides, he moved on.

Under a canopy of brilliant stars on one of the rare nights when all three moons had yet to rise, they passed through a small gap between hillocks and entered a prosperous-looking town. Torches and lanterns blazed at every storefront—an extravagance in all but the wealthiest of towns and cities—and children ran after them, shouting and laughing in the general confusion. Beggars and prostitutes asked favors or offered them respectively, and ramshackle taverns stood open to provide the weary traveler with a cool drink, hot meal, and warm company.

Locklear shouted over the noise, "Quite a prosperous little metropolis growing here."

James glanced about at the dirt and squalor. "Quite. The blessings of civilization," he observed.

Borric said, "Perhaps we should investigate one of these small pubs—"

"No," answered James. "They're certain to offer you refreshments at the Academy."

Erland smiled ruefully. "A sweet and slightly feeble wine, no doubt. What else would one expect from an assemblage of old scholars, poking around in musty piles of manuscripts."

James shook his head. They came to what was obviously the crossroads of the two main streets in the town and turned toward the lake. As James expected, down near the waterfront a large pier had been constructed and several ferries of differing sizes waited to haul goods and people to the island. Despite the late hour, workers still stacked sacks of grain against the need of hauling them the next morning.

Reining in, James called down to the nearest ferryman, "Good evening. We seek passage to Stardock island."

A face, dominated by a hawk-beaked nose, with ill-cut bangs almost hiding the eyes, was revealed as the man glanced over his shoulder and said, "I can make one quick run across, sir. Five coppers a man, sir, but you need stable your horses here."

Jimmy smiled. "How about ten gold pieces for the lot of us, including the mounts?"

The man returned to his work. "No bargaining, sir."

Borric rattled his sword a bit as he said, half-jokingly, "What, you turn your back upon us?"

The man turned again to face them. Touching his forehead, in slightly sarcastic tones, he said, "Sorry, young sir, but no disrespect was intended."

Borric was about to respond, when James tapped his arm with a gloved hand and pointed. In the gloom, just out of the light of a guttering torch, a young man in a plain robe of homespun sat at the dockside watching the interplay calmly.

Borric said, "What?"

"The local constable, I expect."

"Him?" said Borric. "He looks more a beggar or monk than any sort of fighting man."

The ferryman nodded. "Right you are, sir. He's our Peacekeeper." He grinned up at James. "You know your way around, sir. Yes, you do. That's one of the magicians from the island. The council that runs the place keeps it peaceful-like over here in Stardock Town, so they make sure that we have the means. He has no sword, young sir," he said to Borric, "but with a wave of his hand he can stun you worse than a poleax to the noggin'. Believe me, sir, I found that out the hard way." His voice falling to a near mutter, he added, "Or, it could be the magic what sets you to itching so bad you wish to die. . . ." Returning to the topic at hand, he raised his voice, "And as far as hagglin', sir, as much as I do enjoy a good round of lying about how much injury a good profit does my children's diet, the fact is the Academy sets the rates." He scratched his chin. "Suppose you could haggle with that young spellcaster over there, but I expect he'll tell you the same. Given the traffic back and forth, the prices are fair."

"Where is the stable?" James asked, but just then several small boys pushed from the crowd and offered to take their horses.

"The boy's will see your mounts to a clean stable." James nodded and dismounted. The other riders followed suit. Instantly, small hands removed reins from James's grasp as other children did likewise throughout the company. "Very well," said James, "but see they have clean stalls and fresh hay and oats. And have a farrier check shoes, will you?"

James ceased his commentary as something caught his eye. He turned abruptly, reached out, and yanked a small boy away from Borric's horse. James lifted the boy off the ground and looked him hard in the eyes. "Give it back," he said with a calm note of menace. The boy began to protest, then when James shook him for emphasis, thought better of it and held out a small coin purse to Borric. Borric's mouth opened as he patted himself down and then accepted the purse.

James put the boy down but held onto his shirt front, then leaned down so he was eye to eye with the would-be cutpurse. "Boy, before I was half your size I knew more than twice what you'll *ever* know about thieving. Do you believe me?" The boy could only nod, so frightened was he at discovery. "Then take my word on the matter. You haven't the knack. You'll end up at the end of a short rope waiting for a long drop before you're twelve if you keep this up. Find an honest trade. Now, if anything is missing when we leave, I'll know who to look for, won't I?" The boy nodded again.

James sent him scurrying and turned to the ferryman. "Then it'll be twenty-four of us on foot to the island."

At this, the young magician rose to his feet and said, "It's not often we have armed soldiers come to the Academy. May I ask your business?"

"You may ask," said James. "But we'll save our answers for another. If we need your permission, send word to the magician Pug that old friends come to call."

The young magician raised an eyebrow. "Who should I tell him comes to call?"

James smiled, "Tell him . . . Baron James of Krondor and"—he glanced at the twins—"some of his kinsmen."

A small group waited to welcome the company as the ferry came to rest against the shore with a bump. A loading dock was the only sign that this was the entrance to perhaps the strangest community upon Midkemia, the Academy of Magicians. Workers aided the soldiers as they negotiated the dock. Many were unsteady after their first ride on a flat-bottomed ferry. Lanterns hung from the dock posts, illuminating the welcoming committee.

A short man of middle years, wearing only a black robe and sandals, was at the center of the group. To his right stood a striking, dark-skinned woman with iron-grey hair. An old man in robes stood to his left, a large huntsman in leather tunic and trousers at his shoulder. Behind them two younger men, attired in robes, waited patiently.

As James, Locklear, and the twins stepped off the ferry, the short man stepped forward and bowed slightly. "Your Highnesses honor us." Then he said, "Welcome to Stardock."

Borric and Erland stepped forward, and awkwardly held out their hands to exchange a less formal hello with the man. While they were Princes born, used to some degree of deference and awe at their rank at times, here before them stood a man legends and tales had grown around. "Cousin Pug," Borric said, "thank you for receiving us."

The magician smiled and everyone relaxed. Though nearly forty-eight years old, he looked a man in his early thirties. Brown eyes almost shone with warmth and, despite his age, the dark beard couldn't hide an expression that was almost boyish. This youthful face could not belong to the man reputed to be the single most powerful individual in the world.

Erland and he quickly exchanged greetings, and James stepped forward. "Lord Pug . . ." James began.

"Just Pug, James." He smiled. "Around here we have little use for formal titles within our community. Despite King Lyam's generous intentions in creating a tiny duchy out of Stardock and naming me its lord and master, we rarely think of such things." He took James by the arm. "Come; you remember my wife?"

James and his companions bowed slightly and took the woman's slender hand. Upon close inspection, James was surprised at how delicate the woman looked. He hadn't seen her for over seven years, but she had been a robust, healthy woman in her early forties, with suntanned cheeks and raven dark hair. Now she looked ten years her husband's senior. "My Lady," said James, bowing over her hand.

The woman smiled and years vanished from her. "Just Katala, James. How is our son?"

James grinned. "William is happy. He is Acting Captain of Arutha's Guard. He is well thought of, and I expect will hold the office when Valdis steps down. And he courts several lovely ladies of the Princess's retinue. He's a fine officer and will rise high."

Pug said, "He should be here—" Seeing his wife's features darken, he said, "I know, dearest, we have put that argument to rest. Now," he said to the Princes, "may I present the others?"

When Borric nodded, Pug said, "I think you boys will remember Kulgan, my old teacher. And Meecham, who oversees our community's food stores and a thousand other tasks." The two men named both bowed, and Borric and Erland shook each hand in turn. The old magician who had been Pug's teacher moved with difficulty, aided by a cane and the hand of the other man.

Meecham, a powerful-looking man of advancing years, scolded the old magician like a nagging wife. "You should have stayed in your room. . . ."

Kulgan shook off the aiding hand as Erland moved to take Borric's place before Pug's old master. "I'm old, Meecham, not dying." The man's hair was white as winter's first snow, and the skin was lined and tanned like old leather. But the blue eyes were still bright and alert. "Your Highness," he said to Erland.

The Prince smiled back. As boys they had delighted in Kulgan's visits, for the old magician had entertained them with stories punctuated by small feats of magic. "Seems we're informal, here, Uncle Kulgan. It's good to see you again. It's been too long."

The two younger men behind were unknown to James. Pug said, "These are leaders in our community and were among the first of those to come to Stardock to learn the Greater Magic. They are teachers of others, now. This is Körsh." The first man, tall and bald, bowed slightly to the Princes. His eyes shone brightly in contrast to his very dark skin, and gold earrings hung to his shoulders.

The second man looked nearly the twin of the first, save for a full black beard, oiled to ringlets which hung loosely from his cheeks. "And his brother, Watume."

Pug said, "You must all be tired from your journey." He glanced around. "I was expecting our daughter, Gamina, to join us, but she is helping to feed the children and I suppose she was detained. You'll meet her soon enough.

"Now, to your quarters. We have rooms for you in the Academy. You've missed supper, but we'll have hot food delivered to your room. In the morning, we can visit."

The small company moved up the shoreline, to where they could see past the monstrous building that dominated the island. Fully forty stories tall at points, its central focus was a lofty spire that reached another hundred feet above the roof. It seemed little more than an unrailed stairway around a column, topped by a tiny platform. It was illuminated by an odd blue light which shone from below, so that it seemed to almost float upward, rather than be a thing of stone and mortar.

"Everyone is struck by the sight of our Tower of Testing," Pug remarked. "That is where those of the Greater Path learn their first mastery, and leave their apprenticeship behind."

The two dark-skinned brothers cleared their throats in a meaningful way and Pug smiled. "Some of us have differing feelings as to how much 'outsiders' should be allowed to know."

Rounding the shore, they saw a rather busy town at the other end of the building. Cleaner than its twin upon the shoreline, it was still its equal in activity. Despite the advancing hour, many people were in the streets upon one errand or another. "Stardock Town," said Katala, pride evident in her voice.

Locklear said, "I thought the town upon the shore was Stardock Town."

Pug said, "So those who live there call it. But this is the true town upon the island of Stardock. This is where many of our brothers and sisters in magic live. Here is where their families abide. Here we have built a haven for those who have been driven from their communities by fear and hatred." Pug motioned for his guests to enter the main Academy building through a large double door and escorted them inside. At an intersection of two halls, most of the welcoming committee bid the guests good night, while Pug led the travelers down to a series of doors upon each side of a long hall. "We're lacking in regal accommodations, I'm afraid," he said, "but these guest cells are warm, dry, and comfortable. You'll find a basin for washing, and if you leave your dirty travel clothing outside, someone will see it is washed. The garderobe is at the far end of the hall. Now, rest well and we'll have a long talk in the morning."

Pug bid them good night and the twins quickly found the food waiting for them in their cells. Up and down the hall the night was full of the noise of soldiers shedding traveling armor and arms, splashing water, and the clink of knives against serving plates. Soon all were gone from the hall, save a puzzled-looking Locklear standing next to James. "What ails you?"

James shrugged. "Nothing, I guess. Tired, or . . ." he let his voice trail off. He thought of Kulgan's age and Katala's less than healthy appearance. "It's just that the years have not been kind to some fine people." Then his manner brightened, "Or it could be my youthful crimes coming back to haunt me. I'm just not comfortable with the idea of spending the night in any room referred to as a 'cell.' "

With a wry smile and a nod of agreement, Locklear bid his companion good night. A moment later, James stood alone in the long, empty hall. Something was not right. But he left that feeling for the next day. Now he needed food and a wash.

With the sound of a bird chirping outside his window, James was awake. As was his habit, the young Baron of the Prince's court rose before the sun. To his surprise, he discovered his clothing had been washed and folded and left just inside his door. A light sleeper by nature and quick to full wakefulness by training, he was discomforted that anyone could have opened his door and not disturbed him. James pulled on the clean tunic and trousers, foregoing the heavy traveling boots. Since childhood he had preferred bare feet, and over the years it had become something of a common joke among the palace staff that should one enter Baron James's office, one was likely to find his boots removed and tucked away under his desk.

He made his way to the outer doorway, moving soundlessly. He was certain that everyone else was still asleep, but his stealth was not born of consideration, it was habitual. As a boy in the Poor Quarter of the city, James had earned his livelihood as a thief, and moving without sound was second nature.

Opening the outside door, he slipped through and closed it silently behind. The sky had already turned slate grey and the eastern horizon was showing the blush of the approaching sunrise. The only sounds were the calling of birds and the thud of a single axe falling, as someone cut wood for an early morning fire. James moved away from the huge building of the Academy and made his way along the path that led to the village.

The sound of wood being cut fell away as that unknown farmer or fisherman's wife finished the task. After a hundred yards, the path diverged, one part heading toward the village while a smaller path led toward the lakeshore. James decided he was in little mood for idle morning chatter with townspeople, so he moved toward the water.

In the gloom he almost didn't see the black-robed figure until he was nearly upon him. Pug turned and smiled. He pointed eastward. "This is my favorite part of the day."

James nodded. "I thought I'd be the first up."

Pug kept his eyes fastened upon the horizon. "No, I sleep very little."

"The wear doesn't show. I don't think you look a day older than when I last saw you seven years ago."

Pug nodded. "There are things about myself I am just discovering, James. When I took upon myself the mantel of sorcerer . . ." his voice trailed off. "We've never really talked, have we?"

James shook his head. "Not about anything profound, if that's what you mean. It's not exactly as if our paths cross frequently. We first met at Arutha and Anita's wedding," he ticked off on his fingers as he spoke, "and again after the battle at Sethanon." Both men glanced at each other and nothing needed to be said between them about the cataclysmic battle that had taken place there. "Then twice since in Krondor."

Pug returned his attention to the east, where the first hot pink and orange of the sun's rays struck the clouds. "When I was a boy I lived in Crydee. I was nothing more than a Far Coast peasant lad. I worked in the kitchen with my foster family and had ambitions to be a soldier." He fell silent.

James waited. He had little desire to talk about his past, though it was well enough known to anyone of rank in the city of Krondor, and to everyone in the palace. "I was a thief."

"Jimmy the Hand," said Pug. "Yes, but what sort of boy were you?"

James considered the question for a moment, then answered. "Brash. That's the first word that comes to mind." He watched as the dawn unfolded. Neither man spoke for several minutes as each saw the fingers of light striking the clouds hanging in the east. The fiery rim of the disc of the sun began to appear. James said, "I . . . was also foolish at times. I had no idea of there being any limit to what I could do. I have no doubt that had I continued that existence, I'd have finally taken one big chance too many. I'd most likely be dead by now."

"Brash," Pug repeated. "And foolish at times." He indicated with his head the Academy. "Not unlike the royal twins."

James smiled. "Not unlike the Princes."

"What else?"

James considered. Without false modesty, he said, "Brilliant, I suppose you could say, or gifted at least. Things often seemed obvious to me that confused many of those around me. At least the world seemed a more obvious place then. I'm not so sure I wasn't a great deal smarter as a boy than I am now as a man."

Pug motioned that James should walk with him and started slow progress toward the water's edge. "When I was a boy, my modest ambitions seemed the most splendid things. Now . . ."

"You seem troubled," James ventured.

"Not as you would understand it," Pug answered. James turned and in the grey light saw an unreadable expression on Pug's face. "Tell me of the attempt upon Borric. You were closest to him."

James said, "News travels fast."

"It always does. And any coming conflict between the Kingdom and Kesh is of concern for us."

"Given your location, I can understand. You are a window upon the Empire." He gestured south, toward the not-distant border. James told Pug what he knew of the attempt, and finished by saying, "That the assassin was Keshian is hardly in doubt, but all those clues that point to the Royal House of Kesh being at the root of the attempt . . . it's *too* clear. I think someone seeks to dupe us." He turned as they lost sight of the town, regarding the upper stories of the Academy. "You have many Keshians here?"

Pug nodded. "And from Roldem, Queg, the Peaks of the Quor, and other places. Here we pay little attention to matters of nation. We are concerned with other issues."

James said, "Those two who met with us last night . . ."

"Watume and Körsh, yes. They are Keshian. From the city of Kesh itself." Before James could speak, Pug said, "They are not Imperial agents. I would know. Trust me. They think nothing of politics. In fact, if anything, they are too eager for us to be apart from the rest of the world."

James turned for a moment, to regard the hulking edifice of the Academy. "This is a Kingdom duchy, at least in name. But many have wondered aloud what it is you build here. There is something about this place that strikes many in the court as odd."

"And dangerous," Pug added. James turned to study the magician's face. "Which is why I work diligently to see that the Academy never partakes in national conflicts. On *any* side."

James considered his words. "There are few among the nobility who are as comfortable with the idea of magic as our King and his brother. Growing up with Kulgan in the household as they did, they think nothing about it. But others . . ."

"Still would see us driven from cities and towns, or hung, or burned at stakes. I know." Pug said, "In the twenty years we have worked here, much has changed . . . yet so little has changed."

Finally James said, "Pug, I feel something odd in you. I detected it last night. What is it?"

Pug's eyes narrowed as he studied James. "Strange you should observe that, when those closest to me don't see it." He reached the edge of the lake and halted. With an outstretched hand, he pointed. A family of snowy egrets were preening themselves and squawking in the shallow of the lake. "Beautiful, aren't they?"

James could only agree as he took in his surroundings. "This is a beautiful place."

"It wasn't so when I first came here," answered Pug. "The legend is that this lake was formed by a falling star, hence its name. But this island was not the cooled body of that star, which I calculate could have been no larger than this." He held his hands apart about six inches. "I think the star cracked the crust of the earth and lava rose up to create this island. It was rocky and barren when I first came here, with only a bit of tenacious grass at the water's edge, and a few hearty bushes here and there. I brought what you see here, the grass, the trees, the animals." He grinned, and years vanished from his face. "The birds found their own way over."

James considered the groves of trees nearby and the deep meadow grass he saw everywhere. "A not inconsiderable feat."

Pug waved away the comment as if it was a common enough conjurer's trick. "Will there be war?"

James let out an audible sigh. It held the sound of resignation. "That's the question, isn't it?" he asked rhetorically. "No, that's not the question. There is always war. The question is when and between which nations. If I have any say in the matter, there'll be no war between the Kingdom and Kesh in my lifetime. But then, I may not have much to say about the matter."

"You ride a dangerous course."

"It's not the first time. I wish circumstances could have spared the Princes the need to go."

"They are their father's sons," observed Pug. "They must go where duty requires. Even if it means risking much to gain little."

Pug resumed his walk along the shore and James fell into step at his side.

James could only nod at that. "Such is the burden of their birthright."

"Well," said Pug, "there are short respites, such as this one, along the way. Why don't you go over there?" He pointed to a stand of willow trees masking the shore. "On the other side is a small inlet fed by a hot springs. It is a most invigorating experience. Soak in the hot water a bit, then jump into the lake. It will set you right and you can be back in time to join us for the morning meal."

James smiled. "Thank you, it sounds just the thing. I'm so used to having much work before breaking my fast. A pleasant way to fill an hour or so will be welcomed."

Pug turned back toward the town and after a few steps said, "Oh, be careful of swimming in the shore grasses. It's easy to get turned about and lose your way. The wind makes them bend toward the island, so should you get lost, simply swim in that direction until you feel land underfoot. Then walk out."

"Thank you. I'll be cautious. Good morning.

"Good morning, James. I'll see you at breakfast."

As Pug returned to the Academy, James headed toward the stand of trees the magician had indicated.

Passing between large boles, pushing aside hanging greenery like a curtain, he discovered a narrow barren path that led down the side of a small dell, toward the lakeshore. Near the water's edge, he could see steam rising in the morning coolness. James inspected a small pool that was obviously fed from underground, as the steam all rose from that one location only. A small rivulet of water overspilled one side and ran to the shore, joining the lake there. It was but no more than twenty yards from pool to lake. He glanced about. The pool and this small stretch of shoreline were screened on three sides by trees affording him ample privacy. James removed his tunic and trousers and stuck a foot in the pool. It was almost hotter than he cared for in his own bath! He sank in and let the warmth infuse him, relaxing tense muscles.

Tense muscles? He wondered. He had just awoke. Why should he feel tension. His own voice answered, *because much risk is undertaken sending two boys to play at a game of Keshian court politics older than the house of conDoin.* He sighed. Pug was a strange man but a wise and powerful one; he was an adopted kinsman to the King and a Duke. Perhaps James should ask Pug's opinion. Then he thought against it. As much as Pug was reputed to have been a savior to the Kingdom in years past—there was something odd about Stardock and the manner in which it was governed. James decided he'd find out as much as possible about what went on here before speaking in confidence to the magician.

Gods, how I hate waking up tired, he thought. Then he lay back as comfortably as possible to meditate upon his troubles. The soothing heat seemed to creep into his bones, and minutes later his mind floated. He ran down a street, and a hand grabbed him by the arm. He closed his eyes in remembrance. His first memory. He could have been no more than three. It was his mother, pulling him inside her whore's crib, out of the sight of slavers who were prowling the night. He remembered being held tightly while she clamped her hand over his mouth. Later she would be gone. When he was older, he knew she was dead, but all he could remember of that night was the man with the loud voice shouting at her and hitting her and the red everywhere. Jimmy put the ugly memory aside as he fell into the warmth of the water. Soon he dozed.

He awoke without moving. From the angle of the sun, he couldn't have dozed for more than minutes, perhaps a half-hour at best. The morning was quiet, but something had disturbed him. He had somewhat outgrown his childhood habit of coming to his feet with a dagger in his hand—it had proved quite disturbing to the servants in the palace—but he still kept a dagger close by. Opening his eyes he moved them first, and saw nothing in his field of vision. He turned his head and again could see nothing above the rim of the pond. He slowly elbowed himself up, feeling foolish as full wakefulness returned —who would be a threat here upon the island of Stardock?

James peeked up above the rim of the pool and found nothing. There was a strange feeling about the place and he couldn't find a name for it. It was as if he had entered a room a moment after someone had left through another door; without knowing why, he knew someone had just past beyond his view.

Instincts born of city dangers set off a primitive alarm in his head, an alarm that had saved him from danger too many times before to be ignored. Yet this alarm didn't have the echoing ring of danger to it, rather it was excitement. Years before, James had learned the discipline of the night, remaining motionless, keeping one's mind distant from the concerns of the moment so sudden movement wouldn't trigger a response. He relaxed his breathing and kept still. He glanced over the rim again, and the echo of another's passing was gone. The small inlet looked as it had before.

He lay back again and sought to recapture the warm calm that had finally overtaken him, but he couldn't relax his mind. An excitement began to build in James, as if something glorious was approaching, and there was a sadness, too, as if something miraculous had just passed within touching distance and left him behind. Odd feelings of giddy delight and childish tears clashed inside him.

46

Lacking a satisfying answer, he heaved himself out of the pool and raced headlong for the lake, yelling a boy's shout of frustration released. He dove under and came up spitting water. A sound of relief escaped him as the cold lake seemed to shock him to full wakefulness.

He was an indifferent swimmer but enjoyed the occasion from time to time. Like most children of Krondor's Poor Quarter, when the hot winds of summer blew he had sought relief at the harborside, diving from the piers into the salt water and refuse. The sensation of clean water upon his body was something he had remained ignorant of until well into his thirteenth year.

James found himself swimming lazily toward the far side of the inlet. The trees and reeds cut into the water, providing a series of narrow passages to whatever lay upon the other side of the inlet. He picked his way through, half-swimming, half-paddling, until he came to a thick stand of reeds and grasses. He saw the grasses and reeds were wide-spaced, allowing ample vision of the shoreline. He turned upon his back and kicked lazily. Above him, the morning sky turned brilliant, as the sun was now full upon the day. The clouds were white and beautiful as they sped upon their course. Then he was in the grasses, seeing stalks rise high above his head as he felt their ticklish caress while he swam. After a few minutes of swimming this way, he righted himself and glanced about.

Things appeared different and the way back not apparent. Calm by nature, he found the notion of swimming in circles within the reeds an unappealing one but not a fearful one. He remembered Pug's words and saw the grasses all bending to his left. He would simply swim to where he felt ground underfoot and walk out.

Within a minute, he felt the shore under his toes. He walked through thick reeds and tall grasses, toward a line of trees at the water's edge. The hanging branches and thick greenery plunged him into shadows while he was still up to his chest in the water. He could only see a few feet in any direction, and the morning light made everything a pattern of murk and blinding blue-white sky above. James followed the rising bottom until he was in water below his waist. He felt foolish to be striding around naked, but as there was no one about, he would only need a short scamper back to the pool where he had left his clothing.

James took a step and suddenly found himself falling into deep water. A current had eroded a small channel to a depth more than his six feet and he came up sputtering and blind. He paddled to the far side and again felt land under him.

A birdcall above him made him wonder if the creature was laughing at his clumsy progress. Sighing, he continued toward the shore, which was but a few yards away, judging by the glimpses of land he got between the trees. With the water at his knees, he was confronted with an impassable barrier of trees and reeds, a rocky overhang rising up to shoulder height. He moved to his right, toward what seemed a closer exit from the foliage that conspired to trap him, and again felt a drop beneath his feet. He settled down to chest-high water and pushed through a very thick curtain of reeds. His progress was slow and he could only move a few feet at a time. His overwhelming feeling was one of unalloyed stupidity for finding himself so distant from where he wanted to be. Pleasant swim before breakfast, indeed.

As his knees brushed a ridge of lake bottom, signaling an end to the channel he was wading through, he parted the reeds before him. Abruptly, James found himself confronted by a sight totally unexpected. Fair skin, white as a newborn's, was revealed merely a yard before him. And by circumstance of his depressed perspective, he was staring directly at the naked backside of a young woman. Her nearly white-blond hair hung wet from her head as she squeezed water from it, a pose which conspired to display her hips and buttocks in a slightly exaggerated and flattering pose.

James's breath caught in his chest. The same mixed feeling of alarm and excitement struck him like a hammer blow. He felt as embarrassed at his intrusion into her privacy as he would have felt had she found him at his own pool. Conflicting signals to hold motionless, move back, say something, not be discovered, all clashed together and paralyzed him.

Again his boyhood training overroad conscious thought and he froze in place. Then another thought intruded, and he felt his stomach tighten as a hot rush of excitement gathered in his stomach and groin. Almost aloud he said, *It's about the most beautiful bottom I've ever seen.*

Instantly the young woman turned about, her hands flying up to her mouth, as if startled by a noise. In that instant, James discovered that the rest of her was equal to what he had already seen. Her figure was slender, like a dancer's, and her arms and neck were long and elegant, her stomach flat, her breasts not large, but full and lovely. As her hand dropped away from her face, he saw a high forehead, fine cheekbones, and pale, slightly pink lips. Her eyes, wide in astonishment, were the blue of midwinter's ice. All these details were etched in his mind in an instant. A thousand instants of recognition flooded through James, and in each he knew the young woman before him was at once the most wonderful and terrifying sight he had ever beheld. Then those beautiful pale blue eyes narrowed and suddenly pain exploded in James's head.

He fell back as if struck by a weapon, and his voice cried out hollow in his own ears as he went beneath the water's surface. Sharp knives of hot agony filled his mind as water filled his mouth. James sank into the murk of the water as he lost consciousness.

In a place which was not a place James swam, drowning in memories: his playing upon the street cobbles and never a moment passing without the fear. Strangers were a danger, yet every day brought strangers into his mother's house. Men who were loud and frightening passed the boy each day, some ignoring him, others attempting to amuse him for a brief moment with a pat upon the head or an odd word.

Then the night when she died and no one came: the man with the crooked smile had heard him cry and fled. Jimmy had found his way out of the house, his child's feet padding through the sticky blood on the floor.

Then the fights with the other boy for the bone and the bread crust left out behind the inns and taverns, eating the raw wheat and corn that spilled from under the grain wagons at the dockside. And the drops of bitter wine in the almost empty bottle. The occasional coin from a generous passerby to buy a hot pie. Hunger was always there.

A voice in the dark, no face to remember, asked him if he was clever. He had been clever. Very clever. His beginning with the Mockers.

Danger around, at all times. No friends, no allies, only the rules of the guild to protect Jimmy the Hand. But he was gifted; the Upright Man forgave small trespasses from one who brought in so much wealth at such an early age.

Then the man with the crooked smile reappeared. Jimmy had been twelve. It had been nothing of proud honor and hot revenge. A boy thief had crept in and dosed the drunk's wine with a poison purchased from a man dealing in such things. The man with the crooked smile died without knowing his murderer's reasons, his face blackening as his tongue protruded through swollen lips and his eyes bulging, while the son of a murdered whore watched through a crack in the ceiling of the flop house where he lay. Jimmy had felt no triumph, but somehow he hoped his mother rested better. He never knew his mother's name. He felt as if he wanted to cry but didn't know how. He had cried twice . . . no, three times in honesty. When Anita lay stricken and when he thought Arutha dead. That had been grief, and it was not a sign of weakness or shame. But he had cried in the darkness when trapped in the cave with the rock serpent, before Duke Martin had saved him. He could never admit to his fear.

Other images: his incredible, almost inhuman skills in the calling. His discovery that his fate was linked to great things when he helped to hide the Prince and Princess of Krondor from their captors during the reign of Mad King Rodric. His death duel with a Nighthawk upon the rooftops of the city, saving Arutha's life, though he had not known it at the time. His travels twice to the Northlands and the great battles of Armengar and Sethanon, and the peace that followed after the battle to stem the return of the Dragon Host.

Now he was James.

His service to Arutha and his reward by being elevated to a place in his court, his title, and, later, another title, and his being named Chancellor of Krondor, first in rank after Duke Gardan in the Prince's court, all became a haze of pleasant thoughts, the only pleasant thoughts in his life. Faces passed, some named, others nameless. Thieves, assassins, nobles, peasants. Women. He remembered many, for early on he had developed a taste for the attentions of women and, as a rising young nobleman, had his choice of many companions. But there was always something lacking. Something important. Then a nude figure wading in the lake as she squeezed water from her hair. The most stunning vision he had beheld.

Then a face with pale blue eyes, and lips like pink roses. A concerned face, which peered into James's being. Something magical and beautiful burst within James, and again he wanted to cry. A sadness filled him with awful joy and he cringed before those clear eyes. They looked inside and saw things, and he had no secrets. He had no secrets! *I am lost!* he cried out and a child whimpered at the death of his mother, and a boy cried as a young woman lay dying from an assassin's bolt, and a youth cried as the only man he had come to trust lay dead before him in his chambers, and a man cried for all the old pain and torment, the fear and loneliness that had lived within his breast since the day of his birth.

James awoke upon the shore, a cry of pain and fear upon his lips. He sat bolt upright, his arm above his head, a child avoiding a blow from above. He was still damp, and naked. A voice said, "The pain will pass."

James turned, and as he did so the terrible aching inside slipped away. He turned to find the young woman sitting upon the shore a few feet away from him. She sat with her legs pulled up before her, arms around her knees, still without her clothing.

James had never so much wished to flee in his life. No experience filled him with such nameless dread as seeing this beautiful young woman sitting near. Tears rose unbidden to his eyes. "Who are you?" he whispered. Yet as he wished to flee, so much more so did he long to be close to this woman.

Slowly she rose, unself-conscious in her nudity, and came to stand before him. She knelt until her face was before his. A voice sounded inside his mind: *I am Gamina, James.*

Fear again visited James, and he found himself unable to move. He said, "You spoke inside my head."

"Yes," she answered aloud. "You must understand that I can see your thoughts, hear them"—she seemed to grope for a concept— "those words are not right. But I know what you think unless you try to keep your thoughts from me."

He attempted to gather his wits about him as he fought down the aching pain inside. "What happened? Over there . . ." He indicated the reed-filled pool.

"Your thoughts startled me, and I reacted without reason. I can defend myself, as you discovered."

James raised a hand to his head, a memory of pain there. "Yes," was all he could say.

She reached out and touched his cheek softly. "I am sorry. It was not something I would have done knowingly. I can cause much harm to the mind. It is one of the ways my talents could be abused."

James found the touch of her hand both reassuring and disturbing. A fearful thrill ran from his chest to his groin. Softly he asked, "Who are you?"

She smiled and pain and fear fled from James. "I am Gamina. I am Pug and Katala's daughter." Then she leaned forward and softly kissed his lips. "I am who you have been seeking, and you are who I have sought."

James felt hot desire rise up within, but a giddy fearfulness came with it. No stranger to a woman's embrace, he suddenly felt a child with his first stolen moment of love. Words he had never thought to hear himself utter came unbidden. "I am frightened," he whispered.

"Don't be," she whispered back.

Holding him close, she spoke to his mind. *When I stunned you, you fell back into the water. Had I not pulled you out, you would have drowned. As I revived you, your mind was open to me, and mine to you. Had you the ability, you would know me as well as I know you, my Jimmy.*

James's own voice sounded small and wounded in his ears as he spoke. "How can it . . . ?"

"It is," she answered. Then she sat back, rubbing salt tears from his face. "Come, let me show you." Like a baby, he let himself be gathered to her breast, and as her hands caressed his head and shoulders, her voice spoke into his mind. *You will never be alone again.*

Borric and Erland sat beside each other, enjoying the array of foods for the morning meal. Besides the usual Kingdom fare, a large number of Keshian delicacies also were provided. Pug's family as well as Kulgan and Meecham dined with the guests. Two places were empty, next to Katala and Locklear.

Borric chewed a mouthful of fine cheese and wine, while Erland said, "Cousin Pug, how many people live here now?"

Pug picked lightly at his plate, not eating much. He smiled at his wife and said, "Katala attends the daily business of governing this community."

Katala said, "We number nearly a thousand families, both here and on the shore. Here, upon the island—" Her words fell away. All at the table turned to see the cause of Katala's truncated speech.

The door at the end of the hall had opened and James entered, escorting a young woman dressed in a simple lavender dress cinched about the waist with a rainbow-colored belt.

Borric, Erland, and Locklear rose, as the girl hurried to Pug and kissed him upon the cheek. Then she looked into Katala's eyes for a long moment, as if speaking, though no words were exchanged. The older woman's eyes began to brim with tears as a smile spread across her face.

Pug turned to look at James, expectantly.

Locklear said, "James—"

James cleared his throat, and in a self-conscious tone of voice, like a schoolboy reciting before his master, said, "Lord Pug, I—I have the honor to ask permission . . . to ask for the hand of your daughter in marriage."

Borric and Erland's eyes widened in disbelief, then both looked at Locklear. James's life-long companion since coming to the palace sat down heavily with a stunned expression equal to the twins' own. Shaking his head, all he could say was, "Sink me!"

Chapter Four
Concerns

Borric shook his head.

Erland asked, "What's bothering you?"

Borric said, "What?"

"You've been shaking your head 'no' as you've been walking for the last couple of minutes. You're arguing with yourself again."

Borric made a sound between a sigh and a grunt. "I'm worried about Uncle Jimmy."

Erland turned slightly as he picked up the pace so he could examine his brother's face while they walked. The evening sky was turning inky as the middle moon hadn't risen yet. But the balmy evening promised romance for those inclined and able to find willing partners. It was upon such a search the twins were now embarking. As they headed to where the ferry barge was tied, Erland said, "It's not usual for you to concern yourself with others, let alone someone as capable as Uncle Jimmy."

"That's why I'm worried," said Borric, halting to emphasize the point. He poked his finger on Erland's chest. " 'There's nothing dumber in the world than a man with an erection,' he used to tell us, right?"

Erland laughed and nodded. "Except Uncle Locky. It just makes him that much more cunning."

"Only when it comes to finding a warm place to put his great sword. Otherwise he's just as stupid as the rest of us."

"The rest of us *except* Uncle Jimmy."

"Right," agreed Borric. "My point exactly. He's had his share, we both know that. But he's always kept them at a distance and never made stupid promises. Now he meets this woman and . . ." He paused, at a loss for words.

"Like magic."

"Exactly!" said Borric. "And what better place to find magic than an island of magicians."

Erland put a restraining hand on Borric as his brother started to walk again. "You think this is some sort of spell? An enchantment?"

"Ah, a very special enchantment," said a gravelly voice from the dark.

Both brothers turned to see a stout figure sitting upon a tree stump not ten feet away. Because the man had been motionless, he had remained unseen in the gloom until he spoke. Coming closer, the young Princes saw the speaker was the old magician, Kulgan.

"What do you mean?" asked Borric, as if his suspicions had been confirmed.

Kulgan laughed. He stuck out his hand for a moment and then waved it impatiently. "Well just don't stand there. Give an old man some help. My knees are older than creation!"

Erland assisted the old magician as Kulgan pulled himself upright, one hand in Erland's, the other on a large wooden staff. The magician continued, "I'll walk with you to the ferry landing. I assume you're going across to find some trouble. Boys your age always are interested in trouble."

"The enchantment?" said Borric impatiently.

The old man laughed. "You know, when your grandfather was a little older than you, he was just as unwilling to wait. When he wanted an answer, he wanted it right now, by damn. It took a lot of years for him to get over that. Your father has the same flaw, but he hides it better. Arutha always was among the best I've known for recognizing limits."

Erland said, "He has that knack, except when it comes to us."

Kulgan fixed both brothers with a baleful gaze. "Limits? What do you spoiled children know of limits? Oh, maybe you've had to use your swords now and again, but limits?" He halted for a moment, and leaned upon the staff. Tapping his head with one finger, he said, "This. Your brain. When you bring *all* your faculties to bear on a problem, try every conceivable solution in your mind, and still have no solution, then you'll understand what limits I'm talking about."

"Father always said you were one of his most demanding teachers," said Erland with a grin.

"Ha!" snorted Kulgan. "Now Father Tully, there was an exacting taskmaster." His eyes looked off in the distance, reflecting for a moment, then he continued, "It's a pity you never knew him. You were babies when he died. Tragic loss. One of the finest minds I've ever known . . . even if he was a priest," he added, unable to resist the jab at his old debating partner, and feeling sadness at the lack of a rejoinder.

Borric said, "Were you joking about the enchantment on Jimmy?"

Kulgan said, "You are very young, my Prince." With a more than playful whack to Borric's leg for emphasis, he added, "You don't know half of everything yet."

"Ow," Borric said, reflexively dancing back.

As Erland began to laugh, Kulgan gave him a bark on the shins as well, saying, "Just to keep things even."

As both brothers made a show of being in pain, Kulgan said, "Now pay attention. I'm old and I don't have the time to waste repeating myself."

When the twins ceased their little dances of distress, Kulgan said, "The sort of enchantment I am speaking of is nothing you can teach. It's not of the sort of magic men can employ at whim. It's a magic the gods have given to only a few lucky men and women. It's the magic of a love so real and profound that nothing can change you back once you've known it." His eyes again sought distant horizons as he said, "I'm so old I have to work to remember last night's dreams. Yet there are times boyhood recollections come to me as if they were but moments ago." He looked at Borric, as if searching for something familiar in his young face. After a quiet moment, he said, "Your grandfather was a passionate man, and your uncle is, as well. So's your father, though you'd not know it to look at him—he was trapped by your mother almost from the moment they met, though he was too thick to know it. Your Aunt Carline was set upon marrying your Uncle Laurie within days of meeting him.

"The point is that you will feel needs in you as you get older, needs that carousing through alehouses with net-menders' daughters will not satisfy, no matter how rosy their cheeks, sweet their laughter, or soft their arms may be. And the bedsilks of nobility's daughters will lose their luster as well."

Both Borric and Erland exchanged glances, and Erland said, "That will be some time to come, I think."

Kulgan silenced him with another smack to his shins. "Don't interrupt. I don't care if you are a prince. I've whacked better men than

56

you and of higher rank. Your uncle, the King, was a poor student and saw the flat of my hand more than once." He sighed. "Now, where was I? Oh, yes, true love. You'll find as you get older that passion grows and the need for a true mate deepens. Your father found it, Carline found it, your Uncle Martin found it. The King did not."

Borric said, "He loves the Queen, I'm certain."

"Oh, in his way, certainly. She's a fine woman and I'll not hear any man say otherwise, but there's love and there's what your young Baron James has discovered. He's a changed man, no doubt about it. You watch and learn. If you're fortunate, you might see what you will likely not know."

Borric sighed and looked at the ground. "Because I am to be King?"

Kulgan nodded. "Precisely. You're not as thick as I took you to be. You will marry for the good of the nation. Oh, you'll have plenty of opportunity to satisfy itches with willing ladies of many ranks, no doubt. I know your uncle has given you at least a half-dozen cousins born on the wrong side of the blanket. Several of them will no doubt be rising in the ranks of the nobility by the time it's over with and done. But that's not the same thing.

"James has found that person whom the gods placed here to make his life complete. Don't doubt for a moment that it was fated, and don't think for a moment that he was taken unawares. What seems to you to be a hasty act of rash thoughtlessness is in fact a recognition of something so profound that only one who has known it can understand. So, do you understand now?"

"We should let him alone?" said Erland.

"Precisely," said Kulgan, pleased with himself. He smiled as he studied the Princes for a moment. "You know, you two are nowhere near the stupid pair of street thugs you resemble. Blood will tell after all, I guess. Now, you'll most likely forget everything I've told you five minutes after you find an alehouse with a card game and a couple of amply endowed serving women looking to snag a rich gift from a young noble.

"But with luck, at some critical time in your life, you will recall what I've said. It will help you make choices you must make, both of you, for the good of your nation."

Borric shrugged. "It seems that the last few weeks have been dedicated to constantly reminding us of our duty."

"As it should be." Kulgan studied the boys. "You have been placed upon a high seat, Borric, and you one step below, Erland. You are not given all the power your rank carries for your simple pleasures and amusements. They come to you in payment for terrible sacrifices. Your grandfather made them, as did your uncle, and your father. The ghosts of the many men who died under your father's command haunt his nights. And while every one of those men died willingly in service to their King and Prince, still their deaths weigh heavily upon Arutha. That's the sort of man your father is. You will come to know him better as you get older."

Both brothers said nothing. At last Kulgan turned back toward the imposing edifice of Stardock. "It's turning cool. I'll find me a fire to warm myself next to. You go find whatever trouble you can." After he took a few steps, Kulgan halted, turned, and said, "And be cautious of some of our fisher lads. Make free with their women and they'll have their cleaning knives out before they remember you're royalty." He studied the twins' faces a long moment, then added, "Take care of yourselves, boys."

Borric and Erland watched the old magician head back to the entrance of the main building of the Academy, then resumed their walk to the ferry. As they came to the beach, Erland said, "What do you think?"

Borric said, "About what he said? I think he's an old man with a lot of strange ideas."

Erland nodded in agreement as they signaled to the ferryman they wished to cross to the beckoning lights of the distant town.

The wind blew softly as Gamina and James walked along the shore, silently sharing the evening. James felt both invigorated and exhausted. In his thirty-seven years he had shared little of himself with anyone. True intimacy seemed impossible for him, but in Gamina he found someone able to break past previously unbreachable defenses. No, it wasn't that way, he amended silently to himself. She hadn't broken past anything. She simply found the door waiting for her to open.

A scented breeze blew out of the south, the fragrance of distant orchards and fields in bloom across the Vale of Dreams. Middle moon rose in the east, a copper disc in the dark night approaching. James turned to his intended bride. He marveled at the arch of her neck, the way her fine pale hair seemed to float about her face and shoulders, a nimbus of white tinged smoky grey in the twilight. Her pale eyes regarded him, then she smiled and his spirit leaped. "I love you," she said.

"I love you," he said, not quite believing his own joy. "And I must leave you."

She turned to watch the moon for a long moment, then her thoughts came to James. *No, my love. My time here is over. I will journey to Kesh with you.*

James gathered her into his arms. "It's dangerous. Even for one of your gifts, there will be peril." He kissed her neck and felt her shiver slightly in response. "I would be more content within my mind with you safely here."

Would you? she asked. *I wonder.* . . . She stepped slightly away and studied his face in the fading light. "I fear you might retreat within yourself, Jimmy, and after a time you would convince yourself what we have found here was an illusion and those barriers against love and pain would then be restored, stronger, higher, and more firmly buttressed than ever before. You would find a reason to journey back to Krondor another way, and you would find reasons to postpone your return to Stardock. For a time you would convince yourself that you intended to come for me as soon as possible, but there would be one reason then another to keep you away. And always one reason or another to keep you from sending for me. After a time, you would simply put all this away from your heart and forget."

James looked stung. Newly discovered feelings rampaged through him and his usual pose of relaxed confidence was absent. He looked nothing more than the boy he had never truly been, confused and disturbed by the loving attentions of a woman. "Do you think so little of me, after all?"

Touching his cheek, she smiled, and the warmth of her loving gaze swept away the fear again, as it had a dozen times during the day. Gamina had read James's heart and soul when she had revived him upon the lakeshore and had shared herself with him, both her body and heart. Still, trust for James was grudgingly surrendered, even to the woman who had touched him as no other had. "No, love, I do not underestimate you. But I also do not underestimate fear. My talents are not just magic as others upon this island know it. My skills are also in healing the mind and heart. I can share things with those who are weakened in spirit and sick of mind, and help them, sometimes. I can listen to dreams. And I have seen what fear can do. You fear to be left again as you were by your mother."

James knew she was right. Even as she spoke, the feelings of that dreadful night returned, when as a child of six or seven he stole out of his mother's crib, the stickiness upon the floor her blood, the horror of knowing only utter abandonment. Unbidden tears came to James's eyes. Gamina gathered him into her arms and let him vent his pain. *You will never be alone again,* came her thoughts in his mind.

He stood motionless, holding her as if she were his only connection to life. And as it had before, the pain slipped away, leaving behind a tired but warm and relieved feeling. Something angry and festering within him for years had been lanced, and poisonous fear and loneliness were draining away. The wound wouldn't heal in the space of a single day, or even many days, but in time it would heal and James of Krondor would be the better man for the healing. Her voice came to him as she said, *And it is my fear speaking, as well. Doubt can make us all vulnerable.*

"I have no doubt," he answered simply. She smiled as she again hugged him tight.

The sounds of footfalls upon the ground and a pointed clearing of a throat signaled Locklear's arrival. "Sorry to intrude, but Pug would like to see you, James." He smiled apologetically. "And your mother would like you to join her in the kitchen, Gamina."

"Thank you," Gamina answered. She gifted Locklear with a warm smile and kissed James on the cheek. "I will see you at dinner."

He kissed her again, and she headed toward the kitchen. James and Locklear walked toward Pug's study. Locklear cleared his throat in a significant, theatrical manner.

James said, "You've got something on your mind. Out with it."

Locklear's words came in a rush. "Look, we've known each other, what, twenty-two years? In all that time I've never known you to show the least bit of interest in women—" James gave him a strange look and he amended that to, "I mean interest in marriage, at least. Now, out of nowhere, you suddenly walk in and announce to all that you're getting married! I mean, she's certainly a beauty, with that nearly white hair and all, but you've known—"

"I've known no one, nothing, like Gamina," Jimmy interrupted. He stopped his companion with a restraining hand to Locklear's chest. "I don't know if someone like you can understand, Locky, but she's seen *inside* of me. She's seen all there is to see, the bad I've done and felt, the things that I've only hinted at to you, and she loves me despite those things. She *loves* me, *anyway!*" He took a deep breath. "You will never know what that means."

He resumed walking and Locklear hesitated an instant before catching up. "What do you mean 'someone like you'?"

James halted again. "Look, you're the best friend—perhaps the only real friend—I've ever known, but when it comes to women . . . you have no . . . consideration. You're charming, you're attentive, you're persistent, and when the lady in question wakes up in your bed, you're gone. Why some woman's brother or father hasn't run a sword through you . . . When it comes to you and women, Locky, you just are not very constant."

"And you are?"

"I am now," James answered. "As constant as water running downhill."

Locklear said, "Well, we'll see what Arutha has to say about this headlong flight into matrimony. We court Barons need his permission to marry, remember?"

"I know."

"Well, I'll leave you to your meeting with the spellcaster," Locklear said as they reached the door to the Academy building. "I expect he'll also have a thing or two to say about you spiriting away his daughter." Locklear left James alone at the entrance.

James entered the building and made his way down a long corridor to the base of the tower, the top of which housed Pug's study. He mounted a spiral stairway and climbed until he reached the door of the study. As he raised his hand to knock, the door swung open to admit him. Stepping through the portal, he was not surprised to discover Pug alone in the study, some distance away from the door. After he was inside, the door closed behind James without apparent aid.

"We need to speak," Pug said, as he rose and beckoned James to a large window. Looking out, he pointed at small lights which dotted the far shore. "People," he said.

James shrugged. He knew the sorcerer hadn't called him to his presence to discuss the obvious.

"When we came to Stardock over twenty years ago, this was a barren patch of ground in the middle of a deserted lake. The shore was a bit more hospitable, but this Vale was the scene of constant warfare between the Kingdom and the Empire, between rival border lords, or gangs of renegades. Durbin slavers raided, and simple bandits plagued the farmers as much as locust." He sighed as he remembered. "Now people lead relatively peaceful lives. Oh, there are occasional problems, but for the most part, things in the area of the Great Star Lake are quiet.

"And what caused that change?" he asked James.

James said, "It doesn't take a genius to deduce your presence here caused that change, Pug."

Pug turned away from the view of the lake shore and said, "Jimmy, when we first met I was a young man and you were a boy. But in the time between then and now I've encountered more than most men could imagine in a dozen lifetimes." With a simple wave of his hand he created a cloud in the middle of the room, less than two feet in diameter. It shimmered then appeared a hole in the air, through which James could see a strange hall. It was a hall hanging in the midst of a grey nothingness, along the path of which doors were spaced every dozen yards or so. The grey void of nothingness between the doors was so absolute that even the black of night seemed rich and alive in comparison. "The Hall of Worlds," said Pug. "By this path I have ventured to places no human has seen, nor will likely see again. I have visited the ashes of ancient civilizations and seen new races aborning. I have counted stars and grains of sand both, and find that the universe is so vast that no mind, perhaps not even that of a god could encompass it."

Pug waved his hand and the image vanished. "It would become easy to dismiss the concerns of those who live in such a tiny place as the Vale as trivial."

James crossed his arms as he said, "Compared to that, it is trivial."

Pug shook his head. "Not to those who live here."

James sat without Pug's leave and said, "I know there's a point to this, Pug."

Pug returned to his own chair behind his study table and said, "Yes, there is. Katala is dying."

That news, unexpected as well as shocking, caught James by surprise. "I thought she appeared unwell—but dying. . . ."

"There is much we can do here, James, but there are limits. No magic, potion, charm, or prayer can do more for my wife than has already been done. Soon she will journey through a rift back to her homeland, the Thuril Highlands on Kelewan. She has seen no kinsman in nearly thirty years now. She will return home to die."

James shook his head, knowing there was nothing he could say. Finally he asked, "Gamina?"

"I've watched my wife grow old before her time, James, though had this illness not developed I would have had to face this burden eventually. You can see I have not aged measurably. Nor will I in your lifetime. I may not be immortal, but my powers make me long-lived.

62

And I'll not watch my children and grandchildren grow old and wither while I stay as I am.

"I will leave Stardock within hours of Katala's departure. William is firm upon his soldier's path, having forsaken his magic gifts. I wished it were otherwise, but like most fathers I must accept that my own dreams are not necessarily my son's. Gamina has talents, as well, not limited to magic, but rather stemming from an unusual mind. Her mental speech is both magic and natural, but her sensitive nature, her empathy, her caring, these are special gifts."

James nodded. "I can't argue that. Her mind is . . . a miracle."

Pug said, "I agree. I've studied my daughter's talents more closely than any upon this world and know better than even she what the extent of her talents are . . . and her limits. She would have chosen to stay here, had she not met you, to take over the burdens her mother leaves behind—Katala has been the true leader of our community for most of our time here. I wish to spare Gamina this. She was a child burdened with great sadness and pain at an early age— much like you, I suspect."

James gave a slight nod. "We've shared things. . . ."

"No doubt," said Pug with a wry smile. "But that is as it should be with lovers, husbands and wives. I will lose much when Katala departs, more than perhaps even she suspects." For an instant, Pug stood exposed to James and the young Baron saw a man isolated from others by unknowable responsibility, and one of the few who could ease that great weight, one who could give him a few moments of warmth and comfort, was slowly leaving him. For just a moment, Pug revealed the depth of his pain, then the mask was again in place. "For when she leaves I will begin to concern myself with those grand issues I've given you but a glimpse of, and leave behind the 'trivial' concerns of Stardock, the Vale, even the Kingdom.

"But I wish for my loved ones much what any man must wish, safe homes and fine children, lives unspoiled by turmoil and strife. In short, I wish them to be as happy as possible. And Gamina has shown me what is in her heart, and it is you. I wish to grant you my blessings."

James let out a long sigh of relief. "I hope Arutha is as understanding. I need his permission to marry."

"This is no difficulty." Pug moved his hands and created a grey smoky sphere in the air. Within it, shapes began to form, then suddenly James was looking at Arutha in his study in Krondor, as if a window appeared between two rooms but a wall apart. Arutha glanced up as if at them and with an uncharacteristic display of surprise, half-rose from his chair. "Pug?"

Pug spoke, "Yes, Highness. I am sorry to intrude, but I have a favor to ask."

Arutha sat down with obvious relief there was both a reasonable and friendly cause for the sudden apparition in his study. He put down a quill with which he'd been writing and said, "What may I do for you?"

"You remember my daughter Gamina?"

Arutha said, "Yes, very well."

"I would like to see her married . . . to a man of some rank. One of your young court Barons."

Arutha looked past Pug, caught sight of James, and smiled, his eyes revealing a rare amusement. "I suspect we could arrange a state marriage to one of our bright young men, Pug. Do you have anyone in mind?"

"Baron James seems a most promising young man."

Arutha's smile broadened, to what James could swear was almost a grin, something he had never seen his Prince do before. "Most promising," he intoned in mock-seriousness as he returned his attention to Pug. "He stands to be a duke someday if his more impetuous nature doesn't get him killed along the way—or banished by an angry monarch to the Salt Marsh Islands. A wife might be just the thing to rein in some of that recklessness. I had given up on his ever developing an interest in family. I am pleased to be wrong. I was ten years married at his age." Arutha sat an instant, lost in thought as he recalled his own youthful feeling for his wife, then looked past Pug at James, with a rare expression of deep affection apparent. Then he resumed his more familiar stoic demeanor. "Well, if he agrees, then you have my permission."

Pug smiled. "He's agreed, have no worry. He and my daughter are much in agreement on this course."

Arutha sat back in his chair, a more typical half-smile on his face. "I understand. I still remember my own feelings for Anita when first we met. It can come suddenly. Very well, we'll have a state wedding as soon as he returns from his envoy to Kesh."

"Actually, I was thinking of something a bit more timely. She wishes to accompany him on his envoy."

Arutha's features darkened. "I do not think I approve. James may not have told you of the dangers—"

"I have a clear idea of the dangers involved, Arutha," Pug interrupted. "But I think you have no idea of my daughter's talents. I know much of what transpires in Kesh. She will aid your sons and envoy should trouble arise."

Arutha considered this for a moment, then nodded. "Given that you are the girl's father, I expect she has some abilities that may stand her in good stead should things prove difficult.

"Very well, let us do this much. Marry them as quickly as you judge proper, then when they return, we'll have a state wedding and festival in their honor. My wife and daughter would never forgive me for letting an excuse for new gowns pass them by. We shall have to do both."

James looked surprised. "State wedding?"

Arutha nodded once, emphatically. "Gamina's a royal cousin by adoption—unless you've forgotten—all of Pug's family is. Our cousin Willy will be Duke of Stardock. You're marrying into the family." Then in mock doubt, he sighed, "Though that thought brings me only the coldest comfort."

"Thank you, Arutha," said Pug with some amusement at the banter.

"You are most welcome, Pug. And . . . Jimmy," he said, again with a genuine smile.

"Yes, Arutha," said James, returning the smile.

"May you be as happy in your marriage as I am in my own."

James nodded. While Arutha was never a demonstrative man, James remembered years ago when Anita nearly died; the grief Arutha had endured was still keenly recalled. Only a few besides James knew how deep was the Prince of Krondor's love for his Princess. "I think we shall be."

"Then I have a gift for you, an early wedding present." He opened a small chest atop his writing table and withdrew a small parchment scroll. "I shall give it over when you return, but for the present—"

Pug interrupted. "I can bring it to him now, if you wish, Arutha."

If the Prince was surprised by this offer, he showed none of it. He simply said, "If you would be so kind."

Pug waved his hand, closed his eyes a moment, and the document vanished from Arutha's hand, appearing in his own. Arutha's eyes widened slightly, his only reaction to the sorcerer's ability to really move the parchment over such a distance in an instant.

Pug handed it to James. "For you."

James opened the document and read. His eyes widened briefly.

"It's a patent of Office. Earl of the Prince's Court. And King's Minister."

"I was going to give that to you on your return, anyway. You've earned the rank, James. We'll discuss holdings and revenues when you are back in Krondor. You will also assume the duties of Chancellor of the Western Realm when Gardan retires."

James grinned, and Pug and Arutha both remembered the boy thief they had met years before. "I thank His Highness."

"Now, let me return to work," said Arutha.

Pug said, "I bid you good evening, Highness."

"Good evening, to you, my lords Duke and Earl."

Pug waved his hand and the image of the Prince vanished. "Astonishing," James said. "With that trick"—he looked at the parchment he held—"and this . . . armies—"

"Which is why we must talk of things other than your wedding, James." Pug moved toward a table and indicated a decanter of wine. James poured two goblets of a fine fortified red. As he sipped, Pug sat and motioned for James to do likewise. "Stardock will not be allowed to become a tool of any nation. I have plans to prevent that.

"My son will not inherit the title of Duke of Stardock. I think he prefers the life of a professional soldier, in any event. No, the two men you met upon landing, Watume and Körsh will be given sovereignty over this island after I depart, with another yet to be chosen, a triumvirate of magicians who will decide the good of the people here. They may expand that council as they see fit in years to come. But Lyam will not always sit upon the Throne of Isles and I would not give over the power of Stardock to one like Mad King Rodric. I met him, and had he mustered magicians such as we have here to his cause, the world would have trembled. I also remember the havoc created by those magicians on Kelewan who chose to do the Warlord's bidding during the Riftwar.

"No, Stardock must remain apolitical. Always."

James stood up and said, "As a noble of the Kingdom, I fear you come close to treason." He took a few steps toward an open window and looked out into the night. Then he smiled. "As a man who learned to think for himself at an early age, I applaud your wisdom."

"Then you will also understand why I trust you will always remain a voice of reason in the Congress of Lords."

James said, "A small voice, but one that will attempt to speak on behalf of your vision." Then he added, "Still, I will try to make others understand. But you realize many will be of the mind that if you are not clearly loyal to the Kingdom you must be an enemy?"

Pug only nodded. "Now, to other matters. We shall have a priest over from the village on the lake shore—no temples stand upon the island itself, and our relationship with those who practice clerical magic is not, shall we say, entirely cordial."

James smiled. "You poach their lands."

Pug sighed. "So many think. In any event, the only clerics I found reasonable men are either dead or distant. I'm afraid as our power here grows, so does the suspicion of the great temples in Rillanon and Kesh." Then his expression brightened. "But Father Marias who oversees the small Church of Killian in the village is a decent enough man. He'll agree to a wedding." Then Pug's face relaxed into a wide smile. "More to the point, he'll certainly agree to the feasting."

James laughed aloud, and as thought of his wedding to Gamina swept through him, he was both awed and delighted by the sensations thinking of her caused. Then Pug said, "I do not expect you to understand what I'm about to say. But should you ever come to a time when you need to say something upon my behalf, say this, 'The last truth is that there is no magic.' "

James said, "I don't understand."

"I don't expect you to. If you understood what it meant, you would not be traveling to Kesh; I would persuade Arutha to keep you here. Just remember." Pug read his future son-in-law's face and said, "Go find my daughter and tell her we'll hold the ceremony day after tomorrow. No reason to wait another four days to next sixthday— we're breaking enough traditions as it is."

With a smile James placed the half-finished wine upon the table and left the room. As hurried footfalls echoed down the steps of the sorcerer's tower, Pug turned to look out the window and spoke softly to no one, "We could all use a dose of revelry. Too many dark days are coming."

The entire town of Stardock as well as a major portion of those from the shore who could find a way across the lake stood in a large circle around the portly priest. Father Marias smiled and beckoned James and Gamina to stand before him. He was a red-cheeked man, a baby who had never matured, but one whose thinning hair was turning silver-grey. His green robe and golden tabard were threadbare and often washed, but he wore them as proudly as any lord. Marias's eyes were almost alight with pleasure at a wedding. His flock were fisherfolk and farmers in the main, and all too often his duties consisted of burying them. Weddings and dedications of babies to the Goddess of All Living Things were especially delightful.

"Come along, children," he said as Gamina and James advanced slowly. James wore the clothing he had brought along for his presentation to the Empress, a tunic of pale blue, dark blue leggings, and black boots. Over this he wore a white surcoat sewn with gold thread. On his head he wore the latest fashion, a large beret which hung nearly down to his shoulder on his left side, a silver badge and white owl's feather setting it off.

Locklear stood beside him, similarly attired, though his clothes were even more richly fashioned in russet and gold hues. He glanced about, convinced these new fashions appeared ridiculous, but no one seemed to notice. All eyes were upon the bride.

Gamina wore a simple gown of lavender color, set off with an extraordinary string of pearls around her neck. The gown was cinched at the waist by a wide belt studded by matching pearls and a silver buckle. A garland of flowers circled her brow, the traditional "bride's crown."

"Now, then," Marias said, his voice betraying the rich, almost lyrical accent of one who was born along the south coast of the Kingdom Sea, near Pointer's Head, "seeing as you've come before me with the stated intention of marriage, I've a few things to tell you." He motioned for James to take Gamina's right hand in his and he placed his own pudgy hand over theirs. "Killian, the Goddess I serve, looked down upon man and woman when they were created by Ishap, the One Above All, and saw them apart. Man and woman looked heavenward and cried out in their loneliness. Hearing them and pitying them, the Goddess of Green Silence, spoke, saying, 'You shall not abide apart.' She then created the institution of marriage as a bond to bring man and woman together. It is the melding of souls, minds, and hearts. It is when two become as one. Do you understand?" He looked each in the eye and in turn Gamina and James nodded.

To the assembled crowd, Marias said, "James of Krondor, Earl of the Prince's Court and Gamina, daughter of Duke Pug and Duchess Katala, have come to this place and company to pledge themselves one to the other, and we are to bear witness to that pledge. If there is any here among you who knows why this should not be, speak now or go forever in silence." If there was to be any objection, Marias didn't wait to hear it. Plunging on he said, "James and Gamina, understand that from this moment forward, each of you is now a part of the other. No longer separate, you are now as one.

"James, this woman seeks to spend her life with you. Do you take her to you as mate and wife, without reservation and knowing that she is now one with you, holding her to you, and putting away any other, from now until death?"

James nodded, as he said, "I do."

With a wave, Marias motioned for Locklear to hand James a golden ring. "Put that upon your bride's hand." James did as he was asked, placing the ring upon the ring finger of Gamina's left hand.

"Gamina, this man seeks to spend his life with you. Do you take him to you as mate and husband, without reservation and knowing that he is now one with you, holding him to you, and putting away any other, from now until death?"

Gamina smiled and answered, "I do."

Marias instructed Gamina to place a ring upon James's hand, and she did so.

"In as much as James and Gamina have agreed to live as one, in the sight of gods and men, we do hereby bear witness."

The assembled company of guests repeated, "So do we bear witness."

With a grin, the ruddy-cheeked priest said, "Well, that's it, then. You're married."

James glanced around. "That's all?"

Marias laughed. "We keep it simple in the country, my lord. Now, kiss your wife, and let's get on with the feast."

James laughed, grabbed Gamina, and kissed her. The crowd cheered and hats were thrown in the air.

At the edge of the crowd two men did not cheer as they observed the celebration. An angular, thin man with three days' growth of unshaven beard, took the other by the elbow and led him a discrete distance away. Both were wearing clothing best described as ragged and torn, and both would have warranted a wide berth from anyone with an acute sense of smell. Glancing around to see they were not overheard, the first man said, "Earl James of Krondor. Baron Locklear. That means those two red-haired fighting lads are Arutha's sons."

The second man, stout and short, yet powerful in the shoulders, was obviously impressed at his companion's keen observation. His cherubic face appeared almost innocent as he said, "Don't see many Princes in these parts, 's true, Lafe."

"You're a fool, Reese," answered the other in a gravelly voice. "There are those who would pay well to know this. Get to the Inn of the Twelve Chairs at the desert's edge—they are almost certain to ride that route. You know who to ask for. Tell our Keshian friends that the Princes of Krondor and their company ride from Stardock, and travel not in state, but in stealth. Their numbers are small. And wait there for me at the inn. And don't drink up all the money he'll give you or I'll cut your liver out!"

Reese looked at his companion as if such duplicity was unthinkable.

Lafe continued, "I'll follow after them that's here and if they change route, I'll send word. They're surely carrying gold and gifts to the Empress for her birthday. With no more than twenty men at arms, we can be rich for life once the bandits cut their throats and give us our share."

Glancing around the deserted shore, the man named Reese said, "How can I get there, Lafe? The ferryman's at the wedding."

Hissing through teeth black with decay, the taller man said, "Steal a boat, stupid."

A glimmer of delight at the obvious answer shone in Reese's eyes. "Good. I'll get some food, then—"

"You'll go now!" ordered his companion, pushing him off to an uneasy trot toward the shore and the unguarded boats. "You can steal something in the town. With everyone dining here, that should be easy enough. But a few still linger, so be cautious." Reese turned and waved then scampered along the shore, looking for a boat small enough to manage alone.

Snorting in derision, the man called Lafe turned back toward the feasting. His hunger told him that Reese's suggestion wasn't all that bad, but his avarice made him alert to the every move of the wedding party.

The two Princes sat quietly at the dinner table, oblivious to the joy of the newlyweds. Each was intent on their own impatience to be on their way. James had been uncommunicative about when they were leaving, though Locklear had mentioned their stay wouldn't be extended too long, despite the unexpected events of the last two days.

If the twins had been surprised by their mentor's sudden encounter with love, they were equally unsurprised by the hasty permission from their father and the quick wedding. Little in their lives had allowed them to take anything for granted.

The twins lived in a world of the unexpected, where the tranquillity of the moment could be shattered at any time by disaster. Warfare, natural cataclysm, famine, and disease were constant threats, and they lived most of their young lives in the heart of the palace where they had observed their father dealing with such problems on a daily basis. From the most important border clash with Kesh to deciding if one guild or another had jurisdiction over a new trade, their father had dealt with problem after problem.

But as they had when watching their father, their present mood didn't reflect the excitement of the moment. Rather they were bored.

Borric drank deep of a simple ale and said, "Is this the best they have?"

Erland nodded. "I expect so. From what I can see, ale isn't a major concern around here. Let us see if there's something better in the village." The brothers stood up from the bench, bowed slightly at the Baron and his new Baroness, who nodded briefly in return at the Princes' leaving the table of honor.

As they passed by the other tables set up around the square, Borric asked, "Where are you heading?"

Erland said, "I don't know. Around. There must be some fishermen's daughters among all these people. I see a few pretty faces here and there. Every one of them can't be married," he added, attempting a light tone.

Borric's mood seemed to darken rather than improve. "What I really wish is to be quit of this nest of spellcasters and on our way."

Erland put his hand upon his brother's shoulder as they walked and agreed in silence. With the steady lectures they had been getting about responsibility, they felt hemmed in and controlled, and both Princes were eager for anything that resembled movement, change, and the possibility of adventure. Life was just a bit too quiet for their liking.

Chapter Five
Southward

The guards laughed.

James turned to see what caused their mirth and saw the two Princes approaching. Erland was wearing an improbable looking coat of heavy chain, weighing at least five times what his usual leather armor weighed, a bright red cloak tossed rakishly over his shoulder. But the laughter was primarily directed at his brother, who wore a robe which covered him from head to toe. It was a repulsive shade of purple with arcane symbols sewn in gold thread around the hood and sleeves—no doubt once the stunning centerpiece of some magician's wardrobe, it had seen better days. An odd looking wooden staff with a milky-white glass ball mounted atop it, hung in place of the usual sword at his side. On Kulgan or one of the Keshian magicians the robe would have seemed appropriate; on Borric the effect was entirely comic.

Locklear joined in the laughter as he came to James's side. "What are they made up for?"

James sighed. "I have no idea." To the Princes he said, "What is this, then?"

Erland grinned. "We found a game of pokiir—here they call it poker. Our luck was . . . uneven."

James shrugged, absently wondering how long Gamina would keep him waiting. His bride was in her quarters, gathering the last of what she would bring with her to Kesh. The rest of her belongings would be sent to the palace in Krondor, in anticipation of her return there after the Empress's Birthday Jubilee.

Borric said, "I lost my own cloak to a barge-man, and my sword to a fellow who most likely sold it for a bottle of wine. But then I found a magician who believed a little too much in luck and not enough in good card sense. Look at this."

James cast a glance at the elder of the twins and saw him holding out the odd-looking staff. "All right. What is it?"

Borric took the staff out of its sheath and gave it to James to examine. "It's a magic device. The crystal glows when it gets dark, so you needn't bother with lamps or torches. We saw it work last night. It's quite good."

James nodded as if to say that was nice. "What else does it do?"

"Nothing, except it's a rather nice-looking walking stick, I think," answered Erland. To his brother, he added, "But I wager you'll wish you had your sword back if someone comes running at you with a bloody great falchion in his hand."

"I expect," agreed Locklear.

"Well, I'll buy another sword when we reach civilization," said Borric.

James sighed. "And some new clothing. Those outfits look absurd."

Locklear laughed. "You want to see absurd!" To Borric he said, "Show him the boots."

Grinning, Borric pulled up the hem of his robe, and James shook his head in astonishment. Borric wore boots of red leather, rising to mid-calf, each adorned with a yellow eagle. "I won these as well."

"I think the previous owner was pleased to see the losing hand when those were wagered," James said. "You look like you're about to open a traveling carnival. Hide those, if you please. The colors are beyond belief," he added, indicating the clash between the red and yellow boots, and the purple robe. To Erland he added, "And you look like you're about to invade Kesh single-handed. I haven't seen chain like that since the battle of Sethanon."

Locklear who, like James, wore a simple tunic and a leather vest, said, "You're going to love that chain when we reach the edge of the desert."

Erland's retort was interrupted by the appearance of Gamina and her parents. Pug held Katala's arm and it was now clear to James that she was indeed ill. Whether it was due to the demands of her daughter's wedding the day before or her realization that now her children no longer needed her or the illness asserting itself, James could not know. But it was clear to anyone with eyes that Katala's life was numbered now in weeks at the most.

They came to where James waited, and Katala spoke to her son-in-law in quiet tones. "This is good-bye, James."

James could only nod. Katala's people were warriors and proud and always direct. So Pug had impressed on him and so she behaved. "You will be missed," he said at last.

"As I will miss all of you." She placed her hand on his chest, gently, and he could feel the frail fingers touching him lightly over his heart. "We only pass on from view. We live here as long as we are remembered."

James lowered his head and kissed her lightly upon the cheek, a gesture of both affection and respect. "Always remembered," he said.

She returned his kiss, and then turned away to say good-bye to her daughter.

Pug motioned James to walk with him a short distance away. When they were out of earshot of the others, he said, "Katala returns to her homeworld tonight, James. There's no reason to delay any longer, and if we linger, she might not have the strength to make the journey from the site of the rift on Kelewan to the Thuril border. I have friends who will help, but it will still be an arduous trip for someone in her condition to make alone."

James's eyebrows rose in surprise. "You're not traveling with her?"

Pug just shook his head. "I must be about other business."

James sighed. "Will we see you . . .?" He had been about to say soon, but something in Pug's expression caused him to let the sentence fall off.

Pug glanced over his shoulder at his wife and daughter, who stood holding hands silently. Both Pug and James knew they were speaking with their minds. "Probably not. I suspect if I come this way again, few will welcome the sight of me, for I imagine it will herald only the most dreadful circumstances, perhaps something akin to the terrors we faced at Sethanon."

James was quiet a moment. He had been only a boy when the armies of the moredhel, the Brotherhood of the Dark Path, marched under the banner of their false prophet, Murmandamus. But that time was forever etched in stark relief in his memory. He still recalled the battles of Armengar and Sethanon in detail and could vividly recall the sight of the sky torn open by the return of the Dragon Lords, and the nearly catastrophic end of life their return heralded. The seemingly miraculous victory over them, directed by Pug, Tomas of Elvandar, Macros the Black, and Arutha was still something he could not fully comprehend. Finally James said, "That would be when you were the most needed, though."

Pug shrugged, as if to say that wasn't necessarily true. "In any event, I am now dependent upon others to carry forth the work begun under my guidance. You must help."

"What can I do?"

With a faint smile, Pug said, "The first should be no issue between us. Love my daughter and care for her."

James smiled. "No more could any man do."

"And keep an eye on her brother."

"Willy is a competent officer, Pug. He needs little looking after. I expect he will be the Captain of Arutha's guard in a few years."

Pug shrugged again, showing only a small hint of his disappointment that his son was not here to follow after him. Whatever difficulty that had passed between Pug and his son was not discussed. "Secondly, I need your voice in support of Stardock's autonomy."

"Agreed."

"And remember what I told you when you need to speak on my behalf, the secret I shared with you."

James tried to find humor in the sad departure, but could only say, "As you wish. I will remember. Though standing upon an island where men work spells of great art every day makes me wonder at what nonsense I'm to remember."

Pug patted his arm as he moved to return to his wife and daughter. "Not nonsense. Never fall into the trap of judging that which you don't understand as nonsense. That error can destroy you."

James followed after, and then they were leaving. As they walked to where three large barges waited to ferry them across the lake, James glanced over at the Princes.

Borric and Erland stood chatting about the coming trip, obviously relieved to be away from what they judged unwelcome tranquillity, and for a brief moment James wondered if they might not all regret having no more such tranquillity.

Light gusts blew stinging sand, and the twins reined in their horses. Gamina studied the horizon and spoke loudly enough for all to hear. "I don't think it's a serious storm. The sky looks wrong. But it may be bothersome." They rode at the edge of the Jal-Pur, along the road to Nar Ayab, the northernmost city of consequence in the Empire. The rough plateau landscape was almost as desolate as the desert itself, with few trees and bushes, and most of those thickly bunched along the banks of the few small streams that coursed down out of the hills below the mountains called the Pillars of the Stars by the Keshians.

James motioned toward the far end of the road, where it crested a distant hill, as a company of riders slowly made their way toward them. "Keshian border guards," he shouted over the rising wind. "Sergeant! Time to display the guidons." The sergeant of the company motioned two guards forward, and they quickly broke segments of wooden standards out of their saddlebags. Hastily screwing the segments together, they raised two small standards just as the Keshian riders breasted the hill upon which James and his companions waited. Two Royal Krondorian House flags, each with a different cadence mark overlaid, Borric and Erland's royal standards, now greeted the suspicious eye of the advancing Keshian leader.

A dark-skinned man, his knappy beard matted with grey dust, motioned his own company to halt. They were a rough-looking band. Each man had a bow slung over the saddle horn as well as a round hide shield with a metal bosk; each rider wore a curved scimitar at his belt and carried a light lance. All wore heavy trousers tucked into high boots, white linen shirts, leather vests, and metal helms with long linen head coverings hanging over their necks. Borric motioned to Erland. "Clever, isn't it? They keep the sun off their necks and can hook the cloth over their faces if the wind gets vicious."

Erland simply let out a heavy breath and said nothing. He was feeling the heat in the heavy chain-mail coat.

The leader of the Keshian patrol kicked his horse and trotted forward, pulling up before James. He examined the ragged-looking company, unconvinced that such dirty, tired looking travelers would indeed be a royal caravan from Isles. At last he saluted no one in particular, a lazy gesture of bringing his right hand to his head, palm out, then let his hand fall to his horse's neck. "Welcome, my lords . . . and lady."

James moved to the fore. "I am James, Earl of Krondor, and I have the honor of presenting Their Royal Highnesses, Princes Borric and Erland."

The two Princes inclined their heads slightly, and the Keshian patrol leader bowed his head slighting in return. "I am Sergeant Ras-al-Fawi, my lord. What conspires to bring your august company to such a miserable place?"

"We are traveling to the City of Kesh for the Empress's Jubilee."

The sergeant shrugged, indicating that the ways of the gods were not for mortals to understand, nor the ways of nobility clearly sensible to common soldiers. "I would have thought nobles such as yourselves would have been traveling in more . . . stately company."

As the wind increased, the horses began to stamp and shy. James raised his voice over the noise, "It seemed better to move quickly and with stealth than slowly, Sergeant. The storm rises. May we continue?"

The Captain signed his own men forward as he said, "Of course, my lord. I and my men are traveling to the Inn of the Twelve Chairs, to wait out the storm in comfort. I suggest you join us."

"Is it dangerous?"

The Sergeant glanced at the horizon as Gamina had and said, "Who can say? Dust storms that rise in the Jal-Pur may blow quickly or long. If I was a betting man, I would wager this one will be little more than an inconvenience. Still, I would rather be conveniently inside."

"We'll continue," said James. "We stayed longer at our last rest than planned, and it wouldn't do to arrive late to the Jubilee."

The Sergeant shrugged, clearly not caring one way or the other. "Insults to the Empress, blessings be upon her, are to be strenuously avoided. She is often merciful, but rarely forgiving. May the gods guide your travels, my lords."

With a wave, he motioned his patrol to give way as the Kingdom party resumed its journey. James signaled and his small band started down the hard-packed dirt that passed for an Imperial road in the northern frontier.

As they road past the silent Keshians, Borric nodded to Erland, who had also been studying the tired, dirty soldiers. Each man looked a seasoned fighter, with not one youthful face in the company. To his brother, Erland said, "They keep their veterans along our borders."

Jimmy, overhearing, said loudly enough for the entire company to hear, "They have veterans to spare in Kesh. A man who retires in their army has spent twenty years and more putting down revolts and fighting civil wars. They keep but a tenth part of their army near our borders."

Borric said, "Then why do they fear us?"

James shook his head. "Nations fear their neighbors. It's a fact of life, like the three moons in the sky. If your neighbor is bigger than you, you fear invasion and occupation. If smaller, you fear their envy, so you invade them. So, sooner or later, there's war."

Erland laughed. "Still, it's better than having nothing to do."

James glanced at Locklear. Both had seen more than their share of war before they were the twins' age. Both disagreed with Erland's sentiments.

"Riders!"

The soldier pointed to the far horizon, where the wind blew up a dark wall of swirling sand that raced toward the travelers. And within the dusty murk, the shape of approaching riders could be seen. Then, as if the soldier's warning had been a signal, the riders spread out and galloped their horses.

"Gamina! Get to the rear," James shouted, as he drew his sword. The soldiers were but a moment behind in releasing the pack animals and bringing their own weapons to the ready.

"Bandits!" cried one, as he moved to Borric's side. Instinctively, the Prince reached for his sword, finding the odd staff there instead. Cursing fate, he circled his horse away from the attack, moving toward the rear alongside Gamina, who had taken it upon herself to herd the shying packhorses in a circle so they didn't run away. Seeing that the four animals were more than she could manage, Borric leaped from his horse and took two in hand.

The sounds of steel upon steel caused Borric to pull the horses around, back to the wind, in time to see the first bandits intercepted by his own soldiers. In the fray, he sought out sight of Erland, but the milling horses and swirling dust made it impossible.

Then a horse screamed and a rider went down cursing loudly. A clash of sword upon shield and a grunt of effort were followed by a succession of shouts made almost incoherent by the rising shriek of the wind. The bandits had timed the raid with perfection, picking the moment when the travelers would be most vulnerable to the on-slaught, almost blinded by the sandstorm. In the time it had taken to react and draw weapons, the bandits had already succeeded in throwing the men of Isles into confusion.

But the men of Arutha's garrison were tested veterans and quickly they regrouped as the first few bandits rode past. To a man, they sought sight of Baron Locklear, who shouted orders to those closest to him. Then a tremendous blast of stinging sand and dust hit the company and it was as if the sun had vanished.

In the biting sand, Borric fought to control horses terrorized by the sounds of wind and battle and the smell of blood. He could only use his weight to slow their pulling, shouting "Whoa!" repeatedly. A pair of war-trained, riderless horses heard his shouts and halted their trot away from the battle, but the pack animals were ready to bolt.

Borric was suddenly pulled off-balance and released his grip on the lead ropes. He hit the ground and rolled, coming to his feet. He thought of Gamina and wondered if she was in any danger from the spooked horses. He looked about, but all he could see were riders locked in combat. He called her name. In his mind he heard her answer, *I am fine, Borric. See to yourself. I will attempt to keep the pack animals in sight.*

Attempting to "think" back at her, he yelled, "Be alert for raiders! They'll seek the pack animals!" He glanced about, hoping to find a dropped weapon, but saw none.

Then suddenly, a rider was galloping toward him, one of his own guards, shouting at him. Borric couldn't understand him, but sensed something behind. He spun as two bandits bore down upon him, one pointing a scimitar at the guard who raced toward them, the other veering his horse toward the Prince.

As the guard was intercepted by the first rider, Borric braced himself, then jumped at the horse's bridle, causing the mount to stumble and throw his rider. The horse's chest struck the Prince, the impact sending Borric flying back, landing upon the ground with a heavy thud. Quickly he was on his feet, poised for the attack he knew was coming. The raider had also come up ready for a fight, but had the advantage of his weapon. Borric pulled the glowing staff from his belt and attempted to use it to defend himself. The bandit swung wildly, and Borric slipped the blow, moving inside the man's guard. He drove the head of the staff into the pit of the man's stomach, generating a satisfying explosion of breath as the bandit went down, the wind knocked out of him. Borric then broke the staff over the man's head, leaving the raider unconscious or dead. The Prince didn't have time to investigate. He picked up the fallen rider's sword, a short bladed, heavy thing, suitable for hacking at close quarters, not as sharp as the scimitar most of the other raiders used, nor as pointed as a good rapier.

Borric turned and attempted to see what was happening, but all that was visible were milling, cursing shadows in sandy gloom. Then he felt more than heard something behind him. He ducked to one side as a blow intended to crack his skull glanced off the side of his head. Falling heavily, he attempted to roll away from the rider who had taken him by surprise from the rear. He rose to his knees and was almost to his feet, when the chest of a horse struck him, as the rider used his mount as a weapon. Stunned as he lay upon the ground, the Prince barely understood what he saw as the rider leaped from his mount and came to stand over him. Through dust and his own muddled senses, the Prince watched with some detachment as the man drew back a boot and kicked him in the head.

James spun his horse and moved to intercept a bandit heading toward the packhorses. Two soldiers were down by his count, and Locklear was engaged in a running fight with a raider. The raider veered off, and for an instant James was in an island of relative calm in the midst of the struggle. He glanced about, trying to discover the whereabouts of the two Princes and saw Erland clubbing a raider from his horse. There was no sign of Borric.

Through the howl of the sandstorm, James heard Locklear's command, "To me! To me!" Abandoning his search for Borric, James spurred his horse and headed toward the gathering band of Islemen. Quickly commands were given and obeyed, and where moments before a milling band of surprised guards had been fleeing, now a trained unit of the finest horsemen the Kingdom had in service sat ready to receive the next attack by the bandits.

Then the raiders were upon them and the battle was joined in full. Furious cries and screams of pain cut through the constant howl of wind and the sting of sand. James felt the giddy mix of elation and fear, a sensation he hadn't experienced since the Battle of Sethanon. He struck out at a raider, driving the man back as the severity of the storm increased. Then the storm overcame the battle and all was whirling dust and noise. Each man knew he now had a blind spot, for to look into the storm was impossible. Men vainly attempted to cover their faces with cloths and sleeves, but the only relief was to turn away from the storm. After an instant of screaming wind, the storm diminished.

A grunt of surprise and a wet sound of blood filling a throat gasping for breath was followed only by the sound of metal clanking as horses again moved at their riders' commands. Steel upon steel rang out, and again men strove to kill strangers.

Then there was only the storm and the fighting was forgotten. The gusts were literally blinding, for to turn one's face to the shrieking sands was to risk losing sight. Covering his face, James turned himself and his mount away from the wind, conscious of his unprotected back, but there was nothing else to do. He was given at least partial comfort by the knowledge the raiders were as blind as he.

Again the winds lessened, and James spun his mount to face any possible attacker. But like phantoms of dream, the raiders were gone into the storm.

James glanced about and could only see men of Isles. Locklear gave orders and the company dismounted, each man gripping his horse's reins firmly as the intensity of the storm alternately increased and diminished. Turning the animals' backs to the wind, they waited for the seemingly endless howl of wind to stop.

Locklear shouted, "Are you hurt?"

James indicated no. "Gamina?" he asked after his wife.

Locklear pointed to the rear. "She was with the baggage animals. Borric was seeing after her."

Then Gamina's voice sounded in James's mind. *I'm here, beloved. I am unhurt. But Borric and another guard were carried off by the raiders.*

James shouted, "Gamina says that Prince Borric and a guard were carried off!"

Locklear swore. "There's nothing we can do but wait for this storm to blow out."

James tried to look into the dusty murk and could see barely ten feet away. All they could do was wait.

Borric groaned and a rough toe jammed into his ribs brought him to consciousness. Above him, the wind still shrieked as the sandstorm blew itself to full fury, but the sheltered gully where the raiders hid was relatively quiet. He levered himself up on one elbow and found his hands were shackled by a chain of odd design.

Beside him lay an unconscious guard from his own band, tied with ropes. The man mumbled slightly but was not conscious. Matted blood dried in his hair showed he had received a vicious head wound. A rough hand reached out and grabbed Borric by the chin, yanking his face around to face the man who had kicked him. The man squatted before Borric. He was thin, wore his beard cut close so that it looked little more than stubble. His head was covered in a turban that once may have looked fine but now looked only faded and lice ridden. He wore simple trousers and tunic and high boots. Over his shoulder stood another man, wearing an unadorned leather vest over his bare chest. His head was shaved, save a single lock of hair down the middle, and a large gold ring hung in his left ear. Borric recognized these as the trademarks of the Guild of Slavers, from Durbin.

The first man nodded at Borric, then looked at the guard with the bloody face and shook his head in the negative. The slaver pulled Borric roughly to his feet without a word, while the thin man took out a dagger and before Borric realized his intent, cut the unconscious guard's throat.

The slaver whispered harshly in Borric's ear, "No tricks, spellcaster. Those chains will blank out your magic, or Moskatoni the Trader will have my dagger for dinner. We move before your friends can find us. Speak a single word aloud and I'll kill you." He spoke in the northern Keshian dialect.

Borric, still groggy from the blow to his head, only nodded weakly. The slaver pulled him along through the small gully where a group of horsemen were ransacking a bundle of baggage. One of the men swore quietly. The slaver's companion passed where Borric stood and grabbed the man. "What did you find?" he asked, speaking the patois of the desert, a mingling of Keshian, King's Tongue, and the language of the desertmen of the Jal-Pur.

"Women's clothing and some dried meat and cakes. Where is the gold we were promised?"

The thin man, obviously the leader, swore as well. "I'll kill that Lafe. He said nobles brought gold to the Empress."

The slaver shook his head, as if he had expected this sort of disappointment. "You should know better than to trust fools." He glanced up at where the wind shrieked overhead and said, "The storm passes. We're only yards away from this one's companions." He inclined his head at Borric. "We don't want to be found here when the storm is over."

The thin man turned to face his companion. "I lead this band, Kasim." He looked to be on the edge of rage. "I'll say when we move and when we stay."

The slaver shrugged. "If we stay, we will have to fight again, Luten. They will be ready this time. And I see nothing to make me think we'll find gold or jewelry with this band."

The man called Luten glanced around, a near-feral light in his eyes. "These are armed soldiers." He closed his eyes a moment as if about to cry, then opened them and clenched his teeth. Borric recognized a man with a violent temper, who ruled his company through intimidation and threats as much as through any natural leadership. "Ah!" he exclaimed. Nodding at Borric, he said, "Kill him and let us flee."

Kasim moved Borric behind him, as if protecting him, and said, "Our agreement was I would have the prisoners for slaves. Otherwise my men would not have joined with yours."

"Bah!" spat Luten. "We didn't need them. We were more than a match for those guards. We were both misled by that fool Lafe."

As the wind began to lessen, Kasim said, "I don't know who is worse, the fool or he who listens to the fool, but I will have this man for the auction. He is my profit in Durbin. My guild would not look kindly upon returning without at least this small profit."

Whirling to face Borric, the man called Luten said, "You. Where is the gold?"

Feigning ignorance, Borric said, "Gold?"

Luten stepped forward and struck the Prince across the face. "The gold some nobles brought to the Empress's Jubilee."

Borric extemporized. "Nobles? There was a party of nobles we passed along the way. Two, three noblemen with guards, heading for . . . an inn. The Inn of the Twelve Chairs, I think. We . . . hurried because . . . the hide trader was anxious to get his hides to the tanner before they turned rotten."

Luten turned and shrieked his fury into the wind. Two men nearby put hands to swords, startled by the sound. "Quiet," said Kasim.

Luten spun, his dagger out, pointed at Kasim. "Don't order me, slaver." He then pointed his dagger at Borric. "This one is lying and I'll have more than these damn boots to show for three men killed!" Borric glanced down and saw the boots he had won gambling were now on Luten's feet. He had been thoroughly searched while unconscious, it seemed. Luten shoved Kasim aside, coming to face Borric directly. "I'll have the truth out of him, as well." He drew back the dagger, as if to thrust at Borric, then stiffened. A sad, almost apologetic expression crossed his face for an instant, then he fell to his knees.

Behind him Kasim withdrew the dagger he had just stabbed into Luten's back. Kasim then grabbed Luten by the hair and said, "Never threaten me, you stupid man." Then with a quick jerk he pulled back Luten's head and sliced his neck, sending a fountain of blood spurting off to one side. "And never turn your back on me." Luten's eyes turned up in his head and Kasim released him, letting him fall at Borric's feet. "Let this be a lesson to you in your next life."

To the others in Luten's band, he said, "I lead." There was no argument voiced. Glancing around, he pointed to a depression in the small gully, overhung by a clump of boulders. "Dump him in there." Two men picked up Luten and threw him into the depression. "And the other." The dead guard was carried and tossed in beside Luten.

Turning to face Borric, the slaver said, "Show me no trouble, and you'll live. Trouble me, and you'll die. Understand?"

Borric nodded. To the others, Kasim said, "Get ready to leave now." He then jumped up to the edge of the gully, ignoring the howling wind. The powerful slaver put shoulder to one of the larger boulders and shoved it over, starting a small landslide which covered the two bodies. He leaped nimbly down into the depression, and glanced about as if anticipating trouble from one of Luten's men. When no one offered him any difficulty, he rose to his full height. "To the oasis at Broken Palms."

"What are your skills?" The slaver stood above Borric, whose wits were slowly returning to him. He had been dragged to a horse and forced to ride with his hands manacled. The pounding he had taken had added to the disorientation he had felt since his capture. He vaguely recalled the storm suddenly being over and then arriving at an odd oasis, surrounded by three ancient palm-tree trunks, broken off by some cataclysmic storm of years gone by.

Borric shook his head to clear it and answered back in the formal court language of Kesh, "What skills?"

The slaver took his answer as a sign of confusion from the head blow. "What tricks? What magics do you do?"

Borric understood. The slaver judged him a magician from Stardock, which accounted for the magic blanking chains. For an instant, Borric felt an impulse to explain who he was, but thoughts of his father receiving ransom demands on his behalf kept him from answering quickly. He could come forth at anytime between now and the slave auction at Durbin, and perhaps between now and then he could conspire to escape.

Suddenly the man lashed out and struck the Prince a back-handed blow. "I've no time to be gentle with you, mage. Your party is but a few hours away and no doubt will be looking for you. Or even if they have no love of you in their hearts, there are still many Imperial patrols out. We mean to be far from here, quickly."

Another man came to stand over the kneeling man. "Kasim, just kill him and leave him. No one pays a good price for a magician at the slave blocks. Too much trouble keeping them in line."

Kasim looked over his shoulder and said, "I lead this band, now. I'll decide who we kill and who we take to market."

Borric said, "I'm no magician. I won the robes in a game of poker."

The second man ran a hand over his dark-bearded face. "He lies. It's some magician's trick to get free of the manacles and kill us all with his magic. I say kill him now—"

"And I say if you don't shut up and quit arguing, there'll be another worthless carcass for the vultures to feast on. Get the men ready. As soon as the horses have been watered and rested, I want to put as much distance as I can between those guards and us." To Borric he said, "We found some pretty baubles in the bottom of the baggage, mage. The lady you road with had enough gold for me to pay these brigands. You're *my* profit." With an inarticulate grunt, the raider moved away, signaling the others to ready for riding.

Borric managed to sit upright against a large boulder. "I'm no magician."

"Well, you're no fighting man, either. To travel unarmed at the edge of the Jal-Pur, one must either have a great company of guards or a great deal of faith. Faith is for priests, which you're not. You don't look the fool, but then I've never been one for casual appearances." Shifting from Keshian to the King's Tongue, he said, "Where are you from?"

"Krondor"—Borric decided through his aching head he would be best served by obscuring his identity—"but I've traveled a lot."

The slaver sat back on his haunches, arms resting on his knees. "You're not much more than a boy. You speak Keshian like a courtier and your Kingdom tongue is nearly as fair. If you're not a spellcaster, what are you?"

Improvising, Borric said, "I . . . teach. I know several languages. I can read, write, and do sums. I know history and geography. I can recite the line of Kings and Empresses, the names of the major nobles and trading houses—"

"Enough!" interrupted Kasim. "You've convinced me. A tutor, then, is it? Well, there are rich men who need educated slaves to teach their children." Without waiting for any response from Borric, he stood up. As he stepped away, he said, "You are worthless to me dead, teacher, but I am also not a patient man. Do not be too much trouble and you will live. Cause me difficulty, and I'll kill you as soon as spit on you." To his band he said, "Mount up! We ride to Durbin!"

Chapter Six
Dilemma

Erland turned his horse.

"Borric!" he shouted over the still-howling wind.

James and the guards watched from where they stood holding their horses. The newly elevated Earl shouted, "Get off your horse before she runs away with you!"

The already excited mount was snorting and whinnying at the frightening noises and stinging blasts from the sandstorm, despite her training and Erland's firm control. The Prince ignored James's orders and continued to circle away from the others, shouting his brother's name. "Borric!"

Gamina stood beside her husband and said, "It's difficult to concentrate with this wind screaming in my ears, but there are thoughts coming from that direction." She covered her face with her forearm, turned, and pointed to the west.

"Borric?" asked Locklear, who stood next to James, his back to the biting wind.

Gamina held up her arm, letting the sleeve of her gown shield her face. "No. I'm sorry. I don't know these men, but none of the minds I've touched is his. When I attempt to focus on what I remember of his thoughts during the battle . . ."

"Nothing," James finished.

"Could he be unconscious?" Locklear's expression was hopeful.

Gamina said, "If he's stunned or farther away, then I would not sense him. My abilities are limited by the strength and training of the other mind. I can speak to my father from over a hundred miles away and he can speak to me across incredible distances. But those who attacked us are no more than a few hundred feet away; I get images and stray words about the fight." With sadness in her voice, she said, "I can't sense Borric anywhere."

James reached out to her and she came into the comfort of his arm. His horse nickered at the change in pressure on the reins and James gave an impatient yank on the leathers, silencing the animal. Softly, so that only Gamina would hear, he said, "I pray the gods let him be alive."

For an hour the wind blew, and Erland circled his companions to the limit of his ability to see them, while he cried his brother's name. Then the winds ceased, and in the silence that followed, his hoarse cries rang across a desolate landscape: "Borric!"

Locklear signaled to the Captain of his company for a report. The officer said, "Three men dead or missing, m'lord. Two more wounded enough we should get them to shelter. The rest are fit and ready."

James considered his options, then decided. "You remain here with Erland and search the immediate area, but don't wander too far. I'll take two men and ride to the Inn of the Twelve Chairs and see if that Keshian patrol can help us locate Borric." With a glance around the barren landscape, he added, "I'm certain I have no idea where to begin looking."

For the next few hours, through the early afternoon, it took all of Locklear's powers of persuasion, with some not-so-idle threatening, to keep Erland from riding farther into the wastes than Locklear judged safe. The young Prince was frantic to search for his brother, in case he was lying unconscious a few yards away, in a gully or ravine, in need of care. Locklear spread the men out to patrol the surrounding area, always keeping a chain of guards posted so that someone was always in sight of the impromptu camp. Gamina tended the wounded, getting them ready to ride to the closest shelter when James returned.

Finally, James returned, accompanied by the Keshian patrol. Sergeant Ras-al-Fawi was obviously displeased to have his respite interrupted, especially given the potential for personal difficulty should his superiors judge him somehow at fault, as the attack came in his patrol area. He wished to put as much distance between himself and these cursed Islemen as possible, but the possibility of an international incident between the Empire and her largest neighbor gave sufficient reason to put his irritation aside and help in the search for the lost Prince.

Experienced trackers quickly discovered the gully wherein the raiders had hidden. Shouts brought the entire company to the edge of a gully, where two scouts were inspecting a large rock fall. One continued poking about in the rubble while the second scout carried a single boot up to where the Islemen waited. There was no mistaking the scarlet and yellow design of the boot. Pointing back down at the mass of boulders he said, "M'lord, I found this. A little farther in, under the rocks, I can see what's left of the foot that wore it."

Erland sat in silent shock as James asked, "Can we dig him out?"

The Keshian scout at the bottom of the rockfall shook his head. "It would take a company of engineers a day or two at best, m'lord." He pointed up to the place the slide had begun. "It was recently done, from the signs. To cover the owner of this boot, and others, perhaps." Then he pointed to the far side of the gully. "And if too much movement occurred here, the other side might come down as well. I'm afraid it will be risky."

Erland said, "I want him dug out."

James said, "I understand—"

Erland interrupted. "No, you don't. That may not be Borric down there."

Locklear attempted to be understanding. "I know how you must feel—"

"No," said Erland, "you don't know." To James he said, "We don't know that's Borric down there. He could have lost the boot during the struggle. He could be a prisoner. We don't know if that's him under the rocks."

James said, "Gamina, is there any sign of Borric?"

Gamina just shook her head. "The thoughts I detected earlier were in this gully. But there was no pattern of thinking that was familiar."

Erland was unmoved. "That proves nothing." To James he said, "You know how close he and I are. If he were dead . . . I'd feel something." Looking across the broken landscape of the high desert he said, "He's out there somewhere. And I intend to find him."

"And what are you going to do, m'lord?" asked the Keshian Sergeant. "Ride out into the plateau country alone and without water or food? It doesn't look it, but it's as much a desert here as in the great sand ergs of the Jal-Pur. Beyond that rise of ridges over there the true sandy wastes begin, and if you don't know where the Oasis of the Broken Palms is, you'll not live long enough to find the Oasis of the

Hungry Goats. There are thirty or so places out there you can find water and a few with food-bearing plants as well, but you can walk within yards of several and not know them. You would die, young lord."

Turning his horse back toward the way they had come, Sergeant Ras-al-Fawi said, "My lords, I grieve for your loss, but my duty dictates I ride on and discover others bent upon breaking the Empire's peace. I shall file a report on this when I reach the terminus of my patrol. If you would like, I'll leave a scout with you and you may continue your search. When you are satisfied that nothing more can be done, head back to the road." Pointing south, he said, "The road continues past the foothills of the Pillars of the Stars to Nar Ayab. We keep many stations and patrols along that route. Dispatch riders move constantly among those stations and into the heart of the Empire. Send word ahead of your arrival and a state welcome will be mounted by the Governor of Nar Ayab. From there, he will send mounted soldiers to protect you until you reach the city of Kesh." He left unsaid that had this been done from the start, the bandits would never have been able to surprise the Islemen. "In time, the Empress, blessings be upon her, will order engineers out to retrieve your young Prince, and he will be returned home for a fitting burial. Until then, I can only wish you the gods' favor in your travels."

With a wave and heels to the side of the horse, the Sergeant and his patrol headed away from the gully. James skirted the top of the fall and looked down to the lone Keshian scout who remained. "What do you see?"

The scout considered the signs, "Many men, milling about. A murder, there." He pointed to a dark spot upon the already dry ground.

"Murder!" said Locklear. "How can you be certain?"

"Blood, m'lord," answered the scout. "Which would not be unusual after a struggle, save this is in a large pool, with no signs of a wounded man approaching this spot. I would guess a throat was cut." He pointed to two lines of faint scratches in the dust leading from the bloodstain to the rockfall. "Two heels as someone was dragged to where the rocks were pushed." He pointed again to the top of the gully. "One climbed there." He glanced about once more, then scampered up the incline to where his horse waited. "They move south, to the Oasis of the Broken Palms."

Locklear said, "How do you know?"

The guard smiled. "It is the only place they can go, m'lord, for they move into the desert, and without baggage horses they cannot carry enough water to see them through to Durbin."

"Durbin!" Erland almost spat the word. "That rat hole. Why would they risk the dangers of the desert to go there?"

"Because," James answered, "it is a safe harbor for every cutthroat and pirate from every nation bordering the Bitter Sea."

"And the best market for slaves in the Empire," said the scout. "In the heart of the Empire, slaves are plentiful, but up here very difficult to find. Only Kesh and Queg have open markets for slaves. In the Free Cities and the Kingdom, the practice is discouraged."

Erland said, "I don't follow."

James turned his horse toward the direction the scout had indicated and said, "If only two guards—" quickly he added, "or Borric and one guard remain alive, there's enough profit at the Durbin slave auction to make the raid profitable. If they are taken into the Empire, the money is less than a third what it is in Durbin, and then the leader has an angry crew to govern, and that can be dangerous." James spoke with authority.

Erland said, "Then why wouldn't Borric just tell them who he is? He's certainly worth more in ransom than he'd ever fetch as a slave."

James looked out thoughtfully across the wastelands at the late afternoon sun. Then he said, "If he is alive, I would have expected a message from the raiders, something telling us he is well and for us not to follow, and that a ransom demand would be made within a short time. It's what I would have done. . . . I would have made sure I didn't have a company of soldiers dogging my heels."

The Keshian scout ventured, "These raiders may not be as clever as you, m'lord. Your Prince, should he live, may feel it dangerous to tell them who he is. They might cut this throat to avoid trouble and flee into the wastes. He may be unconscious, yet not injured enough for them to abandon. There may be other answers, m'lord."

Erland said, "Then we must hurry."

The scout said, "We must proceed cautiously to avoid ambush, Highness." He pointed into the sandy landscape. "If slavers attack the road, then out there at an oasis or in one of the wadis a slave caravan gathers. Many raiders with many guards will bring their catch to be taken to Durbin—many more fighters than we could face, even had my Sergeant remained—more than both our companies could face. Perhaps a hundred guards."

Feeling the heavy weight of despair begin to descend upon him,

Erland said, "We'll find him. He isn't dead." But his own words sounded hollow in his ear.

The scout scrambled up the wall of the gully to where his horse waited. "If we ride quickly, m'lord, we shall reach the Oasis of the Broken Palms at sundown."

James detailed two guards to accompany the two wounded men back to the inn where they would recuperate until they were ready to return to the Kingdom. He did a swift calculation and realized he now had only a dozen healthy soldiers. Feeling vulnerable and somewhat foolish, he ordered that small band into the desert.

The sun was touching the horizon when the scout rode at a gallop toward the Islemen. James signaled a halt. Reining in his mount, the scout said, "In the Wadi al Sáfra, a caravan gathers—one hundred guards, maybe more."

James swore. Erland said, "Any sign of my brother?"

"I could not get close enough to tell, my Prince."

"Is there any place nearby where we could get close to the camp?" asked Locklear.

"A shallow ravine courses along one side of the wadi, and at the far end it becomes a gully running close to the camp, m'lord. Four, maybe five men could approach unobserved, be they stealthy. But it is dangerous. At the far end it becomes shallow enough for a standing man to see into the camp, but it is also close enough for a standing man to be noticed."

Erland began to dismount, but James said, "No, you'll clank like an armorer's wagon in that chain. Wait here."

Gamina said, "I should go, James. I can tell if Borric's in the caravan if I can get close enough."

"How close is close enough?" asked her new husband.

"A stone's throw," answered Gamina.

James asked the scout, "Can we get that close?"

The scout said, "We shall be close enough to see if any of the pigs have boils upon their faces, m'lord."

"Good," said Gamina, picking up the hem of her riding gown so it stayed clear of the ground. She tucked it in her wide leather belt, in the fashion of the Stardock fisherwomen when they waded into the shallows.

James ignored the unseemly display, exposing two slender white legs very high up on the thighs, as he attempted to think of a good reason to object to her coming along; he couldn't. *It's the problem* with having a logical mind and giving women the same credit for ability as men, he mused to himself as he dismounted. You can't contrive reasons to keep them safe.

Locklear signaled a pair of guards to accompany James, Gamina, and the scout and the five set out down the trail on foot. They moved slowly, as the sun fell below the western horizon. By the time they approached the near end of the ravine, the sky was slate grey and the desert was alive with highlights of crimson and pink as the reflected sunlight off the clouds over the distant sea bathed the landscape in rose twilight.

Noise from the caravan echoed through the deepening gloom and James glanced around to see if everyone had stayed close. Gamina touched his arm lightly and her thoughts came to him. *I can sense many minds in the wadi, my love.*

Borric? he asked silently.

Nothing, she admitted. *But I must get closer to be certain.*

Gripping the scout's arm, James whispered, "Can we get closer?"

Whispering back, he answered, "There is a bend ahead, and if we follow it, we shall be close enough to urinate upon the dogs. But be cautious, my lord, for it is a likely place to dump offal and garbage and there may be guards nearby."

James nodded and the scout led them into the gloom.

James could remember several times in his past when he had taken short journeys that seemed to take forever, but none seemed to take so long as it took to travel the short distance to the end of the gully. As they reached it, the voices of the guards could be heard in soft conversation as they walked easily along the perimeter of the camp. Not only was the journey nerve-wracking for the danger, but the end of the gully was being used as a garbage dump and privy trench; the Islemen had to creep through garbage and waste, both human and horse.

James stepped in something wet and soft and from the odor which hung in the ravine like a noisome fog he was certain he didn't want to know what it was. He could guess. He signaled to the scout who signaled back that they were as close as they dared get.

Cautiously James peeked over the edge of the gully. Standing no more than ten paces away, two silhouettes stood outlined against the campfires. Huddled near them for warmth were at least thirty misera-ble-looking people, but nowhere in the group could James see Borric. Not every face could be seen, but James was certain his red hair would be easily noticeable in the sea of dark heads, despite the flickering firelight.

Then a man in a purple robe approached the two guards and for a moment, James's chest constricted. But it wasn't Borric. The wearer of the robe had the hood tossed back and the darkly bearded face that scowled at the two guards was one James had never seen before. He wore a sword at his hip, and ordered the two men to cease their chatter and move on.

The robed man turned as another joined him, a large man in a leather vest, wearing the caste mark of the Durbin slavers on his arm. It was a mark James hadn't seen since he was a boy, but like all members of the Mockers, Krondor's Guild of Thieves, he knew it by reputation. The Durbin slavers were not men to trouble lightly.

James chanced another glimpse of the camp, then hunkered down next to his wife. Her eyes were closed and her face was set in an expression of concentration as she sought out Borric among the prisoners in the camp. Finally she opened her eyes and her mind's voice came to James. *There is no thought I recognize as Borric's in the camp.*

Are you certain? he asked.

Sadly, she said, *If he were in that camp, as close as we are, I would find him. Even were he sleeping, I could sense his presence were he in that camp.* She silently sighed and he caught the echoes of sorrow in her mind. *There can be no explanation for it save he lay buried beneath the rubble back where we found the boot.* There was a moment of silence, then she said, *He is dead.*

James was motionless for an instant, then he motioned to the scout. By sign he gave the order to return the way they had come. The search was over.

"No!" Erland's face was harsh as he refused to accept Gamina's pronouncement. "You can't know for certain."

James recounted his observations for the third time since returning to where Erland and the balance of the company waited. "We saw another bandit wearing the robe, so we can assume that it's possible they took the boots from him as well, I grant that. But there was no sign of him in the camp." To the Keshian scout he said, "Is there any chance the bandits who raided us were not part of this slaver caravan?"

The scout shrugged, as if to say anything was possible. "Probably not, my lord. By carrying off some of your men it is unlikely it was but a coincidence you were raided. Any of your men who remain alive are for certain in that camp."

James nodded. "If he had been alive, Erland, Gamina would have been able to speak to him."

"How can you be so certain?"

So that all in the camp could hear her, Gamina said, *I have control over my talents, Erland. I can choose how many or few I wish to speak to, and once I touch a mind I can recognize its thoughts. Borric's thoughts were not among those in the camp.*

"Perhaps he was unconscious."

Gamina shook her head sadly. "I would have sensed his presence, even if he were unconscious. There was an . . . absence of him. I can't explain it better than that. He was not among them."

The scout said, "My lord, if I may remain with you this night, I shall have to move on to find my Sergeant. He will wish to know of these Durbinites. The Governor of Durbin is little better than a pirate and renegade himself, and sooner or later, word of this outrage will reach the Court of Light. When the Empress, blessings be upon her, at last decides to act, retribution shall be forthcoming, and it shall be terrible indeed. I know it can not ease your burden, but to assault the person of a royal family enroute to her Jubilee is beyond insult. The Empress, blessings upon her name, will no doubt take it as a personal insult and act to revenge your family."

Erland's anger was not soothed in the least. "What? The Governor of Durbin reprimanded? Then a formal letter of apology, I suppose."

"More likely she will ordered the city surrounded and burned to the ground with all the citizens within, sire. Or if she is feeling merciful, perhaps she will only send the Governor of Durbin, with his family and retainers of course, to your King for punishment, sparing the city. It will depend upon her mood at the time she decides."

Erland was overwhelmed. The shock of Borric's apparent death at last setting over him and the blasé attitude of the guard as he recounted such power on the part of one woman, conspired to render him without wit. He just nodded dumbly.

James, seeking to turn talk away from the terrible diplomatic situation that would arise out of Borric's death, said, "We shall ask you to bear letters to be forwarded back to the Prince of Krondor, so that we may mitigate any difficulties between our two nations."

The scout nodded. "As one who serves along the border, I would do so gladly, m'lord." He then left to see to his horse. James nodded at Locklear, who in turn motioned with his head toward Erland. Both young nobles moved away to speak in private.

Locklear said, "This is a fine mess."

"Well, we have faced difficulties in the past. This is what we were trained for, to make choices."

Locklear said, "I think we should consider returning to Krondor."

James said, "If we do, and Arutha orders Erland back to the Jubilee, we risk insulting the Empress by arriving late."

"The festival will last more than two months," Locklear pointed out. "We would be there before it's over."

"I still would rather have us there at the beginning." He glanced around at the black night. "Out there something's going on. I can't help feeling that." He put a finger on Locklear's chest. "It's just too much a coincidence that we were the ones raided."

"Perhaps," agreed Locky in part, "but if we were the target for a raid, then those behind it were those who attempted to assassinate Borric in Krondor."

"Whoever they are." James was silent for a long moment, then said, "It makes no sense. Why would they wish to kill the boy?"

"To start a war between our Kingdom and the Empire."

"No, that's obvious. I mean *why* would anyone wish war?"

Locklear shrugged. "Why does anyone ever wish to start one? We must discover who within the Empire will profit most from a destabilized northern border, and that is our likely culprit."

James nodded. "We will not be able to do that in Krondor."

Turning to find Erland alone, facing out into the desert night, James crossed to stand beside him. In quiet tones he said, "You must come to terms with this, Erland. Your grief must quickly be abandoned and you must accept the change in circumstances fate has forced upon you."

Erland blinked in confusion, as one suddenly thrust into the light. "What?"

James turned and stood before him. With firm hand upon the younger man's shoulder, he said, "You are now Heir. You will be our next King. And you will carry the fate of your homeland with you when we ride to Kesh."

Erland seemed not to hear him. The Prince said nothing as he returned his gaze to the west, to the distant slaver caravan. At last, he turned his horse slowly away and rode to where the others were waiting to resume their trek southward, into the heart of Great Kesh.

Chapter Seven
Captive

Borric awoke.

He lay motionless, straining to hear through the confusion of voices and sounds that were ever-present in the camp, even at night. For an instant, while still half-dozing, he had thought he heard his name being faintly called.

Sitting up, he blinked as he looked around. Most of the captives still sat huddled near the campfire, as if its light and warmth would somehow banish the cold fear in their souls. He had chosen to lay as far from the stench of the waste trench as possible, on the opposite side of the band of slaves. As Borric moved, he was again reacquainted with the manacles that bound his wrists, the odd-looking flat silver metal with the reputed property of blanking out all magic powers of whoever was forced to wear them. Borric shivered, and realized the desert night was indeed turning cold. His robe had been taken from him and his shirt as well, leaving him with only a pair of trousers to wear. He moved toward the campfire, eliciting an occasional curse or complaint as he forced his way between captives reluctant to move. But as all the fight was gone from them, his inconsiderate shoving through the mass of slaves got him nothing more than a glare of anger or a muttered oath.

Borric sat down between two other men, who attempted to ignore his intrusion. Each lived moment to moment in his own world of misery.

A scream cut through the night as one of the five women captives was again assaulted by the guards. Earlier a sixth woman had struggled too much, biting out the neck artery of the guard who was raping her, earning both of them death, his the swifter and less painful.

From the sound of the pitiful wail that trailed on after the scream, Borric considered her the lucky one. He doubted any of the women would be alive by the time they reached Durbin. By turning them over to the guards, the slaver avoided problems for many days to come. Should any survive the trip, she would be sold cheaply as a kitchen drudge. None was young enough nor attractive enough that it was worth the slave master's trouble to keep them out of the guards' reach.

As if summoned by Borric's thoughts of him, the slaver appeared at the edge of the campfire. He stood there in the golden red glow of the firelight and made his tally. Pleased by what he saw, he turned toward his own tent. Kasim. That's what Borric had heard him called. He had marked him well, for someday the Prince was certain he would kill Kasim.

As he moved away from the closely guarded slaves, another man called his name and approached. The man's name was Salaya, and he wore the purple robe Borric had won two nights before in Stardock. When Borric had first come to camp in the dawn hours that morning, the man had demanded the robe at once and had beaten the Prince when he appeared slow to remove it. The fact Borric was wearing manacles at the time seemed to make no difference. After the Prince had been struck repeatedly, Kasim had intervened, pointing out the obvious. Salaya was hardly mollified as Borric had one wrist, then the other, freed while he removed the robe. He seemed to blame Borric for that embarrassment before the others his own impatience had caused, as if it had been the Prince's fault somehow that Salaya was a stupid pig. Borric had marked him for death as well. Kasim gave some instructions to Salaya, who seemed to listen with a surly half-attention. Then the slaver was gone, heading off toward the string of horses. Most likely, thought Borric, he's off to supervise another band of slaves being brought to the impromptu caravansary.

Several times during the day, he had considered revealing his identity, but caution always overruled him. There was a good chance he would not be believed. He never wore his signet, always finding it inconvenient when riding, so it was locked away in his baggage, among those packs the bandits did not conspire to capture. While red hair might make them pause to consider the probability of his claim, it was in no way unique among those who lived in Krondor. Blond hair might be the norm for fair-skinned people living in Yabon and along the Far Coast, but Krondorians numbered as many redheads as blonds among their citizenry. And proving he was not a magician would take some doing, for what difference was there between someone who doesn't know any magic and someone who knows magic but pretends he doesn't.

Borric was decided. He would wait until he reached Durbin then seek to find someone a little more likely to understand his circumstance. He really doubted Kasim or any of his men—especially if they all were as bright as Salaya—would either understand or believe him. But someone with the intelligence to be the master of such as these might. And if so, Borric could most likely ransom himself to freedom.

Taking what comfort he could from thoughts like these, Borric pushed a half-dozing captive, moving him a few inches, so Borric might lie down again. The blows to the head had made him very groggy and sleep beckoned often. He closed his eyes, and for a moment the sensation of the ground spinning beneath made him nauseous. Then it passed. Soon a fitful sleep descended.

The sun burned like the angry presence of Prandur, the Fire God, himself. As if hanging only a few yards above him, the sun beat down on Borric's fair skin, searing it. While Borric's hands and face had been lightly tanned when serving at the northern borders, the scorching desert sun burned him to weakness. Blisters had erupted along Borric's back the second day, and his head swam from the pain of his burn. The first two days had been bad enough, as the caravan had moved from the rocky plateau country down into the sandy wastes the local desert men called the ergs of the Jal-Pur. The five wagons moved slowly over what was less dirt than hard-packed sand baked to brick finish by the same sun that was slowly killing the slaves.

Three had died yesterday. Salaya had little use for weaklings; only healthy, strong workers were wanted on the slave blocks at Durbin. Kasim had still not returned from whatever business he was upon, and the deputized caravan leader was revealed for the sadistic pig Borric had marked him in their first minute of meeting. Water was handed out three times a day, before first light, at the noon break when the drivers and guards halted to rest, and then with the evening meal—the only meal, Borric corrected himself. It was a dried mush bread, with little flavor and little that gave strength. He hoped the soft things in the bread were indeed raisins; he had not bothered to look. Food kept him alive, no matter how distasteful it might be.

The slaves were a sullen group, each man lost in his own suffering. Weakened by the heat, few had anything to say to each other; talk was a needless waste of energy. But Borric had managed to glean a few facts from one or two of them. The guards were less vigilant now that the caravan was into the wastes; even should a slave escape, where would he go? The desert was the surest guard of all. Once in Durbin, they would rest for a few days, perhaps as long as a week, so bloody feet and burned skins could heal, and weight could be regained before they were offered upon the block. Travel-weary slaves brought little gold.

Borric attempted to consider his choices, but the heat and sunburn had weakened him, made him ill, and the lack of food and water was keeping him dull and stupid. He shook his head and tried to focus his attention on ways to escape, but all he could manage was to move his feet, one then the other, pick them up and let them fall before him, over and over, until allowed to halt.

Then the sun vanished and it was night. The slaves were ordered to sit near the campfire as they had been for the last three nights and listened to the guards having sport with the five remaining women captives. They no longer struggled or screamed. Borric ate his flat piece of bread and sipped his water. The first night after entering the desert, one man had gulped his water, then vomited it a few minutes later. The guards would give him no more. He had died the next day. Borric had learned his lesson. No matter how much he wished to tilt back his head and drain the copper cup, he lingered over the stale, warm water, sipping it slowly. Sleep came quickly, the deep dreamless sleep of exhaustion, with no real rest obtained. Each time he moved, angry sunburns brought him awake. If he faced away from the fire, his back smarted at any touch of heat, yet if he moved from the fire, the cold brought him chills. But no matter how close or far the source of his discomfort, he soon was overcome by his fatigue, until he moved, when the cycle began again. And then suddenly, spear butts and boot kicks roused Borric to his feet with the others.

In the cool of the morning, the almost damp night air seemed nothing so much as a lens for the sun, bringing the searing touch of Prandur to torment the slaves. Before an hour was passed, two more men were fallen, left where they hit the sand.

Borric's mind retreated into itself. An animal consciousness was all that remained, a cunning, vicious animal that refused to die. Every iota of energy he possessed was given over to but one task, to move forward and not to fall. To fall was to die.

Then after a time of mindless moving forward, hands seized him. "Stop," commanded a voice.

Borric blinked and through flashing yellow lights, he saw a face. It was a face composed of knots and lumps, angles and planes, skin dark like ebony over a curly beard. It was the ugliest face Borric had ever beheld. It was magnificent in its repulsiveness.

Borric began to giggle, but all that came from his parched throat was a dry wheeze. "Sit," said the guard, helping Borric to the ground with a surprising gentleness. "It's time for the midday halt." Glancing around to see if he was being observed, he opened his own water skin and poured some out upon his hand. "You northerners die from the sun so quickly." He washed the back of Borric's neck and dried his hand by running it through Borric's hair, cooling his baking head slightly. "Too many have fallen along the way; Kasim will not be pleased." Quickly he poured a mouthful for the young Prince, then moved on, as if nothing had passed between them.

Then another guard brought around the water skin and cups and the clamor for water began. Each slave who could still speak announced his thirst, as if to remain silent was to chance being ignored.

Borric could barely move, and each motion brought waves of bright yellow and white light and red flashes behind his eyes. Yet, almost blindly, he pushed out his hand to take the metal cup. The water was warm and bitter, yet sweeter than the finest Natalese wine to Borric's parched lips. He sipped the wine, forcing himself to hold it in his mouth as his father had taught him, letting the dark purple fluid course around his tongue, registering the subtle and complex components of the wine's flavor. A hint of bitterness, perhaps from the stems and a few leaves left in the vat of must, while the winemaker attempted to bring his wine to just the proper peak of fermentation before barreling the wine. Or perhaps it was a flaw. Borric didn't recognize the wine; it lacked noticeable body and structure, and was deficient in acid to balance the fruit. It was not a very good wine. He would have to see if Papa was testing him and Erland by putting a poor local wine on the table, to see if they were paying attention.

Borric blinked and through eyes gummy from heat and dryness, he couldn't see where the tip was. How was he to spit the wine if there was no tip bucket to spit into? He mustn't drink it, or he would be very drunk, as he was only a small boy. Perhaps if he turned his head and spit behind the table, no one would notice.

"Hey!" shouted a voice. "That slave is spitting out his water!"

Hands ripped the cup from Borric's hands and he fell over backwards. He lay on the floor of his father's dining hall and wondered why the stones were so warm. They should be cool. They always were. How did they get so warm?

Then a pair of hands lifted him ungently from his sitting position, and another helped to hold him up. "What's this? Trying to kill yourself by not drinking?" Borric opened his eyes slightly and saw the vague outline of a face before his.

Weakly, he said, "I can't name the wine, Father."

"He's delirious," said the voice. Hands lifted him and carried him and then he was in a darker place. Water was daubed over his face and poured over his neck, wrists, and arms. A distant voice said, "I swear by the gods and demons, Salaya, you haven't the brains of a three days' dead cat. If I hadn't ridden out to meet you, you'd have let this one die, too, wouldn't you?"

Borric felt water course into his mouth and he drank. Instead of the bitter half-cup, this was a veritable stream of almost fresh water. He drank.

Salaya's voice answered: "The weak ones fetch us nothing. It saves us money to let them die on the road and not feed them."

"You idiot!" shouted the other. "This is a prime slave! Look at him. He's young, not more than twenty years, if I know my business, and not bad looking under the sunburn, healthy—or at least he was a few days ago." There was a sound of disgust. "These fair-skinned northerners can't take the heat like those of us born to the Jal-Pur. A little more water, and some covering, and he'd have been fit for next week's block. Now, I'll have to keep him an extra two weeks for the burns to heal and his strength to return."

"Master—"

"Enough, keep him here under the wagon while I inspect the others. There may be more who will survive if I find them in time. I do not know what fate befell Kasim, but it was a sorry day for the Guild when you were left in charge."

Borric found this exchange very odd. And what had happened to the wine? He let his mind wander as he lay in the relative cool, under the wagon, while a few feet away, a Master of the Guild of Durbin Slavers inspected the others who in a day's time would be delivered to the slave pens.

"Durbin!" said Salman. His face of dark knots split in a wide grin. He drove the last wagon in the train, the one in which Borric rode. The two days since Borric was carried into the shade of the wagon had returned him from the edge of death. He now rode in the last wagon with three other slaves who were recovering from heatstroke. Water was there for the taking, and their burned skins were dressed with a soft oil and herb poultice, which reduced the fiery pain to a dull itch.

Borric rose to his knees then stood upon shaky legs as the wagon lurched across the stones in the road. He saw little remarkable about the city, save the surrounding lands were now green rather than sandy. They had been passing small farms for about a half-day. He remembered what he had been taught about the infamous pirate stronghold as a boy.

Durbin commanded the only arable farm land between the Vale of Dreams and the foothills of the Trollhome Mountains, as well as the one safe harbor to be found from Land's End to Ranom. Along the south coast of the Bitter Sea the treacherous reefs waited for ships and boats unfortunate enough to be caught in the unexpected northern winds that sprang up routinely. For centuries, Durbin had been home to pirates, wreckers and scavengers, and slavers.

Borric nodded to Salman. The happy little bandit had proved to be both friendly and garrulous. "I've lived there all my life," said the bandit, widening his grin. "My father was born there, too."

When the desert men of the Jal-Pur had conquered Durbin hundreds of years before, they had found their gateway to the trade of the Bitter Sea, and when the Empire had conquered the desert men, Durbin was the capital city of the desert men. Now it was the home of an Imperial governor, but nothing had changed. It was still Durbin.

"Tell me," asked Borric, "do the Three Guilds still control the city?"

Salman laughed. "You're a very educated fellow! Few outside Durbin know of this thing. The Guild of Slavers, the Wreckers Guild, and the Captains of the Coast. Yes, the Three still rule in Durbin. It is they, not the Imperial Governor, who decide who is to live and die, who is to work, who is to eat." He shrugged. "It is as it has always been. Before the Empire. Before the desert men. Always."

Thinking of the power of the Mockers, the Guild of Thieves, in Krondor, he asked, "What of the beggars and thieves? Are they not a power?"

"Ha!" answered Salman. "Durbin is the most honest city in the world, my educated friend. We who live there lay at night with doors unlocked and may walk the streets in safety. For he who steals in Durbin is a fool, and either dead or a slave within days. So the Three have decreed, and who is foolish enough to question their wisdom? Certainly not I. And so it must be, for Durbin has no friends beyond the reefs and sands."

Borric lightly patted Salman on the shoulder and sat down in the back of the wagon. Of the four sick slaves, he was the quickest to recover, as he was the youngest and fittest. The other three were older farmers, and none had shown any inclination to quick recovery. Despair robs you of strength faster than sickness, Borric thought.

He drank a little water and marveled at the first hint of ocean breeze that came into the wagon as they headed down the road toward the city gate. One of his father's advisors, and the man who had taught Borric and Erland how to sail, Amos Trask, had been a pirate in his youth, rading the Free Cities, Queg, and the Kingdom under the name Captain Trenchard, the Dagger of the Sea. He had been a renowned member of the Captains of the Coast. But while he had told many tales of the high seas, he had said almost nothing of the politics of the Captains. Still, someone might remember Captain Trenchard and that might stand Borric in good stead.

Borric had decided to keep his identity hidden a while longer. While he had no doubt the slavers would send ransom demands to his father, he thought he might avoid the sort of international difficulties that would arise should it come to pass. Instead, he might bide his time in the slave pens a few days, regain his strength, then flee. While the desert was a formidable barrier, any small boat in the harbor would be his passage to freedom. It was nearly five hundred miles of sailing against prevailing winds to reach Land's End, Baron Locklear's father's city, but it could be done. Borric considered all this with a confidence of one who, at the age of nineteen, did not know the meaning of defeat. His captivity was merely a setback, nothing more.

The slave pens were sheltered by shingle roofs rested upon tall beams, protecting the slaves from the noon heat or unexpected storms off the Bitter Sea. But the sides were open slats and crossbeams, so the guards could watch the captives. A healthy man could easily climb over the ten-foot fence, but by the time he reached the top and crawled through the space between the fence and the crossbeams supporting the roof three feet above, guards would be waiting for him.

Borric considered his plight. Once he was sold, his new master might be lax in his security, or he might be even more stringent. Logic dictated he attempt to escape while confined close to the sea. His new owner could be a Quegan merchant, a traveler from the Free Cities, or even a Kingdom noble. What would be worse, he could be carried deep into the Empire. He was not sanguine about letting fate make the choice.

He had a plan. The only difficulty lay in getting cooperation from the other prisoners. If a long enough diversion could be arranged for, then he could be over the fence and out into the city. Borric shook his head. He realized as plans go, it wasn't much.

"Pssst!"

Borric turned to see from where the odd sound came. Seeing nothing, he turned back into himself as he considered improvements on his plan.

"Pssst! This way, young noble." Borric looked again through the bars of the pen, but this time down, and in the scant shadows he saw a slight figure.

A boy, no more than eleven or twelve years old, grinned up at him from the meager shelter of a large roof support. If he moved more than inches in any direction, he would certainly be spotted by the guard.

Borric glanced around, seeing the two guards at the corner speaking to one another. "What?" he whispered.

"Should you but divert the guards' attention for an instant, noble sir, I will be indebted to you for ages," came the answering whisper.

Borric said, "Why?"

"I need but a moment's distraction, sir."

Counting no harm from it, save perhaps a blow for insolence, Borric nodded. Moving to where the guards stood, he said, "Hey! When do we eat?"

Both guards blinked in confusion, then one snarled. He jammed the butt of his spear through the staves of the fence, and Borric had to dodge not to be struck. "Sorry I asked," he said.

Chuckling to himself, he moved his shoulders under the rough shirt they had given him, fighting the impulse to scratch. The sunburn was healing after being dressed for the last three days, but the peeling skin and the itching were making him doubly cross. The next slave auction was over a week away, and he knew he would be on the block. He was regaining his strength quickly.

A tug at his sleeve caused him to turn and there beside him was the boy. "What are you doing here?"

The boy gave him a questioning look. "What do you mean, sir?"

"I thought you were trying to escape the pens," said Borric in a harsh whisper.

The boy laughed. "No, noble youth. I needed the distraction you so magnanimously provided, so I might enter the pen."

Borric looked heavenward. "Two hundred prisoners all dreaming continuously of a way out of here, and I have to meet the one mad-man in the world who wishes to break in! Why me?"

The boy looked up to where Borric's gaze went, and said, "To which deity does my lord speak?"

"All of them. Look, what is this all about?"

The boy took Borric's elbow and steered him to the center of the pen, where they would be the least conspicuous to the guards. "It is a matter of some complexity, my lord."

"And why do you address me as 'my lord'?"

The boy's face split with a grin, and Borric took a good look at him. Round cheeks burned red by the sun dominated a brown face. What he could see of the boy's eyes, made narrow slits by merry amusement, suggested they were dark to the point of being black. Under a hood several sizes too large, ill-cropped coarse black hair shot out at differing lengths.

The boy made a slight bow. "All men are superior to one as low as I, my lord, and deserve respect. Even those pigs of guards."

Borric couldn't help but smile at this imp. "Well, then, tell me why you, alone among sane men everywhere, would wish to break into this miserable company?"

The boy sat upon the ground and motioned Borric to do likewise. "I am called Suli Abul, young sir. I am a beggar by trade. I am also, I am ashamed to admit, under threat of punishment from the Three. You know of the Three?" Borric nodded. "Then you know their wrath is great and their reach long. I saw an old merchant who had paused to sleep in the midday sun. From his torn purse, some coins had fallen. Had I waited until he had awoke, and chanced he would not miss his coins, then I would have but found them upon the ground, and none would think the worse of me. But not trusting the gods to keep the man from noticing his loss, I sought to pick them up while he dozed. As the Lady of Luck decreed, he did awake at the worst moment, and cried 'thief!' to all who were nearby. One who recognized me added my name to the shout, and I was pursued. Now I am being sought after by the Three for punishment. Where better to hide than among those already condemned to slavery?"

Borric was silent for a moment, at a loss to answer that. Shaking his head in wonder, he asked, "Tell me, in nine days when we are to be sold, then what shall you do?"

With a laugh, the boy said, "By then, gentle lord, I shall be gone."

"And where shall you go?" asked the Prince, his eyes narrowing.

"Back to the city, young sir. For my transgressions are slight and the Three have much to concern their attentions. Some great issue is being decided now, at the Governor's palace, or so the rumors in the streets tell. Many officials of the Three as well as Imperial envoys come and go. In any event, after a few days, those who are searching for myself will be about other business and I may safely return to my craft."

Borric shook his head. "Can you get out as easily as you got in?"

The boy shrugged. "Probably. Nothing in life is certain. I expect I shall be able to. If not, it's the gods' will."

Borric gripped the young beggar's shirt, pulling him close. In whispers, he said, "Then, my philosophical friend, we shall cut a bargain. I helped you in, and you shall help me out."

The boy's dark face paled. "Master," he said, almost hissing between his teeth, "for one as adroit as I, we might contrive a means to release you from your captivity, but you are the size of a mighty warrior, and those manacles upon your wrists confine your movement."

"Have you the means for my release of these?"

"How could I?" asked the frightened boy.

"You don't know? What kind of a thief are you?"

The boy shook his head in denial. "A poor one, master, if the truth be known. It is the height of stupidity to steal in Durbin, therefore I am also a stupid one. My thievery is of the lowest order, the most inconsequential of thefts. Upon the soul of my mother, I so swear, master! Today was my first attempt."

Shaking his head, Borric said, "Just what I need—an incompetent thief. I could get free myself if I had a pick." He took a breath, calming himself so as not to frighten the boy more. "I need a hard piece of wire, so long. A thin nail might work." He showed the boy by holding up thumb and forefinger, two inches of length. The manacle chain made the gesture difficult.

106

"I can get that, master."

"Good," said Borric, releasing the boy. The instant he was released, he turned as if to flee, but anticipating just such a reaction, Borric's foot went out and tripped the beggar. Before the boy could scramble to his feet, the Prince had him by the shoulder of his garment. "You make a scene," said the Prince, indicating the guards a short distance away with a nod of his head. "I know what you are going to do, boy. Don't seek to flee my grasp. If I'm to be sold at auction in a week's time, I might as well not go alone. Give me one more excuse to turn you over to the guards and I will. Understand?"

"Yes, master!" whispered the boy, now completely terrified. Borric said, "I know you, boy. I've been taught by one who was to you as you are to the fleas who live in your shirt. Do you believe me?" Suli nodded, unwilling to trust his voice. "If you seek to betray me or leave me, I will insure I don't go to the block alone. We are in this as one, do you understand?" The boy nodded, and this time Borric saw his agreement wasn't just to gain his freedom, but to show he believed Borric would indeed turn him over to the guards if he attempted to abandon the Prince. Borric released him, and the boy fell hard upon the ground. This time he didn't attempt to run, but simply sat upon the hard-packed dirt, a look of fear and hopelessness upon his face. "Oh, Father of Mercies, I pray you, forgive my foolishness. Why, oh, why did you cast me in with this mad lord?"

Borric settled to one knee. "Can you get me the wire, or were you just lying?"

The boy shook his head. "I can get it." He rose to his feet and motioned Borric to follow.

Borric followed him to the fence. The boy turned his back so the guards would not see his face should they look in his direction. Pointing to the boards, the boy said, "Some of these are warped. Look for what you need."

Borric turned his back as well, but studied the fencing from the corner of his eye. About three boards down, a warp had bowed the fence outward slightly, pushing a nail out. The Prince leaned against that board and could feel the nailhead poking him in the shoulder.

Borric turned suddenly and pushed the boy against the board. The boy leaned into it and, in one motion, Borric hooked the edge of his metal cuff over the nail. "Now pray I don't bend it," he whispered. Then with a quick yank, the nail was free.

Stooping to pick it up, he moved to hide his prize from any watching eyes. Glancing around, he saw with relief that no one had bothered to take note of his odd behavior.

With little movements, he had one, then the other manacle off. He quickly rubbed his chafed wrists, then put the manacles back on.

"What are you doing?" whispered the young beggar.

"If the guards see me without the bracelets, they'll come investigate. I just wanted to see how difficult it was going to be to get them off. Obviously, not very."

"Where has a noble son such as yourself learned such a thing?" asked Suli.

Borric smiled. "One of my instructors had a . . . colorful childhood. Not all his lessons were standard teaching for—" He had almost said "Princes," but at the last instant, he said, "noble sons."

"Ah!" said the boy. "Then you are one of noble birth. I thought as much from your speech."

"My speech?" asked Borric.

"You speak like one of the commons, most noble lord. Yet your accent is that of one from the highest born families, even royalty itself."

Borric considered. "We're going to have to change that. If we are forced to hide in the city for any length of time, I must pass as a commoner."

The boy sat. "I can teach you." Looking down at the manacles, he said, "Why the special confinement, son of a most noble father?"

"They think I'm a magician."

The boy's eyes widened. "Then why have they not put you to death? Magicians are most troublesome to confine. Even the poor ones can visit boils and harry warts upon those who displease them."

Borric smiled. "I've almost convinced them I am a poor tutor."

"Then why have they not removed the chains?"

"I've *almost* convinced them."

The boy smiled. "Where shall we go, master?"

"To the harbor, where I plan to steal a small boat and make for the Kingdom."

The boy nodded his approval. "That is a fine plan. I shall be your servant, young lord, and your father will reward me richly for helping his son escape this evil den of black-souled murderers."

Borric had to laugh. "You're given to a noble turn of phrase yourself, now, aren't you?"

The boy brightened. "One must be gifted in the use of words to earn one's living as a beggar, my most glorious lord. To simply ask for alms will bring nothing but kicks and cuffing from all but the kindest of men. But to threaten them with curses of the most elaborate sort will bring gifts.

"If I say, 'May your wife's beauty turn to ugliness,' what merchant would bother to hesitate in his passing. But should I say, 'May your mistress grow to resemble your wife! And may your daughters do likewise!' then he'll pay many coppers for me to remove the curse, lest his daughters grow to look like his wife and he can find no husbands for them, and his mistress grow to look like his wife and he lose his pleasure."

Borric grinned, genuinely amused. "Have you such powers of cursing that men fear you so?"

The boy laughed. "Who's to say? But what man would hoard a few coppers against the chance the curse *might* work?"

Borric sat down. "I shall share my meals with you, as they account the bread and stew. But I must be free of this place before they finally tally for auction."

"Then they will raise alarm and search for you."

Borric smiled. "That is what I wish them to do."

Borric ate his half of his dinner and gave the plate to the boy. Suli wolfed the food down and licked the tin plate to get the last bits.

For seven days they had shared Borric's rations, and while they both felt hunger, it was sufficient for them; the slavers gave generous portions for those heading toward the auction. No dark circles under eyes, nor hollow cheeks, nor shrunken frames would lower price if a few meals would prevent it.

If any others had noticed the unorthodox manner in which the boy had joined the company in the pen, no one commented upon it. The slaves were quiet, each man lost in his own thoughts, and little attempt was made to converse. Why bother to make friends with those you would most likely never see again?

Whispering so that no one would overhear, Borric said, "We must flee before the morning tally." The boy nodded, but said, "I don't understand." For seven days, he had been hiding behind the assembled slaves, ducking to not be included in the head count. Perhaps he had been seen once or twice, but the guards would not bother to recheck the number if they had one too many heads, simply assuming they had miscounted. If there had been too few, they would have recounted.

"I need as much confusion in their search for us as possible. But I

109

want most of the guards back at the auction the day following. You see?"

The boy made no pretense of understanding. "No, master."

Borric had spent the last week profitably picking the boy's brain for every piece of information he could about the city and what lay in the area surrounding the Slavers Guild. "Over that fence is the street to the harbor," Borric said, and Suli nodded to show he was correct. "Within minutes, dozens of guards will be racing down that street to find us before we can steal away on a boat for Queg or elsewhere, right?"

The boy nodded. It was the logical assumption. "No one in his right mind would risk the desert, right?"

"Certainly."

"Then we're going to head toward the desert."

"Master! We will die!"

Borric said, "I didn't say we'd go into the desert, just we'd head that way and find a place to hide."

"But where, master? There are only the houses of the rich and powerful between here and the desert, and the soldiers' barracks at the Governor's house."

Borric grinned.

The boy's eyes widened. "Oh, gods preserve us, master, you can't mean . . ."

Borric said, "Of course. The one place they'll never look for two runaway slaves."

"Oh, kind master. You must be joking to torment your poor servant."

"Don't look so crestfallen, Suli," said Borric, glancing around to make sure no one was watching. "You gave me the idea."

"I, master? I said nothing about delivering ourselves up to the Governor."

"No, but if you hadn't been trying to hide from the slavers in the slave pen, I'd have never thought of this."

Borric slipped the manacles and motioned for the boy to stand. The guards at the far end of the pen were playing a game of knucklebones and the one delegated to keep watch was dozing. Borric pointed upward and the boy nodded. He stripped his robe, leaving himself unclothed save for his breechcloth, and Borric made a cup with his hands. The boy took one step and Borric half-lifted, half-threw him up into the overhanging beams of the roof supports. The boy moved agilely along the beams to the farthest corner from the gambling guards, near where the single guard dozed.

Hesitation and any sort of noise would undo them, so Borric found himself holding his breath while the little beggar scampered to the corner of the pen. There Borric quickly climbed a few feet of fence, and reached up to grip the robe the boy had tied around the beam. Hauling himself over the fence with two pulls, he swung down to where the sleeping guard lay. Suli Abul climbed down to hang almost directly over the sleeping guard.

In a coordinated movement, the boy lifted the guard's metal helm from his head as Borric swung the manacles. The iron struck the guard on the side of the head with a dull crack, and the man slumped down.

Not waiting to see if they were observed—if one of the other guards noticed they might as well give up now—Borric leaped and grabbed the hanging robe.

Pulling himself up beside the boy, he paused a second to gulp his breath back into his lungs, then motioned. Suli set off in a crouched-over, silent walk, along the beam that ran the length of the roof. Borric followed, though his bulk forced him to move on hands and knees, crawling behind the slight boy.

Over the gambling guards they moved, then into the gloom. At the far end of the compound, they dropped to the top of the last pen, then leaped to the outside wall. Half-falling, half-jumping, they hit the ground and were off in the night, running as if the entire garrison of Durbin was on their heels, heading straight for the home of the city's Governor.

Borric's plan had worked as he had thought it would. In the busy house of the Governor of Durbin, there was much confusion and many people moving. A nameless pair of slaves crossing the courtyard to the kitchen elicited no comment.

Within ten minutes, the alarm had been raised, and many of the city's watchmen were in the streets, crying that a slave had escaped. By then, Borric and Suli had found a nice attic in the guest wing of the house, vacant and, from the amount of dust on the floor, unused for years.

Suli whispered, "You are certainly a magician, my lord. If not of the sort they thought, of a different kind. No one will think to search the Governor's home."

Borric nodded. He held up his finger to indicate silence, then lay back as if to sleep.

The excited boy could hardly believe his eyes when the young man fell into a fitful doze. Suli was too tense and excited—and afraid—to try to sleep. He glanced through the small roof window they had used to enter the attic, one which gave them a clear view of part of the Governor's courtyard and some of the other wing of the house.

After watching the occasional comings and goings of the household, the beggar turned to inspect the rest of the attic. He could stand easily enough, though Borric would have to stoop. He walked carefully upon the beams of the room, lest any who might happen to be beneath the attic hear movement.

At the far end of the attic, he found a trapdoor. Putting his ear against it, the boy heard nothing. He waited a long time, or at least what he felt was a long time, before prying the door up slightly. The room below was empty and dark. The boy moved the trap carefully, attempting not to cause dust to fall in the room below, and stuck his head through the trap.

He almost cried out as he turned to see a face inches from his own. Then his night vision adjusted and he saw he was nose to nose with a statue, the sort imported from Queg, life-size and carved from marble or some other stone.

The boy put his hand upon the stone head and lowered himself into the room. He glanced around and was satisfied the room was being used for storage. In a corner, under some bolts of cloth, he found a dull kitchen knife. A poor weapon was better than none, he thought, and he stuck the knife in his robe.

Moving as quietly as possible, the boy inspected the only door in the room. He tested it and found it unlocked. Opening it slowly, he peered through a tiny crack, into an empty, dark hall.

He moved cautiously into the hall and slowly walked to where the hall met with another, also dark. After listening, Suli was certain no one was using this wing of the Governor's large home. He scurried along, checking in rooms randomly, and found that all were deserted. Many were empty, and a few had furnishings covered with canvas tarps.

Scratching his arm, the boy glanced around. Nothing suggested itself to him as likely plunder, so he determined to return to the attic, to see if he could get some rest.

Then, at the far end of the hall he was leaving, he noticed a faint line of light. At the same instant, the silence was broken by the distant sound of an angry voice.

Caution and curiosity fought. Curiosity won. The boy stole down the hall, to find a door through which muffled voices could be heard. Putting his ear to the wood, the boy heard a man shouting. ". . . Fools! If we had known ahead of time, we could have been prepared."

A second, calmer voice answered. "It was chance. No one knew what that idiot Reese meant when he brought word from Lafe that a princely caravan with few guards was ripe for the taking."

"Not 'princely,'" said the first voice, anger barely contained. "'Princes' caravan.' That's what he meant."

"And the prisoner who escaped tonight was the Prince?"

"Borric. Or the Goddess of Luck is having more sport with us than I care to imagine. He was the only redheaded slave we took."

The calmer voice said, "Lord Fire will be displeased that he lives. With Borric thought dead, our master's mission is completed, but should a living Prince of Isles make his way home . . ."

The angry voice said, "Then you must insure that he does not, and for good measure, that his brother dies, as well."

Suli attempted to peek through the crack of the door and saw nothing, then he looked through the keyhole. He could only see a man's back and part of a man's hand resting upon a desk. Then the man at the desk leaned forward, and Suli recognized the face of the Governor of Durbin. His was the angry voice. "No one outside this room can know the escaped slave is Prince Borric. He must not be allowed to identify himself to anyone. Circulate the rumor he killed a guard while escaping, and order that the slave be killed the instant he is caught."

The man with the calm voice moved, blocking Suli's view. The beggar stood back, fearing the door was about to be opened, but the voice said, "The slavers will not like a kill-on-sight order. They will want a public execution, preferably death by exposure in the cage, to warn others against attempting to escape."

The Governor said, "I will placate the guild. But the fugitive must not be allowed to speak. Should any discover we had a hand in this—" He left the thought unfinished. "I want Lafe and Reese silenced, as well."

Suli moved away from the door. Borric, he thought to himself. Then his new master was . . . Prince Borric, of the House of con-Doin, son of the Prince of Krondor!

Never before had the boy known fear as he knew this minute. This was a game of dragons and tigers and he had stumbled into the middle of it. Tears ran down his face as he hurried to the attic, barely keeping his wits about him enough to close the door silently when he passed through into the storage room.

Using the Quegan statue, he boosted himself back into the attic and carefully put the trap back. He then scampered to where the dozing Prince lay. Softly, he whispered in his ear, "Borric?"

The young man was instantly awake, and said, "What?"

With tears running down his face, Suli whispered, "Oh, my magnificent lord. Have mercy. They know who you are and they are searching for you in force. They seek to kill you before others discover your identity."

Borric blinked and gripped the boy by the shoulders. "Who knows about me?"

"The Governor and another. I could not see who. This wing connects to where the Governor holds counsel with others. They speak of the slave with red hair who escaped this night, and they speak of the Prince of Isles. You are both."

Borric swore softly. "This changes nothing."

"It changes everything, gentle master," cried the boy. "They will not stop searching for you after a day, but will hunt you down for as long as they must. And they will kill me for what I know, too."

Borric let go of the frightened boy and swallowed his own fear. "Then we'll just have to be more clever than they are, won't we?"

The question sounded hollow in his own ears, for if the truth were to be known, he had no idea what he would do next.

Chapter Eight
Escape

The boy shook his head no.

"Yes," repeated Borric.

Suli again shook his head. He had been almost speechless since returning to the attic. In a hoarse whisper, he said, "If I go back they shall kill me, my Prince."

Borric leaned forward and firmly took the boy's shoulders. He attempted to fill his voice with as much menace as possible while whispering. "And if you don't, I will kill you!" From the terror that shone from the boy's eyes, he must have succeeded.

The debate was over the boy's refusal to return to his listening post near the Governor's chambers to discover more of what was said there. Borric had told him that the more information they possessed, the better their chances of survival. The theory seemed lost upon the terrified boy.

Discovering that the prisoner who escaped was a royal prince from a neighboring kingdom was a shock, enough of a shock to push the boy to the brink of hysteria. Then by the time the boy had returned to the attic, it had sunk in that every power in the city of Durbin was being turned toward finding that Prince, with one thought in mind, to kill him! That had him teetering over the edge of hysteria. Then it hit him that whoever was found in the company of said Prince would be disposed of at the same time, to insure his silence, and the boy found himself hanging out over the brink of hysteria, his feet churning in air as he clung with all his might to what remained of his wits.

115

He sat silently crying, only his fear of discovery keeping him from wailing like a scalded cat.

Borric at last saw the child was beyond reason. Shaking his head in disgust, he said, "Very well. You remain here and I'll go. Which way was it?"

The prospect of this large warrior knocking over statues and banging into furniture in the dark and making enough noise to wake the city hit the boy like cold water. It was an even more fearful choice than risking capture one more time. Shivering, the boy swallowed his fear and said, "No, my good master, I'll go." He took a moment to collect himself, then said, "Stay quiet, and I will go listen to what is said."

Once he had made the choice, the boy acted without hesitation, and moved back to the trapdoor. He levered it up and slipped through silently. Borric thought that despite everything, the boy showed a particular type of courage, doing what had to be done regardless of how frightened he was.

Time passed slowly for Borric and after what seemed an hour, he began to worry. What if the boy had been caught? What if instead of a round-faced little beggar coming through that trap, an armed warrior or assassin climbed into the attic?

Borric picked up the dull kitchen knife and held it tightly. It was scant comfort.

More minutes passed, and Borric was left alone with the sound of his own heartbeat. Someone wanted him dead. He had known that since the football match in Krondor. Someone named "Lord Fire." A silly name, but one designed to hide the identity of the author of that order to kill the son of the Prince of Krondor. The Governor of Durbin was part of the plot, as was a man in a black cloak. Probably a messenger from this Lord Fire. Borric's head ached from stress, fatigue, hunger, and the aftereffects of his journey across the desert. But he forced himself to concentrate. For the Governor of even a pest-hole city like Durbin to be involved in such a plot meant two things: the author of the plan to plunge the Empire into war with the Kingdom was placed highly enough to influence many people of rank, and the plot was far flung, as there were few places within the Empire farther away from the capital city as Durbin.

The trap opened and Borric tensed, bringing his knife to the ready. "Master!" a familiar voice whispered. Suli had returned. Even in the dark, Borric could sense his excitement.

"What?"

The boy hunkered down close to Borric, so he could whisper the news. "Much consternation in the city from your escape. The auction is closed tomorrow! This is an unprecedented thing. All wagons and packtrains from the city are to be searched. Any man with red hair is to be arrested at once, gagged so he may not speak, and brought to the palace for identification."

"They really want to insure no one knows I'm here."

Borric could almost sense the boy's grin as he said, "Difficult, master. With so much alarm in the city, sooner or later someone will discover the cause. The Captains of the Coast have agreed to sweep the sea-lanes between the reefs and Queg, from here to Krondor, to find the runaway slave. And every building in the city is to be investigated, the search is underway even as we speak! I do not understand this thing."

Borric shrugged. "I don't know either. How they could get so many people to agree to this sort of business without telling them what they were after . . ." Borric moved toward a tiny gap in the support beam of the roof, where he could peek into the courtyard. "It's another five, six hours to dawn. We might as well get some rest."

"Master!" hissed the boy. "How can you rest? We must flee!"

Borric said softly, "Fleeing is what they expect. They are looking for a man who is fleeing. Alone. A red-haired man."

"Yes," agreed the boy.

"So we wait here, steal a little food from the kitchen, and wait for the search to wind down. In a household as big as this, we should be able to pass unnoticed for a few days."

Sitting back on his haunches, the boy let out a long sigh. It was clear Suli wasn't pleased to hear this, but having nothing more intelligent to offer, he remained silent.

Borric awoke with a gulp of breath, his heart pounding in his chest. It was still dark. No, he corrected himself as he spied a bit of light entering through the crack at the roof line, it's still dark in this attic.

He had been dreaming, of a time when he and his brother had been playing in the palace as children, using the so-called secret passages that were used by servants to move unseen between the different suites. The boys had split up and Borric had become lost. He had waited a long, lonely time before his Uncle Jimmy had come looking for him. Borric smiled as he remembered. Erland had been the more upset of the two.

117

Moving to peer through the tiny crack at the sliver of courtyard he could see, Borric had little doubt it was much the same now. "Erland must think me dead," he muttered to himself.

Then he realized he was alone. The boy, Suli, was gone!

Borric patted around in the dark for the knife and found it where he left it. Feeling only slightly better for the presence of the indifferent weapon, he wondered what the boy could be up to. Perhaps he figured to bargain his own life in exchange for knowledge of the whereabouts of a certain red-haired slave?

Borric felt close to panic. If the boy had indeed tried to bargain for his own safety, both were as good as dead. Forcing himself to calmness, he again peered through the little crack. It was nearly sunrise, and already the Governor's household was busy, with servants hurrying between the outbuildings, the kitchen, and the main house. Still, there was nothing to suggest other than the normal morning's activities. No armed men were in sight, no shouting voices would be heard.

Borric sat back and thought. The boy might not be terribly educated, but he was not stupid. No doubt he knew his own life was forfeit if anyone learned of his involvement with the escaped slave. He most likely was hiding in another part of town, or perhaps even on a ship heading out of the city, working as a common seaman.

Always a hearty eater, Borric felt his stomach knot. He had never truly been hungry before in his life, and he didn't care for the feeling. He had been too miserable while traveling to Durbin to dwell much on his hunger; it was merely one among many afflictions. But now with his sunburn turned to a deep reddish tan and his strength almost returned in full, he was *very* aware of his empty stomach. He wondered if he could slip out into the early morning bustle, and decided against trying. Redheaded slaves over six feet tall were certainly not common in this city and he would probably be caught before he got within a hundred paces of the kitchen. As if fate conspired to torment him, a familiar odor came wafting in on the morning breeze. The kitchen cooked bacon and ham for the Governor's household. Borric's mouth began to water, and he sat for a miserable minute, thinking of breakfast cakes and honey, boiled eggs, fruit with cream, hot slabs of ham, steaming fresh bread, pots of coffee.

"No good can come from this," he scolded himself, forcing himself back from the crack. Hunkering down in the dark, he attempted to discipline his mind away from the torment of hunger. All he need do was wait for night to fall and then he could steal into the kitchen and nick some food. Yes, that's all he need do. Wait.

Borric discovered, that like hunger, waiting was not to his liking. He would lay back for a time, then cross over to the crack in the roof, peer through, and wonder how much time had passed. Once he even dozed for a while, and was disappointed to discover that—judging from the nearly unchanged shadow angles—only minutes had passed when he had hoped for hours. He returned to his place of resting, a section of attic where the floor seemed a little less uncomfortable than the rest of the floor, more likely due to his imagination than any real difference. He waited and he was hungry. No, he corrected himself. He was ravenous.

More time passed and again he dozed. Then to break the routine, he practiced some stretching exercises a Hadati warrior had once taught him and Erland, designed to keep muscles loose and toned at times when there was no room for sword practice or the other rigors common to warcraft. He moved one way then another, balancing tension and relaxation. To his astonishment, he discovered that not only did the exercises take his mind off of his stomach, they made him feel better and calmer.

For the better part of four hours, Borric sat near the crack, observing the comings and goings of those in the Governor's courtyard. Several times, soldiers running messages hurried through Borric's field of vision. He considered: if he could stay hidden here long enough—assuming he could steal food and not get caught—in a few more days they would assume he had somehow slipped out of their grasp. At that time he might be able to sneak aboard an outbound ship.

Then what? He thought upon that prickly issue. It would do little good to return home, even if he should find a way. Father would only send fast riders south to Kesh with warnings to Erland to be cautious. No doubt he could be no more cautious than he already was. With Borric's disappearance, Uncle Jimmy was sure to assume the worst and count Borric dead. It would take a gifted assassin to win past Earl James's notice. As a boy, Jimmy had rightly been counted something of a legend in the city. When years younger than Borric's present age, he was already a master thief and counted an adult by the Mockers. No mean feat that, Borric thought.

"No," he whispered to himself. "I must get to Erland as quickly as possible. Too much time will be lost if I return home first." Then he wondered if perhaps he should attempt to reach Stardock. The magicians could do astonishing things and perhaps could provide him with a faster way yet to reach Kesh. But Jimmy had mentioned Pug was leaving the day after they departed, so he was already gone. And the two Keshian magicians he left in charge were not men who appeared to Borric as likely candidates for generous help. There was something decidedly off-putting about both of them. And they *were* Keshian. Who knows how far this Lord Fire's plotting reaches? Borric considered.

Looking up from his musing, he realized that night was falling. The evening meal was being prepared in the kitchen and the smell of meat roasting over a spit was nearly enough to make him mad. In a few hours, he told himself. Just relax and let the time pass. . . . It won't be long. In just a few more hours, the servants will be in their own beds. Then it will be time to steal out and—

Abruptly the trap moved and Borric's heart raced as he readied the knife to defend himself. The trap raised up and a slight figure pulled himself into the trap. Suli Abul said, "Master?"

Borric almost laughed from relief. "Here."

The boy scurried over and said, "I feared you might have been found, though I suspected you were wise enough to stay here and await my return."

Borric said, "Where did you go?"

Suli was carrying a sack that Borric could barely make out in the gloom. "I stole out before dawn, master, and as you were sleeping soundly I chose not to disturb you. Since then I have been many places." He opened the bag and brought forth a loaf of bread. Borric tore off a hunk and ate without having to be asked twice. Then the boy handed over a block of cheese and a small skin of wine.

Through his full mouth, Borric asked, "Where did you get this?"

The boy sighed, as if being back in the attic was a relief. "I have had a most perilous day, my kind master. I fled with the idea of perhaps leaving you, then considered what fate has offered. Should I be caught, I will be sold for a slave because of my incompetent theft. If I am linked with your escape, I will be dead. So, what are the risks? By hiding until you are caught and hoping you will not speak the name of Suli Abul before they kill you, I wager a death sentence against the possibility of regaining the life I had before these recent turns of events, which upon consideration is not a very grand thing. Or I can risk that poor life and return to help my young master against the day you return to your father, to reward your faithful servant."

Borric laughed. "And what reward shall you have if we get safely back to Krondor?"

With a solemnity that almost made Borric laugh again, the boy said, "I wish to become your servant, master. I wish to be known as the Prince's body servant."

Borric said, "But what about gold? Or perhaps a trade?"

The boy shrugged. "What do I know of trade, master? I would be a poor merchant, and perhaps be ruined within a year. And gold? I would only spend it. But to be the servant of a great man is to be close to greatness in a way. Do you not see?"

Borric's laughter died in his throat before it was voiced. He realized that to this boy of the street, the position of a great man's servant was the highest attainment he could imagine. Borric thought about the countless and nameless bodies that had surrounded him all his life, the servants who had brought this young son of the Royal House his clothing in the morning, who washed his back, who prepared his meals, each day. He doubted he knew more than one or two by name and perhaps only a dozen by sight. They were . . . part of the landscape, no more significant than a chair or a table. Borric shook his head, and sighed.

"What is it, master?"

Borric said, "I don't know if I can promise you a position that close to me, personally, but I will guarantee that you'll have a place in my household and that you will rise as high as your talents will take you. Is that fair enough?"

The boy bowed with solemn formality. "My master is most generous."

Then the boy pulled some sausage from the sack. "I knew you would be a generous, kind master, so I returned with many things—"

"Hold a moment, Suli. Where did you get all this?"

The boy said, "In one of the rooms below, a woman's sleeping chamber from its look, I found a comb with turquoise set within silver, left behind by a thoughtless maid when the quarters were last vacated. I sold this to a man in the bazaar. I took the coins he gave me and purchased many things. Not to worry. I moved along and purchased each item from a different merchant, insuring no one knew what business I was upon. Here." He handed Borric a shirt.

It was nothing fancy but obviously a significant improvement over the rough homespun the slavers had given him. Then the boy passed over a pair of cotton trousers, the kind worn by sailors throughout the Bitter Sea. "I could not find boots, master, that I could purchase, yet have enough left for food."

Borric smiled at the boy. "You did well. I can go without the boots. If we're to pass as sailors, bare feet will not bring us any notice. But we'll have to sneak to the harbor at night and hope no one sees this red hair of mine under a lamp."

"I have taken care of that, master." The boy handed over a vial of some liquid and a comb. "I have this from a man who sells such to the older whores down by the waterfront. He claims it will not wash out nor run with water. It is called oil of Macasar."

Borric opened the vial and his nose was assaulted by a pungent, oily odor. "It better work. The smell will have people marking me."

"That will pass, according to the merchant."

"You'd better put it in my hair. I wouldn't want to pour it over half my head. There's barely enough light for you to see what you're doing."

The boy moved behind him and ungently rubbed the vial's contents into the Prince's hair. He then combed it through, many times over, spreading it as evenly as possible. "With your sunburn, Highness, you will look every inch the Durbin sailor."

"And what of you?" asked Borric.

"I have trousers and a shirt in the bag, too, my master. Suli Abul is known for his beggar's robe. It is large enough for me to hide limbs when I play at being deformed."

Borric laughed as the boy continued to work on his hair. He sighed in relief as he thought, Just maybe we do have a chance to get out of this trap.

Just before dawn, a sailor and his younger brother ventured into the streets near the Governor's estate. As Borric had surmised, there was little activity near the Governor's home, as it was logical to assume the fugitive was unlikely to be anywhere near the heart of Durbin authority. Which is why they made back toward the slave pens. If the Governor's house was an unlikely place for the fugitives to hide, the slave quarters were even less likely. Borric was not entirely comfortable being in a rich part of town, as the presence of two obviously shabby figures near the residences of the wealthy and powerful was in and of itself sufficient to bring unwanted scrutiny upon them.

When they were but a block from the slave quarters, Borric halted. Upon the wall of a storage shed was a newly hung broadside. Painted by skilled craftsmen, it proclaimed in red letters a reward. Suli said, "Master, what does it say?"

Borric read aloud. " 'Murder most foul!' it says. It says that I killed the wife of the Governor." Borric's face went pale. "Gods and demons!" He quickly read the entire broadside, then said, "They say a Kingdom-born house slave raped and killed his mistress, then fled into the city. They've put a reward of one thousand Golden Ecu on me." Borric couldn't believe his eyes.

The boy's eyes widened. "A thousand? That is a fortune."

Borric tried to calculate the worth. It came out to roughly five thousand Kingdom Sovereigns, or the income from a small estate for a year—a staggering sum indeed for the capture, dead or alive, of a runaway slave, but one who had murdered the city's foremost lady of society. Borric shook his head in pained realization. "The swine murdered his own wife to give the guards a reason to kill me on sight," he whispered.

Suli shrugged. "It is no surprise when you understand that the Governor has a mistress who demands more and more from him. To put aside his first wife and marry his mistress—after the appropriate period of mourning, of course—will ease two sources of concern for him: keeping his mistress and Lord Fire happy. And while astoundingly beautiful, the mistress would do well to consider the future of one who marries a man who killed his first wife to make her his second. When she becomes older and less fair of face—"

Borric looked around. "We better keep moving. The city will be at full speed within the hour."

Suli seemed unable to stifle his incessant chatter, except under the most dire circumstances. Borric didn't attempt to shut him up, deciding the garrulous lad would look less suspicious than one who was sullenly glancing in all directions. "Now, master, we know how the Governor convinced the Three to help apprehend you. The Three and the Imperial Governor have little love amongst them, but they have less love for slaves who murder their lawful lords."

Borric could only agree. But he found the Governor's means to achieve that reaction chilling. Even if he hadn't loved the woman, he had lived with her for some number of years. Wasn't there any compassion in him? wondered Borric.

Rounding a corner, they saw the side of the slave pens. Because the auction had been canceled, the pens were especially crowded. Borric turned his face toward Suli and moved steadily, but not so hurried as to attract attention. To any guards who might be looking, he was simply a sailor speaking to a boy.

A pair of guards walked around a corner and approached them. Instantly, Suli said, "No. You said I would have a full share this voyage. I am grown now. I do the work of a man! It was not my fault the nets fouled. It was Rasta's fault. He was drunk—"

Borric hesitated only an instant, then replied in as gruff a voice as he could muster, "I said I would consider it. Be silent or I'll leave you behind, little brother or not! See how you like another month working in Mother's kitchen while I'm gone." The guards gave the pair a quick glance, then continued on.

Borric resisted the temptation of looking to see if the guards were paying attention. He would know quickly enough if they became suspicious. Then Borric turned another corner and collided with a man. For a brief instant the stranger looked into his eyes with a threatening mutter, his alcohol-ladened breath in Borric's face, then the man's expression turned from drunken irritation to murderous hatred. "You!" said Salaya, reaching for the large dagger in the belt of his robe.

Reacting instantly, Borric put his fingers together in a point and drove it as hard as he could into Salaya's chest, right below the bottom-most ribs. As his fingers smashed into the nerves there, Salaya's breath was driven from his lungs. As he struggled to catch his breath, Salaya's face turned crimson and his eyes went unfocused. Borric then struck hard into his throat, pulled him forward, and smashed down as hard as he could manage on the back of the slaver's neck, at the base of the skull. Borric had him by the arm before the slaver hit the ground, and if any more guards chanced to glance their way a moment after the encounter, they would see nothing more suspicious than two friends, a man and boy, helping home a friend who had had too much to drink.

Halfway down the street they came to an alley and turned into it, dragging the now-unconscious man along like so many sacks of rotten vegetables. Borric deposited him on a pile of refuse and quickly had his purse off. A fair number of Keshian and Kingdom coins weighed down the heavy leather pouch. That went inside Borric's shirt. He removed the belt knife and sheath, wishing the slaver had carried a sword as well. As he hesitated as to what to do next, Suli stripped Salaya of his rings, four from his hands, two from his ears. Then the boy took off the slaver's boots and hid them. "If we leave anything of value behind, it will look suspicious." Stepping back, he said, "You can kill him now, master."

Borric halted. "Kill him?" Suddenly it registered. He had dreamed of revenging himself upon this swine, but all those visions had involved killing him in a duel, or bringing him before a magistrate on charges. "He's unconscious."

"All the better, master. There will be no struggle." Seeing Borric hesitate, he added, "Quickly, master, before someone chances upon us. The city stirs and this alley will be traveled shortly. Someone is bound to find him soon. If he is not dead . . ." He let the consequences of that go unspoken.

Steeling himself, Borric withdrew the knife he had taken from Salaya and held it. But then he was confounded by a completely unexpected concern: how to do it? Should he drive the knife into the man's stomach, cut his throat, or just what?

Suli said, "If you wish not to kill a dog, master, let your servant do it for you, but it must be done *now!* Please, master."

The thought of letting the boy kill was even more repugnant to Borric, so he pulled his arm back and drove the knife into the slaver's throat. There was not the slightest movement from Salaya. Borric stared in astonishment, then with a bitter laugh, he said, "He was already dead! The second blow must have broken his neck." Borric shook his head in astonishment. "The punch to the chest and throat was one of the dirty fighting tricks taught me by James—not the sort of things noble sons usually learned—but one which I am glad to have been taught. I didn't know the blow to the neck would be lethal."

Not caring for explanations, Suli said, "Let us go now, master! Please!" He tugged on Borric's tunic, and the Prince let the boy pull him out of the alley.

When he was clear of the sight of the dead slaver, Borric turned his thoughts away from revenge and back toward escape. Putting his hand upon Suli's shoulder, he said, "Which way to the harbor?"

Suli didn't hesitate. He pointed down a long street and said, "That way."

"Then lead on," was Borric's answer. And the beggar boy led the Prince through a city ready to kill them both at a moment's notice.

"That one," said Borric, indicating a small sailboat tied to a relatively lonely dock. It was a pinnace, the sort used as a tender, to run to and from larger ships in the harbor, carrying passengers, messages, and very small cargo. But if handled right, it would do well upon the open sea, as long as the weather remained fair. As the entire fleet of Durbin pirates had put out the day before to intercept the murdering slave, there was almost no activity in the harbor. But that condition wouldn't last long, Borric was certain, as there were common citizens who had no concerns with the hunt for the murderer of the Governor's wife. Soon the docks would be busy and the theft of the boat would be observed.

Borric looked about and pointed to a coil of old, filthy rope that lay nearby. Suli picked it up, and slung the wet, foul-smelling coil over his shoulder. Borric then picked up a discarded wooden crate, pushing the open slats closed. "Follow me," he said.

No one paid any attention to two sailors walking purposefully toward the small boat at the end of the docks. Borric put the crate down and jumped into the boat, quickly untying the bow line. He turned to find Suli standing in the rear of the boat, an open look of perplexity upon his face. "Master, what do I do?"

Borric groaned. "You've never sailed?"

"I have never been on a boat before in my life, master."

Borric said, "Bend down and look like you're doing something. I don't want anyone to notice a confused sailor boy on board. When we're underway, just do what I tell you."

Borric quickly had the boat pushed free of the dock, and after a fitful start, the sail was up and the boat moving steadily toward the harbor mouth. Borric gave Suli a quick list of terms and some duties. When he was done, he said, "Come take the tiller." The boy moved to sit where the Prince had, and Borric gave him the tiller and the boom hawser. "Keep it pointed that way," the Prince instructed, pointing at the harbor mouth, "while I see what we have here."

Borric went to the front of the boat and pulled a small boat's locker out from under the foredeck. The box was unlocked and inside he found little of value: a single sail, a rusty scaling knife left over from when the boat had belonged to an honest fisherman, and some frayed line. He doubted any fish caught on that line would be big enough for more than bait. There was also a small wooden bucket bound in iron, used as a bailer or to pull up water to keep a catch wet, back when this boat was used for fishing. A rusty lantern without oil was his only other discovery. Turning to face the boy who studied the sail and held the tiller with fierce concentration on his face, Borric said, "I don't suppose you have any more bread or cheese left?"

With a look of sincere apology, the boy said, "No, master."

One thing about this change in his circumstances, Borric commented to himself: hunger was becoming a way of life. . . .

The wind was a brisk nor'easter, and the pinnace was fastest in a broad beam reach, so Borric turned her north by northwest as he left the harbor mouth. The boy looked both terrified and exhilarated. He had been babbling most of the way through the harbor, obviously his means of dealing with his fear, but as they had exited the harbor mouth, with no more than a casual glance by the deck crew of a large lateen-rigged caravel, the boy's fear had vanished. Borric had sailed intentionally close to the ship, as if unconcerned by its presence, but rather irritated by the need to sail around it.

Now with the harbor mouth behind them, Borric said, "Can you climb?"

The boy nodded, and Borric said, "From the front—and mind the sail—climb the mast to that ring up there and hang on. Look in all directions and tell me what you see."

The boy shinnied up the mast like one born to it and gripped the observation ring at the top of the small mast. It swayed dramatically with the additional weight at the top, but the boy didn't seem to mind. Yelling down, he said, "Master! There are small white things along that way!" He pointed eastward, then swept with his hand toward the north.

"Sails?"

"I think so, master. They mark the horizon as far as I can see."

"What about to the north?"

"I think I see some sails there, too, master!"

Borric swore. "What of to the west?"

The boy squirmed and shouted, "Yes, there are some there, too."

Borric considered his choices. He had thought to escape to Ranom, a small trading port to the west, or if needs be, LiMeth, a modest city high up on the southern peninsula below the Straits of Darkness. But if they had some pickets established just against that choice, he would have to put out farther north, perhaps reaching the Free Cities eventually—if he didn't starve first—or brave the straits. This time of the year the straits were only moderately dangerous, unlike the winter when they were impassable, save for an exceptional brave, or stupid, sailor.

Borric signaled for Suli to climb down and when the boy was near, the Prince said, "I think we'll have to run to the northwest and get around the pickets. He glanced at the sun and said, "If we steer away from those western pickets, they're sure to come running, but if we hold a steady course as if we're simply going about our business, we may fool them." He looked down. "See how the water changes color from here"—he pointed—"to there?"

The boy nodded. "That's because this is a deep channel, and that is a coral reef. This boat has a very shallow draft, so we can slip above those reefs, but that big ship we saw at the harbor would bottom out here and crash. We must also be cautious; some of these reefs are too near the surface for even our small boat, but if we are alert, we can avoid them."

The boy looked at Borric with fear in his eyes. He obviously felt overwhelmed by what the Prince was saying and didn't understand. "That's all right," said Borric. "I'll tell you what to look for if we have to flee." He glanced at the distant western horizon, where he could barely see a single white dot on the surface of blue-green. "Anything in close to shore will have just as shallow a draft as we have and probably be faster." Checking the luff of the sail to make sure he was at the proper angle to the wind for maximum speed, Borric said, "Just keep watching that white speck on the western horizon, Suli, and tell me if it starts to get bigger."

With concentration that bordered on the single-minded, the boy hung over the windward side of the boat, using the angle of the craft as a means to sit at the highest perch possible, short of climbing the mast again. For the better part of an hour the white spot appeared to neither shrink nor grow, then suddenly it was heading straight at them. "Master!" the boy yelled. "They are coming!"

Borric turned the craft, attempting to get the maximum angle to the wind for speed, but the sail slowly grew. It was a faster craft. "Damn," he swore. "They'll overtake us if we keep running."

Suli shouted, "Master, another!"

As if summoned by the first ship to intercept the pinnace, a second sail appeared upon the northern horizon. "We're cut off," yelled Borric. He swung the tiller hard about, cursing himself for a fool. Of course the guards at the harbor mouth had been lax. They were instructed to intercept only those who looked like the runaway, and could clearly see that the two sailors were neither redheaded. But the ships on picket would only know a sail was on the horizon. They would intercept, and Borric wanted nothing to do with close inspection. In Durbin, he might have tried to bluff his way out with a contrived story, but out here, with freedom so close, he wasn't going to chance another capture. To be caught was to be killed, he reminded himself.

Borric looked about and said, "Come here!"

The boy hurried to Borric's side and the Prince gave him the tiller and boom line. "Hold on this course."

Borric moved quickly to the front of the boat and took the second sail from the locker. He attached it to the front of the mast, but didn't raise it. "Hurry, master!" cried the boy.

"Not now. It would only slow us down. We're at the wrong angle." Borric returned to the tiller.

The two other boats were turning to give chase and now Borric could make them out. The northern interceptor was a large two-masted galleon, fast running before the wind, but slow to maneuver and with a deep draft. He knew that captain wouldn't follow him into the reefs. But the first boat they had seen was a fore-and-aft-rigged, sleek-looking sloop. Newly found upon the Bitter Sea over the last twenty years, they were favored by pirates working the shoals of the southern coast. Faster than the pinnace in a light wind, they were more maneuverable and had almost as shallow a draft. Borric's only hope was to get past the sloop, put on more canvas, and get into the shallowest water possible. Only in a very heavy wind in a broad reach could his pinnace possibly outrun that boat.

The larger boat moved to cut off Borric's smaller craft and he eased off the tiller, turning more and more upwind. Then he jibbed his boat and left the galleon wallowing close-hauled into the wind, its speed evaporating like water on a hot stone.

The sloop turned to cut him off as he sailed back toward the reef, and Borric spilled wind from his sail, letting the captain of the larger boat think he had cut off the fugitives. Borric concentrated, as it was going to be a very close thing, and any miscalculation would leave him either too much room between the sloop and pinnace, so the larger boat could turn again and intercept him, or bring them too close, so they could be grappled and boarded. Borric pulled hard over on the tiller, as if attempting to turn back away once more. Sailing just shy of directly into the eye of the wind was the only point of sailing he was faster than the sloop in this light breeze, but not by much. And if he attempted to stay that course he would end up sailing directly back to the galleon.

Borric let the pursuing craft get near enough to make out the crew, nearly thirty unsavory-looking thugs, all armed with sword and pike.

If there are archers on the boat, he thought to himself, we'll never make it alive.

Then he surprised the crew of the sloop and Suli both, by jibbing his boat directly toward the larger craft. Suli cried out and threw his arms before his face, expecting a collision, but rather than the crack of splitting timbers, the only sound above the sounds of the sea were the loud oaths from the sailors on the sloop, taken by surprise. The sloop's helmsman reacted as Borric hoped he would, turning his wheel hard over. The sloop's captain's curses filled the air. The helmsman was now steering away from the boat they wanted to come alongside and grapple, and he started to turn the wheel back. But the damage had been done.

Borric's pinnace stood still, trembling in the teeth of the wind, then started moving slightly backwards. Like a dancer spinning on her heels, the boat swung away from the sloop, coming quickly around. The sound of the canvas snapping taut echoed across the waters as the pinnace seemed to jump away, running before the wind. Astonished-looking sailors stood at the rail of the sloop with their mouths open. Then one made so bold as to attempt to leap across the narrow gap between. He fell only a few feet short of the stern of Borric's craft.

Borric yelled, "Suli! Come here!"

The boy scampered to take the tiller from Borric, while the Prince raced the mast. The instant he was sure they were on a running broad reach again, he hauled the second sail aloft, making a crude spinnaker. He hoped it would give the pinnace just enough extra speed to stay away from the sloop.

The captain of the sloop, swearing mightily, ordered his men to come about. Quickly, the nimble boat turned and gave chase. Borric divided his attention fore and aft, watching to see if the larger boat was overtaking them, and then looking to see they stayed clear of dangerous shoals.

Suli sat with eyes wide with terror, listening as Borric shouted, "A little more to starboard!"

The boy yelled, "What, master?" He stared at the Prince in confusion, not understanding the nautical term.

Borric yelled back, "More to the right!" Borric turned his attention back to the dangers ahead. He shouted to Suli, directing him first to come a little right, then left, then right again, as they steered a maddening course through the shoals.

Borric glanced back and saw the larger boat had closed some distance, and he cursed. Even with the spinnaker, they were not moving fast enough. He yelled, "Turn toward shore!"

The boy reacted instantly, turning so hard Borric almost lost his footing. Borric looked for rocks, rocks just below the surface of the water that they could avoid but that would bring their pursuer to a nasty halt.

As they moved closer to shore, the boat's up and downward movement became more pronounced, as the ground swells moved toward the breaker line. The sound of surf could now be heard clearly. Borric pointed with one hand. "There! Steer there!"

Praying to the Goddess of Luck, Borric said, "Let us hit that on the crest!"

As if the Laughing Lady had heard him, Borric felt the boat on the rise as they passed over the spot he had marked. Even so, as they started to feel the boat come down, a groaning, tearing sound of the bottom scraping rock could be heard and a teeth-jarring vibration came up through the hull of the boat.

Suli's face turned ashen as he crouched, holding on to the tiller as if it were his only connection to life. Borric shouted, "Come left!" and the boy yanked upon the tiller. Again the sound of wood scraping over rock filled their ears, but the boat settled down into a trough and rose without further difficulty.

Borric glanced back and saw the sloop heeling over as the captain gave orders to his frantic crew to turn away from shoals too lethal even for his shallow craft. Borric gave a low whistle of relief.

Turning his mind to what to do next, he signaled Suli to head slightly away from the coast, picking up speed as they moved out of the tide's pull and into a better angle away from the wind. The freshening breeze moved the boat along, and Borric could see the sloop fall farther behind with every minute as the captain had to stay outside the reef that now lay between the two boats.

Borric lowered the makeshift spinnaker and took the tiller from Suli. The boy grinned at him with an expression that was half-delight, half-terror. Perspiration soaked the lad's tunic and Borric found himself wiping his drenched brow.

Borric pointed the boat slightly upwind and could see the sloop's sail falling off even farther as the reef ran off toward the northwest. He laughed. Even with the headsail jib the sloop's crew was running out, it was too late. By the time they rounded the reef, the pinnace would be so far ahead they could be anywhere upon the sea. It would be nightfall before the distance could be made up, and Borric planned on being far away by nightfall.

The next two hours passed uneventfully, until Suli left his place at the bow and came toward Borric. Borric noticed water splashing under the boy's feet.

Borric looked down and saw water was gathering in the bilge. "Start bailing!" he yelled.

"What, master?"

Realizing the boy didn't understand that term either, he said, "Get the bucket from the locker and start scooping up the water and pouring it out!"

The boy turned, got the bucket, and began bailing out the water. For an hour or so it seemed the boy kept even with the incoming water, but after another hour of the exhausting work, the water had gathered about his ankles. Borric ordered him to switch places and took over. After another hour, it was clear that even when bailing at a furious rate, it would prove an eventually hopeless undertaking. Sooner or later the boat was going to sink. The only question seemed to be when and where.

Borric glanced to the south and saw that not only had the coastline been running southwest, away from them, but their course was northwest, toward the Straits of Darkness. By his reckoning, they were now as far away from the coastline as they could get, slightly northeast of Ranom, where the coastline would turn northward. Borric had to make a quick choice, either head for the south shore, or hope that between Suli and himself they could keep the boat afloat long enough to reach the coast somewhere south of LiMeth. As he was about equal distance between either part of the shoreline, he decided his best choice was to keep as much speed as possible and hold his present course.

As the sun sped westward, Borric and Suli alternated bailing out the boat and keeping it pointed toward LiMeth. Near sundown, a scattering of clouds appeared in the north and the wind turned, now blowing into their faces. The pinnace was decent enough traveling into the eye of the wind, but Borric doubted they would survive long enough to reach land if it started to rain. As he considered this, the first drops hit him in the face, and less than an hour later, the rain began to fall in earnest.

As the sun rose, a ship was upon them. Borric had seen its approach for the last quarter hour, as it suddenly had appeared out of the predawn gloom. Both the Prince and Suli, exhausted from a night's bailing to keep afloat, could barely move. Yet Borric mustered what little reserve of energy he possessed and stood up.

They had taken down the sail at sundown, decided it was better to drift in the dark and have both of them bail for periods, than to sail blindly in the dark. The sound of breakers would alert them to any chance of coming too close to shore. The only problem was that Borric didn't have any idea of how the currents in this part of the Bitter Sea ran.

The ship was a small three-masted merchantman, square-rigged with a lateen sail on the back. It could have come from any nation on the Bitter Sea, so it could be their salvation or their doom.

When the ship was close enough for him to be heard, Borric called out, "What ship?"

The Captain of the vessel came to the rail as he ordered the helm put over, bringing the ship to a slow pace as it passed Borric's sinking pinnace, wallowing in the chop. *"The Good Traveler,* out of Bordon."

"Where are you bound?"

"Bound for Faráfra," came the reply.

Borric's heart began to beat again. It was a Free Cities trader bound for an Empire city on the Dragon Sea. "Have you berths for two?"

The Captain looked down at the ragged pair and their rapidly wallowing boat and said, "Have you the price of passage?"

Borric did not wish to part with the coins he had taken from Salaya, as he knew they would need them later. He said, "No, but we can work."

"I've all the hands I need," called back the Captain.

Borric knew by stories that the Captain would not likely leave them to drown—sailor's superstition forbade it—but he could exact a price of an indenture for several cruises; seamen were an inconstant lot and keeping a steady crew was difficult. The Captain was bargaining. Borric pulled out the rusty fishing knife and brandished it. "Then I order you to strike your colors; you are all my prisoners."

The Captain stared in wide-eyed disbelief, then began to laugh. Soon every sailor on the ship was laughing uproariously. After a moment of genuine amusement, the Captain called out, "Bring the madman and the boy aboard. Then make for the Straits!"

Chapter Nine
Welcome

The trumpets sounded.

A thousand soldiers came to attention and presented arms. One hundred drummers on horseback began a rhythmic tattoo. Erland turned to James, who rode to his left, and said, "This is unbelievable!"

Before them stood the Imperial City, Kesh. They had entered the "lower city" an hour earlier, to be met by a delegation from the City Governor and his retinue. It was the same ceremony they had been forced to endure at each stop along the wearisome journey from Nar Ayab to the capital. When the Governor of Nar Ayab had met them at the outskirts of town, Erland found the welcome a relief from his black mood. He had been numb with Borric's death for nearly a week, giving himself over to dark bouts of depression, interspersed with rage at the unfairness of it all. The pageantry of the Governor's welcome had taken his mind off the ambush for the first time, and the novelty of seeing such a display had kept him diverted for over three hours.

But now, the displays wore upon his patience. He had received another extravagant welcome at the cities of Kh'mrat and Khattara, and a half-dozen other welcomes that might have been smaller in scale, but were just as formal and tedious at smaller towns along the way. From any official from Regional Governor down to town elderman, Erland had been forced to endure welcoming speeches from them all.

Erland glanced behind to where Locklear rode with the Keshian official sent to meet them at the lower-city gates. The Prince signaled, and both men set heels to their mounts, trotting them to where Erland rode. The official was one Kafi Abu Harez, a noble of the Beni-Wazir, one of the desert people of the Jal-Pur. Many desertmen had come to Imperial service over the last hundred years, with a marked preference and talent for diplomacy and negotiations. Kesh's old Ambassador to the Western Realm, Abdur Rachman Memo Hazara-Khan, deceased for ten years now, had once told Erland and his brother, "We are a horse people, and as such we are rigorous horse traders." Erland had heard his father curse the man with grudging respect enough times to believe it so. He knew that whatever else this protocol officer might be, he was no man's fool and he needed to be watched. The desertmen of the Jal-Pur were terrible enemies.

Kafi said, "Yes, Your Highness. How may I serve you?"

Erland said, "This is a bit of a change from what we've been seeing. Who are these soldiers?"

Kafi pulled his robe around him slightly as he rode. His outfit was similar to those Erland had seen before in Krondor, head covering, tunic, trousers, long vest, knee-high boots, and belt. But where this costume differed from those Erland had seen before was in the intricate designs sewn into the fabric. Keshian court officials seemed to display an almost unnatural affection for gold thread and pearls.

"These are the Imperial Household Guard, Highness."

Erland casually said, "So many?"

"Yes, Highness."

"It looks almost like a full city garrison," observed Locklear.

The Keshian said, "It would depend which city, m'lord. For a Kingdom city, it is. For a Keshian city, not quite. For the city of Kesh, but a small part."

"Would it be giving military secrets away to ask how many soldiers guard the Empress?" asked Erland drily.

"Ten thousand," answered Kafi.

Erland and Locklear exchanged glances. "Ten thousand!" said the Prince.

"The Palace Guard, which is a part of the Household Guard, which is but again a part of the city garrison—that is the heart of Kesh's armies. Within the walls of the upper and lower city, ten thousand soldiers stand ready to defend She Who Is Kesh."

They turned their horses along the route lined by soldiers, and curious citizens, who stood and observed the passing Islemen in relative quite. Erland saw the road turn upward and climb an incline, a gigantic highway of stone that wound its way up to the top of the plateau. Halfway up the ramp, a gold-and-white banner flew and, Erland took note, the uniform of the soldiers above and below changed. "These are different regiments, then?" he asked.

Kafi said, "In ancient times, the original people of Kesh were but one of many nations around the Overn Deep. When pressed by enemies, they fled to the plateau upon which the palace rests. It has become tradition that all who serve the Empire, but who are not of true Keshian stock, live in the city below the palace." He pointed up the ramp to where the banner flew. "All the soldiers you see here in Kesh are of the Imperial garrison, but those above the Imperial banner are all soldiers of true blood. Only they may serve and live in the palace." There was a faint edge to his voice as he added, "No one who is not of the *true* Keshian blood may live within the palace." Erland looked close, but there was nothing to indicate any feelings one way or the other in the protocol officer. He smiled, as if to say it was a mere fact of Keshian life.

As they neared the bottom of the ramp, Erland also could see that those who stood guard along the route were much as he had seen throughout the Empire so far: men from all races and of all appearances—more dark skins and hair coloring than in the Kingdom, to be certain, but a few redheaded and blond citizens. But those above the banner were of nearly uniform appearance: dusky skin, but not black or dark brown, nor fair. Hair uniformly black or dark brown, with an occasionally red cast to it, but no real redheads, blonds, or light browns in sight. It was clear that this company of soldiers came from bloodlines with little intermixing with the other peoples of Kesh.

Erland studied the wall that ran along the edge of the plateau above, noticing the many spires and towers visible from where he rode. Considering the size of the plateau, he said, "So then all who live in the city above, but outside the palace, are also of 'true' blood?"

Kafi smiled indulgently. "There is no city atop the plateau, Your Highness. All you will see atop the plateau *is* the palace. Once there were other buildings atop the plateau, but as the palace grew and expanded over the centuries, they were displaced. Even the great temples were relocated below so that those not of true Keshian blood could worship."

Erland was impressed. Under the rulership of Mad King Rodric, the city of Rillanon had been beautified to become the most splendid city on Midkemia, or that was Rodric's stated ambition. But Erland was forced to admit that even had Rodric's plan come to fruition, even with the marble facings on all public buildings, the gardens along the walking paths throughout the city, the waterways around the palace, even with all that, Rillanon was a poor thing next to the city of Kesh. It was not that Kesh was a lovely city; it wasn't. Many of the streets they had ridden were packed tight with dirty little buildings thick with the odors of life—cooking, the acrid smell of the forge, the pungent leather of the tanner, and the ever-present stink of unwashed bodies and human waste.

There was little that was lovely in the city of Kesh. But it was ancient. It held the echoes of centuries of history, a mighty nation rising to become a great empire. There was a culture that produced artists and musicians here when Erland's own ancestors were fishermen who had just turned their hand to raiding their neighboring islands from their safe harbor at Rillanon. The point had been made to him by his history teacher as a child, but now he could see exactly what his teacher had meant. The stones under his horse's hooves were worn with the passage of raiders, captive chieftains, and triumphant captains before Rillanon had come under conDoin rule. And conquering armies under legendary generals passed here to bring subjugation to other nations when Rillanon and Bas-Tyra first began their trade wars, two city-states seeking dominance over what would come to be called the Kingdom Sea. Kesh was old. Very old.

Kafi said, "Of course, Your Highness, those who are guests of the Empress, will be housed in a special wing of the palace, overlooking the Overn Deep. It would be unkind to require you to ride this route daily."

Erland came out of his reverie and said, "But you ride this route each day, do you not?"

There was a tiny tightening around the man's mouth as he said, "Of course, but those of us not of true Keshian blood understand our place in the scheme of things. We serve gladly, and such a small inconvenience is not even to be discussed."

Erland took the clue and let the subject drop. Coming down to meet him was an assortment of officials, each more colorfully dressed than the one before. The thundering drums ceased, and a band of musicians played something that sounded suspiciously like a Kingdom tune but played by those who had never heard such.

To James, he said, "Welcomed in grand fashion."

James nodded absently. Since reaching the city, he had let old habits of watchfulness come to the fore. His eyes constantly scanned the crowd, looking for any sign that trouble was coming at Erland.

Messages had been dispatched to Krondor and an answer had overtaken them, as the Keshian rider post had operated with amazing efficiency in carrying word to Arutha of Borric's death and bringing his answers. There had been many letters in the pouch the rider had carried. The Kingdom rider was exhausted as he had been ordered not to surrender the contents of the diplomatic pouch to any but Earl James, Baron Locklear, or Prince Erland. He had been escorted by a changing succession of Keshian post riders, changing fresh horses at stations along the way. The man had ridden without stopping for over three weeks, halting only when exhaustion was overwhelming, otherwise napping in the saddle as well as eating while riding. James had commended the man and sent back word to Krondor with him, along with an order to return at a more sedate pace, as well as a recommendation for promotion and reward for his heroic ride.

Arutha's reply to the news of Borric's death had been what James expected: closed off, all personal reaction to the news absent. The Prince of Krondor let nothing sway him from the hard choices he faced as ruler of the Western Realm. He had cautiously instructed Earl James to see to recovering Borric's body, but that under no circumstances was there to be any significant change in their demeanor. The envoy's first duty was to pay the Kingdom's respects to the Empress, on the event of her seventy-fifth birthday Jubilee, and nothing was to cause more friction between the two nations. James smelled trouble. Borric had been murdered to plunge the Empire into war with the Kingdom, but Arutha had refused to rise to the bait. This could only mean an escalation in the provocations. And the only thing James could imagine more provocative than killing one Prince of the Blood would be killing both of them. He felt personally responsible for Borric's death, and he had put his own grieving aside for a time while he protected Erland. Glancing at his side, he noticed his wife watching him. To Gamina, he thought, *How are you doing, my love?*

I will be glad to be off this horse, at last, my love, came the answer, as Lady Gamina showed no outward signs of discomfort. She had born up under the rigors of the long trip without complaint, and each night as she lay at James's side, she was well aware that their happiness at being together took away the day's discomfort but could not eradicate James's pain at Borric's death, nor his concern for Erland's well-being. She nodded toward the front of the procession. *The most official welcome yet, my darling.*

At least a hundred officials stood just a short distance beyond the white-and-gold banner, to welcome the Prince and his retinue to the upper city. Erland's eyes opened slightly at the sight. The first impression was disbelief, as if some odd joke was being perpetrated upon him. For standing before him were men and women wearing very little clothing and a great deal of jewelry. The common dress was a simple skirt or kilt, fashioned from gauzy silk, wrapped once about the hips, from waist to mid-thigh. Ornate belts held the kilt in place, with golden clasps of complex designs common throughout the party. But both men and women alike were bare-chested, and the footgear of choice was an unadorned cross-gartered sandal. All the men had their heads shaved and the women wore their hair cut short, at the shoulder or at the ear, with magnificent rows of gems and gold woven into the tresses.

Kafi spoke with his head turned slightly toward Erland. "Perhaps Your Highness didn't know, but the nudity taboo common to your nation and some of the people of the Empire does not exist among those of the true Keshian blood. I also had to become accustomed to the sight—among my people, to see another man's wife's face is to die." With an ironic note, he said, "These people are from a hot land, Highness, but not so hot as my home desert, where to dress such would be to invite death. When you experience the long, hot, windy nights up on the plateau, you will understand why here clothing is a matter of fashion only. And the Keshian truebloods have never been terribly concerned with the sensibilities of their subject peoples. 'In Kesh you do as the true Keshians do,' goes an old adage."

Erland nodded, attempting not to stare at so much skin. A man stepped forward, not much older than Erland, powerfully muscled and carrying a shepherd's crook and a bow, both which appeared ceremonial rather than functional. His head was shaved like the others, but for a lock of hair, tied with loops of precious stone, gems, and gold. An instant later, another man, stout and obviously discomforted by standing in the hot sun, stepped to the first's side. Ignoring the perspiration which coursed off his reddening skin, he said, "We welcome our guests."

To the heavy man, Kafi said, "My lord Nirome. I have the honor of presenting His Highness, Prince Erland, Heir to the Throne of Isle, Knight-Captain of the Armies of the West, and envoy to She Who Is Kesh."

"Your Highness," said the stout Nirome. "To honor your arrival, one of the Imperial blood comes to greet you. It is my great honor to present Prince Awari, son of She Who Is Kesh."

The young man stepped forward again, and spoke directly to Erland. "We welcome our brother Prince. May your stay here be happy and for as long as it pleases you, Prince Erland. For the King of Isles to send his heir is an honor indeed. She Who Is Mother To Us All is pleased enough to have sent her poor son to bid you welcome. I am to tell you that all Kesh's hearts are gladdened the moment you come to us and that each moment of your stay is as riches in our treasury. Your wisdom and valor are unrivaled and She Who Is Kesh waits with anticipation at welcoming you to her court." So saying, Prince Awari turned and began walking up the road. The men and women of the Imperial welcoming committee stepped aside so the Prince and Lord Nirome could pass, then Kafi indicated the Prince and Baron Locklear should follow, with himself and Earl James behind.

As they moved up the ramp, James turned to Kafi and said, "In truth, we know so little about the Empire, save what we see along its northern border. It would please His Highness if you could guest with us and perhaps tell us more of this wondrous place."

The man smiled and James saw something in his eyes. "Your wish has been anticipated. I shall be outside your door at first light each day and not be gone from your side until you have given me leave to depart. The Empress, blessings be upon her, has ordered it so."

James smiled and inclined his head. *So, he's our watchdog.*

Gamina smiled at those nearby and said *Among many, I'm sure, beloved.*

James turned his attention to the front of the company, where Erland followed the Imperial welcoming delegation. His wits and talents might be tested in the next two and a half months, he knew. And he had but two basic tasks: keep Erland alive and the Kingdom out of war.

Erland was almost incapable of words. His "apartment" was a six-room complex set off in the "wing" of the palace set aside for them, which itself was nearly as large as his father's palace in Krondor. The Imperial palace was indeed a city unto itself. And the guest apartments were opulent beyond imagining. The stone walls had all been faced with marble, polished to a brilliance that reflected back torchlight like the sparkle of a thousand jewels. Rather than the Kingdom fashion of many small rooms, all the rooms in the apartment were large, but able to be partitioned by hanging curtains of varying opacity. Right now, the only curtains were to his right and left, and both were transparent gauze, allowing him to see that divans and chairs were arrayed in anticipation of his need for holding conferences. And at his left, a large terrace permitted a stunning view of the Overn Deep, the gigantic freshwater lake that was the heart of this Empire. The sleeping chamber lay just beyond a pair of doors in this, the audience chamber, where he could meet with his advisors if needed.

Erland signaled one of his two guards, detailed to act as servants, to open the large door. Before they could react, a young woman appeared at his side. "M'lord," she said, clapping her hands loudly, once.

The doors swung open and Erland nodded absently as he stepped through to what was his sleeping chamber. The Prince halted at the sight which greeted him. Everywhere he glanced, he saw gold. It was used on the tables and divans, stools and chairs that were arrayed around the room, for whatever needs he might have while dressing, composing messages, or eating a solitary meal. High upon the wall, the marble ceased and was replaced by sandstone, upon which murals of bright color had been painted against the muted ocher of the sandstone. In the stylized Keshian fashion, they showed warriors, kings, and gods, many depicted with animal heads, as the Keshians gave aspects to the gods that differed markedly from how they were perceived in the Kingdom.

Erland stood silently taking in the splendor of the room. A giant bed dominated the chamber, surrounded on three sides by gauzy silk curtains, hanging from a ceiling twenty feet above his head. The bed was twice the size of his own large bed at home, which had seemed immense when he and Borric had returned from their service with Lord Highcastle, given what they had been used to sleeping on, the narrow cots of Highcastle's barracks.

Thinking about Borric made Erland wistful for a moment, as he wished he could share his astonishment with his brother. For a countless time again since the attack, Erland could not admit to his brother's death. Somehow it just didn't feel within as if Borric was dead. He was out there somewhere, Erland was certain. The young woman who had entered with them clapped again, and suddenly the room was filled with activity.

The Prince's guards stood in mute amazement at the seemingly endless parade of Keshian servants who paraded through the suite, first for their quick efficiency in unpacking the Prince's baggage and laying out formal clothing upon an armoire nearby, but mostly for the fact they were women, all beautiful and all clad in the same scanty fashion as the welcoming committee. The only difference was the lack of jewelry. The plain kilt was bound about the waist with a linen belt. Other than that, the women were naked.

Crossing to where the two guards stood, Erland said, "Go get something to eat. If I need you, I'll send word."

The two saluted and turned, obviously uncertain of where to go, but as if reading the Prince's mind, a young woman said, "This way," and led them off.

Another young woman, with eyes mahogany brown, came to stand before Erland. "If it pleases m'lord, your bath is ready." Erland noticed her belt was red, with a gold clasp, instead of the common white one, and assumed her to be the one in charge of this host of young women.

Feeling suddenly both overdressed in the still hot air in the palace, and dirty from two days' ride, Erland nodded and followed the woman into the next chamber. There a pool at least thirty feet long awaited. At the far end a gold statue of some sort of water spirit held a vase pouring water into the pool. Erland glanced around, for at least five women waited for him in the pool, all without clothing.

Two others stepped to his sides, while the one who led him turned and began unfastening his tunic. "Er . . ." began Erland, reflexively stepping away.

"Is there something amiss, m'lord?" asked the young woman with the mahogany eyes. Erland was suddenly aware that her dark skin was several hues: a reddish warmth of suntan over the naturally dark olive-tinged duskiness. Her black hair was pulled back in a tight braid, and Erland noticed her very long neck.

Erland started to speak, then stopped, uncertain of what to say. Had Borric been with him, he was sure the two of them would both be splashing about in the pool, testing the limits of their prerogatives with the lovely serving women. But alone . . . he felt awkward. "What is your name?"

"Miya, m'lord."

"Ah, Miya . . ." He glanced at all the lovely ladies waiting for him to make his requirements known. ". . . In my land it is not the custom for so many servants to . . . so many are not needed."

The young woman's eyes searched his for an instant. Softly she answered, "If m'lord would indicate which servants he finds pleasing, I will send the rest away." She hesitated a second, then added, "Or should you wish but one, I would be most honored to . . . care for your needs, m'lord." The last was said with clear meaning.

Erland shook his head. "No, I mean . . ." He sighed in resignation. "Just get on with it."

Deft hands stripped him of his clothing, and when he was nude he stepped quickly into the pool, feeling awkward and self-conscious. The water was hot, he was surprised to discover, when he descended the steps into the shallow pool. Feeling foolish, he sat upon the bottom step, the water coming to his chest. Then Miya unclasped her own belt and her small kilt fell to the floor. Unself-consciously she entered the water and sat upon the step just behind Erland. Clapping once, another bath attendant signaled those outside of the pool to begin bringing oils, soaps, and unguents.

With gentle pressure on his shoulders, Miya drew him back until his head was resting upon her soft breasts. Then he felt her fingers working upon his scalp as she rubbed scented oils into his hair. Two other servants were now at his side, rubbing his chest with soaps that smelled faintly of flowers. Another two then began to clean and trim his fingernails, while two more were busy kneading the tired muscles in his legs.

After the first moment of tension at being handled so intimately by seven strange women, Erland took a deep breath, willing himself to relax. This was not much different from having one of the serving men scrub his back at home, he told himself. Then he glanced around at the dozen beautiful women standing on the side of the pool, and the seven in the water with him, and chuckled, Sure it was just like back home.

"M'lord?" asked Miya.

Erland let out a long breath. "This takes some getting used to."

The woman ceased washing his hair, rinsing his head with water from a golden bowl, then she began to knead the muscles of his neck and shoulders. Despite his self-consciousness at being in the pool with the nude servants, he found that the persistent massage was causing his eyelids to feel heavy. Smelling the lovely sun-touched fragrance of Miya's damp skin along with the soft aromas of the oils, he closed his eyes and felt fatigue and worry begin to slip away from him.

He sighed deeply, and Miya spoke softly. "Does m'lord desire anything?"

Erland smiled for the first time since the bandits' attack and said, "No, I think I could get used to this."

"Then rest, my handsome young lord with the fire hair," she whispered in his ear. "Rest and refresh yourself, for tonight She Who Is Kesh will receive you."

Erland settled back against the soft body of the servant and let the warmth of the pool and the kneading fingers of the women, as they probed tense and tired muscles, overtake him. Soon he felt himself drifting off into a hazy, sensuous doze, and as he relaxed, he felt himself responding to the gentle caresses of the women. Through lowered lashes he saw smiling faces looking at him with expectation, as two of the servants exchanged whispers and stifled a giggle. Yes, he thought, I could get used to this.

One of the servants shook his foot, as she whispered, "M'lord!"

Erland elbowed himself up to see what was occurring and blinked through sleepy eyes. Rousing himself fully awake, Erland said, "What?"

"The Lord James sends word he will be here within the half-hour, m'lord. He advises you to be ready for your presentation to the Empress. You must get dressed."

Erland looked first right, then left, and found himself hemmed in on both sides by two motionless bodies; on his right, the sleeping Miya made soft breathing sounds, while on the left, another servant —the one with the startling green eyes, he remembered, but he couldn't recall her name—watched him through half-closed eyelids. Slapping Miya playfully on her bare buttocks, he said, "Time to get ready, my darlings!"

Miya responded by coming fully awake and out of the huge bed in one fluid motion. She signaled by clapping her hands once and instantly a half-dozen more slaves appeared with Erland's wardrobe, cleaned and ready to wear. Erland jumped out of bed and motioned for them to wait and hurried into the room with the pool. Motioning the servants to stay out of his way, he walked down the three steps, dunked himself under, and rinsed off. To Miya, who had followed him, he remarked, "I was drenched. And I needed this."

The woman smiled slightly. "You were . . . very active for a time, m'lord."

Erland returned the slight smile. "Is it always so hot?"

The girl said, "This is the summer season, so it is like this. Fans are used to cool those who wish them. In the winter, it is really very cold at night and many furs are needed upon the beds to keep warm."

Erland found that hard to imagine as he left the pool. Three women dried him quickly, and he returned to the bed chamber.

Being helped to get dressed turned out to be more difficult than he had imagined. He kept trying to do things for himself and that interfered with the women attempting to fasten laces or buckle clasps. But he was fully dressed when Earl James was announced. Erland nodded permission for him to enter.

James appeared and said, "Well, you look better. Have a nice nap?"

Erland glanced about at the abundant female flesh on display and said, "Quite nice, actually."

James laughed. "Gamina was not pleased to see so many beautiful young women in our suite, so they sent some handsome young men. She became very distressed when they offered to help her bathe." He glanced about. "I would call them a wanton people, but to them this is normal. To them, we must appear . . . I don't know how we must appear."

Motioning Erland to come with him, the Earl led the young man into a large hallway, where Locklear and Gamina were speaking. As they entered the hall, Gamina's mind spoke to Erland: *Erland, James has already marked two listening posts in our chambers. Be wary of what you say aloud.*

I would be willing that at least one of my "servants" is a Keshian intelligence officer, he thought back at her.

There was a silence as a Keshian court officer, in the same dress they had seen everywhere, the white kilt and sandals, came for them. But he also wore an ornate torque of gold and turquoise and carried a staff of office. "This way, Your Highness, m'lords, m'lady."

He led them down a long hall, where the entrances to vast chambers and apartments were alternated with open breezeways. Through the breezeways, fountains and small gardens would be illuminated by standards with torches placed atop them. As they passed many such gardens, James said, "You might as well get used to those naps, Highness. It's the custom here. Court business in the morning, the Empress and her privy officers, an afternoon meal, nap from after lunch to evening, court business from sundown to about the ninth hour, then supper."

Erland glanced at several serving women passing by, again wearing nothing but the small kilt. "I'll manage," he said.

A thought came from Gamina, not a vocalized word, but an attitude, and it was wholly disapproving.

At the end of the hallway, they intersected and entered an even larger hallway. Columns of stone were all faced with marble and rose to a height of three stories over head. The walls on both sides of the hallway were painted with stylized renderings of great events and mythical battles between gods and demons. Down the center of the hall they walked, their feet treading on a carpet of fabulous design and weave, impossibly long, yet without apparent flaw.

Every twenty feet or so, a Keshian guard stood at the ready. Erland noticed how little these men looked like the famous Dog Soldiers who manned the frontier with the Kingdom. These soldiers seemed to have been chosen for their appearance more than their experience, Erland thought. Each wore only the short kilt, though of different design, cut away in front so that the legs might move more freely. Each man wore a breechcloth of the same white linen as the kilt, and an ornate belt fashioned of many colors, closed in front by a silver clasp. Each soldier wore the plain cross-gartered sandals, as well. Upon their heads were helms of fascinating design to Erland, barbaric, primitive looking. One wore a leopard skull atop his head, with the skin of the animal allowed to fall around his shoulders. A few others wore elk heads and bear heads in a similar fashion. Many wore hawk or eagle feathers attached to ivory rings set upon their heads, or helms fashioned from brightly colored parrot plumes, and a few high conical helms made of reeds dyed bright colors, that looked far from functional for battle.

James spoke aloud, "A grand display, isn't it?"

Erland nodded. Nothing he had seen so far in the upper city of Kesh spoke of anything less than excess. In contrast with what they had seen in the lower city, it was even more overwhelming. In even the most minor detail, richness and opulence was the order of the day. Where something base could suffice, it was replaced by something noble: gold in place of common iron, gems in place of glass, silk where cotton would be expected. And after passing through more chambers and halls, he knew the same held true for the servants. If a man was needed, he not only must be fit and able, he had to be handsome. If a woman were to be seen walking through the halls, even by chance, then she must be lovely and young. A few more days of this, thought Erland, and I'll welcome the sight of a plain face.

Reaching a massive pair of doors, gold leafed over all, the officer who led them brought the metal butt of the staff down on the floor, announcing, "The Prince Erland, the Earl James, the Countess Gamina, and the Baron Locklear!"

The doors swung open wide, and through them Erland could see a vast hall, at least a hundred yards from where they stood to the opposite wall, and against that distant wall, a high dais rose, upon which sat a golden throne.

Out of the side of his mouth, Erland said, "You didn't tell me it was a formal reception."

James said, "It isn't. This is a casual, intimate dinner."

"I can hardly wait for formal court." Taking a deep breath, Erland said, "Well, then, let us take a bite with Her Majesty." Stepping forward, Prince Erland led his advisors into the hall of the Empress of Great Kesh.

Erland marched purposefully and directly down the center of the hall. The sound of boot heels cracking against the stone floor seemed alien, a loud and brash intrusion in this hall where the soft leather of sandals and slippers were the norm. Silence drank the noise, as no one in the hall spoke and all eyes were upon the retinue from the Kingdom of the Isles.

Upon the dais, before a golden throne, a pile of cushions had been placed. Laying upon this was an old woman. Erland tried to look directly at her, yet not stare, and found the task impossible. Here, reclining upon cushions before the mightiest throne in the known world, was the single most powerful ruler in the known world. And she was a tiny, withered woman of unremarkable appearance. Her costume was similar to the customary short white kilt, though hers was long, reaching past the knees. Also her belt was studded with magnificent gems which caught the torchlight and sent sparkles dancing upon the walls and ceiling. She wore a loose vest of white fabric, clasped in front by a golden brooch set with a stunning pigeon's-blood ruby. Upon her head a diadem of gold rested, set with sapphires and rubies equal to any the Prince had ever seen before. The ransom of a nation rested upon the body of this old woman.

Her dusky skin couldn't hide the pallor of age. And her movements were those of a woman ten years more than her seventy-five, but it was her eyes that made Erland sense greatness, for they still had fire.

Dark eyes, with lights as brilliant as those in the sapphires and rubies upon her brow dancing in them, regarded the Prince as he walked along the aisle between the diners who shared the evening with the Empress. Around the base of the dais a dozen low tables had been placed in a semicircle, and around each round table, reclining upon cushions, were those whom the Empress deemed worthy of such honor.

147

Erland came to stand before the Empress and bowed his head, no more than he would do to his own uncle, the King. James, Gamina, and Locklear bent their knee, as they had been instructed by the protocol officer, waiting the signal to rise.

"How fares our young Prince of the Isles?"

The woman's voice was lightning cutting through a languid summer's afternoon, and Erland almost jumped at the tone of it. That simple question contained nuances and meanings beyond the young man's ability to articulate. Overcoming an unexpected attack of panic, Erland answered as calmly as possible, "Well, Your Majesty, my uncle, the King of the Isles, sends his wishes for your continued good health and well-being."

With a chuckle, she answered, "As well he should, my Prince. I am his best friend in this court, have no doubt." She sighed, then said, "When this business of Jubilee is over with, return Kesh's fondest wishes for Isles' continued well-being. We have much in common. Now, who is this with you?"

Erland made introductions, and when that was done, the Empress surprised them all by sitting up slightly and saying, "Countess, would you do me the courtesy of approaching."

Gamina flashed a quick glance at James and then moved up the ten steps that put her before the Empress. "You of the North can be so fair, but I have never seen your like," said the old woman. "You are not from the area near Stardock, originally, are you?"

"No, Your Majesty," answered Gamina. "I was born in the mountains north of Romney."

The Empress nodded, as if this explained everything. "Return to your husband, my dear. Your looks are lovely in their exotic fashion."

As Gamina descended from the dais, the Empress said, "Your Highness, a table has been set aside for your party. You will do me the pleasure of dining with us."

The Prince bowed again and said, "It is our honor, Your Majesty."

When they were seated at the indicated table, that one closest to the Empress, save one, another courtier appeared and announced, "Prince Awari, son of She Who Is Kesh!" The Prince who had met Erland that afternoon made his entrance from a side door that Erland assumed came from another, different wing of the palace than the one in which his party was housed.

"If I may advise His Highness," came a voice from Erland's right, and he turned to find that Kafi Abu Harez had insinuated himself between the Prince and Earl James. "Her Majesty, may she prosper, considered your potential for discomfort at so many new things and instructed me to sit at your side and answer whatever questions you might have."

And discover what it is we are curious about, came Gamina's thoughts.

Erland nodded slightly, and to Kafi it appeared he was merely considering this, but Gamina knew he was agreeing with her. Then the courtier cried, "The Princess Sharana!" Behind Awari came a young woman, near Erland's age from her appearance. Erland felt his breath catch in his throat at sight of the Empress's granddaughter. In this palace of beautiful women, she was stunning. Her dress was in the fashion of all others he had seen, but like the Empress, she also wore the linen vest—and her allure was heightened by more of her being hidden from view. Her arms and face were the color of pale almonds, turned golden by the hot Keshian sun. Her hair was cut at the forehead and shoulders, square and without fashion, but she wore a long braid in back, interwoven with gems and gold. Then the courtier shouted, "The Princess Sojiana."

Locklear almost came out of his seat. If the Princess Sharana was loveliness in its first bloom, then her mother, Sojiana, was beauty at its height. A tall woman of athletic stature, she moved like a dancer, each step designed to show her body to maximum advantage. And an exceptional body it was, long-limbed, flat stomach, and ample breasts. She had the look of fullness without hint of fat, of softness over firm muscle. She wore only the white kilt, with a golden girdle rather than the white belt. Around her arms two golden serpents coiled and around her neck she wore a golden torque set with fire opals, all of which set off her dusky tan skin. Her hair was the brown of wine-soaked wood, red as abundant as brown. And from a face as striking as her body, eyes of the most startling green regarded her mother.

"Gods," said Locklear, "she is astonishing."

The desertman concurred. "The Princess is conceded among the most beautiful of the trueblood, m'lord Baron." There was a guarded tone in his observation.

James looked at Kafi with an odd, questioning expression on his face, but the desertman seemed unwilling to speak. After enduring James's stare a moment, he took note of Locklear's rapt attention to the Princess as she came to stand before her mother, and at last said, "Lord Locklear, I feel the need to add a note of caution." He glanced back at the Princess Sojiana as she reached the dais, and whispered, "She is the most dangerous woman in their court after the Empress.

And that makes her the second most dangerous woman in this world."

With a defiant grin, Locklear said, "I can well believe that. She is breathtaking. But I think I could rise to the challenge."

Gamina gave him a dark look at the crude joke, but the desertman forced a smile. "She may give you the opportunity. It is said her tastes are . . . adventuresome."

James didn't miss Kafi's true message, even if Locklear was too enamored of the woman to listen. James gave Kafi a slight nod of thanks for the warning.

Unlike Awari and Sharana, Sojiana did not simply bow before the Empress and retire to the table set aside for the Imperial family, but she bowed and spoke. "Is my mother well?" she asked in a formal tone.

"I am well, my daughter. We rule another day in Kesh."

The Princess bowed and said, "Then my prayers are answered." She then moved to sit beside her brother and daughter, and the servants entered the hall.

Dishes of remarkable variety were presented one after the other, and Erland had to consider what to try every minute or two. Wines were brought forth, dry and sweet, red and white, the latter chilled by ice brought down from the peaks of the Guardian Mountains.

To the Keshian, Erland said, "Tell me, then, why were the Imperial family members last to enter?"

Kafi said, "In the strange way we in Kesh do things, those of the least importance enter first, the slaves and servants and minor court officials, who make all ready for the highborn. Then, She Who Is Kesh enters and takes her place upon her dais, then come the others of noble birth or special merit, again in the order of least to most important. You're the only ranking noble in attendance besides the Imperial family, so you entered just before Prince Awari."

Erland nodded, then found himself struck by an oddity. "That would mean his niece, Sharana, is—"

"Higher in rank in this court than the Prince," finished Kafi, glancing about the room. "This is something of a family dispute, my Prince."

And something he doesn't wish to speak of here, added Gamina. Erland gave her a glance and she said, *I'm not reading his thoughts, Highness. I would not do that with anyone who did not give me permission, but he's . . . announcing it. I can't explain it better, but he is straining to not speak about many things.*

Erland let it drop, and began asking questions about the court. Kafi answered in much the same way a bored history teacher might, save when questions could lead him into funny, embarrassing, or scandalous anecdotes. He was revealed to be something of a gossip.

James chose to let the others do most of the speaking, while he sifted through the answers Kafi gave. While the meal continued, he pieced together hints and tantalizing bits of this and that and fitted them into the pattern of what he already knew. Kesh was as complex as an anthill, and it was only the presence of this hill's queen, the Empress, that maintained order. Factions, old national rivalries, and age-old feuds were facts of Keshian court life, and the Empress kept her Empire intact by playing off one faction against another.

James sipped a fine dry red wine and considered what part they were to play in this drama, for he knew as certain as he knew boots hurt his feet that their presence would be seized upon by someone to further his own political ends. The question would be who would try the seizing and what his motives would be.

To himself, he added, not to mention how such a person would attempt to employ Erland's presence in court. It was clear that at least one faction in court wanted Erland dead and war between the Kingdom and the Empire. James glanced around the room, and then tasted the dry red wine again. As he savored it, he considered that he was a stranger in a very strange land and he would quickly have to learn his way around. He let his gaze wander, studying faces here and there and found more than a half-dozen faces studying him in turn.

He sighed. There would be time, and he doubted much trouble would arrive the first night they were in the palace. For if he were in charge of murdering Erland, he would do so when there were more guests to throw off suspicion and the effect of the death would do more to ruin the Empress's Jubilee. Unless, of course, he amended, it's the Empress herself who wishes Erland dead.

He picked up a delicately seasoned piece of melon off his plate and ate it. Savoring the taste, he decided to let matters of state go for a few hours. But less than a minute later, he found his gaze wandering again about the room as he sought some clue, some hint of from where the next attack might originate.

Chapter Ten
Companion

The lookout pointed.

"Faráfra!"

The captain called to trim sails as they rounded the headlands and came into view of the Keshian seaport. A sailor at the rail turned to Borric and said, "Some fun tonight, eh, Madman?"

Borric smiled ruefully. From behind, the Captain said, "Get aloft and make ready to reef in sail!" The sailors jumped to obey. "Two points to port," commanded the Captain, and Borric turned the large ship's wheel to bring the ship to the indicated heading. Since joining the crew of *The Good Traveler,* he had earned the grudging respect of the Captain and crew. Some tasks he did well, while others he seemed to have no understanding of, but learned quickly. His sense of the ship, and shifts in current and wind, learned while sailing small boats as a boy, had earned him the job of helmsman, one of three sailors the Captain allowed the task.

Borric glanced upward, where Suli ran along a spar, negotiating the sheets and hawsers like a monkey. Suli had taken to the sea like one born to it. In the month they had been at sea, his child's body had put on a little bulk and muscle, made strong by constant exercise and the plain but filling food, hinting at the man he would be someday.

The Prince had kept his identity to himself, which probably wouldn't have mattered. After his lunatic behavior with the knife, he was called by crew and Captain alike "the Madman." Claiming to be a Prince of Isles was unlikely to change their minds, he was sure. Suli was just "the Boy." Nobody had pressed them for why they had been drifting at sea in a boat near to sinking, as if to know such things was to invite trouble.

From behind, the Captain said, "A Faráfran pilot will take us into harbor. Bloody nuisance, but that's the way the Port Governor likes it, so we must heave to and wait." The Captain called out to reef sails and made ready to drop anchor. A pair of green and white pennants were run up, a request for a pilot. "Here's where you leave us, Madman. The pilot will be here within the hour, but I'm putting you over the side and will have you rowed to a beach outside the city."

Borric said nothing. The Captain studied the Prince's face and said, "You're a fit lad, but you were no kind of real sailor when you came aboard." His eyes narrowed as he said, "You know a ship like a sailing master knows one, not like crew; you knew nothing of the most common sailor's duty." As he spoke, the Captain kept glancing about, insuring everyone was performing his tasks as he should. "It's like you've spent your days upon the quarterdeck and never a minute below or aloft, a boy captain." Then his voice lowered, "Or the son of a rich man who owns ships." Borric moved the wheel slightly as the ship's speed dropped off, and the Captain continued, "Your hands showed calluses, but those of a horseman, a soldier, not a sailor." He glanced about to see if anyone was shirking his duty. "Well, I'm not asking to know your story, Madman. But I do know that the pinnace you had was from Durbin. You'd not be the first pair to want out of Durbin in a hurry. No, the more I think on it, the less I wish to know. I can't say you've been a good sailor, Madman, but you've given your best, and been a fair deck hand with no complaining, and no man can ask for more." He glanced aloft, saw the sails were all in, and called out for the anchor to be dropped. Lashing the wheel while Borric held it steady, the Captain said, "Normally, I'd have you bursting your liver hauling cargo until sundown with the rest of the men, not counting your work for passage finished until then, but there's something about you which tells me trouble's following in your wake, so I'll have you off and unnoticed." He looked Borric up and down. "Well, get below and get your things. I know you robbed my men blind with your card tricks. It's a good thing I haven't paid them yet, or you'd have all their earnings, as well as the rest."

Borric saluted and said, "Thank you, Captain."

He turned toward the companionway and slid down the ladder to the main deck, yelling up to Suli, "Boy! Come below and get your things!"

The Durbin beggar boy swung down the ratlines and met Borric at the entrance to the forecastle. They went inside and gathered together their few belongings. Besides the sheath knife and belt, Borric had won a small stake of coins, a pair of sailor's tunics, a second pair of trousers, and a couple of like pieces of clothing for Suli.

By the time they emerged from below, the crew was idly standing around, waiting upon the arrival of the Faráfran pilot. Several bade the two good-bye as they crossed to the rope ladder which hung off the lee side of the ship. Below, a small captain's boat waited, with two sailors to row them to shore.

"Madman. Boy!" said the Captain as they turned to descend the ladder. Both hesitated. He held out a tiny pouch. "It's a quarter wages. I'll not turn a man penniless into a Keshian city. It would be kinder to have left you to drown."

Suli took the pouch and said, "The Captain is kind and generous."

As the boat was rowed toward the breakers, Borric took the pouch of coins and hefted it. He put it inside his tunic, next to the pouch he had taken off of Salaya. Letting out his breath, he considered his next action. To get to the city of Kesh, obviously, but how, that was the question. Deciding not to dwell on that until land was underfoot, he asked Suli, "What did the Captain mean he'd not turn a man penniless into a Keshian city?"

It was one of the two sailors who answered, before the boy could speak. "To be penniless in Kesh is to be a corpse, Madman." He shook his head slightly at Borric's ignorance. "Life is cheap in Kesh. You could be the bloody King of Queg and if you didn't have a coin upon you, they'd let you die in the street, step over you as they go about their business, and curse your soul to the Seven Lower Hells for your corpse being in the way."

Suli said, "It's true. Those of Kesh are animals."

Borric laughed. "You're of Kesh."

The boy spit over the side. "We of Durbin are not truly of Kesh, no more than the desert men. We have been conquered by them; we pay their taxes, but we are not Keshians." He pointed toward the city. "Those are not Keshians. We are never allowed to forget this. In the city of Kesh the true Keshians are found. You shall see!"

"Boy's right, Madman," said the talkative sailor. "True Keshians are a strange lot. Don't see many along the Dragon Sea or anywhere else 'cept near the Overn Deep. Shave their heads and walk around naked they do and don't care if you make free with their women. It's a fact!" The other sailor grunted, as if this was but another story yet to be

154

proven to his satisfaction. The first said, "They ride in their chariots, and they think they're better 'en us. They'd kill you as soon as look at you." Both sailors pulled hard as they neared the breaker line, and Borric felt the boat rising on the back of a comber. The first sailor returned to his narrative. "And if one of 'em does kill ya, why the courts'll just turn 'im loose. Even if'n he's just as common as you are, Madman. It's being *trueblood.*"

The second sailor said, "That's fact enough. Watch yourself with the truebloods. They think different than the rest of us. Honor's different. If you challenge one, he might fight you, might not, won't care a fig about honor. But if he figures he's a grievance agin' you, why he tracks you, like you'd hunt an animal."

The first sailor added, "And he'll follow you to the edge of the world if he has to; that's a fact, too."

The breaker caught the boat and propelled it into the beach. Borric and Suli jumped out into waist-high water and helped the two rowers turn the boat around, then when the tide began to surge back out toward sea, they gave the boat a shove, so that the rowers would have some momentum to carry them over the breakers. Wading out of the water, the Prince turned to the beggar boy and said, "Not the sort of welcome to Kesh I had anticipated, but at least we're alive"—he jiggled the pouch under his tunic—"have some means to eat, and are free of pursuit." He glanced back to where the ship waited for the Keshian pilot. He knew that sooner or later one of the seamen would mention the man and boy picked up outside of Durbin, and those who might be in this part of the Empire seeking news of him would connect that fact with his escape. Then the hunt would be on again. Taking a deep breath, Borric said, "At least no pursuit for the moment." Slapping the boy playfully upon the back, he said, "Come along and let's see what this Keshian city has to offer by way of a good, hot meal!"

To that prospect, Suli agreed vigorously.

Where Durbin had been crowded, dirty, and miserable, Faráfra was exotic. And crowded, dirty, and miserable. By the time they were halfway to the center of the city, Borric understood exactly what the Captain had meant by his remark. For within twenty yards of the sea gate, next to the docks where they entered the city, a dead body lay rotting in the sun. Flies crawled over it and from the mangled appearance of the torso, dogs had feasted sometime before dawn. People passing the corpse ignored it, the only noticeable reaction being an occasional averting of the eyes.

Borric looked around and said, "Doesn't the city watch or someone do something?"

Suli was peering in every direction, constantly on the lookout for any opportunity to make a coin or two. Absently he said, "If some merchant nearby decides the stink is bad for business, he'll pay some boys to drag it to the harbor and toss it in. Otherwise it will lie there until it's no longer there." Suli seemed to take for granted that eventually some magic agency would dispose of the corpse.

A few feet away, a man in a robe squatted, ignoring those who passed by. As Borric watched, the man stood, and moved into the flow of traffic, leaving behind fresh proof he hadn't been squatting to say devotions to some god, but rather to answer the call of nature. "Gods above," said Borric. "Aren't there public jakes in this city?"

Suli looked at him with a curious expression. "Public? I've never heard of such a thing. Who would build them and clean them? Why would anyone bother?"

Borric said, "Never mind. Some things are just hard to get used to."

As they entered the flow of traffic from the docks into the city, Borric was astounded by the impossible variety of people. All manner of speech could be heard, and all fashions of dress could be observed. It was unlike anything he had seen before or expected to behold. Women passed by dressed in desert garb, covered from head to foot in plain blue or brown robes, nothing shown but their eyes, while a few feet away, hunters from the grassy plains stood inspecting goods, their dark, oiled bodies naked save for a simple thong breechclout, but their vanity showed in the copper bracelets, necklaces, and earrings they wore and in their choice of weapons. Clan tattoos marked faces here, and odd temple robes marked beliefs there. Women with skin as dark as morning's coffee passed wearing brightly colored cloth wrapped round from under-arm to knee, with high conical hats of the same cloth. Babies with serious eyes seemed to guard the rear from slings hung over their mothers' backs. Children of every possible description raced through the street, chasing a dog who dodged through the forest of human legs before him. Borric laughed. "That dog runs as if his life depended upon it."

Suli shrugged. "He does. Those street boys are hungry."

Borric could hardly take it all in. There was just too much that was too new to comprehend. Everywhere he looked, hundreds of people moved by, going one way or another, some strolling, others hurry-ing, but all oblivious to the throng surrounding them. And more than the press of bodies and the constant babble of voices, there was the smell. Unwashed bodies, expensive perfumes, human excrement, cooking, exotic spices, animal odors, all filled his nose with the reek of this alien land. The street was packed, with little room to move without coming in contact with strangers. Borric was aware of the weight of his two purses in his tunic, as safe a place for them as he could manage. Any pickpocket was going to have to stick his arm down the front of Borric's shirt, which seemed unlikely. Borric felt his senses assaulted, and he needed a respite.

They came to an open-front alehouse and the Prince motioned the boy to turn in. In the relative dark, they saw a pair of men speaking softly at a corner table, but otherwise the room was empty. Borric ordered a bitter ale for himself and a light ale for the boy, paying from the meager purse the Captain had given him, preferring to keep his more ample purse hidden in his shirt front. The brew was average in quality, but welcome for the long interval since Borric had tasted such.

"Clear the way!" A woman's shriek was followed by the clatter of hooves and more shouts, punctuated by the crack of a whip. Borric and Suli both turned to see what the fuss was. Before the open front of the alehouse, a strange scene was unfolding. A pair of splendid bay horses pulling an ornate chariot were rearing and whinnying as they were halted by their driver.

The cause of the sudden stop was a large man, who stood fore square in the center of the street. Behind the driver, the charioteer shouted, "Fool! Idiot! Get out of the way!"

The man in the street walked toward the two horses and grabbed the bridle of each. He clucked with the side of his tongue and pushed, and the horses moved backwards. The driver cracked his whip behind the ear of one of the horses, shouting loudly. But the horses obeyed the constant pressure from the front, rather than the noise from the back. The chariot was being backed up despite the driver's curses and protestations, while the charioteer behind him looked on in stunned disbelief. The driver drew back to crack a whip again, and the man pushing the horses said, "Crack that thing once more, and it will be the last stupid act of your life!"

"Fascinating," Borric remarked. "I wonder why our large friend is doing that?"

The "large friend" was a mercenary soldier by his look, wearing leather armor over his green tunic and trousers. Upon his head rested an old metal helm, much dented and in desperate need of a wire brush and polish, and across his back was a leather sheath, containing what appeared to be a half-and-a-half-, or bastard-sword. Upon his sides, two long dirk handles showed weapons at his belt.

The man behind the chariot driver looked upon the man blocking his way in outrage. He was undressed, save for a white kilt and an odd weapons harness, crossed leather straps over his shoulders, forming an *X* across his chest. Spears were within easy reach of him, tied to the side of the chariot, looking like a boat's mast as they pointed straight up. A bow was also slung to the side of the vehicle. With his face turning crimson, the charioteer shouted, "Make way, you idiot!"

Suli whispered to Borric, "The man in the chariot is of true Keshian blood. He is also a member of the Order of Imperial Charioteers. He is therefore upon the business of the Empire. The man who has halted them is a very brave man or a fool."

The man who held the horses merely shook his head and spit. He forced the horses to retreat until the chariot began to turn to the right, backing into a pot dealer's small shop. The pot merchant shouted in alarm and jumped to get out of harm's way, but the man with the large sword ceased pushing the horses just short of wreaking havoc on the man's livelihood. The mercenary released the bridle and bent down to pick something up, then sauntered aside. "You can go now," he said.

The chariot driver was about to start the horses on their way again, when the charioteer pulled the whip out of his hand. As if anticipating the move, the warrior wheeled about as the leather lash sang through the air and let it catch upon a leather bracer he wore on his left arm. Quickly grabbing the whip, he yanked hard and almost pulled the charioteer over the side of his chariot. Then just as the man was regaining his balance, the mercenary drew one of his two long dirks and cut the lash. The charioteer fell backwards and almost went over the other side. As the angry charioteer started to right himself again, the mercenary struck the nearest horse on the flank, shouting "Ya!" at the top of his lungs. Caught unawares, the driver was barely able to pull them around and head them down the street without driving through a packed mob of merchants and shoppers.

Laughter filled the boulevard as the enraged charioteer called back curses upon the large warrior. The warrior watched the departing chariot, then entered the ale shop and came to stand beside Suli.

"Ale," he said, putting down what he had picked up in the street. It was a copper coin.

Borric shook his head. "You were almost run down because you stopped to pick up a copper?"

The man removed his metal helmet, revealing damp hair clinging to his head, where he had hair, for the man was at least in his forties or fifties and had lost most of the hair on top. "You can't take the chance of waiting, friend," he said slowly, his accent giving him a full-mouth sound as he spoke, as if he was speaking around cotton wadded in his cheeks. "That's five luni, it's more money than I've seen in a month."

Something in his accent sounded familiar upon Borric's ear, and he said, "Are you from Isles?"

The man shook his head. "Langost, a town in the foothills of the Peaks of Tranquillity. Our people were from Isles stock, though. My grandfather's father was from Deep Taunton. I take it you're from Isles?"

Borric shrugged as if it really didn't matter. "Most recently from Durbin," he said. "But before that I was in Isles."

"Faráfra isn't paradise, but it's a better place than that pest-hole Durbin." The man stuck out his hand. "Ghuda Bulé, caravan guard, late of Hansulé, and before that Gwalin, and before that Ishlana."

Borric shook the man's hand, heavily callused from years handling both sword and livestock. "My friends call me Madman," he said with a grin. "This is Suli."

Suli solemnly shook hands with the fighter, as if one among equals.

"Madman? Must be a story about that name, or didn't your father like you?"

Borric laughed. "No, I did some crazy things once and the name stuck." Borric shook his head. "Caravan guard? That would explain why you knew how to move those chariot horses."

The man smiled, little more than curling his lip slightly, but his blue eyes danced. "Charioteers and their drivers give me gas. And one thing I *do* know about horses is that when someone is pushing on their faces, they don't like it and will back up. You can try that with a fool wiggling their reins and trying to flick a whip behind their ear, but I wouldn't try it with a rider on their back with a strong leg and a pair of spurs." He chuckled. "Pretty stupid, wasn't it?"

Borric laughed. "Yes, it was."

Ghuda Bulé drained the last of the ale from his cup and said, "Well, best be off to the caravansary. My most recent woman threw me out of her crib this morning when she finally figured out I wasn't going to marry her and get a job in the city, after all. So, I'm without funds and that means time to find work. Besides, I've about had my fill of Faráfra and could do with a change of scenery. Good day to you both."

Borric hesitated an instant, then said, "Let me buy you one."

Ghuda put the helm he had just retrieved back on the bar. "You talked me into it, Madman."

Borric ordered another round. When the barkeep had put the drinks down, Borric turned to the mercenary and said, "I need to get to the city of Kesh, Ghuda."

Ghuda turned about as if looking to see where he was. "Well, first walk that way," he said, pointing down the street, "until you reach the southern tip of the Spires of Light—it's a large mountain range; you'll notice them right away. Then turn left to bend around them, then right where the River Sarné runs along the north tip of the Guardians. Follow the river to a place on the Overn Deep where a lot of people live, and that's the city of Kesh. Can't miss it. If you start now, you should get there in six or eight weeks."

"Thanks," said Borric drily. "I mean I need to get there and I'd like to hire on a caravan heading that way."

"Uh-huh," said Ghuda noncommittally, nodding.

"And it would help if I had someone known around here to vouch for me."

"Uh-huh," said Ghuda. "So you'd like me to take you along to the caravansary and tell some unsuspecting caravan master that you're my old friend from home, a truly cracking good swordsman, who, by the way, is called the Madman."

Borric closed his eyes as if he had a headache. "Not quite."

"Look, friend, I thank you for the drink, but that doesn't entitle you to risk my good name by making recommendations that are bound to reflect badly on me in time."

Borric said, "Wait a minute! Who said it would reflect badly on you. I'm a competent swordsman."

"Without a sword?"

Borric shrugged. "That's a long story."

"It always is." Ghuda picked up his helm and put it crookedly upon his head. "Sorry."

"I'll pay you."

Ghuda took his helmet off and put it back on the bar. He signaled to the barman for another round. "Well, then, let's cut to the heart of it. Reputations have a certain value, don't they? What do you suggest?"

"What will you earn on a trip from here to Kesh?"

Ghuda considered. "It's a pretty uneventful route, well patrolled by the army, so there's little pay, which is why there are always caravans needing guards. A large caravan, perhaps ten ecu. A small one, five. And food on the trip of course. Maybe a bonus if there are bandits along the way we have to fight."

Borric did a quick calculation in his head—he could only think in terms of Kingdom coins—and reviewed the money he had in his purse from Salaya and his poker winnings on ship. "I'll tell you what. Get the three of us hired on to guard a caravan and I'll double whatever is paid you."

"Let me get this right: we get you on a caravan to Kesh and you'll give me your wages when we get there?"

"That's right."

"No," he said, drinking down his ale. "What guarantee do I have you'll not skip out with the money before I can collect?"

Borric gave him an exasperated look. "You'd doubt my word?"

"Doubt your word? Sonny, we've just met. And what would you think if you were me and this was being proposed to you by someone who's called 'Madman.' " He looked significantly down at his empty cup.

Borric signaled for another round. "All right, I'll pay you half on account before we leave and the rest when we get there."

Ghuda still wasn't convinced. "And what about the boy? No one will consider him a likely guard."

Borric turned to look at Suli, who was now clearly wobbling from the influence of three ales. "He can pass work. We'll hire him on to the caravan as a cook's monkey."

Suli just nodded, bleary-eyed. "Cook."

"But can you handle a blade, Madman?" asked Ghuda, seriously.

Borric said matter-of-factly, "Better than any man I've met."

Ghuda's eyes widened. "That's a boast!"

Borric grinned. "I'm still alive, aren't I?"

Ghuda stared at Borric a moment, then threw back his head and laughed. "Ah, that's good." Killing what was left of his ale, Ghuda pulled out his two long dirks, and reversed the one in his left hand, handing it to Borric. "Show me what you've got, Madman."

Suddenly Borric was twisting and parrying a vicious lunge, barely able to avoid a potentially killing stroke. He didn't hesitate as he struck the mercenary as hard a blow to the head as he could with his left hand. As Ghuda shook his head to clear it, Borric lunged, and the mercenary was falling away from the point, striking a table with his back.

The barman shouted, "Here you two! Stop breaking up my shop!"

Ghuda sidled along the table, as Borric measured him. "We can stop any time you're convinced," said the Prince, balancing his weight on the balls of his feet, shoulders hunched, the point of the dirk aimed at Ghuda.

The mercenary grinned, his manner playful. "I'm convinced."

Borric flipped the dirk, catching the blade between thumb and forefinger, and handed it back to Ghuda. The mercenary took it and said, "Well, we'd better find a weapons dealer and get you set up. You may know how to handle a weapon, but it does you little good if you don't have one."

Borric put his hand down the front of his baggy tunic and pulled out his purse. He took out a pair of copper coins and handed them to the furious barkeep. "Suli, let's be off—" He discovered the boy was slumped down at the foot of the bar, snoring loudly.

Ghuda shook his head. "Can't say as I trust anyone who can't hold his drink."

Borric laughed as he pulled the drunken boy to his feet. Shaking him severely, he said, "Suli, we have to go."

Through bleary eyes, the boy said, "Master, why is the room spinning?"

Ghuda grabbed his helm and said, "I will wait for you outside, Madman. You tend the boy." The mercenary exited the shop and stood next door examining some copper jewelry while the sounds of a boy being very sick emerged from the ale shop.

Three hours later, two men and a very pale boy passed through the eastern city gate, and entered the caravansary. The large field, surrounded on three sides by tents and sheds, was located just to the east of the city, less than a quarter mile from the gates of Faráfra. Close to three hundred wagons of varying sizes were spread around the meadow. Dust filled the air as horses, oxen, and camels moved from one place to another.

Suli hefted the large sack he carried, full of various items Ghuda had insisted they buy. Borric had followed the mercenary's lead in the matter, save when it came to his own armor. Borric now wore an old but serviceable jacket of leather, with leggings and bracers. He couldn't find a light helm, so rather than one he didn't care for, he chose a leather band with a cloth headcover, to keep his lengthening hair back and perspiration out of his eyes. The covering also protected the back of his neck from the harsh Keshian sun. A longsword hung from his left hip, and a dirk from his right. He'd have preferred a rapier, but they were rarer in Faráfra than in Krondor and beyond his means. The day's shopping had eaten away at his meager supply of coins and he was aware that he was still a long way from the city of Kesh.

As they moved along past the corrals where horses were kept, they came to the main concourse, a series of wagons arrayed in two lines. Strolling along between them were a full score of armed men, as well as merchants seeking transport for their goods.

Moving down the concourse, the three were called to by a man atop each wagon. "Bound for Kimri. I need guards for Kimri!" At the next, a man shouted to them, "Ghuda! I need guards for Teléman!" The third called, "Top price paid. We're leaving tomorrow for Hansulé!"

Halfway down the concourse, they found a caravan bound for the city of Kesh. The caravan master looked them over and said, "I know you by name, Ghuda Bulé. I can use you and your friend, but I don't want the boy."

Borric was about to speak, but Ghuda cut him off. "I don't go anywhere without my Good Luck Cook."

The stout caravan master looked down upon Suli, perspiration beading upon his hairless head as he said, "Good Luck Cook?"

Ghuda nodded, as if it was something so obvious he needn't comment upon. "Yes."

"What, O Master of Ten Thousand Lice, is a Good Luck Cook?"

"When I was guard on Taymus Rioden's caravan from Querel to Ashunta, seven years back, we were raided by bandits. Struck as if by lightning. Had no time to even get out a prayer to the Death Goddess." He made a good luck sign, as did the caravan master. "But I survived as did my Good Luck Cook. Not another man did. I have always had my Good Luck Cook with me since."

"As that boy can be no more than twelve summers, Father of Prevaricators, he must have been precocious indeed to have been a caravan cook seven years ago."

"Oh, it wasn't him," said Ghuda, shaking his head as if that should be obvious. "Different cook. You see, I was down in the gully with

163

my britches around my ankles with the worst case of runs in my life when the bandits struck. Couldn't even get up to fight. They just never found me."

"And how did the cook survive?"

"He was squatting a few feet away."

"And what happened to him?" asked the caravan master, squinting down at Ghuda with interest.

"I killed the bastard for almost poisoning me."

The caravan master couldn't help himself but laugh. When he was through, Ghuda said, "The boy'll cause you no trouble. He can help the cook around the campfire at night and you needn't pay him. Just let him eat a full meal every day until we reach Kesh."

"Done!" said the master, spitting in his hand and extending it. Ghuda spit in his and they shook. "I can always use a good liar around the fire at night. Makes the journey pass quickly." To Suli he said, "Go find my cook, boy." He hiked his finger over his shoulder to where a cook wagon could be seen amidst a dozen freight wagons. "Tell him you're to be his new cook's monkey."

Suli looked to Borric, who nodded he should go. As Suli left, the caravan master said, "I am Janos Saber, trader from Kesh. We leave at first light tomorrow."

Ghuda unslung the small bundle he carried over his shoulder. "We'll sleep under your wagons tonight."

"Good. Now, leave me, as I need four more guards before night-fall."

Borric and Ghuda wandered from the spot, and found some shade under a widely spreading tree. Ghuda took his helm off and ran his hand over his sweaty face. "Might as well rest now, Madman. Tomorrow it gets really miserable."

"Miserable?" asked Borric.

"Yes, Madman. Today we're merely hot and bored. Tomorrow we will be thirsty, dirty, tired, hot, and bored."

Borric crossed his arms on his chest and tried to rest. He knew that it had been drilled into him since boyhood that a soldier steals rest whenever the opportunity appears. But his mind raced. How was Erland faring and what was transpiring in Kesh? By his estimate, Erland and the others should be in Kesh by now. Was Erland safe? Did they count Borric dead, or merely missing?

Sighing aloud, he settled down. Soon he was dozing in the afternoon heat, the noise of the busy caravansary becoming lulling in its own fashion.

Chapter Eleven
Hunting

The lion stood motionless.

Erland watched with interest as the cat waited with eyes fixed upon a grazing herd of grassland antelopes. Erland sat on his horse, next to James and Locklear, and the desertman, Kafi Abu Harez. Arrayed nearby were a half-dozen chariots, the traditional centerpiece to Kesh's army. The Commander of the Imperial Charioteers, Lord Jaka, watched as his son Diigaí made ready to hunt the cat. The elderly commander's face was set in stoic repose, as if carved from weathered black stone, showing no emotion at his son's approaching confrontation.

Kafi pointed to where the lion hunkered down in the tall grass. He said to Erland, "This young male has no pride." Erland took note of the huge animal, much larger than the small lion that hunted the mountains in parts of the Kingdom. Also this one had a huge mane that was nearly black, while the lions Erland had seen were completely tawny. This was a truly magnificent animal. "He hunts for himself," continued Kafi. "If the lion survives this day, he will someday be a fat, lazy fellow with lionesses to hunt for him."

"Might he survive?" asked Locklear.

Kafi shrugged. "Most likely not. It is as the gods will. The boy may not leave the field unless he is disabled, which is much the same as death for one of his rank. His father is among the most important lords in the Empire, so to be reduced to the rank of a *sah-dareen*—a nonhunter—would be more shame than the family could endure and retain its influence. The boy would most likely go out and do something terribly foolish, and brave, but die nevertheless, to expiate the shame."

The lion padded forward silently, head low and eyes fixed upon his quarry. He had already marked a weak herd member, a young calf or a sickly old buck or doe. Then the wind shifted and, as one, the heads of the antelopes came up. Black noses twitched as the herd tested the wind for the scent of approaching danger.

Abruptly, one buck sprang up in a seemingly impossible four-footed jump, and the herd was off. The lion sprang after, using an uncustomary burst of speed to overtake the rear of the herd. An old doe, weakened by age, kicked at the lion, causing the animal to veer a moment. The young lion stood in confusion. Antelope weren't supposed to do that, he was certain. Then the lion picked up a new scent on the breeze and realized suddenly that he was no longer the predator but the prey.

At that moment, Diigaí gave a shout and his driver cracked his whip and called for his horses to give pursuit. That was the signal, and the hunt was on. Borric and his companions put heels to their mounts and galloped to keep up with the chariots.

In a military maneuver, the chariots fanned out to intercept the lion if it broke right or left. Hunting calls filled the air as the young Keshian hunters cried ancient invocations of their hunting god, Guis-wa. Seen as a dark god in the Kingdom, the Red-Jawed Hunter was a major deity in Kesh and patron god of all Keshian hunters.

The lion raced over the grassy plane. The lion could not run long effectively, and there was no clear hiding place in sight. Diigaí and the other charioteers moved after the fleeing cat.

Suddenly James reined in, calling Erland to halt. The Kingdom riders pulled in, as did Kafi Abu Harez. "What?" asked Erland.

James said, "Just give that organized confusion a moment to get ahead of us that's all. I wouldn't want you to find yourself in front of it accidentally."

Erland was about to protest, then realized what James was telling him. It was the sort of scene that would lend itself to an "accident." He nodded, and turned his mount, bringing her to a canter, fast enough to see what was occurring ahead without the risk of being caught up in the hunt.

Suddenly the chariots were reining in, giving Diigaí ample room to face the lion. By the time Erland's party caught up, Diigaí was off his chariot, stalking the lion with a long spear and hide shield.

Erland said, "Those are pretty primitive weapons to be hunting a cat of that size. Why not use a bow?"

Kafi said, "This is his manhood rite. He is a very important boy, being the eldest son of Lord Jaka. The trueblood will use a bow to kill an animal raiding his herd, but to be a great hunter—a *simbani*— to have a lion's-main headdress for formal occasions, you must use the weapons of your ancestors."

Erland nodded and moved his horse next to Diigaí's chariot. His driver, a boy of about the same age, looked on anxiously, obviously concerned for the young noble's safety. The young hunter was now about fifty yards ahead of his chariot, halfway to where the lion crouched.

The lion crouched, his tongue lolling in his mouth as he panted to catch his breath. His eyes darted and his head turned as he attempted to determine if danger was approaching and if so from where. Then he reared up on his haunches and looked around. There was no avenue of escape, as a ring of chariots stood ready to block his flight on all quarters. Then he spied the approaching figure. The lion roared a scream of anger and fear.

Several horses nickered and attempted to move, but their drivers held them steady. Erland turned to Kafi and said, "What if he misses on his throw?"

Kafi said, "He won't throw. It's too dangerous. He'll attempt to goad the lion into charging and set spear and impale it, or get close enough to stab it."

That made sense to Erland, as much as any of this barbaric ritual made sense. To hunt down lions, bears, wolves, and wyverns that were raiding herds made sense. To hunt something you couldn't eat so you could wear its head as a trophy, didn't.

Then the lion charged. A slight sound of surprise escaped the lips of several of the charioteers, and it was obvious to Erland and his companions this was unusual behavior for this breed of lion. Diigaí hesitated, and in that instant he lost his opportunity to be ready. His spear was incorrectly set when the lion charged and he gave it only a glancing blow. Suddenly all was confusion: the boy was knocked back, his shield saving him a terrible raking as the lion lashed out blindly at the source of his pain. Then the animal was biting at his flank, as if some enemy was biting him there. The young man's spear protruded from his side.

The lion knew only two things, pain and blood. It roared, and the young man attempted to back away while covering himself with the shield. The lion spun in a circle, attempting to bite the spear, then the weapon was dislodged. And Diigaí discovered he was on one side of an angry wounded lion with his spear on the other.

"He'll be killed!" Erland shouted.

Kafi said, "No one will interfere. It's his right to kill or be killed." The desertman shrugged. "I don't see much logic in it myself, but it is the trueblood way."

Suddenly, Erland pushed back in the saddle, kicking his legs out of his stirrups. He reached under the right knee roll and quickly unbuckled his right stirrup leather. Pulling it free of the saddle, he rebuckled it, and pulled his left stirrup iron up so it wouldn't strike his horse. Erland wrapped the leather of his right stirrup around his right hand twice, swung the heavy iron in his hand to test the weight and how far he could strike with it. James began to say, "What are you—" but before the question was finished, Erland had his horse off toward the young hunter.

The lion crouched and snarled, and began to move at a fast crawl, keeping low until the moment to spring, but as he neared the young man who held his shield to take the charge a new attack materialized.

Erland charged the lion, striking downward with the heavy stirrup iron. The lion roared in pain and Erland's horse instinctively danced sideways. The lion spun and swung out with a huge paw, but the horse was away. The big cat began to move after, then remembered there was another enemy to face.

Erland's distraction was enough. Diigaí sprinted to where his spear lay, and made ready. As Erland returned to his companions, the young Keshian noble shouted his hunter's cry and the lion turned. Crazed with pain and confused with the attacks from all quarters, the young cat sprang at Diigaí. This time the spear was correctly set and it took the lion full in his massive chest. His own momentum carried the lion forward, driving the spearhead into his heart.

The charioteers shouted and the young man stood over the twitching cat. Erland turned his horse, who was shying at the smell of blood. It took a moment to control him without stirrups, but being an excellent horseman, the Prince quickly had the mount turned and trotting away from the shouting trueblood men. A chariot approached and Erland found Lord Jaka passing by. Suddenly the enormity of his impulsive act struck Erland. Had he violated some fundamental law of theirs by distracting the lion? As they passed one another, Erland and Jaka's eyes met. Erland looked for something in the old man's glance, approval or condemnation, but as the Master of

Charioteers passed, he revealed nothing, gave no sign or gesture to the young Prince. James came to where Erland sat, reattaching his leathers and irons and said, "Are you mad? What possessed you to do something that foolish?"

Erland said, "He would have been killed. The others would have then killed the lion. Now only the lion is dead. Made sense to me."

"And if your horse had shied a moment earlier, you could have been the lion's first victim!" James grabbed Erland's tunic and pulled him almost off his horse as he drew him closer. "You are not some stupid son of a nameless noble. You are not the idiot child of a wealthy merchant. You are Isles' next *King,* for mercy's sake. If you ever try anything that foolish again, I will personally beat you within an inch of your existence."

Erland pushed James's hand away. "I haven't forgotten that." Erland circled his horse, anger on his face. "I haven't *forgotten* that for an instant, my lord Earl. Not since my brother died!" Suddenly, Erland kicked his mount and was riding at a fast gallop back toward the city. James signaled and the Kingdom honor guard gave chase. They wouldn't try to stop him, but they wouldn't let him ride unprotected either.

Locklear came to where James sat, now alone, and said, "The boy's not making it easy, is he?"

James shook his head. "It's the sort of thing you or I would have tried at his age."

Locklear said, "Were we really that stupid?"

"I'm afraid so, Locky." James glanced around. "They're taking the lion's head, so we'll be heading back to the palace. And they'll be inviting us to another celebration."

Locklear grimaced. "Has anyone ever told these people that it's acceptable for less than fifty people to eat together at one time?"

"Apparently not," answered James, kicking his horse into motion.

"Let's go soothe our Prince's wounded pride," said Locklear.

James looked off toward where Erland rode, closely followed by his guard, and said, "It's not his pride that's wounded, Locky." Glancing at the ceremonial dismemberment of the lion, he said, "Diigaí is the same age as Erland . . . and Borric. Erland misses his brother." James let out a long breath, almost a loud sigh. "As do we all. Come on, we still need to talk to him."

Together, the two advisors approached the waiting Kafi Abu Harez, who turned his mount and joined in with them to ride back to the city. As they left the celebrating Keshians, Locklear asked, "Kafi, what has Erland done by taking a hand?"

The desertman said, "I do not know, my lord. Had your young Prince killed the lion, then he would have not only shamed Diigaí by showing the world the boy could not hunt, he would have made a powerful enemy in Lord Jaka. As it is, he only distracted the animal, allowing the boy to regain his weapon and kill the cat." Kafi shrugged and smiled as he spurred his horse to a canter, along with James and Locklear. "Perhaps nothing will come of this. With the trueblood, who can say?"

James said, "I'm sure we'll find out soon enough."

They rode the rest of the journey back to the city in silence.

Miya sat behind Erland in the pool, rubbing the tension from his neck and shoulders. They were alone, as Erland had sent away the others. While he had taken advantage of the willingness of the Keshian serving women available to him, he had discovered himself returning more and more to Miya's company. He felt nothing he would call love for the young Keshian servant, but with her he felt the comfort of being able to relax and speak of what bothered him. She seemed to know when to stay silent or when to ask the probing question that cleared up his own confusion. And their lovemaking had progressed from the excitement of newness and raw clashing of desire to a more sedate familiarity of two people who understood one another's need.

Another servant entered and said, "Highness, the Lord James asks permission to enter."

Erland felt like refusing, but realized he would have to speak with James sometime today, so he nodded once. A moment later, James entered the bathing room.

James looked down upon the nude pair, and if he was startled to discover the girl with Erland, he hid it. He didn't ask anything of the servant who remained in the room, but removed his cloak and handed it to the young woman, who took it from him. He then crossed over to a small stool, carrying it himself to the pool's side.

Sitting down, James said, "Well, then. Feeling better?"

Erland said, "No. I'm still angry."

"Who are you mad at, Erland?"

For a silent moment the frustration was clearly etched on the young man's face. Then it seemed to wash away as Miya continued to probe at the knots of tension in his neck and shoulders.

170

"The universe, I guess. The gods of fate and chance. You. My father. Everyone." Then his voice fell away. "Mostly I'm furious with Borric for getting himself killed."

James nodded. "I know. I feel that way, too."

Erland let out a long sigh of tension released and said, "I guess that's why I did what I did. I just couldn't see that boy killed by that lion. Maybe the boy's got a brother—" Words failed him as tears came unbidden. For a moment, Erland sat in the warm pool, his grief manifested for the first time since the bandit attack. James waited while the young Prince cried for his dead brother, neither showing or feeling embarrassment at the display. James had done his crying a week before, in the arms of his wife.

After a moment, Erland looked at his teacher with red-rimmed eyes. "Why, damn it?"

James could only shake his head. "Why? Only the gods know and they aren't talking. At least not to me." He reached down and stuck his hand into the water. A moment later he withdrew it and wiped his brow. "Some things make sense, others don't. I don't know."

James was reflective a while, then said, "Look, I've not told you this. Your father saved my life. A couple of times. Now I'm no more an expert on why a Prince of Isles should save the life of a boy thief than I am on why another Prince of Isles should die in an ambush on the way to a birthday party. I can only tell you that no one ever told me, *ever told me,* that life makes sense. It just is."

Erland sank back against Miya's soft body and let warmth infuse him. He sighed and felt something leave from within, an ache that had been there every minute since the ambush. "It's so odd," he said quietly. "It just hit me now that Borric must be dead. Yet . . ."

"What?" James asked quietly.

"I don't know." Erland looked at James and there was a question in his eyes. "How is it supposed to feel? I mean, Borric and I haven't spent more than a few days apart ever. It's like we were . . . just part of each other. I thought that if I lost him, or he me, we'd . . . feel it. Do you know what I mean?"

James got up. "I think so. At least, I think I know as much as anyone can who has never had one in their life to be as close with as you two were with each other. But I've watched you since you were babies and I've seen you fight and play. I think I know what you mean."

Erland sighed again. "I just thought it would feel different. That's all. It's not like he's dead, you know, just very far away." Erland's eyes got heavy and he closed them. A moment later his breathing became more regular and he dozed.

James motioned for the servant who held his cloak to return it. To Miya he said, "We dine with the Empress again, tonight. Wake him when it's time?"

She nodded, not speaking so as not to wake the sleeping Prince. James folded his cloak over his arm and departed.

Erland finished dressing as Miya announced Lord Jaka. The Prince was not surprised, as he had a feeling there would be a reaction from Diigaí's father over this afternoon's business. Erland motioned for the servant to admit the Keshian noble and a few moments later the tall warrior entered. Miya moved a discreet distance away, out of earshot but close enough should Erland need her.

Jaka bowed before Erland, then said, "My lord Prince, I trust I have not come at an inopportune minute?"

"No, Lord Jaka. I was just finishing my dressing in anticipation of dining with your Empress."

Jaka made a gesture with both his hands, held parallel and moving them downward and out, the meaning of which Kafi had told him was, "May heaven protect," or "May heaven give bounty," an all-purpose benediction.

The old warrior said, "I have come to speak to you of this thing you did this afternoon."

"Yes?"

Jaka seemed to struggle with the words he wished to say. "As a hunter of great reputation, it would have been a shameful thing for my son to have failed in his manhood hunt, today. It is difficult to accept such a thing.

"There are those who will say that you robbed my son of a courageous death, or that his kill is tainted because of your interference."

Here it comes, thought Erland. He had half-expected something like this.

"Yet," continued Jaka, "you did but annoy the animal, distracting it long enough for my son to recover his spear."

Erland nodded. "The kill was his."

"This is true. So, while I am partially mixed in my feelings as to the elegance of the kill, as a father of a boy I love deeply, I wish to thank you for allowing him his manhood." Softly he added, "And for saving his life."

Erland stood motionless an instant, struggling with what he

should say. Then he took the course that would allow the father the most pride possible under the circumstances. "Perhaps he would have regained the spear without my aid. Who can say?"

"Who, indeed?" said the old man. "It was a young cat, inexperienced and in great pain. A more experienced hunter would have struck it in the face with the flat of the shield, no damage, but noise and pain. If the cat attacks the shield, the experienced hunter lets him and attempts to recover the spear. It is a thing we teach, though in the heat of the moment, it is easily forgotten. *Easily forgotten*, Your Highness.

"I must leave, my lord Prince. But before I do, know that should you have need, I am in your debt."

Erland could think of nothing appropriate to say to such a straightforward offer of thanks, so he merely said, "Thank you for the courtesy of your call, and the honor of your presence, Lord Jaka."

The Commander of the Imperial Charioteers bowed to Prince Erland and departed. Erland turned to where Miya stood, and said, "I will see you later this evening, I expect."

Miya came to Erland and stood a moment, adjusting his tunic, more for the closeness it brought than for any true need, and said, "I will see you sooner, my Prince. I am ordered to the Empress's presence."

"Something's amiss?"

Miya shrugged. "Nothing. All who serve in the palace of She Who Is Kesh are occasionally permitted to share the glory of the Empress's court."

"Good. I will see you there."

Erland motioned for the doors to his apartment to be opened and two young women swung them wide. Outside, four Krondorian Palace Guards stood waiting, in formal uniform. They fell in around Erland, and in lock step they marched down the large halls of the palace.

Along the route, they were joined by James and Gamina, then Locklear, and finally Lord Kafi. When they reached the Imperial complex of the palace, the Krondorian Guards halted, as it was not permitted for soldiers of a foreign nation to approach the Imperial presence.

Erland entered to the fanfare of trumpets. Leading his small band, as senior most in rank he was required to address the Empress first. The Keshian Master of Ceremonies intoned the long list of praise for the approaching Prince, and Erland knew from his coaching this signaled that the court was a formal one. He refrained from smiling as he thought that the difference between formal dining and informal was a matter of label with the Empress. He was sorely wishing to be back in Krondor, eating at a simple table with Borric in the corner of the kitchen, something they had done often, rather than endure state dinners with their parents.

Reaching the foot of the dais, Erland bowed and the Master of Ceremonies, said, "O She Who Is Kesh, I have the honor of presenting to you His Highness, Prince Erland, Heir to the Throne of the Kingdom of the Isles, Knight-Captain of the Western Realm."

Erland stood upright and said, "Your Majesty, I thank you for the kindness of sharing your bounty with myself and my companions. May I present—" and he went through the formality of presenting his companions, as he had each time they had come before the Empress. He wondered if this nonsense went on at every meal of the day for the Empress.

The Empress said, "Your Highness had a busy day, from all reports." Erland waited for her to say more, but all she said was, "It is our pleasure that you join us again, Your Highness. Please, enjoy the bounty of our tables."

Entering the hall as Erland turned was Prince Awari, with several of his companions. One, closest to Erland as he passed, spat upon the floor before the Prince.

Erland halted, his eyes widening and his face reddening. The young man who had spat began to move on, when Erland turned and said, "You!"

All eyes turned to watch the two young men. The young man looked at Erland with narrow eyes. He was a trueblood, probably an important noble's son, given his proximity to the Prince, and his body was muscular and strong. Erland smelled a fight coming, and was in no mood to avoid it.

"Erland!" James's voice hissed in the Prince's ear. "Back off!"

The Empress watches, came Gamina's warning.

Erland glanced at the throne as the young noble came to stand before him. The Empress's attention was riveted upon the two who stood facing each other. A court noble moved to intercede, and the Empress ordered him to her side. She seemed disinclined to interfere. Rather, there was an avid glint in her eye. Erland wondered if this was some sort of test, to determine what sort of ruler of Isles Kesh would face in years to come. If that were so, thought Erland, they find a staunch opponent if needs be.

174

When the young man was inches from the Prince he said, "What, *sah-dareen?*"

A few voices could be heard muttering. In this court, to be a nonhunter was to be less than noble, and to be called such was a deadly insult.

Erland glanced at Prince Awari, to see if he would interfere. The Prince looked on, interest in his eyes, and a slight smile upon his lips. Erland then knew the young man had insulted him at Prince Awari's bidding. Erland took a breath, then as quickly as he could, he brought his hand across his chest, and delivered a punishing back-handed blow to the young man's face.

The youth staggered as his knees buckled. He collapsed to the floor, but before he could complete the fall, Erland grabbed the ornamental torque around his throat and lifted him by it.

"He who insults me in Kesh's court insults the Kingdom of the Isles. I cannot let that pass." He released the young man's torque, pushing him away. The youth staggered but regained his feet. Erland said, "You have the choice of weapons."

James gripped Erland's arm. He whispered. "You cannot fight this duel. It is what they want."

But the young man only said, "I do not understand what you mean."

Erland said, "I've struck you. You have the right to name the weapons we shall use when we duel."

The young man's face knotted in an expression of unfeigned perplexity. "Duel? Why would I fight you? You would surely kill me."

Erland did not know what to say. He was spared the need of saying anything by the Empress. "Lord Kiláwa."

A man of middle years stood up, at a table located near the back of the room. "My Empress's command?"

"Your son is a buffoon, Kiláwa. He insults a guest in my house. What is to be done with him?"

The man's face went pale. But he stood erect as he spoke. "Your wish, Majesty?"

The Empress hesitated, then said, "I should have his head presented to Prince Erland in a jar of honey and wine, as a trophy, but as our ways are not His Highness's, I think this would only serve to cause him more discomfort." She paused, then said, "Young Rasajani."

Instantly, the youth who had insulted Erland bowed his head toward the Empress. "Your Majesty?"

"The sight of you causes me discomfort. You are banished from the upper city. Never set foot upon the plateau so long as the light shines from my eyes. When I have gone to the Hall of Eternal Beauty, then the one who rules after me may prove merciful and allow your return. That is as much forbearance as you'll get from me—and only because your father is dear to me—I don't have much mercy left in my bitter old bones. Now, begone!"

When he reached the table set aside for his party, Erland turned to Kafi and said, "What was that about?"

The desertman seemed uncertain of the question. "My Prince?"

"Why did he insult me if he didn't wish to fight?" Erland said as he sat down.

Sitting, Kafi said, "It is a trueblood thing, Highness. You must understand: they are not a warrior people. They are hunters. Warriors are little more than dogs to be turned loose upon an opponent. Oh, they'll fight if necessary and with ferocity, but they count no honor in it. No, honor is in the ability to track down your prey, to bring it to bay, and kill it with a single blow. That is honor to a trueblood. For young Rasajani to fight you would be unreasonable. You are a warrior of undoubted talents. You would quickly kill him. He knew that, so to fight you would be sheer folly."

Erland shook his head as he said, "This is a difficult thing to understand."

Kafi shrugged. "To them it is difficult to understand how a man would allow circumstances to force him into fighting someone he knew was a finer warrior over a matter of honor. It is, from their point of view, tantamount to suicide."

The party of Princess Sharana entered, and walking a step back was Miya. Erland drank in the sight of the golden-skinned Princess, then said to Kafi, "Why is my serving maid with the Princess tonight?"

Kafi smiled. "Because your 'serving maid' is Lady Miya, Sharana's cousin."

Erland's eyes widened. "Cousin? To the Princess? You're joking?"

Kafi said, "Of course not, Highness. The Empress would not allow slaves nor 'inferiors' such as myself to attend your personal needs in your own quarters." The word *inferiors* snarled with barely hidden bitterness. "So only young men and women of noble birth—lesser sons and daughters—may serve the Empress and her guests."

Now Erland's eyes grew round. "All of them!"

Kafi said, "Yes, every servant in your chamber is a daughter of nobility." He waved absently at the others around the table, who were watching Erland's discomfort. "Of course all in *your* apartment, Your Highness, are related to the Empress and of royal blood."

Erland said, "Gods and demons. I've bedded half the royal daughters in the Empire, I fear."

Kafi laughed. "Not by a tenth, Highness. Many are related, albeit distantly, to Her Majesty. And what if you did? The trueblood look upon questions of the body differently than you or I. Their women are as free to take lovers as the men. It comes from having as many Empresses as Emperors." Again there was a hint of bitterness in the last observation.

As protocol dictated, the Princess Sojiana and her retinue were the last to enter, and she made formal enquiry as to her mother's health. The forms were met as required, and the meal commenced.

Servants appeared when the Princess's party was seated and the dinner began. Little talking occurred around Erland's table, as both the Prince and Locklear seemed content to stare across the room, Erland at Princess Sharana and Lady Miya, and Locklear at their mother.

Later that evening, James requested Erland accompany Gamina and himself upon a stroll through one of the many palace gardens. Assuming there was a reason for the odd request, the Prince agreed.

As they were entering the garden, Gamina's voice entered Erland's mind. *James asks that you speak through me, as he is certain that even in the center of this garden we are likely to be overheard.* Aloud she said, "Not like home, but lovely, don't you think?"

Erland said, "I agree, completely."

James's voice came into Erland's mind, with Gamina's aide. *I have finally been contacted by our agent in the palace.*

Finally? Has there been a problem?

A problem? There was a feeling of humor with James's answer. *Only that we're under constant supervision. Half the "servants" in our quarters are most likely Keshian spies—which is a faint differentiation, as anything we do would be reported as a matter of course by those who are not spies. I think something* very *important is happening.*

Erland asked Gamina how her day passed, and they chatted about inconsequential things, as they found a magnificent marble water fountain: three demons of comic aspect seemed to be trapped in motion, and above them beautiful nude women hunted them from chariots. Water poured out of the rear of the three chariots as the demons were herded toward the center of the pool. Somehow a light shone from below, by what means Erland couldn't guess, and the effect was truly wonderful.

Aloud he said, "I must ask how this light effect is done. I must have one like it built in Krondor." Mentally, he said, *What do you think is going on?*

I'm not sure yet, answered James. *I've pieced together this much. The Empress's health fails. She is more ill than is apparent. That is common gossip in the palace and the city below. What isn't known is that she is expected to name Prince Awari her heir, but every sign points to her naming Sojiana, or even Sharana, before her own son. The Empress and her son have had differences for years and at times have barely spoken.*

So there's a question of inheritance of the throne?

Apparently, answered James. *The throne usually passes to the eldest child.*

"Lovely night," said Erland aloud. *But that's Sojiana.*

True, but there is a major faction of nobles who would see Awari upon the throne. First because the last two rulers have been women, and many of the subject nations of Kesh are fiercely patriarchal and fear that three women rulers in a row might turn Kesh into a matriarchy. In ancient times, the people of Kesh went through such a period. But the major reason for wanting Awari named heir is he's seen by many as simply being more able. Sojiana is . . . seen as weak by many. Her late husband was a powerful voice in the Gallery of Lords and Masters, their equivalent to our own Congress of Lords. But others fear her as being . . . dangerous. She is able to manipulate Awari and other lords . . . enough so that if Awari is named the next Emperor, she could still cause difficulties in the Gallery.

Does this have anything to do with the attempt . . . the killing of my brother? "Let's see what other marvels this garden offers."

"Yes," said Gamina. "It is so lovely here."

James said, "For a while. I fear we have a terribly busy day tomorrow. It is the official welcome and beginning of the Jubilee. All the rulers of the Empire will be here and gathered together for the first time. We must look our best."

James's thoughts then came to Erland. *It possibly has something to do with the attack in the desert. Awari's faction is very strong in the heart of the Empire, while Sojiana's strength lies primarily upon this plateau. Should war erupt in the north and the usual companies of Dog Soldiers be sent against us, it weakens Awari's presence here. Also, he is the likely choice to oversee the army sent against us. Aber Bukar, Lord of Armies, is getting too old. Lord Jaka would make a logical choice, but the Brothers of the Horse and a few other factions already count the Imperial Charioteers too influen-*

tial, so it's unlikely the Empress would risk an open breach by giving him command. No, the Prince would be the only binding figure they would all follow without question. Also, another lord wishes preeminence in the Gallery.

Who? asked the Prince.

Lord Ravi, Master of the Brothers of the Horse. But he is not trueblood, and while his cavalry units are critical for the success of any move against us the Empire might make, they lack the prestige of the charioteers.

You paint a picture of a court in shambles.

Perhaps, but remember, as long as the Empress rules, all obey her. It is possible that when she does die, chaos, even civil war, may come. But whoever is trying to start a war is obviously not waiting for her death. Parts of this puzzle are still unclear.

Aloud Erland said, "Well, if we are to be fresh tomorrow, we should be getting back." Turning back toward the hallway that led to his apartments, he seemed to lapse into silence. *Most of this puzzle is unclear. Let us hope we can solve it before we come to any conflict.*

There was silent agreement.

Chapter Twelve
Evasion

Borric pointed.

"What in the world is that?" asked Ghuda.

The caravan was traveling the well-used Imperial highway from Faráfra to Kesh, passing through miles of farm land. The journey had proven uneventful, until now.

To the north of the road, three men on horseback were attempting to capture another man on foot, a strange-looking fellow wearing an unadorned knee-length yellow robe. His head was shaved in the fashion of monks, but his garment was unlike any of those worn by any order in the Kingdom Borric had ever seen. And he appeared to be having too much fun for, and making a great deal more noise than any monk Borric had ever observed. For as the horsemen attempted to grab hold of the man's robe, he would dodge away, occasionally ducking under the horse's necks, keeping up a terrific whooping and laughing the entire time.

All this was accomplished despite the fact he carried a wooden staff and a rucksack of some size slung over one shoulder, its cloth broadband across his chest. He ran, laughing and chittering nonsense to torment his would-be captors. The insane caper had Ghuda and Borric laughing. One of the riders turned at the sound and the humor seemed to enrage him more.

The rider pulled a club of exotic fashion and rode at the dancing man, attempting to strike him, but the man ducked under the blow, rolling on the ground, and before the first rider could turn the horse, he was up and dancing again. He turned his backside to all three and wiggled it, making a flatulent noise to show his contempt for the three.

"Who are they?" asked Borric, laughing at the comedy.

Ghuda said, "That cavorting character is an Isalani by his dress. They're a people from Shing Lai, south of the Girdle of Kesh. Strange bunch.

"The others are plainsmen from Ashunta. You can tell by the way they wear their hair and the ceremonial war club that one there is trying to brain the Isalani with." Borric then saw all three men wore their hair in similar fashion, despite a wide variation in dress; one wore buckskin breeches, no shirt, and a leather vest, while another was dressed in leather armor, and the third favored cavalier boots, an ornate shirt, and a hat with a plume. Each man had his hair bound back, tied off with a ring set with a feather and allowed to fall in a long tail, down to mid-back, but with two long ear locks left free.

"What do you think this is about?"

Ghuda shrugged. "With an Isalani, who can tell? They're mystics—seers, shamans, fortune-tellers, and visionaries; they are also the biggest bunch of thieves and swindlers in Kesh. He probably bilked those three."

With a shout of frustration, one of the men drew a sword and swung in earnest at the Isalani. Borric jumped off the wagon, which was moving slowly as the road was gently rising into the foothills of the Spires of Light, and Janos Saber, the caravan master, was keeping his horses to a slow walk to preserve them. Sabér shouted, "Madman, get back to your wagon! Leave this alone."

Borric gave a vague, reassuring wave and hurried toward the odd game of tag, crying out, "What passes here?"

The odd-looking man on foot didn't halt his dodging and ducking for an instant, but one of the horsemen—the one with the plumed hat—turned and shouted, "Stay out of this, stranger."

"I know your temper grows short, *friend,* but using a sword against an unarmed man seems excessive."

The rider ignored him and spurred his horse with a shout, riding directly at the Isalani. Another rider had begun a similar attack, and instantly the Isalani was moving between the two. The first rider veered, and realized too late he had made the wrong decision. As the Isalani danced away, the two horses collided, and as horses will, one decided it was time to bite the other, which resulted in the second horse deciding it was time to kick the first, the net effect of which was the second rider being thrown. Swearing an oath, the first rider waved the third back, lest the accident be repeated. Then he turned to discover the butt of the Isalani's staff in his face and in a moment he, too, was on the ground.

The third rider—the one with the leather vest—didn't hesitate, but came cantering toward the fray, and turned sideways at the last instant. He dodged in his saddle as the Isalani attempted to dislodge him with his staff. The rider avoided being dumped by the Isalani, who stood to his left, but suddenly found strong hands on his tunic, reaching up from the right side. Borric pulled the rider out of his saddle, and half-tossed, half-pushed him to where the other two were regaining their feet.

"That was a mistake," said the first rider, who had a longsword out and ready. And from his expression as he advanced, he meant to have blood.

"Well," said Borric, getting ready for the fight as the other two riders turned their attention to the armed mercenary, "it wouldn't be the first one I've made." Under his breath he said, "Let's hope it's not the last one."

The first warrior raced forward, attempting to overwhelm Borric by surprise. Borric adroitly stepped aside, slicing the man across the back of the thigh—one of the few places unprotected by his leather armor—as he passed, sending him to the ground with a painful and incapacitating wound, but one which would eventually heal.

The second and third riders realized they faced a very skilled opponent. They split up, the man with the plumed hat circling to the right, and the man in the leather vest moving left, forcing Borric to guard two quarters from attack. Borric began talking to himself, a habit Erland had been poking fun at since they were boys. "If they have the brains of a pound of pepper, the lout on my right will feign an attack while the thug on the left comes at me."

Suddenly Borric took the fight to them, pulling his parrying dirk and springing left, moving the off-side attack back. He was instantly around as the man who had been on his right attempted to seize the opportunity presented by an exposed back. But at the moment he sought to strike a blow, Borric spun and took the blow upon his dirk, counterthrusting a second later, delivering a serious stomach wound to the man in the ornate shirt and cavalier boots.

As the man fell away, a gurgling cry of pain on his lips, Borric whirled and found the last remaining rider approaching him cautiously. Borric swore to himself. "Damn. This one knows what he's doing." The Prince had hoped the man in the leather vest would make the same mistake as the other two, and rush him.

The rider approached the Prince warily. What he had seen told him he indeed faced a very skilled warrior. The two men circled one another, not sparing any attention for anything else. Then the Prince saw a pattern of steps. Softly to himself, Borric said, "Step, slide, step, slide, cross over. Come on, you beauty, repeat it. Step, slide, step, slide, cross over." Borric grinned, and when the man again cross stepped, Borric leaped to the attack. The slight turning of the body was the opening Borric needed. He drove the man back with a furious combination of slashing blows and thrusts with the dirk.

Then the rider countered and took the offensive, and Borric found himself being driven back. Cursing the fate that put a longsword in his hand instead of a rapier, he attempted to parry and regroup. Muttering under his breath, he said, "This bastard is good!"

For what couldn't have been more than five minutes, but seemed hours to Borric, the two men evenly traded blows, answered every thrust with a counterthrust, every parry with a riposte. Sweat drenched both men as they struggled under the hot sun. Borric attempted every combination he had learned, only to find his opponent equal to the challenge.

Then there was a lull, as both men stood in the hot afternoon sun gasping for breath, the only sound the buzzing of flies and the rustle of wind in the tall prairie grass. Borric gripped the hilt of his sword tightly, feeling fatigue begin to nip at him. Now the struggle was becoming more dangerous, for beyond issues of skill, both men were weary, and fatigue could cause a fatal mistake. Seeking to end it, Borric leaped forward with a high blow to the head, followed by a snap blow toward the man's legs. But even with the advantage of being able to parry with his dirk and free himself from the need of protecting his left with his sword, he still could not gain enough of an edge to bring the contest to an end.

Back and forth the advantage swung, first to Borric, then the plainsman, but each man successfully took the other's measure. Perspiration ran down the plainsman's bare chest and drenched Borric's shirt, making fingers unsure on hilts. Breath came in ragged pants as the sun continued to be the most merciless opponent of all. Kicked-up dust clogged noses and made throats raw, and still neither man could end the fight. Borric tried every trick he had been taught since boyhood and came close several times to wounding his opponent. But close was all he got. And he narrowly avoided being wounded on as many occasions. Then Borric realized with a chilling clarity that at last he had overstepped himself; he faced as good a swordsman as he had ever seen, one perhaps with less native ability than the Prince, but one with a great deal more experience.

For a moment, they paused, each man facing the other, both crouched, panting for breath as exhausted bodies trembled with fatigue and tension. Both men knew the first to make a mistake would now be the one to die. Borric drew in gasping breaths of air, trying to find one last reserve of energy. He stared at his opponent, knowing the man did the same. Neither man wasted breath on conversation, as each waited for the moment when enough strength would return to press the attack again. Then, with a loud intake of breath, the plainsman rocked forward on his feet, gave out a cry of anger, and forced himself to a running charge. Borric sidestepped and brought his sword and dirk up, to block the cut, then he drove his knee into the man's stomach. As the plainsman's breath erupted from him, Borric pushed him away with a boot to his side, disengaging his sword. The plainsman fell over backward, hitting the ground with another explosion of breath. Springing after, Borric brought his sword down on the dirt, as his opponent rolled away. Then he felt something behind his heel and his balance was lost.

Borric had gotten too close, and the man had hooked his heel with his foot. Now Borric was on the ground and rolling, seeking to get clear and regain his feet. Spinning around, Borric came to his knees, only to find the point of a sword coming at his face. Then another sword interposed itself, and the first blade was knocked away.

Borric looked up into the bright glare of the sky and saw Ghuda standing with his hand-and-a-half sword interposed between the two combatants. "If you two boys are finished . . . ?" he said.

The horseman looked up and the fight seemed to drain away from him. It was obvious that a fresh opponent stood ready to act if he continued being combative, and from Ghuda's appearance and the size of the sword he carried, one willing and able to cause much damage. Borric relented by simply holding up his hand and waving it weakly. The rider backed away a few steps, then simply shook his head. "Enough," he croaked, through a dust-caked throat.

Suli peeked out from behind the large warrior and came to give Borric a drink from a waterskin.

To the rider, Ghuda said, "Your two friends are in need of help. One of them is in some serious danger of bleeding to death. It would probably be to his benefit if you got him to a chirurgeon.

"And you," he said, turning to Borric, "had better look down the road to see where you're supposed to be instead of larking about with these silly children."

Borric watched the other swordsman turn his attentions to his friends. The man with the leg wound he helped to his feet, and they both examined the man who was wounded in the stomach.

"Where's that capering lunatic?" asked Borric, taking another drink of water.

"I don't know," said Ghuda quizzically. "I lost track of him when I stepped in between you two prodigies."

"Well, he couldn't have vanished, could he?" said Borric.

"Gods' truth, Madman, I don't know. Nor do I care. Janos Sabér was less than amused to see you go scampering off like that. What if this lot had been a diversion for an ambush on the other side of that hill? Could have been a nasty turn, and that's a fact."

Putting away his large sword, Ghuda motioned for the younger swordsman to give him his hand, and as he helped Borric up, one of his big gloved fists struck Borric in the side of the head, driving him back to the ground.

Shaking his ringing head, Borric said, "What was that for?"

Ghuda shook his fist at Borric, "For being a stupid son of misery! Damn it, boy, it's so you'll learn to act like a responsible guard and *do your job!* It *could* have been an ambush, couldn't it?"

Borric nodded, and said, "Yes, I suppose it could."

Borric got to his feet unaided and Ghuda motioned for the Prince and the boy to come along. As they stepped onto the road, Borric said, "I just wish people would stop thinking the best way to teach is to beat the lesson into me."

Ghuda ignored the remark and said, "You spent too much time with the rapier, Madman."

"Huh?" said the exhausted Prince. "What do you mean?"

"You kept trying to skewer that fool, and with the longsword that's a bit of a task. No damn point, and unless you grab the forté with your off hand and really drive the thing, all you'll do with the point against an armored opponent is irritate him. You missed a half-dozen chances to hand that bloke his head, if you ask me. If you're going to live a long life, you'd better learn to use a sword with an edge on it, as well as one of those Krondorian pig-stickers."

Borric smiled. The rapier had never been a popular weapon until his father, as fine a swordsman as ever held a sword, had become

Prince. Then it had become fashionable, but obviously not south of the Vale of Dreams. "Thanks. I'll practice with it."

"Just don't pick an opponent who's quite so determined to kill you next time." Looking down the road at the dust of Janos Sabér's wagons, he added, "Now that they're heading downhill, it'll be half the day catching up. Let's get a shake on."

"Oh, let's not," answered Borric, expended from the exertion in the heat. He had gradually been getting used to the savage Keshian midday sun, but he was still not as adept at moving about as those born to it. He drank lots of water and fruit juice, as did Ghuda and Suli, but still found himself weakening quickly in the heat. He wondered how much was due to his brush with death in the Jal-Pur Desert.

Cresting the hill, they saw the caravan of Janos Sabér moving sedately down the road. And sitting on the end of the last wagon was the Isalani, feet dangling off the tailgate, as he ate a big, bright orange. Ghuda pointed and Borric shook his head. "He's the clever one, isn't he?"

Ghuda started trotting down the road, and Borric forced himself to do likewise, though his arms and legs felt like damp cotton. After a few minutes, they overtook the last wagon and Borric managed to pull himself up on the tailgate, while Ghuda climbed up next to the driver, and Suli scampered ahead to the cook wagon.

Borric let out a long sigh, then took a good look at the man he had rescued from the three plainsmen. The Isalani was nothing to look at: a bandy-legged, short fellow, with the features of a vulture. His head was a thing of squat asymmetry, almost square, and perched oddly atop a gangly neck, giving him a comic appearance. A fuzz of hair sprouted around the base of his head and over his ears, showing he needed only aid nature a little in his depilatory duty. His eyes were narrow slits as he grinned at Borric, and his skin was a golden hue, a color Borric had only seen a few times on some citizens of LaMūt who were of Tsurani heritage. With a merry note in his gravely voice, the Isalani said, "Want an orange?"

Borric nodded and the strange-looking man took one out of the rucksack he had been so fiercely hanging on to during the encounter with the three riders. Borric peeled back the orange and pulled out a wedge and sucked the sweet juice from it, while the odd man handed another one up to Ghuda. The old caravan guard asked, "What was all that about back there?"

The man shrugged, his grin staying in place. "They think I cheated them at cards. They were very angry."

"Did you?" asked Borric.

"Perhaps, but it was of little matter. They were cheating me."

Borric nodded as if this all somehow made sense. "I'm called Madman."

The grin broadened. "So am I at times. At other times I am called Nakor the Blue Rider."

Ghuda said, "The Blue Rider?"

An emphatic nod yes was followed by, "At times I have been known to ride about on a fine black steed of most impressive conformation, dressed in robes of the finest weave died vivid blue. I am very famous in some places."

"But this is not one of those places," said Ghuda.

"Alas, no. Here I am relatively unknown. However, at those times when I have my blue finery and my fine steed, then I quickly gain fame wherever I pass, for there are few who rival my beauty."

Borric regarded the faded orange robe and said, "I take it this is not one of those times."

"Again I must say alas, for this also is so. My horse died, which made riding him most difficult, and the robe was lost to a man who cheated at cards better than I."

Borric laughed at the last. "Well, at least you're more forthright a cheat than those I usually encounter."

Nakor shared the laugh. "I only cheat those who attempt to cheat me. I deal honestly with those who are honest with me. The difficulty, usually, is in finding honest men."

Borric nodded, amused by this strange little man. "And how many honest men have you dealt with lately."

Nakor shrugged, an exaggerated moving of the shoulders with a slight bobbing of his head. "None, so far. But I still have high hopes one day of meeting such a one."

Borric shook his head and laughed, as much at himself for going to the trouble of saving this lunatic as he was at the lunatic.

When night approached, the wagons were circled around the campfire, a tradition as old as caravans. Janos Sabér had let Borric know in no uncertain terms what he thought of any guard that would go looking for troubles that didn't concern him, and questioned Ghuda as to his lack of brains in going after him. The boy he forgave, insofar as he was still a boy and boys were expected to do witless things.

For some reason, he didn't seem to be in the least bit troubled by the Isalani's having joined his caravan unasked. Borric was reasonably certain the strange little man had somehow bemused the usually stern caravan master, but that suggested the little man had some magic power or another. Unless he was a confidence trickster of sufficient guile to run his confidence game while on the back of a moving wagon five vehicles behind the one upon which his victim rode. Borric thought that even his uncle Jimmy wouldn't claim being that good.

At thought of James, he was once again visited with the frustration of his situation. How to safely reach the palace of the Empress and get word to James he was still alive? The facts learned at the Governor of Durbin's house showed that important men, placed very highly in the Imperial house, were involved with this plot on his life. And the closer he got to the palace, he was certain, the more difficult it would be to reach.

Settling back near the fire, Borric considered that he would dwell on it as they traveled. There was still a great deal of road between where he was now and the gates of the palace. In the warmth of the evening, after a hot meal, he dozed until Ghuda came and kicked him to alertness. "Your duty, Madman."

Borric rose and assumed his post with another two guards, each spaced a third of the way around the perimeter, with the muttering and oaths appropriate to such men in similar situations throughout history.

"Jeeloge!" called Ghuda.

Borric levered himself up on his arm, peering between Ghuda and the teamster who drove the wagon, and looked to where the older guard pointed. As the extra guard at this end of the caravan, he could get away with laying atop bales of silk imported from the Free Cities, dozing in the afternoon sun. A town appeared upon the horizon as they crested a hill. It looked to be of good size. In the Kingdom, it might even count as a small city, but Borric had long since discovered that in relation to Kesh, the Kingdom was sparsely populated. The Prince returned to his doze. They would lay over for the night in Jeeloge before continuing on to Kesh, and most of the caravan's drivers and guards planned on a night of celebration and gambling.

A day earlier they had rounded the northern edge of The Guardians: the mountains bordering the Overn Deep on the west. They now followed the River Sarné toward the city of Kesh. Little towns and farming communities dotted the landscape. Borric could understand now why caravan duty in the interior of Kesh was considered a low-risk profession. Things tended toward the quiet this close to the capital of the Empire.

"I wonder what that's all about?" mused Ghuda.

Borric looked up and saw a company of mounted men had set up an inspection point near the edge of the town. Moving to the far right so he could speak in Ghuda's ear without the driver overhearing, Borric whispered, "They may be looking for me."

Turning toward the younger guard, Ghuda's eyes almost blazed in anger as he said, "Isn't that interesting? Do you have any other wonderful news I should know about before I'm hauled into an Imperial court?" His angry tone cut through his whisper. "What did you do?"

"They say I killed the wife of the Governor of Durbin," whispered Borric.

Ghuda's only reaction was to close his eyes a minute and press forefinger and thumb to the bridge of his nose. "Why me? What have I done to displease the gods so?" Looking Borric directly in the eyes, he said, "Did you do it, Madman?"

"No, of course not."

Ghuda's narrow eyes searched Borric's for a long moment, then he said, "Of course you didn't." With a big sigh, he said, "We could take a band of ragged bandits, if bump came to push, but if push came to shove, those Imperials would have us trussed up like a game bird for the table in less time than it takes to tell about it. Tell you what: if you're asked, you're my cousin from Odoskoni."

"Where is Odoskoni?" asked Borric as the wagons drew near the horsemen.

"A little town in the Peaks of Tranquillity, nearest city is Kampari. You have to go through a hundred miles of the Green Reaches to get there, so few do. Very little chance of any of these boys having been within a year's march of the place."

The first wagon slowed, then stopped, and by the time the others followed suit, Borric, along with Ghuda and the other guards, were off their respective wagons and coming to stand behind their master, which was expected in case these guardsmen were false. But from the manner their officer approached Janos Sabér, it was obvious it was really an Imperial troop; this officer *expected* to be obeyed, instantly. Each man in the company wore a splendid tunic of red silk, a metal helm with a fur band around the base—this company's being leopard skin. Each held a lance and had a sword at his side and a bow slung behind the saddle. Borric agreed with Ghuda's assessment. The men of the company had the look of seasoned veterans. Whispering in Ghuda's ear, Borric said, "Doesn't Kesh have any green troops?"

Ghuda whispered back. "Many, Madman. The cemeteries are full of them."

The officer spoke to Sabér. "We're looking for a pair of runaway slaves, from Durbin. A young man, perhaps twenty years of age and a boy of eleven or twelve."

Janos said, "Sir, my men are all caravan guards and drivers, either known to me or vouched for by those known to me, and the one boy we have is our cook's monkey."

The officer nodded, as if anything the caravan master had to say was of little consequence. Ghuda stroked his chin, as if thinking, but hiding his face as he whispered to Borric. "Interesting, they're searching wagons here. Why would a slave escaping from Durbin run *into* the heart of the Empire, instead of out of it?"

If Janos connected Borric and Suli to the pair the guards looked for, he said nothing. A guard came to where Ghuda and Borric stood. The guard looked Ghuda over quickly, but lingered to inspect Borric. "Where are you from?" he asked Borric. He asked as if one who felt the need to go through the motions, for not knowing the truth he would assume he was looking for a runaway slave. For a slave to be standing before him calmly, armed and armored, was very improbable to the guard, but duty required he ask.

Borric said, "Here and there. I was born in Odoskoni."

Something in Borric's speech or the way he carried himself sparked an interest in the guard. "You speak with an odd inflection."

Borric didn't miss a beat when he answered, "You sound foreign to me, soldier. My people all talk like I do."

"You have green eyes."

Suddenly the guard snatched the headgear from Borric's head, revealing his black-dyed hair. "Hey!" complained Borric at the treatment. Borric and Suli had used the last of the dye a few days before, and he hoped his red roots weren't long enough to give him away.

"Captain!" shouted the soldier. "This one matches the description."

Then Borric thought that while those who were trying to kill him knew he had red hair, the description of the runaway slave would be altered to fit the description given by the sailors who had pursued him from the harbor. What a fool I've been, he thought. I should have found another dye.

The Captain slowly came to inspect Borric and said, "Your name?"

Borric said, "Everyone calls me the Madman."

One eyebrow lifted as the Captain said, "Odd. Why?"

"Not many leave my village and before I left I was known for doing—"

"Stupid things," finished Ghuda. "He's my cousin."

"You have green eyes," said the Captain.

"So does his mother," answered Ghuda.

The Captain turned to face Ghuda. "Do you always answer for him?"

"As often as I can, sir. Like I said, he does stupid things. The people of Odoskoni don't call him Madman out of affection." He pantomimed a man with little wits, crossing his eyes and sticking his tongue out of the side of his mouth.

Another guard approached, pulling Suli along by the arm. "What have we here?" said the Captain.

"That's the cook's monkey," answered Janos.

"What's your name, boy?" asked the Captain.

Ghuda said, "Suli of Odoskoni."

The Captain turned. "Quiet!"

Borric said, "He's my brother."

The Captain struck out, the back of his gloved hand smashing into Borric's face. Tears came to Borric's eyes, but he held himself in check, despite a sudden urge to skewer the Captain of the Imperial Keshian Guards.

The Captain grabbed Suli by the chin and inspected him. "You have dark eyes."

Suli stammered, "My . . . mother had dark eyes."

The Captain looked hard at Ghuda. "I thought you said his mother had green eyes."

Without missing a beat, Ghuda retorted, "No, *his* mother had green eyes," he said, pointing at Borric. Pointing at Suli he said, "His mother had dark eyes. Different mothers; same father."

Another guard approached and said, "No one else matches the description, sir."

The soldier holding Suli demanded, "Who is your father?" Suli glanced at Borric but the soldier said, "Answer me!"

"Suli of Odoskoni," the boy squeaked. "I was named for him."

The Captain struck the soldier. "Idiot." He pointed at Borric. "The other one could hear the name."

Borric said, "Captain, take the boy away and ask him the name of our other brother."

The Captain motioned for it to be done, while Borric whispered to Ghuda, "He's going to hold us."

"Then why this nonsense?" asked Ghuda in hushed tones.

"Because the minute he's certain he has the right pair, we're dead before another minute follows."

"Kill on sight?" hissed Ghuda.

Borric nodded yes, while the Captain came to stand before them. "Now, who is this mythical brother of your two liars?"

"We have a brother Rasta, who is a drunkard," answered Borric, silently praying the boy remembered the impromptu dialogue he had engaged in just before they encountered Salaya in Durbin.

A moment later the soldier returned and said, "The boy says they have an older brother named Rasta who is a drunkard."

Borric could have kissed the boy but held his smile in check. The Captain said, "There is something about you two I don't like." He glanced over to where Janos Sabér waited. "You and the rest of your men can go, but I'm taking these two into custody." He then looked at Ghuda and said, "Bring this one along, too."

Ghuda said, "Wonderful," as guards disarmed him and bound his wrists. Borric and Suli were likewise bound, after all weapons were taken from them, and soon the three captives were being led along on lead ropes, trotting after the horses as best they could.

The town of Jeeloge had a constable's office, which in turn had a poor excuse for a cell, used mostly to hold troublesome farmers and herdsmen when arrested for brawling. Now it was the Imperial Captain and his company who used it, to the acute discomfort of the local constable. A retired soldier, with grey in his beard and a belly that hung over his belt, he was just the sort to keep rowdy farm boys in line, but unlikely to be up to any serious fighting. He had quickly agreed to the Captain's demand that he absent himself from the premises.

Borric had overheard him instructing his sergeant to send a post dispatch rider as quickly as possible to the city of Kesh, a request asking what to do with the three prisoners. Borric only made out part of the conversation, but it was obvious the orders came from one high up in the army, and certain precautions were being taken to prevent any undue attention being turned to this massive search. One thing about Kesh, Borric thought, it was a nation of so many people doing so many things, that this sort of operation could continue for a long while with perhaps only one citizen in a hundred even hearing about it. The day had gone and now the night was dragging out. An hour earlier, Suli had fallen asleep, any hope for an evening meal vanished with the constable. The Imperial Guard seemed to have little concern over something as trivial as the prisoners' hunger.

"Hello!" came the cheery voice from the window. Suli awoke with a jump.

They all looked up and saw a grinning face at the small window above in the cell they were occupying. "Nakor!" Borric whispered.

Motioning Ghuda to give him a leg up, Borric pulled himself up by the bars of the window, standing upon Ghuda's shoulders. "What are you doing here?"

"I thought you might want another orange," said the grinning little man. "Jail food is never very good."

Borric could only nod dumbly as the little man handed an orange through the bars. Borric tossed it to Suli who hungrily took a bite and spit the peel out. "We'll have to take your word for that," said the Prince. "They haven't bothered to feed us."

Then suddenly Borric said, "How did you get up here?" The window was a good eight feet up in the wall, and the little man didn't seem to be hanging by the bars.

"Never mind that. Do you want to get out?"

Ghuda, who was beginning to wobble a bit under Borric's weight, said, "There's one of the all-time stupid questions asked by mortal man in the last thousand years. Of course we want out!"

Grinning widely, the Isalani said, "Then stand over in that corner and cover your eyes."

Borric jumped down from Ghuda's shoulders. Moving to the corner, they covered their eyes. There was a silent moment when nothing happened, then suddenly a shock hit Borric, as if a large hand slammed him against the wall and a loud boom deafened him. He winced at it, then opened his eyes. The wall was now breached. The constable's jail was full of fine dust and the reek of sulphur. Several guards stood holding on to whatever gave them support, while others lay upon the floor, obviously blinded by whatever had opened the wall.

Nakor stood next to four horses, all with saddles bearing the Imperial Army's crest. "They won't need these, I'm certain," he said, handing over the reins to Borric.

Suli stood fearfully, saying, "Master, I don't know how to ride."

Ghuda picked the boy and lifted him up into the saddle of the nearest animal. "Then you'd better learn quickly. If you start to fall, just grab the horse's mane and don't!"

Borric was in the saddle and said, "They'll be after us in a moment. Let's—"

"No," said Nakor. "I cut all their saddle girths and bridles." Seemingly from nowhere he produced a wicked-looking knife, as if to illustrate the point. "But it still might be wise to move along, lest those alerted by the sound come investigate."

To that no one had any argument, and they rode out, Suli barely able to hang on for his life. A little way down the road, Borric dismounted and fixed Suli's stirrup leathers for him. Suli's horse, sensing an inexperienced rider, was full of nasty tricks, so Borric could only hope the boy would survive any falls that were certain to come as they hurried away.

As they left the now-awake town of Jeeloge, Borric said to Nakor, "What was that?"

"Oh, a little magic trick I learned along the way," said the grinning man.

Ghuda made a sign of protection, and said, "Are you a magician?"

Nakor laughed. "Of course. Don't you know that all Isalanis are capable of magic feats!"

Borric said, "Is that how you were able to get to the window? You floated up using magic?"

Nakor's laughter increased. "No, Madman. I stood on the back of the horse!"

Feeling relief and exhilaration at this escape, Borric put heels to his horse, and the animal broke into a canter. A moment later, the others could be heard behind him, until a yell and unpleasant thud told them Suli had been tossed.

Turning around to see if the boy was seriously hurt, Borric said, "This may be the slowest escape in history."

Chapter Thirteen
Jubilee

Erland stood silently.

No matter how hard he tried, he just couldn't accept the scope of what he saw: the site of the first day's ceremonies for the Empress's Seventy-Fifth Jubilee. For centuries Kesh's finest engineers had refurbished, expanded, added to it, until it stood out as the single most impressive feat of construction Erland had witnessed. It was a gigantic amphitheater carved into the side of the plateau upon which the upper city—the Imperial palace—rested, built by the skill of artisans, the sweat of builders, and the blood of slaves, vast enough to comfortably seat fifty thousand people, more than the populations of Rillanon and Krondor combined.

Erland motioned his companions to walk with him, for it was still almost an hour before his own part in the formal drama of court was to commence. Kafi Abu Harez, his ever-present guide, was at his elbow, to answer questions.

Finally Erland said, "Kafi, how long did it take to build this?"

"Centuries, Highness," answered the desertman. He pointed to a place in the distance, near the base of the gigantic wedge that had been cut from the plateau. "There, near the edge of the lower city, in ages past, an Emperor of Kesh, Sujinrani Kanafi—called the Benevolent—decided that the prohibition against those who were not of true blood remaining upon the plateau at night prevented his citizens from observing some necessary Imperial functions, most notably those ceremonies to affirm Sujinrani's benevolence, as well as public executions of traitors. He felt the object lesson was lost on many who would benefit from observing it firsthand.

"So he decreed that all that was of this plateau, including the lowest part of it, was, in effect, part of the upper city. He then had a small amphitheater created down there, about a dozen feet higher than it is today." With a small sweep of his hand, Kafi illustrated his next remark. "A wedge of rock was then carved out, so that a court could be held in view of those not permitted to ascend to the upper city."

"And it's been enlarged several times since," said Locklear.

"Yes," said Kafi. "The entrance alone has been enlarged on five occasions. The Imperial box has been repositioned three times." He pointed to the large area overhung by a giant canopy of fine silk, at the middle point of the large stone crescent upon which Erland and his party walked. Kafi halted the Prince with a gentle touch to the arm and pointed to the Empress's private viewing area. "There She Who Is Kesh, blessings be ever upon her, will oversee the festival. Her throne of gold sits upon a small dais, around which her family and servants, and those of royal blood will rest in comfort. Only those of the highest nobility within the Empire are permitted in that area. To enter without Imperial writ is to die, for Her Majesty's Izmali guards will stand at every entrance."

Pointing out a row of boxes, each slightly lower than the one preceding as they moved away from the Imperial box, he said, "Those closest to Her Majesty are the highest born in the Empire, those who make up the Gallery of Lords and Masters." He indicated the entire level they walked upon.

Erland said, "Five, six thousand people could stand upon this level alone, Kafi."

The desertman nodded. "Perhaps more. This level reaches down and embraces the floor below, like arms surrounding a body. At the distant end we will be a full hundred feet below the Empress's throne. Come, let me show you more."

The desertman, wearing robes of the darkest blue and starkest white for the formal ceremonies, led them to a railing looking down upon another level. As they walked, nobles who would proceed Erland's party in being presented to the Empress hurried past, a very few taking a moment to offer the Prince of the Kingdom of the Isles a slight bow. Erland noted the half-dozen tunnels that opened onto the broad walkway behind the boxes. "All of these can't originate in the palace alone, can they?"

Kafi nodded. "Ah, but they do."

Erland said, "I would think the safety of the Empress would supercede the convenience of those nobles needing to come down here once or twice a year. Those tunnels are an invitation to any invader seeking to enter the palace."

Kafi shrugged. "It is academic, my young friend. For you must understand, that for an invader to threaten the tunnels, they must hold to the lower city, and should any invader hold the lower city, the Empire is *already* lost. For if they hold the lower city, the might of Kesh is already dust. This is the heart of the Empire, and a hundred thousand Keshian soldiers would lie dead before an invader came within sight of the city. Do you see?"

Erland considered this, then nodded. "I guess you're right. Being a nation born upon an island, in a sea sailed by a dozen other nations . . . we look at things differently."

"I understand," said Kafi. He pointed to the area between the down-sweeping boxes and the floor of the amphitheater. The stone had been cut in descending, concentric crescents, so that a grandstand had been chiseled from the rock of the plateau. A dozen stairways from the floor upward to the level just below the boxes were already filled to capacity with colorfully dressed citizens. "There is where the lesser nobles, masters of guilds, and influential merchants of the city will sit, upon cushions or the bare stone, all around. The center is kept clear for those being presented to the Empress."

Kafi said, "You and your party will enter there, Highness, after the nobles of Kesh and before the commoners, as Ambassadors of all nations will. The Empress has favored you by placing your delegation before all others, an admission that the Kingdom of the Isles stands second only to the Empire of Great Kesh in majesty upon Midkemia."

Erland cast James a wry look at the offhanded complement, but only said, "We thank Her Majesty for the courtesy."

If Kafi shared the sarcasm, he kept that fact well hidden. Moving on as if nothing impolitic had been said, he continued, "The common people of Kesh are permitted to view the festivities from across the entrance, atop roofs, and many other vantage points."

Erland looked out over the lower city, where thousands of commoners were held back by a line of soldiers. Beyond the street that crossed before the amphitheater people crowded upon the rooftops of buildings and into every window providing a vantage point. Erland found the sheer number of people in one place breathtaking.

Gamina, who had been silently walking beside her husband, said, "I doubt they can see much."

Kafi shook his head. "Perhaps, but then, before the rule of Sujinrani Kanafi, they saw nothing of court ceremony."

"My lord Abu Harez," said Locklear, "before we continue, could you and I discuss the speech my Prince has prepared for this day, so that we might not inadvertently give offense?"

Kafi saw the transparent request for his absence, but given there was no reason not to agree, he let Locklear lead him away, leaving James, Gamina, and Erland relatively alone. Several Keshian servants hovered nearby, taking care of the many details of preparation. A few of them were agents of the Imperial Court, no doubt, thought Erland as he regarded James. "What?"

James turned and leaned upon the marble railing of the gallery, as if looking out over the vast amphitheater. "Gamina?" he said softly.

Gamina closed her eyes, then her voice came into Erland's head. *We are being watched.*

Erland had to force himself not to look around. *We expected that,* he replied.

No, by magic arts.

Erland forced himself not to swear. *Can they hear us speaking this way?*

I don't know, she replied. *My father could, but there are few with his power. I don't think so.*

James's voice said, "Spectacular, isn't it?" while his mental message was, *I'm going to assume they can't or you'd sense it. And I don't think we're going to be under any less scrutiny any time soon, so we might as well hope that we're right.*

Yes, agreed Gamina. *I wasn't aware of the magic until I went looking for it. It's very subtle. And good. I think whoever is using it can hear what we say, perhaps even see how we act. But if they could hear our thoughts, I think I would know.*

Gamina closed her eyes a moment, as if dizzy from the heat. James steadied her for a moment. *I don't think it's a mind, or I would have sensed purpose behind it.*

What do you mean? asked Erland.

I think we are under the focus of a device. Perhaps a crystal or mirror. My father has used several in his studies over the year. If that is so, then we can be seen for certain, and either our lip movement is being read by one so trained or we are being heard aloud. Our thoughts are safe, I'm certain.

Good, said James. *I've finally gotten word from our agents down here. It was a demon's own time getting word to me.*

"I wonder how long we'll be expected to stand during this cere-mony?" said Gamina absently.

"Hours, no doubt," commented James. To Erland he said, *We've walked into a stew and it's rapidly coming to a boil. There's a plot to overthrow the Empress's rule, that's our agents best guess.*

Feigning a yawn of boredom, the Prince said, "I hope I can be alert throughout." Mentally, he said, *What does that have to do with plung-ing Kesh and the Kingdom into war?*

If we knew that, we'd have a better idea who's trying to start this revolt. I have a bad feeling about this, Erland.

Why?

Besides the obvious dangers, there are going to be a lot of soldiers in this city this afternoon. Each subject ruler will be bringing companies of honor guards. There will be thousands of soldiers not under the Empress's direct command within the walls of Kesh for the next two months.

Charming, was Erland's response. "Well, perhaps we should rest before this ordeal begins."

James said, "Yes, that would be best, I think."

Gamina spoke in both men's minds, *What should we do, James?*

Wait. That's all we can do, was his reply. *And remain alert.*

Kafi returns, observed Gamina.

The desertman said, "Highness, your remarks will be doubly appre-ciated for their sincerity and brevity. After the ceremonies of this day, I fear you shall see that economy of speech is not an Imperial trait."

Erland was about to answer, when Kafi said, "Look! It begins."

A tall man, old but still muscular, entered the Imperial box, and came to the very edge. He was dressed as all trueblood, in kilt and sandals, but he also wore a solid gold torque, which Erland estimated had to weigh as much as a suit of leather armor. He carried what looked to be a wooden staff covered in gold leaf, with an odd-looking golden design at the top. A falcon perched upon a golden disc.

Kafi whispered, though it seemed impossible to Erland anyone would overhear them, "The Falcon of Kesh, the royal insignia. It is only seen publicly at the highest festivals. The falcon gripping the sun's orb is holy to the trueblood."

The old man lifted the staff and brought it down upon the stones, and Erland was astonished at how loud the sound was. Then he spoke. "O Kesh, Greatest of Nations, harken to me!"

The acoustics were perfect in the amphitheater. Even those across the boulevard, sitting atop the buildings, could hear the man perfectly as the sounds of the crowd died away to a hush.

"She is come! She is come! She Who Is Kesh has come, and she graces your lives by her presence!" At this a procession of hundreds of the trueblood began slowly entering the Imperial box. "She walks and the stars yield to her splendor, for she is the heart of glory! She speaks and the birds cease their singing, for her words are knowledge! She considers and scholars weep, for her wisdom is certain. She judges and the guilty despair, for her gazes see into the hearts of men!" The enumerations of the Empress's wondrous attributes continued in similar vein as more and more truebloods, of all ages and ranks, entered the Imperial box.

Erland thought he had met a great many of those who were important to the Empire, but just the Imperial party alone numbered dozens of strangers. And the only one he had spoken to on more than one occasion was Lord Nirome, the stout and inadvertently comic noble who had greeted them at the boundary of the upper city as aide-de-camp to Prince Awari. Erland was surprised to discover Nirome was related to the royal family. Then, upon reflection, it seemed a reasonable explanation for why a man so obviously maladroit would have a high post in the government. The men and women of the royal blood continued to enter the box and take their places as the Master of Ceremonies continued to intone the Empress's virtues. *Impressive,* Erland thought, trying to establish contact with Gamina.

James's wife lightly touched him on the arm, as she answered, *Yes. James thinks so, as well.*

"Kafi," said Erland.

"Your Highness?"

"Would it be permitted for us to remain here a while?"

"As long as you make a timely entrance, there is no reason why not, Highness."

"Good," said Erland, smiling for the desertman's benefit. "Would you answer a few questions?"

"If I am able," he answered.

And if you could chime in with what you know, James, he added.

Gamina relayed the message, for James nodded slightly.

"How is it there are so many in the Imperial box, yet I have not seen any of the great lords and masters yet?"

Kafi said, "Only those related to the Empress by blood may join her in the Imperial box, servants and guards notwithstanding, of course."

"Of course," replied Erland.

Which means that there are at least a hundred people with a recognized, legitimate claim to the throne, added James.

Providing enough people die in the proper order, Erland added drily.

There is that, answered James.

When the relatives had entered, the first discordant note intruded: suddenly black-clad warriors appeared. Each wore turbans of black, with face coverings that left only the eyes exposed. Long flowing robes were designed for easy, quick movement, and each had a black scabbard scimitar at his belt. Erland had heard tell of these: Izmalis, the nearly legendary Shadow Warriors of Kesh. Tales had grown in the telling until they were regarded as almost supernatural. Only those most highly placed in the Empire could afford such as body-guards. They were counted superior warriors, as well as spies of superior ability—and assassins if needs be, it was whispered.

James attempted to sound casual as he said, "My lord Kafi, wouldn't it be usual for the Empress to be surrounded by her own Imperial Guards?"

The desertman's eyes narrowed slightly, but without any change in inflection he said, "It is considered more prudent to use Izmalis. They are without peer."

Which means, thought James to Erland through Gamina, *the Empress can no longer trust even her own Imperial Guards.*

When the Izmalis were in place, a dozen husky slaves, bodies oiled, entered carrying a litter, upon which sat the Empress. Throughout the entrance of the Imperial party, the old man with the golden staff had been intoning a long ritual introduction, citing great feats accomplished under Lakeisha, the Empress. Suddenly Erland caught a shift in tension and began listening to the introduction.

". . . crushed the rebellion of Lesser Kesh," intoned the old man. Erland remembered from his study of Keshian history that about the time of his birth all of the nations south of the two mountain ranges that transverse the continent—the Girdle of Kesh—had been brought to heel after twenty years of successful revolt. The self-pro-claimed Keshian Confederacy had been made to pay dearly for their rebellion. Thousands had been put to death and from the few reports that had made their way to the Kingdom, the devastation had been unequaled by anything in Kingdom history—entire cities were put to the torch and their populations sold into slavery. Entire peoples, races, languages, and cultures had ceased to exist, except among the slaves. And from the angry muttering that could be heard from the crowd—not just the commoners in the street, but from many of the lesser nobles in the amphitheater below—bad blood still existed between those subject peoples and their ruler.

Gamina went pale, and Kafi noticed. "Is my lady feeling ill?"

Gamina gripped James's arm and stood on wobbly legs a moment. She shook her head, and said, "The heat, my lord. If I could please have some water."

Kafi merely motioned and instantly a servant was at their side. Kafi instructed him, and a moment later the servant offered a cool cup of water to Gamina. She sipped it, while speaking silently to James, Locklear, and Erland. *I was caught unprepared for that. The sudden flow of anger and hatred. Many of those here would happily murder the Empress. And many, many of the angry minds are in the Imperial box.*

James made comforting sounds as he patted his wife on the arm, and Locklear said, "If you think it would be too much for you to stand here for the rest of the day, Gamina . . ."

"No, Locky. I'm fine. I just need to drink a bit more water, I think."

Kafi said, "That is wise."

Erland returned his attention to the next group to enter. The Prince and both Princesses of Kesh had entered after their mother, and now the most powerful lords and masters in the Empire were being announced.

Lord Jaka, Commander of the Imperial Charioteers, entered. "How important are the charioteers, Kafi?" asked Erland.

"I'm not certain I understand, Highness."

"I mean, is their position only tradition, or do they really stand as the heart of the army? On those occasions in the past where our two nations have . . . had differences, we've always faced your dreaded Dog Soldiers."

Kafi shrugged. "The Charioteers were the vanguard of those who crushed the Confederacy, Highness. But your borders lie far to the north and the Charioteers would be dispatched that far from the capital upon only the greatest need."

Jaka's the man who can make or break any attempt to overthrow the Empress, offered James.

Erland nodded, as if considering Kafi's words. To Gamina, Locklear, and James he thought, *He seems pretty solid, from outward appearances.*

202

He's an important man, Erland, answered James. *No coups d'etat would succeed without him either participating or neutralized.*

Kafi touched Erland upon the arm. "Speaking of the Dog Soldiers, here is their master. Sula Jafi Butar, Prince Regent of the Armies, and hereditary ruler of Kistan, Isan, Paji, and the other states where our armies are recruited."

The man who entered was fairly nondescript, save that he looked a black-skinned version of the trueblood. His dress was identical, white kilt, sandals, and shaved head, but his skin shown like ebony in the sun. Most of his followers were equally dark, though a few could pass as trueblood to Erland's inexperienced eye.

Erland looked at James, who answered, *He's an unknown player, Erland. He seems openly loyal. His peoples were the first to be conquered by their neighbors, so they are among the oldest lines in the nation, second only to the trueblood. Aber Bukar, Lord of the Armies, is the true commander, but this man has a lot of influence with the army.*

Kafi said, "Perhaps we should begin moving downward, Prince Erland. That way we shall not have any risk of a breach of courtesy."

Erland said, "Please. Lead on."

A group of guards fell in around Erland and his companions, and the Prince was momentarily startled. He did not notice them approaching in the crowd. They made no cry nor did they need to. People on the ramp behind the boxes seemed to sense their approach instinctively and give way. James observed, "At this social strata, people seem to be alert to the possible approach of someone of greater rank."

Kafi gave a shrug with a gesture of his hands down and outward, and said *"Ma'lish,"* which Erland knew was Beni—Kafi's native language—for, "I'm sorry," but actually meant, "Disasters happen." It was what the Beni-speaking people called kismet or fate, the will of the gods.

The name Lord Ravi intruded upon Erland's awareness and he glanced back to see another colorful group of men entering. Each man in front had a shaved head, save for a scalplock down the center, combed high and kept erect by a pomade or wax. A fall of horsehair was died to match the wearer's natural color and tied by a leather thong woven into the scalplock. The men wore only a loincloth and their bodies were oiled to a gloss. Their skin was sunburned, but seemed lighter than most Keshians, with a reddish cast. Most of the men were dark haired. Then behind came younger men, who wore their hair long, tied behind in imitation of the horsehair fall, but with ringlets loose at the ears. These wore brightly colored leather armor, with wide flaring at the top, giving them an exaggerated breadth of shoulders. They also wore only loincloths, rather than trousers. All wore soft leather boots tied at mid-calf.

Erland stopped his party a moment. "Kafi, who are they?"

Kafi could barely conceal his contempt. "Ashuntai horsemen, my Prince. Lord Ravi is Master of the Brothers of the Horse. They are an order of cavalry who are descended from the finest warriors the nation of Ashunta could field. They are among the most difficult people—" Kafi realized he almost let an opinion slip and said, "They were conquered with great difficulty, lord, and still hold strongly to their own national identity. It is only because they have been allowed to rise highly in the court they remain loyal to the Empire."

And because their city-state is on the wrong side of the Girdle of Kesh, added James, with a humorous feeling to his thoughts. *Aber Bukar, the Empress's General, had to threaten them to get them to put cavalry in the field against the rebellious Confederacy, according to our reports.*

As the group resumed their travel to the bottom of the amphitheater, Erland said, "I don't see any women. Is there a reason for that?"

Kafi said, "The Ashuntai are a strange people. Their women"—he glanced at Gamina, as if not wishing to give offense—"their women are considered property. They are bartered and bought and sold. The Ashuntai do not count them human." If Kafi found this distasteful, he hid it well.

Erland couldn't resist the opportunity. "Isn't it true that your own people give women little freedom?"

Kafi's dark skin colored as the blood rose in his cheek. "It does appear so, Highness, as we have been taught by our forefathers. But we are also a people who have learned from our neighbors, and we no longer trade our daughters for camels." He glanced over his shoulder to the box where Lord Ravi's company sat.

"But those sell their female children, and if a woman troubles a man, he is free to do with her as he wishes, including killing her. They are taught to despise warm feelings, and to love a woman is to be weak. Desire and lust they count necessary for breeding sons, but love is . . ." Kafi shrugged. "Among my own people we have a saying, 'Even the most high born man is but a servant in his own bedchamber.' Many of our best rulers took counsel in the arms of their wives, to the benefit of their nation.

"But those—" Kafi glanced down. "Forgive me. I do not mean to lecture."

"No," said Gamina. "By all means. I find this fascinating." To the others, she said, *He has a personal dislike for the Ashuntai that goes beyond any objection to their social customs. He hates them.*

Kafi said, "A long time ago, when I was a boy, my father served She Who Is Kesh, honors upon her line, before me. Here, I came to know one who was Lord Ravi's son. We were boys in the palace, that is all we knew. Ravi's son, Ranavi, was a fine boy and we used to ride together. It is an open question who are the best horsemen in the Empire, the Ashuntai or we of the Jal-Pur. We would often race our horses on the grasslands beyond the city gate, his Ashuntai pony, my desert horse. We became friends after a fashion.

"There was a girl. An Ashuntai girl who I came to know." Keeping his face a mask, Kafi said, "I attempted to barter for her, in their fashion, but Ravi made her a prize for one of their festivals. She was won by one of their warriors and he took her to his home. It was this warrior's third or fourth wife, I believe." He waved his hand, as if this were a long ago, nearly forgotten incident. "They bind their women with collars of leather and lead them on chains in public. They do not let them wear clothing, save a loincloth, even in cold weather. The fact of their being without clothing is of little importance to the trueblood, but the Empress, as her mother before, finds their treatment at the hands of their husbands, sons, and fathers personally distasteful. Lord Ravi and the others have enough political acumen not to bring down the Empress's disapproval, so their women are never brought to the palace. It has not always been so. The Empress's grandfather, it is said, had a decided preference for very young Ashuntai girls. It is said that it is for the Ashuntai's willingness to provide him with as many as he required for his . . . amusement, that the Brotherhood of the Horse was allowed to rise so high in the court of the Empire."

"Upon such things are the strengths of nations founded," Locky remarked drily.

"It is so," replied Kafi.

They reached the bottom of the long ramp and a line of guards stood upon either side, keeping the crowds away from the staging area for those who would enter and be presented to the court. Erland's guards were waiting for him below, wearing the full dress uniform of the Kingdom, and the badge of the Royal Krondorian Palace Guard upon their chest. Erland noted with some amusement the Quegan delegate stood behind his men, fuming at the Kingdom of the Isles being given precedence over his own nation.

Erland returned his attention to Kafi's story. "Ranavi sought to steal the girl for me, as a gift. It is also part of their culture that if you can successfully steal a woman from a rival—carrying her away to your own home—you may keep her. Ranavi was not quite seventeen years of age when he attempted to steal his own sister from the man who had won her at the festival. He died in the attempt."

Without a note of bitterness or emotion as he spoke, Kafi said, "This, you can see, is why I have some difficulty appreciating the better qualities of the Ashuntai." Softly, he added, "Whatever they may be."

Gamina looked at the desertman with sympathy, but said nothing.

They had been standing in place for ten minutes, waiting to move up to the entrance to the amphitheater. No one had spoken since Kafi had related the story of his friend. Locklear decided it was a good time to change the subject. "My lord Kafi, where are the delegates from the Free Cities?"

"Absent, my lord," answered Kafi. "They would not send anyone to the Jubilee. Those people who once were Imperial Bosania still have no official dealings with the Empire."

"Old grudges die hard," said James.

Erland said, "I don't understand. Queg and the Empire have had three wars in my lifetime, and there have been several border skirmishes between Isles and Kesh. Why is it different with the Free Cities?"

As they moved into place in the procession, Kafi said, "Those who live in what you call the Free Cities were once our loyal subjects. When the first revolt of the Confederacy occurred, ages past, Kesh stripped all her garrisons north of the Jal-Pur, leaving those colonists to fend for themselves. Queg, on the other hand, had successfully revolted a decade before. Queg is a successful revolutionary nation. Your own Kingdom were always foreign, but the Free Cities are a people who were betrayed by their own rulers. They were farmers and tavernkeepers, left to defend themselves."

Erland thought about this as they moved forward a few steps in anticipation of being announced. He glanced at the upper gallery, and saw it was quickly filling up as the last of the lords and masters were entering. What was Bosania, part of which was now the Kingdom's own duchy of Crydee, conquered by Erland's own great, great grandfather, was a terribly harsh land, inhabited by goblins, trolls, and the Brotherhood of the Dark Path. Without soldiers, it must have been years of constant struggle just to survive. Erland could understand why those of the Free Cities could still hold a grudge against the Empire.

Then he heard his name announced and Kafi said, "Highness. It is time."

As one, the entire company set off, only Gamina not walking in military lockstep, as they trod the flat stone floor of the amphitheater. It took a full five minutes to cross the vast base of the bowl, but at last, under the scorching sun of Kesh, the Prince of the Isles was formally presented to the Empress of Great Kesh. And not until this moment did Erland really understand what had been true since Borric's disappearance. He, not his brother, now stood before the mightiest ruler in the world, and he someday might find her successor his deadliest enemy, for he, not Borric, would someday be King of the Isles. And not since he had been a little boy held in his mother's arms had Erland felt so frightened.

The presentation went by in a blur. Erland hardly recalled being introduced to the formal court, and could hardly remember speaking the words he had been forced to memorize. As no one remarked or laughed, he assumed he said them properly, and he couldn't remember what the delegations behind him had said. He now sat at the lowest level of the amphitheater, on the bench of stone set aside for the delegates who came to offer wishes of health and prosperity to the Empress on her Seventy-Fifth Jubilee. Trying to focus himself, despite his unexpected attack of fear, he said, "Kafi, why has the festival been held off this long past Banapis?"

Kafi said, "Unlike your people, we of Kesh do not count the Festival of Midsummer as the date of our birth. Here, each man who knows it, celebrates the event of his birth on the day he was born. So, as She Who Is Kesh was given to the world by the gods on the fifteenth day of Dzanin, so her birth is celebrated upon that day. It will be the last day of Jubilee."

Erland said, "How odd. To celebrate your birthday on the actual day you were born. Why there must be dozens of little celebrations each day. I would feel cheated if I were to miss the great festival at Banapis."

"Different customs," Locklear remarked.

A servant, wearing the garb of the trueblood, appeared before the Prince and bowed low. He held out a scroll, sealed with a golden ribbon. Kafi, acting as the official guide and protocol officer, took the scroll. He glanced at the wax seal and said, "I suspect this is personal."

Erland said, "Why?"

"It bears the chop of the Princess Sharana."

He passed it to Erland, who pulled on the ribbon, breaking the seal. He read the immaculate script slowly, as he had never been gifted with the written high language of Imperial Kesh. As he read, Gamina began to laugh.

James turned suddenly, fearful for an instant that his wife was inadvertently revealing her ability to hear thoughts, but as he did, Gamina said, "Why, Erland, I swear you're blushing."

Erland smiled, putting the scroll into his belt. "Ah . . . just the sun, I suspect," he said, but he couldn't hide the embarrassed smile that refused to leave his mouth alone.

"What is it?" said Locklear playfully.

"An invitation," said Erland.

"For what?" asked Locklear. "We dine in formal reception with the Empress tonight."

Unable to keep from grinning, Erland said, "It's for . . . after dinner."

James and Locklear exchanged knowing glances. Then Locklear said, "Kafi, is that how the trueblood make . . . arrangements? To . . . call on each other, I mean."

Kafi shrugged. "It is not unheard of, though the Princess, being so highly born, can stretch the boundaries of . . . decorum more than others, if you follow."

"What about the Princess Sojiana?" asked Locklear.

James grinned. "I was wondering when you'd get around to that one."

Gamina narrowed her eyes a bit. " 'That one?' "

"A figure of speech, my love. Locky is known in court for trying . . . er, to get to know every pretty woman that comes into view."

Kafi said, "If you send a note requesting a meeting of the Princess, be prepared for it to be but one of many. Besides, it is said that these days she is . . . spending time with Lord Ravi, so I expect your note would be politely . . . ignored."

Locklear sat back, attempting to find a comfortable position upon the stone, hard and unyielding despite the ornate cushion placed atop it. "Well, I'll just have to find a way to get to meet her, I expect. Once I have a chance to speak with her . . ."

Kafi made the gesture for "things happen" again. *"Ma'lish."*

James glanced at Erland, who was off in a world of his own. To Gamina, James silently said, *Kafi isn't saying something about the Princess Sojiana. Can you tell what it is?*

No, she answered. *But I have an impression at the mention of her name.*

What is it?

Extreme danger.

Chapter Fourteen
Bargain

Borric rubbed his jaw.

"I wish people would stop hitting me to make a point," he grumbled.

Ghuda, who stood over him, said, "That's for costing me my pay. I can't go looking for Sabér now with half the Imperial Army looking for me, and even if I found him, I doubt he'd pay me what he owes me. And it's your fault, Madman."

Borric could only agree, though sitting on damp straw in an abandoned barn in the middle of a nation of people seemingly bent on killing him at every opportunity, he felt he deserved at least a little sympathy. "Look, Ghuda, I'll make it up to you."

The mercenary turned to remove a saddle from one of the horses they stole and, over his shoulder, said, "Oh, really? And how, pray tell, do you plan on doing that? Are you going to send a polite note to the Office of Aber Bukar, Lord of the Armies, saying, 'Please, kind lord, let my friend off with a stern talking to. He didn't know I had the kill-on-sight order on my head when he met me'? Right!"

Borric stood, wiggling his jaw to make sure it wasn't broken. It hurt and popped in and out of the socket on one side, but he was fairly certain it was intact. He glanced around the old barn. The farmhouse that had stood nearby was burned out, either by bandits or guardsmen for whatever reasons the Empire judged sufficient, but in either case, it gave Borric's little band a chance to rest up the horses. Like most good cavalry provided, there was grain in the saddlebags, so Borric set about giving a handful to his horse. Suli sat tenderly upon a half-rotten pile of straw, a study in misery. Nakor had already unsaddled his horse and was wiping it down with the cleanest handful of straw he could find. He was absently humming a nameless tune as he went about his work. And his grin had not vanished even for an instant.

Ghuda said, "When the horse is rested, Madman, you and I are quits. I mean to get myself back to Faráfra somehow and take ship down to Lesser Kesh. Things are a little less Imperial down there, if you catch my meaning. Just maybe I'll live through this."

Borric said, "Ghuda, wait."

The large mercenary dumped the saddle on the ground and said, "What?"

Borric motioned him away from the others and quietly said, "Please. I'm sorry to have gotten you into all of this, but I need you."

"You need me, Madman? For what? So you'll not die alone? Thanks, but I'd rather die in the arms of a whore many years from now."

"No, I mean I can't get to Kesh without you."

Ghuda glanced heavenward. "Why me?"

Borric said, "Look at the boy. He's terrified and so sore he can't think. He might know the back allies of Durbin, but he knows nothing else. And the Isalani . . . well, he's not exactly what I'd call reliable." Borric put a finger to his head and made a circular motion.

Ghuda glanced at the sorry-looking pair and was forced to agree. "So, that's your lookout. Why should I care?"

Borric thought and couldn't come up with a single reason. Circumstances had thrown them together, but there was no real friendship. The older mercenary was likable in his own fashion, but not what Borric would call a comrade. "Look, I *really* will make it worth your while."

"How?"

"Get me to Kesh, and see me to the people I must reach to clear this mess up, and I'll pay you more gold than you'll see in a lifetime of caravan duty."

Ghuda's eyes narrowed as he considered Borric's words. "You're not just saying this?"

Borric shook his head. "I give you my word."

"Where are you going to get your hands on that kind of gold?" asked Ghuda.

Borric considered telling him the entire story but couldn't bring himself to trust Ghuda that much. A nameless man blamed for a crime he didn't commit was one thing; a prince being hunted was another. Even though Borric knew anyone who guessed his identity was as good as dead should the guards find him in Borric's company, Ghuda might be tempted enough by thoughts of reward to push his luck. Borric's experience with mercenaries in the past didn't argue for their sense of personal loyalty.

Finally Borric said, "I was accused of the murder of the wife of the Governor of Durbin for political reasons." Ghuda didn't blink an eye at that, so Borric felt he was on the right track; political murders in Kesh didn't seem improbable. "There are people in Kesh who can clear me of that, and more, they have resources—substantial re-sources—and can provide you with"—he quickly calculated a suffi-ciently impressive figure by Kingdom standards into Keshian currency —"two thousand golden ecu."

Ghuda's eyes widened a second, then he shook his head. "Sounds good, Madman, but then so do a whore's promises."

Borric said, "All right, three thousand."

Looking to call Borric's bluff, he said, "Five thousand!"

"Done!" replied the Prince. He spit in his hand and held it out.

Ghuda looked at the outstretched hand, offered in the old trader's fashion, and knew he was obliged to either take it or be known as oathbreaker. Reluctantly, he spit in his own hand and shook. "Damn your eyes, Madman! If this is a lie, I'll have your guts on my sword, I swear! If I'm to die for stupidity, at least I'll have the pleasure of seeing you dead the instant before I meet the Death Goddess!"

Borric said, "If we make it, you'll die a rich man, Ghuda Bulé."

Ghuda threw himself down upon the damp straw to rest as well as he could. "I would have preferred it had you chosen to put that a different way, Madman."

Borric left the mercenary muttering to himself and sat down next to Suli. "Are you going to make it?" he asked.

The boy said, "Yes. I only hurt a little. But this beast has a back like a sword blade. I am split in two."

Borric laughed. "It's hard at first. We'll try a little instruction, here in the barn, before we leave tonight."

Ghuda said, "Not that it will do him much good, Madman. We're going to have to lose those saddles. The boy's going to have to ride bareback."

Nakor nodded his head vigorously. "Yes, that is true. If we are to sell these horses, we must not have anyone suspect they are Imperial property."

"Sell them?" said Ghuda. "Why?"

"With the Jubilee," replied Nakor, "it is easier for us to reach the city by river travel up the Sarne, on a boat for hire. We will be but four among multitudes. But to travel so requires payment. So we must have funds."

Borric considered the little money he had remaining after buying his clothing and armor in Faráfra, and knew Nakor was right. They didn't have enough funds among them to buy a first-class meal for one at a decent inn.

"Who would buy them?" asked Ghuda. "They are branded."

"True," said the Isalani, "but that can be dealt with. The saddles, alas, cannot be altered without damaging them to the point of worthlessness."

Ghuda levered himself up on one arm. "How can you change that brand? Do you have a running iron in your rucksack?"

"Better," said the little man, reaching into his sack and pulling out a small, stoppered jar. He rummaged around in the sack and came up with a small brush. "Observe." He pulled the cork from the jar and dipped the brush into the solution in the jar. "A running iron leaves a crude, easily detected alteration of the brand. This, however, is for an artist." He approached the nearest horse. "The army brands all livestock with the Imperial Army glyph." Dabbing at it with the brush, he began to apply fluid to the horse's flank. A faint sizzling sound could be heard, and the hair where he touched with the brush began to blacken, as if being touched by flame. "Hold the horse, please," he said to Borric. "This does not harm them, but the heat can alarm the animal."

Borric went and grabbed at the animal's bridle, holding it while the animal's ears turned this way and that, as it tried to decide whether or not to get upset with the proceedings.

After a moment, Nakor said, "There. It is now the glyph of Jung Sût, horse trader of Shing Lai."

Borric came around and looked. The brand had changed, and Nakor was right. It looked as if the brand had been made with a single iron. "Will anyone in Kesh know this Jung Sût?"

"Unlikely, my friend, as he does not exist. However, there are, perhaps, a thousand horse traders in Shing Lai, so who can claim to know them all?"

Ghuda said, "Well, then, when you're done with that, and we're ready to leave, wake me, will you?" So saying, he lay back on the damp straw and tried to make himself comfortable.

Borric looked at Nakor and said, "When we reach the river, it would probably be better if you left us."

"I don't think so," he said with a grin. "I intend to travel to Kesh in any event, as the occasion of the Jubilee will make it easy to earn money. There will be many games of chance and many opportunities for my small magics to serve me. Besides, if we move together, with Ghuda and the boy traveling a few hours behind or ahead, we will not be those the guards are seeking."

"Perhaps," said Borric, "but they have a pretty good description of the three of us by now."

"But not me," grinned the Isalani. "No guard caught sight of me when they stopped the wagon."

Borric thought back and remembered that somehow when the Imperial Guards were looking over everyone, Nakor had been absent. "Yes, now that you mention it, how did you do that?"

"It is a secret," he said with an affable grin. "But it is no matter. What does matter is that we must do something about your appearance." He cast a knowing eye upon Borric's uncovered head. "Your dark hair grows suspiciously red at the roots. So we must devise another look for you, my friend."

Borric shook his head. "Another surprise from that bag of yours?"

Bending over the bag, Nakor's grin widened more than usual. "Of course, my friend."

Borric awoke to Suli's pushing his shoulders emphatically. He came instantly awake and could see that it was growing dark outside. Ghuda was alert by the door, his sword drawn, so Borric was at his side with his own weapon at the ready an instant later.

"What is it?" hissed Borric.

Ghuda held up his hand for silence, listening. "Horsemen," he whispered. He waited, then put up his sword. "They ride west. This barn is far enough back from the road that they're likely to miss it, but once they meet up with the bunch we left on foot back at Jeeloge, they'll be over this place like flies on dung. We better get moving."

Borric had decided which of the four horses was likely to be the most agreeable for Suli and gave the boy a boost up. Giving him the reins, he said, "Hold on to her mane with your left hand if we have to go anywhere in a hurry. And keep your legs as long as you can; it's balance, not gripping with your knees. Understand?"

The boy nodded, but it was clear from his expression the idea of going anywhere on a horse in a hurry was a notion only slightly less terrifying than running into more guards. Borric turned and found Nakor carrying the saddles out of the barn. "Where are you taking them?"

The grinning Isalani said, "There is an old compost pile in back. They'll not look under it, I'm thinking."

Borric had to laugh, and in a minute the chronically happy little man was back in the barn, nimbly leaping to his horse's back, despite his ever-present rucksack and staff. Borric caught the aroma of decomposing compost and said, "Whew. If you're an example of that pile, you're right. They'll not be poking around in there soon."

Ghuda said, "Come on. Let's get as far up the road as possible by dawn."

Borric motioned and the mercenary pushed open the barn door, then jumped to his horse's back. He kicked it firmly and set off at a trot, with Borric, Suli, and Nakor coming behind. Borric put aside a terrible feeling that every turn in the road hid another ambush, and focused on one fact: every passing minute brought him that much closer to Kesh, and to Erland and the others.

The town of Páhes was busy, as it squatted upon the bridge across the River Sarne, where the road beginning at Faráfra and ending at Khattara, in the northeast, joined. Just east of the bridge, on the south bank, a huge warehouse and riverfront district had grown over the years, as teamsters pulled heavy wagons up close to barges and riverboats, which carried goods into the heart of the Empire. A few shallow-draft sailing boats could be seen, as the prevailing winds were from the west, so that it was possible to sail upriver most times of years, save when there was flooding, from Kesh to Jamila and the other towns that dotted the shore. And shipping upon the vast lake, the Overn Deep, was as plentiful as upon any sea of Midkemia.

Borric glanced around, still feeling foolish in his present costume. He was wearing the *dahá,* traditional costume of a Bendrifi, hillpeople of the Rainshadow Mountains. The garment consisted of a colorfully died piece of cloth tied around his waist, then drawn over the shoulder, like a toga. His sword arm was bare, as were his legs. Instead of boots, he now wore cross-garter sandals. Borric felt both ridiculous and vulnerable without armor. But it was a good choice as far as the Bendrifi being one of the few fair-skinned races native to Kesh. Borric's hair had been cut close to his scalp and dyed with a foul-smelling concoction that Nakor had obtained the night before, and now he was a startlingly near-white blond color; the hair was standing straight up—held in place by a sweet-smelling pomade—while shaved over the ears. The Bendrifi were also a standoffish, aloof tribe, so it was unlikely anyone would wonder at his reticent manner; Borric prayed he never ran into one this far from home, for their language was also unrelated to that of the other peoples of Kesh and Borric couldn't speak a single word. Though while Borric had been undergoing the transformation, Suli revealed he could curse a little in Ghendrifi, their language, so Borric had the boy teach him a few phrases.

Where Nakor had found the outlandish costume, Borric had no idea, but like anything else the Isalani tried, it usually meant astonishing results. The little man had gotten at least double what Borric thought the horses were worth and had managed to find the Prince a new rapier in this modest town, when Borric had failed to obtain one in one of Kesh's largest cities. Against any reasonable expectation, Nakor had produced exactly what Borric needed to change his appearance to a startling degree.

Suli was now garbed as a boy of the Beni-Sherín, a large tribe of desertmen in the Jal-Pur, with a sword at his side. He wore a robe and head covering, with only his eyes visible, and if he remembered to walk erect, could pass for a short adult. The boy had resisted giving up his old familiar rags until Ghuda threatened to cut him out of them with his sword. Given Ghuda's lack of patience since their arrest, Borric wasn't sure if he was only jesting.

Ghuda had sold his armor and purchased a finer rig, an almost new leather harness and a matching pair of bracers. His old dented helm was gone, replaced by one similar to that worn by the Dog Soldiers, a metal pot with a pointed spike at the crown, rimmed in black fur, with a chain neck guard down to the shoulders. It could be hooked across the face, revealing only the eyes, and this is how Ghuda wore it for the moment.

Nakor had somehow managed to lose his faded yellow robe and now wore one that was almost as disreputable, but of a blotchy peach color. And he didn't look one whit less ridiculous to Borric. But the Isalani felt this was a sufficient change in costume, and given his resourcefulness, Borric was unwilling to argue.

Nakor had secured passage for them on a barge heading downriver to the city of Kesh. They would be four among about a hundred passengers.

As Borric expected, there were guards everywhere. They attempted

216

to look unobtrusive, but there were too many, spending too much time peering into every passing face, for them not to be there for a purpose.

Turning a corner, Borric and Suli walked a few yards ahead of Nakor and Ghuda, toward a tavern only a few yards from the dockside. The boat would be leaving in two hours' time. They would act the part of travelers forced to idle their time away in the company of strangers.

They passed an open door and Suli faltered a step. Hissing to Borric, he said, "Master, I recognize that voice."

Borric shoved the boy into the next doorway and motioned to Ghuda and Nakor to continue past as they approached. "What do you mean?" Borric asked.

Suli pointed back to the next door. "I heard only a few words, but I know the voice."

"Who was it?"

"I don't know. Let me return and perhaps I can remember." The boy turned back and walked past the door, halting a moment on the other side, then turned the corner and looked down it as if expecting to see something. He then made a display of waiting a moment, turned, and shrugged to Borric, then walked back. As soon as he was past the door, he hurried to Borric and said, "That was one I heard in the Governor of Durbin's house that night I overheard the plot to kill you!"

Borric hesitated. If they passed by again and glanced in the doorway, they would call unwanted attention to themselves, but he wanted to know who this bloodhound on his trail was. "Wait here," Borric said, "and see who comes out. Then make for the inn and tell us."

Borric left the boy and hurried to where his companions waited, already drinking ale. He paused at their table for a moment, saying, "Someone who knows me may be in town," then turned and sat at the table next to them.

A short time later, Suli came and sat next to Borric. "It was the man in the black cloak. He wears it still, master. It was his voice," whispered the boy.

"Did you get a look at him?"

The boy said, "Enough that I might know him again."

"Good," whispered Borric, knowing Ghuda and Nakor were listening. "If you see him again, let us know."

"Master, there is something else."

"What?"

"I saw enough of him to know he is of the trueblood."

Borric nodded. "That is not surprising."

"But that is not all. He gathered the front of his cloak before him, and as it shifted, I saw around his neck the glint of gold."

Borric said, "What does that mean?"

It was Ghuda who answered, hissing angrily over his shoulder. "It means, you mush-brained maniac, that that trueblood is not just a trueblood, but he's also a member of the Royal House of Kesh! They're the only ones allowed to wear the golden torque! He's maybe only a very distant cousin to the Empress, but she still sends him a gift on his birthday! Just what the hell kind of mess have you gotten us into?"

Borric fell silent as a large, sullen serving woman approached. In a raspy voice he ordered two mugs of ale and when she left, he half-turned to Ghuda. "It's a very deep and twisted mess, my friend. As I said, it is politics."

When the serving woman brought ale to them and left, Ghuda said, "My dear dead mother wanted me to go into an honorable trade, like grave robbing. Would I listen? No. Be an assassin, like your uncle Gustav, she said. Would I pay heed? No. Apprentice to the Necromancer—"

Borric tried to appreciate the gallows humor, but found himself chewing over the implication. Who was trying to kill him and Erland? And why? It was obvious that this plot came down from the very highest levels in the Empire, but from the royal family? He sighed and drank his bitter ale, and tried to relax his mind as he waited for the call that the boat was ready to leave.

The call to board rang across the dockside, and Borric and his companions, as well as a half-dozen others in the inn, rose, gathering together bundles and packages, and crowded through the door. Outside, Borric saw a company of Imperial Guards waiting at the boarding ramp, watching everyone who climbed onto the boat. These were the Guards of the Inner Legion, the command given dominion over the heart of Kesh. Each man wore a metal helm and breastplate enameled in black. Short black kilts and black greaves and bracers gave them an intimidating appearance. The officer in charge of the company wore a helm topped with a red horsehair crest, with another long red tail falling down his back. Borric said, "Quietly now, and act like you have nothing to hide." He gave Suli a slight push, indicating the boy should move on alone, and then waved Ghuda and Nakor ahead. Borric hung back, watching.

The guards consulted a parchment from time to time, probably a detailed description of the three of them. They let Suli aboard without a second look. Ghuda was halted and asked a question. Whatever answer he gave seemed to satisfy them, for they waved him aboard.

Then Borric's heart seemed to go cold as he saw Nakor turn and speak to a guard, pointing at him across the crowd. The guard said something and nodded, and then spoke to a second guard. Borric felt his mouth go dry as three guards left the ramp and started walking purposefully toward him. Deciding he might need room to break free, Borric moved toward the ramp as if nothing unusual was occurring.

As he attempted to move out of the guards' way, one put a restraining hand upon his arm. "Hold a moment, Bendrifi." It was not a request.

Borric did his best to look irritated and disdainful. He then glanced to where the officer stood on the ramp, observing the exchange. "What?" he said, sounding as surly as he could manage.

"We heard about the fight you almost started on the road from Khattara. Maybe the caravan guards couldn't keep you in line, but you'll have six legionaries on the boat with you. Any more trouble of that sort and we'll pitch you into the river."

Borric stared the man in the eye, made a slight snarling sound as he curved his lip, then said one of the phrases Suli taught him. He yanked his arm out of the legionary's grip, but when three hands went to the hilts of their swords, he held up his own, palm outward, showing he intended no trouble.

Turning his back on them, he attempted to maintain the pose of being a touchy, rude hillman, and hoped his knees weren't looking as wobbly as they felt. He boarded the boat among the last to climb the ramp, and found himself a seat on the opposite side of the wide craft from where his three companions sat. The six guardsmen were the last to board and they stationed themselves at the stern, in a group, talking among themselves. Silently, Borric vowed that when they reached the city of Kesh he would happily throttle the little Isalani.

A day and a half later, stopping three times along the way, they saw the skyline of the city of Kesh in view. Borric had recovered from the shock the Isalani had handed him, and had fallen into sullen brooding, a pose which took almost no effort on his part. The situation

219

looked hopeless and yet he must somehow force himself to continue. As his father had taught him and Erland when they were still young that the only thing they could guarantee in life was failure; to achieve success you had to take risks. He had not truly understood what his father had been talking about—Erland and he were both Princes of the Blood Royal, and there was really nothing they couldn't do, but that was because of what they were.

Now Borric understood much of what his father had tried to explain before, and now the stakes were his own life, his brother's, and perhaps the life of the Kingdom, as well.

As they approached the upper docks of Kesh, Borric saw companies of soldiers upon the boat landing. They might be taking passage across the Overn Deep or upriver, or they might be the normal guard for this city, but they also might be screening passengers into the city, one more barrier between himself and his brother.

As the boat began nosing in to the dockside, Borric made his way back toward the legionaries. The guardsmen were making ready to exit, and as the boat was tied off to the dockside, Borric moved to stand beside the man he had spoken with before boarding. The guardsman gave him a quick glance then turned away.

While the first passengers disembarked, Borric did nothing, but when he saw they were being halted and inspected as they left, he knew he couldn't chance being singled out again. So as it came time to leave, he turned to the guardsman and said, again in his gruff voice, "I said a rude thing to you at Páhes, guardsman."

The legionary's eyes narrowed as he said, "I assumed that, though I don't speak your babble."

Borric mounted the gangplank in step with him and said, "I come to celebrate the Jubilee, and to make devotions at the temple of Tith-Onaka." Borric had noticed the man wore the good-luck charm common to those soldiers who worship the War God with Two Faces. "At such a holy time, I wish no bad blood with any soldier. The Isalani cheated me at cards. That is why I was vexed. Will you take my hand and give pardon for the offense I gave."

The guardsman said, "No man should enter the Planner of Battle's Temple with an affront to a warrior on them." At the foot of the ramp, before the guards who were questioning the other passengers, the legionary and Borric gripped each other's right forearm, and shook. "May your enemy never see your back."

Borric said, "May you sing victory songs for many years, legionary."

As if they were old friends saying good-bye, they shook again, and Borric turned and shouldered past two soldiers on the dock. One had observed the farewell and started to say something to Borric, but thought better of it and turned his attention to another man trying to push past, a strange little Isalani from Shing Lai.

Borric crossed the street, then paused, waiting to see what was occurring. Nakor and the guard seemed to be in some sort of an argument, and several other guardsmen turned to see what the problem was. Ghuda materialized beside Borric, seemingly having come to that spot by chance. A few moments later, Suli came to stand next to Borric. Nakor now had a circle of guards and one pointed at the rucksack he always carried.

Finally, as if relenting on some point, the Isalani handed the rucksack over to the first guard, who stuck his hand in the bag. After a moment, the guard turned the bag upside down and then pulled it inside out. It was now empty.

Ghuda gave a low whistle. "How in the world did he do that?"

Borric said, "Maybe all his magic isn't just sleight of hand."

Ghuda said, "Well, Madman, we are in the city of Kesh. Where to now?"

Glancing about, Borric said, "Turn right and walk along the dockside. At the third street, turn right again and keep going until you find an inn. We'll meet at the first inn we encounter." Ghuda nodded and headed off. "Suli," Borric whispered, "wait for Nakor and tell him."

The boy said, "Yes, master," and Borric left him, and made his way leisurely after Ghuda.

The inn was a seedy riverfront establishment with the grandiose name the Emperor's Standard and Jeweled Crown. Borric had no idea what event in Keshian history had prompted this odd name, but there was nothing in the least bit Imperial nor jewel-like about this establishment. It was like a hundred other dark and smoky establishments in a hundred cities on Midkemia. Languages and customs might differ, but the patrons were all cut from the same cloth, bandits, thieves, cutthroats of all stripe, gamblers, whores, and drunkards. Borric felt at home for the first time since entering Kesh.

Glancing around, he saw that the usual respect for privacy prevailed here as in the other like inns he and Erland used to frequent in the Kingdom. Casually, looking down at his mug, he said, "We can assume that at least one of these customers is either an Imperial agent or an informer."

Ghuda removed his helm, scratched his scalp, itching from perspiration, and said, "That's a safe bet."

"We won't stay here," said Borric.

"That's a relief," said Ghuda, "though I would like a drink before we seek lodgings."

Borric agreed and the big man caught the attention of a serving boy, who returned with four chilled ales. Borric sipped his and said, "I'm surprised it's chilled."

Ghuda stretched. "If you bother to glance north the next time you're outside, Madman, you'll notice a tiny range of mountains called the Spires of Light. They are called such because their highest peaks are constantly coated with ice, which when conditions are right, reflect the sunlight with an impressive effect. There is a thriving business in ice in this city. The Guild of Ice Cutters is among the richest guilds in Kesh."

"You learn something new every day," said Borric.

Nakor said, "I don't like it. Ale should be warm. This makes my head hurt."

Borric laughed. Ghuda said, "Well, then, we're in Kesh. How do we reach these friends of yours?"

Borric lowered his voice. "I . . ."

Ghuda's eyes narrowed. "What now?"

"I know where they are. I'm just not sure how to get there."

Ghuda's eyes became angry slits. "Where?"

"They are in the palace."

"Gods' teeth!" Ghuda exploded, and several of the inn's patrons turned for a moment to see what caused the outburst. Lowering his voice to a whisper, but not losing his angry tone, he said, "You are joking, aren't you? Please say that you are joking."

Borric shook his head. Ghuda stood up and put his long dirk in his belt, and picked up his helm. "Where are you going?" asked Borric.

"Anywhere but where you are going, Madman."

Borric said, "You gave your word!"

Looking down, Ghuda said, "I said I'd get you to Kesh. You're in Kesh. You didn't say a thing about the palace." Pointing an accusatory finger at Borric he said, "You owe me five thousand golden ecu, and I'll never see a tenth of one coin of it."

Borric said, "You'll get it. You have my word. But I have to find my friends."

"In the palace," hissed Ghuda.

"Sit down, people are watching."

Ghuda sat. "Let them watch. I'm going to be on the first boat for Kimri I can find. I'll get to Hansulé and take ship for the Eastern Kingdoms. I will be sitting caravan watch in some foreign land for the rest of my life, but I'll be alive, which is more than I can say for you if you try to get into the palace."

Borric smiled. "I know a trick or two. What will it take to keep you with us?"

Ghuda couldn't believe Borric was serious. After a moment, he said, "Double what you promised. Ten thousand ecu."

Borric said, "Done."

"Ha!" snapped Ghuda. "Easy enough to promise anything when we're all going to be dead in a day or two."

Turning to Suli, Borric said, "We need to get in touch with certain people."

Suli blinked uncomprehendingly. "Master?"

Whispering, Borric said, "The Guild of Thieves. The Mockers. The Ragged Brotherhood, or whatever they're called in this city."

Suli nodded as if he understood, but his expression showed he didn't have a hint as to what Borric wanted. "Master?"

Borric said, "What sort of a street beggar are you?"

Suli shrugged. "One from a city without such a group, master."

Borric shook his head. "Look, get out of here and find the nearest market. Find a beggar—you'll be able to do that, won't you?" Suli nodded. "Just drop a coin in his hand and say there's a traveler who needs to speak to someone on a matter of urgency and that it is a matter worth the time of people who can get things done in this city. Understand?"

"I think so, master."

"If the beggar asks any more questions, just say this . . ." Borric sought to remember some of the stories James had told him about his own boyhood with the thieves of Krondor and after a long moment he added, ". . . one is in town who wishes not to cause difficulty by being here, but who wishes to make arrangements so that all may benefit. Can you do that?"

Suli repeated his instructions and when Borric was satisfied he had them correctly, he sent the boy off. They drank in relative silence, until Borric saw Nakor reach into his rucksack and pull out some cheese and bread. Looking pointedly at the Isalani, Borric said,

"Hey, wait a minute. When the guard examined that bag it was empty?"

"That's right," said Nakor, his white teeth looking as if they didn't quite fit his face.

"How'd you do that?" asked Ghuda.

"It's a trick," answered the laughing little man, as if that explained everything.

At sundown, Suli returned. He sat down next to Borric and said, "Master, it took a while, but at last did I find such a one as you required. I gave him a coin and said as I was instructed. That one asked many questions, but I only repeated what you said, and refused more. He bid me wait for him and vanished. With much fear I waited, but when he returned all was well. He said those you wish to speak with will meet us and named the time and place."

"Where and when?" asked Ghuda.

To Borric, Suli said, "The time is the second ringing of the watchbell after sundown. The place is but a short walk from here. I know it because he made me repeat the directions several times. But we must go to the market, and find it from there, for I would not tell this beggar where we were staying."

"Good," said Borric. "We've been here too long as it is. Let's go."

They rose and left, following Suli to the nearest market square. Borric was again astonished at the press of humanity around him, and the diversity of it. If he felt foolish, no one took note of his impersonation of a Bendrifi. The array of costumes, and lack thereof, he saw in Faráfra was even more varied in the Empire's capital. The blackest skin Borric had ever seen gleamed in the late afternoon sun as lion hunters of the grassy plains walked by, and yet there were enough fair-skinned people to show that those who once lived in the Kingdom had come to Kesh over the years. Many had the narrow eyes and yellowish skin that Nakor possessed, but their dress was in different fashion than the Isalani—some wearing silk jackets and knee breeches, others wearing armor, and still others in simple monk's robes. Women in all states of dress, from the most modest to almost naked passed by, and few took notice, unless the woman was unusually striking.

A pair of Ashuntai plainsmen sauntered by, each leading a pair of women on chains—the women were nude and walked with eyes downcast. A company of brawny-looking men with red and blond hair, wearing furs and armor despite the heat, passed them by, and insults were exchanged.

Borric turned to Ghuda and said, "What was that?"

"Brijaners—seamen from Brijané, and the towns along the shore below the Grimstone Mountains. They're raiders and traders who ply the Great Sea from Kesh to the Eastern Kingdoms in their long ships —and even across the Endless Sea, the stories claim. They are proud, violent men, and they worship the spirits of their dead mothers. All Brijaner women are seers and priestesses, and the men believe their ghosts come to guide their ships and therefore hold all women sacred. The Ashuntai treat women worse than dogs. If it wasn't for the Empress's peace seal being on the city, they'd be trying to kill one another on sight."

Borric said, "Wonderful. Are their many such feuds in Kesh?"

Ghuda said, "No more than usual. About a hundred such, give or take a few, on any given festival. That's why the Palace Guards and the Inner Legion are here in strength. The Legion has dominion over the Inner Empire, all that surrounds the Overn, inside the ring of mountains formed by the Mother of Waters, Spires of Light, Guardians, and Grimstones. Outside of that, local lords run things. Only on the Imperial highways and at these sort of festivals is peace enforced. At other times"—he made a "wipe clean" motion with his hand—"one side or the other is dogmeat."

Kesh was a wonder to Borric. The throng in the streets was both familiar and alien. So much of what a city was was familiar to him, but *this* city was overlaid with ages of an alien culture.

When they entered the market, Borric said, "This is pretty impressive."

Ghuda snorted. "This is a local market, Madman. The big one is across from the amphitheater. That's where most travelers will go."

Borric shook his head. Glancing around, he said to Suli, "When should we leave?"

"We have a while, master." As he spoke, a dozen chimes and gongs around the city rang, as the sun vanished over the horizon. "The second bell, so it will be an hour."

"Well, then, let's find something to eat."

They agreed on that, and set off in search of a street vendor whose wares weren't too costly.

As the second bell of night sounded, they entered the alley. "This way, master," said Suli, keeping his voice low.

Despite the early hour of the night, the alley was deserted. The narrow corridor was cluttered with trash and garbage, and the stench was overwhelming. Trying to keep the greasy meat and flatbread he had eaten down, Borric said, "A friend once told me that thieves will often put garbage and"—stepping on what appeared to be a dead dog, Borric continued—"other things along their private escape routes to discourage casual inspection."

At the end of the alley was a door, wooden with a metal lockplate. Borric tried it and found it locked. Then from behind, a voice said, "Good evening."

Borric and Ghuda turned, and pushed Suli and Nakor behind them. A half-dozen armed men were approaching them down the alley. Ghuda hissed. "I have a very bad feeling, Madman!"

Borric said, "Good evening. Are you the one I arranged to meet?"

"That depends," answered the leader, a thin man with a grin too big for his face. His cheeks were heavily pockmarked, to the point of the disfigurement being apparent in the dim light in the alley. The others behind him were shadowy silhouettes. "What is your proposal?"

"I need entrance into the palace."

Several men laughed. "That is easy," said the leader. "Get arrested and they will take you before the High Tribune, assuming you break an Imperial law. Murder a guard—that always works."

"I need to get in unseen."

"Impossible. Besides, why should we help? You may be Imperial agents for all we know. You do not speak like a Bendrifí, despite your dress. The city has been crawling with agents looking for someone— who we don't know, so you may be him. In any event," he said, drawing a longsword, "you have about ten seconds to explain why we shouldn't just kill you and take your gold now."

As he and Ghuda drew their own swords, Borric said, "For one thing, I can promise you a thousand golden ecu if you tell us of an entrance, twice that if you take us there."

The leader motioned with his blade, and his companions spread out, forming a wall of swords across the alley. "And?"

"And I bring greetings from the Upright Man of Krondor."

The leader paused a moment, then said, "Impressive."

Borric let out a breath of tension, then the leader of the thieves said, "Very impressive. For the Upright Man has been seven years dead in Krondor and the Mockers are now ruled by the Virtuous

Man. Your introduction is less than timely, spy." To his men, he said, "Kill them."

The alley was too narrow to allow Ghuda to draw his bastard sword, so he pulled both dirks as Borric unsheathed his rapier and Suli his shortsword. Forming a three-man front, Borric took a second to say to Nakor, "Can you open that lock?"

The Isalani said, "It will take but a moment," and the attackers were full upon them.

Borric's sword took the first man in the throat, as Ghuda was forced to use his two dirks to parry his attacker's longer sword. Suli had never used a sword before, but he flailed about with enough conviction that the man opposite him was reluctant to try to get past the blurring weapon.

The attackers fell back a step at the death of one of their number. They were reluctant to rush Borric's sword point again. The cluttered alley gave no one an advantage, save time. The attackers could hang back and let Borric's party tire then take them, for they had no place else to go, so the thieves were content to feint and withdraw, feint and withdraw.

Nakor rummaged through his rucksack and found what he was looking for. Borric glanced over his shoulder for an instant, to see the Isalani pry the lid off a flat jar. "What . . . ?" he began, then he was forced to pay the price of his inattention as a broadsword almost took his left arm off. He dodged and thrust, and a second attacker was out of the fight, this one with a ragged cut to his own right arm.

Nakor poured a small pile of white powder in his left hand, then put the lid back on the jar. Kneeling before the lock plate, the diminutive man blew on the powder. Rather than scattering randomly, the powder left his hand in a thin line, straight to the keyhole on the lock plate. As the powder passed through the lock, a series of audible clicks could be heard. Nakor stood up with a satisfied smile, put away his jar, and opened the door. "We can go now," he calmly announced.

Instantly, Ghuda shoved him unceremoniously through the door and followed after, as Borric launched a flurry of blows that drove back the thieves, allowing Suli to bolt through the door after the mercenary. Then Borric was through and Ghuda slammed the door behind him. Nakor held out a large, ornate chair, which Borric jammed against the door handle, barring the door for a moment.

Borric turned and was suddenly aware of two facts: the first was a nearly nude girl regarded him with eyes years older than the rest of her, from where she sat outside a door, waiting the bidding of whoever was inside that door. The second was the sweet smoke that hung in the air, unmistakable once smelled. It was opium, cut with other smells, julé weed, hashish, and sweet-smelling oils. They had broken into the back of a joy house.

As Borric expected, the moment after they had broken in, three large men—the establishment's resident bruisers—each armed with clubs in hand, knives, and swords at their belts, materialized in the hall. "What passes here, scum?" shouted the first, his eyes wide in anticipation of a little free bloodletting. Borric was instantly convinced that whatever he said, the man's intent was bloody.

Borric pushed himself past Ghuda, shoving the mercenary's dirk point down in clear message not to start trouble. Glancing over his shoulder, Borric said, "City watch! Trying to break in that door."

He slid past the first man, just as the thieves outside obliged by hitting the door, causing the chair to move a foot.

"Those thieving bastards!" said the first bruiser. "We're paid up this month."

Borric gave the man a friendly shove toward the door saying, "The greedy scum are trying to shake you down for more." As the second bruiser sought to hold onto Borric, the Prince grabbed that man's elbow and turned him after the first. "There's ten of them out there, armed! They claim there's a Jubilee surcharge you haven't paid."

By now several clients of the establishment were opening doors and peeking into the halls to see what was happening. At sight of armed men, several doors were slammed, then one girl screamed, and the panic was on.

The third bruiser said, "Wait a minute, you," to Borric and took a swipe with his club.

Borric barely got his left arm up in time, and took the blow on his left bracer, but the shock still numbed his arm to the elbow. Thinking of nothing else to do, the Prince shouted, "Raid!" at the top of his lungs, and every door in the hall flew open. The third bruiser tried to take another swipe at Borric, but Ghuda struck him behind the ear with the hilt of his dirk, stunning the man.

Borric shoved the third bruiser hard into a fat merchant attempting to leave with his clothing in his hands, shouting at the merchant, "It's the girl's father! He's come to kill you, man!"

The merchant's eyes widened in horror, and he dashed through the outside door, still nude and holding his robes in a bundle. A sleepy-looking woman easily in her forties stood in the door, saying, "My father?"

At that moment, Suli shouted, "City watch!" as loud as he could.

Then the rear door flew open and the thieves barged in, collided with naked girls and boys, drugged men, and two very angry bruisers. The commotion in the hall was redoubled with another pair of large men appeared at the top of the hall, demanding to know what was going on. Borric shouted, "Religious fanatics! Trying to free your slave girls and boys. Your men are being attacked, back there. Help them!"

Somehow, Ghuda, Suli, and Nakor extricated themselves from the confusion in the hall and bolted for the entry of the building. The nude merchant running down the street had piqued the curiosity of the city watch, and two armed guardians of the peace were standing before the door as Borric pulled it open. Without hesitation he said, "Oh, sirs! It's horrible! The house slaves have revolted and are killing the customers. They're crazed on drugs and their strength is superhuman. Please, you must send for help!"

One guardsman pulled his sword and dashed inside, while another took a whistle from his belt and blew it. Within seconds of the shrill whistle sounding, ten more city guardsmen were hurrying to the riot and dashing through the door.

Two blocks away, in a dark inn, Borric and his companions sat at a table. Ghuda took off his helm and almost bounced it off the table, so hard did he put it down. Pointing his finger at Borric, he said, "The only reason I don't knock your head off now is that we'd certainly get arrested."

"Why do you keep wanting to hit me?" said Borric.

"Because you keep doing stupid things which threaten to get me killed, Madman!"

Nakor said, "That was fun."

Ghuda and Borric both stared at him in astonishment. "Fun?" said Ghuda.

"Most excitement I've had in years," said the grinning man.

Suli looked as if he was close to exhaustion. "Master, what do we do now?"

Borric thought a moment, shook his head, and said, "I don't know."

Chapter Fifteen
Snares

Erland approached the door.

A dozen guards stood without, but none sought to question him about his approach to the Princess Sharana's private quarters. At the entrance to the reception area, Erland discovered Lord Nirome, the noble who had acted as Master of Ceremonies when Prince Awari had greeted him at the entrance to the upper city.

The stout man smiled affably as he bowed, and said, "Good evening, Your Highness. Is all here to your liking?"

Erland smiled and returned the bow with a deference beyond what Nirome's rank entitled him to, saying, "Your generosity is at times overwhelming, my lord."

Glancing backwards over his shoulder, the pudgy trueblood took Erland by the arm and said, "If I might have but a brief moment with you, sire."

Erland allowed himself to be steered to an alcove out of view of the guards and servants, saying, "Only a moment. I would not like to keep the Princess waiting."

"Understood, Highness, understood." He smiled and something in Erland said to beware of this friendly bungler, that no one could be this highly placed and not have some guile. "What I wished to say, Highness, is that it would be a kind and generous act, a kingly act, if you would communicate to Her Imperial Majesty your desire to see young Rasajani, Lord Kiláwa's son, pardoned for his offense against you." Erland said nothing, and when it was obvious he wasn't going to speak, Nirome continued. "The boy is stupid; on that point we

230

agree. However, the fault lies not with him but with certain provoca-
teurs in Prince Awari's camp." Glancing around as if wary of being
overheard, Nirome said, "If I may elaborate a brief instant." Erland
nodded. Nirome whispered, "Awari is second born to Sojiana, so by
rights the Princess should inherit. But it is known that many fear
three generations of sitting Empresses—a patriarchal bias exists in
many of the nations which make up the Empire. To that end, some
misguided souls have sought to exacerbate the differences between
Awari and his sister. Young Rasajani thought—or rather without
thought was only trying to show his Empress that Awari is not some
weakling, fearful of Isles simply because he is foremost in insisting
peace be kept between our two nations. It was a rash and foolish act,
one which really was unforgivable, but I am certain others put him up
to it, thinking Awari would approve. If you could somehow find it in
your heart to forgive. . . ."

Erland said nothing for a few moments, then at last spoke. "I shall
consider the matter. I will discuss it with my advisors, and if we are
certain no loss of prestige for my nation is involved, I will speak to
your Empress."

Nirome grabbed Erland's hand, and kissed his royal signet. "Your
Highness is most gracious. Perhaps someday I may be privileged to
visit Rillanon. When I do, I shall gladly tell all there that a gracious
and wise ruler is destined to govern them."

Erland had about all the fawning he could stand, so he nodded and
left the portly court noble, moving purposefully toward the entrance
to the Princess Sharana's suites. Presenting himself to the servant
who waited, he was ushered into the receiving area, a private chamber
equal in size to his father's own audience hall in Krondor.

A young woman with a strong reddish cast to her hair—unusual
for a trueblood—bowed low to Erland and said, "Her Highness re-
quests that you join her in her private garden, m'lord."

Erland indicated she should lead him and as she did, he found
himself admiring the graceful sway of hips barely covered by the short
kilt. Feeling himself becoming aroused at thoughts of this evening's
encounter, Erland focused on James's parting words to him, just after
dinner. The Earl of his father's court had said, "Remember, like yourself, she's destined to rule her nation, so don't take *anything* for
granted. She may look like a twenty-two-year-old girl, and even act
like one, but she may be Empress of Kesh in your lifetime, and I
suspect her education is as extensive, or more so, than yours." James
had revealed an unusual level of concern, even for one as cautious by

nature as he was. And he had taken the moment to tell Erland, "Be wary. Don't be led astray by pretty promises in soft arms, my friend. There's murder in these people as much as in the soul of any street thug in the Poor Quarter of Krondor."

Reaching Sharana's pavilion, Erland admitted he would have to work hard to keep that idea foremost in his thoughts. The Princess lay upon a pile of cushions under a silken panoply, with four serving women nearby to answer any call she made. Rather than the short kilt and vest he had seen her wear on public occasions, Sharana wore only a simple robe, clasped just above her breasts by a golden falcon in the same design he had seen upon the Royal Keshian standard. The robe was almost transparent and fell open in front as she rose to greet him, giving Erland a tantalizing view of the young woman's body. The effect was considerably more powerful than the commonplace nudity in the palace. Erland bowed slightly, the deference given a host by a guest, rather than the bow of a subject to a ruler. Sharana extended her hand and he took it as she simply said, "Come, walk with me."

Erland found his reaction upon first seeing the Princess returning. In a flower garden of exotic blossoms, she was both the most lovely and exotic. Unlike most of the trueblood women he had encountered so far, she was not lithe and long-legged, but more voluptuous. Her legs were thicker than Miya's, but not unpleasantly so, and she was easily the most large-breasted woman he had met so far. There was an odd tilt to her nose which, combined with her full lips, gave her a pouty expression. Her large sable eyes had a slightly alien cast to them, almost like the yellow-skinned people from Shing Lai he had seen at court. Her shoulders and hips were broad, her waist narrow, and her stomach rounded in a pleasing way. Erland was finding himself totally captivated by the young woman.

When the silence became oppressive to the nervous Prince, he said, "Your Highness, are there any . . . unattractive women at court?"

Sharana laughed. "Of course." Her voice was sweet and feminine and her smile brought her face alive and made Erland's pulse beat faster. "But my grandmother has a terror of old age and death, so at her command all those not young and beautiful are relegated to the lower levels of the palace. They are there, to be sure." Sharana sighed. "If I come to rule, I will abolish that silly order. Many fine and capable people work in obscurity, while those less gifted but fairer to look upon achieve high office."

Erland didn't really understand what the girl was saying. His mind was fixed upon the lovely scent of her mixing with the exotic aroma of the garden's flowers. He said, "Uh . . . I noticed Lord Nirome somehow managed to stay aboveground."

Again she laughed. "He's wonderful. He just manages to somehow stay on everyone's good side. He's such a dear. Of all my uncles—"

"Uncle?"

"He's my mother's cousin, actually, but I call him my uncle. He's the only one who could get me to stop crying when I was left alone as a baby. Grandmother has constantly had to scold him to do something about his love of eating and look more like a trueblood hunter, but she puts up with him anyway. I often think he's the only one who keeps this Empire together—he really does his best to disarm potential conflicts. He's tried to be a good influence upon my uncle Awari. . . ." She left it unsaid that most would have considered that undertaking a failure.

Erland nodded. "Why are your uncle and grandmother estranged?"

"I'm not sure, really," answered the girl, taking Erland's hand in hers, a natural and unself-conscious act. With fingers interlaced, they walked along, the girl speaking in a matter-of-fact tone. "I think it's because Awari thinks he should rule instead of my mother, which is silly. He's too young—he's only three years older than me. Grandmother's fifth or sixth husband fathered him, I think. Mother is eldest and she should be unquestioned heir, but there are some who fear the Empire becoming a matriarchy."

Erland felt his blood pounding but he forced himself to concentrate on matters of politics, which was difficult with the scantily clad Princess constantly brushing against him. "So, ah, some of your people wish a male ruler?"

"Silly, isn't it?" Sharana halted and said, "What do you think of my garden?"

"It's impressive," Erland admitted, without any flattery. "Nothing like this in Isles."

"Many of these blooms are cultivated here, for the Imperial gardens, and do not exist anywhere else upon Midkemia. I'm not sure how that's done, but I've been told it's so." She reached across her own body with her left hand and squeezed his forearm, holding onto his left hand with her right. It was a familiar gesture, of lovers, and Erland was both aroused and discomforted by it.

As they continued to walk through the garden, Sharana said, "Erland, tell me of your home, of this legendary Kingdom of the Isles."

"Legendary?" laughed the Prince. "To me it's commonplace, while Kesh is the legendary land."

Sharana giggled. "But you have so many wonders. I have been told that you have spoken to elves, and that you have fought the Dark Brotherhood. Is this true?"

Erland himself had never spoken to elves or fought the Brotherhood of the Dark Path, as most people referred to the moredhel—the dark elves—but he decided it wouldn't help to embellish the truth a bit. He had fought goblins at Highcastle and they were the next best thing.

He spoke a bit and found Sharana to be fascinated by his stories, or at least give a convincing performance as one fascinated. After a while, they had circled the garden and returned to Sharana's pavilion. Sharana indicated the large bed outside her sleeping quarters. "I prefer sleeping under the stars most nights during the summer. The palace holds the heat."

Erland agreed. "It takes some getting used to. Having the pool close by helps. I've grown quite accustomed to taking long baths before retiring."

Sharana giggled as a servant pulled aside the gossamer hangings which protected the sleeping pavilion from flying night insects. "So Miya told me." Erland felt himself blush as Sharana said, "She said that you are quite . . . gifted in some respects. And quite a lot of fun." Motioning for Erland to recline at her side, she ran a finger around the collar of his tunic. "You wear so many clothes, you men of the North. You're almost as bad as our fierce Brijaner sea rovers. They refuse to remove their fur cloaks, even to growing faint in the heat. And they think their lives are ruled by the ghosts of their dead mothers, and only take one wife in their lifetime. They are very strange. You would be more comfortable if you took some clothing off, don't you think?"

Erland found himself actually blushing. He had assumed from the timing of the meeting and his previous experience with Keshian trueblood girls that the Princess might have something more personal than an informal state visit in mind when she asked him to visit her quarters, but now he felt suddenly awkward.

Sensing his reluctance, Sharana unfixed the clasp that held her scant robe in place and let it fall open. "See, it's easy."

Erland leaned forward and offered a kiss, ready to retreat if he mistook the girl's intentions. She answered with a strong kiss, and suddenly two pair of hands were removing his clothing. When Erland removed his last garment, Sharana rolled over on her back. As he took position over her, he realized the four serving women were still stationed around the pavilion, and the gauzy hangings offered only an illusion of privacy. Borric felt a momentary hesitation as he saw one of the servants standing only a few inches away, but as the Princess pulled him to her, he gave no more thought to her presence. I must be getting used to these people, he thought, before he lost himself in a warm and sensuous world. Their lovemaking was intense and hurried, as if neither could wait to reach satisfaction.

When they were both spent, Erland moved to Sharana's side and the girl playfully ran her hand over his chest and stomach. "Miya said you start quickly."

Erland felt himself blush again and said, "Do . . . did you and Miya discuss me . . . in great detail?"

Sharana laughed, her ample breasts bouncing with the movement. She put her head upon Erland's chest. "Of course. I ordered her to tell me everything, *everything* about you after you took her that first night."

Not sure he wanted to hear the answer, Erland said, "Ah . . . what did she say?"

Sharana began doing interesting things with her left hand while lying next to Erland, her right arm forming a triangle as she rested her head on her right hand. "Oh, she said that you were . . . enthusiastic . . . and a little impatient . . . the first time . . . but that the second time was well worth the effort."

Erland laughed as he reached out and grabbed Sharana, pulling her to him. "Let's see if she was right."

The heralds blew their long horns, and the drums began beating. Erland and his company sat in one of the boxes used by the Keshian nobility the previous night, the guests of Prince Awari and Lord Nirome. As the second day of the Empress's Jubilee got underway, contests and exhibitions were scheduled. The Empress might or might not appear in her private box, overlooking the amphitheater, but the games continued as if she were there. Short, muscular men were dressed in the costumes of their warrior ancestors. Each man wore a white breechcloth, leaving buttocks bare. Some wore carved and painted demon masks, while others had painted their faces with blue patterns. Many had shaved heads or their hair pulled back into a warrior's queue. Ancient instruments, skin-covered drums, rattles made from animal skulls, and horn trumpets were played with enthusiasm as the warriors began their ancient contest.

A stone of seven feet in height was pulled out to the center of the amphitheater by a dozen men, singing a strange repetitive chant. Others urged them on with cries, grunts, and exaggerated gestures.

Erland turned to his host and said, "I am pleased for the opportunity to spend some time with Your Highness."

Awari smiled graciously and said, "The pleasure is mine, Your Highness."

Lord Nirome, sitting behind Erland, and next to James and Gamina, said, "Anything to build bridges between our two nations, Your Highnesses."

Awari glanced at Nirome for a moment then said to Erland, "It is as my lord Nirome says, Erland. Your Kingdom has been growing steadily in power since the time of your grandfather and with those Quegan pirates properly chastised—"

"Quegan pirates?" interrupted Erland.

Awari said, "I guess news has not been swift in reaching you. A fleet of Quegan galleys had been raiding the Free Cities and even being so bold as to raid some of your coastal towns near Questor's View. Your father ordered Admiral Bruhall's fleet to find and sink them. He did."

Nirome chimed in. "A squadron of the raiders was blown by squall past their own island and were intercepted by a squadron of Imperial ships out of Durbin and were also crushed."

At this, James and Erland exchanged glances, and Erland heard Gamina's voice in his mind. *James is fascinated by that.*

Why? Aloud the Prince said, "Then the Bitter Sea should be safe to travel for some time to come. Barring a Durbin pirate or two."

Awari smiled indulgently. "Some of our more distant cities are difficult to control on that level, Erland. If a ship's captain raids outside of Imperial waters . . ." He shrugged, as if saying, what can we do? "It's easier to send the Inner Legion or an army of Dog Soldiers to crush Durbin and hang the Governor than it is to replace a corrupt judge there, do you see?" The tone of the question showed clearly it was rhetorical.

Then James's voice came to Erland. *This is intriguing. What was an "Imperial squadron" doing in Durbin? Those pirates usually can't agree on anything, let alone how to organize ten or more ships into a squadron.*

Gamina spoke to Nirome. "My lord, what are these men doing?"

"These are men from Shing Lai, Dong Tai, and Tao Zi, many villages and towns in the region, who in ancient times were known as the Pô-Tào. They are no longer warriors, but they still practice the ancient arts and craft of war. These men are wall jumping."

As he spoke, the first man in line raced for the large stone, then as he came within a stride of it, he sprung as high as he could, placing his foot on the face and flipping backwards, and landing on his feet. The crowd cheered.

"Impressive," said James.

Awari said, "The object is to clear the stone. He was just warming himself to the task."

James said, "That stone is how tall? Seven feet?"

"Yes," said Awari. "An adequate warrior will leap to the top, touching the stone, then land on the other side. A true warrior will clear the height without touching the stone. In ancient days, this was training for their soldiers, so they might jump the protective walls of rival villages."

"That *is* impressive," said Erland.

Awari smiled. "They used to plant spears on both sides of the wall stone, giving the contestants a bit more motivation in making the jump clean. Anyway, as I was saying, now that that nest of pirates up in Queg has been slapped down, I'm hoping things will stay calm along the northern borders. I don't mean to bother you with the details of our domestic difficulties, but with my mother's age . . ." He watched a moment as a strong-looking man in a wooden demon's mask, with a spear in his left hand, leaped high over the stone to the roar of the crowd. ". . . well, the situation in the heart of Kesh is such that it would be to no one's advantage for there to be any conflict between our two people. You are now clearly our strongest neighbor, and from this time forward, I hope our good friend."

Erland said, "As long as I live, I hope that is so."

Awari said, "Good. Let's hope you live a long, full span of years."

A flourish of trumpets announced the arrival of a member of the royal family, and Erland turned, hoping it was Sharana. Instead, the Princess Sojiana entered with her retinue, and Erland could barely contain his laugh of astonishment. Escorting the beautiful woman to her place in the box next to the one he occupied with Awari was Baron Locklear.

James's amusement came behind his thoughts, too. *Well, it seems that no barrier is insurmountable for our friend, doesn't it?*

It does appear that way, replied Erland.

The Princess was the first to enter the box, and behind her came Locklear, who couldn't resist tossing a grin Erland's way. Gamina's only reaction was to raise one eyebrow and fix him with a look of disapproval. Then her eyes widened a bit and she spoke to both Erland and James. *Locky is putting on a charade.*

What? asked Erland.

He's trying to keep up appearances, but he's deeply disturbed about something.

What is that? asked James.

He said he'll speak to us later, that right now he's having difficulty concentrating. But he's saying one thing now. He thinks Sojiana may have been behind the attempt on Borric in Krondor.

Erland nodded absently to some observation Lord Nirome was making. To Gamina, and through her James and Locklear, he said, *Then that makes her a prime candidate behind the raid that killed Borric.*

As if she somehow overheard, the Princess turned and regarded Erland with a frankly appraising look, as if trying to measure him against whatever reports her spies brought her from her daughter's garden, or as if speculating as to his suitability for her own amusement. But when she smiled at him, her beautiful face looked nothing more to the Prince than mocking.

The festivities wore on, and while Keshian nobles came and went at their leisure, Erland remained. He found himself concerned with things that a few months before he hadn't dreamed of, and he wished he could speak with his father.

The various exhibitions had followed a martial theme, with warriors from distant corners of the Empire showing their Empress and her court their finest young men. The last exhibition was less a demonstration of martial arts as much as it was a ritual. Two companies of warriors were competing in a contest, the origins of which were lost in time. Two villages had been selected by the Governor of Jandowae to present the Battle of Dragons. Two large dragons, marvelously fashioned from rope, tied in coils and knots to the actual size of the creature, were carried upon the backs of hundreds of warriors. The rival villagers were wearing cane and bone armor, centuries old in design and nothing that would withstand modern iron weapons. Each man's helm was bedecked in bright ribbons, one side red, the other blue, and each rope dragon had a brightly carved mask on the front of the same color. Upon the back of each of the two dragons riders in ornate and brightly painted armor directed their companies. The two competing groups would pick up the massive creatures, easily ten feet in circumference at the widest part of the body, behind the head, and run. They would run until they reached the speed they felt was sufficient for their purposes, then charge, bringing the drag-ons together in a clash. The two rope monsters would then be furi-ously pushed upward, the tension between them forcing them higher and higher, until the riders were easily fifty feet in the air. Then the large figures would fall to the ground. Eventually, Erland had been told, one of the two riders would gain a height advantage over the other and seize the plume from his opponent's helm, ending the contest.

Erland found it strangely compelling. The two forces had closed a half-dozen times, with one side or the other feigning and dodging away before the first clash. They had actually come in contact three times now, without either rider getting the other's plume before be-ing forced to jump away and try again. Erland was also impressed on how the riders could make the jump, from a height of twenty-five or so feet, in armor, and not be hurt.

At last the contest ended, with the red side prevailing, and the festivities were over for the afternoon. After a recess for a long nap and refreshments, the dinner festivities would commence. Erland was thinking about sending a runner to the Princess, requesting a repeat of the previous night's encounter, when Gamina's voice came to him. *James would like you to dine with us this evening.*

Erland had gotten so used to the mind speech that he almost answered aloud. He covered by feigning a cough, then said, "Perhaps we should have a quiet meal tonight, my lord Earl?"

James shrugged as if it was nothing important. "Well, we've an-other fifty-eight days of festivities, so we should marshal our re-sources. Perhaps that would be best, after all."

Kafi, who had been at his usual post, said, "Then, Highness, I shall bid you good evening and return to my quarters in the lower city. I shall return at dawn for your pleasure."

"Thank you, Lord Abu Harez," said Erland, with a slight bow.

As Erland's party returned to its quarters, nothing of consequence was said, either aloud or by mind-speech. Reaching the entrance to the wing they were housed within, Erland said, "I guess the Empress felt her time was spent better elsewhere."

James shrugged and Gamina said, "It's a long festival and she is elderly, Erland. It may be wise for her only to attend those functions which are absolutely vital. Today was not much different than a har-vest festival, really."

"True—"

Further conversation was cut off by the appearance of a soldier, dressed in trueblood fashion, but without the colorful headdress. This one wore a very functional-looking helm, and his sandals were replaced with boots and greaves. Upon his chest he wore a leather vest, and a very well-tended sword hung from his belt. "My lords," he said, without waiting for permission to speak. "She Who Is Kesh commands your presence at once."

Erland felt himself flush in surprise and irritation. "Commands—?"

James put a restraining hand upon Erland's shoulder, preventing him from making any rash statement to the guard. "We shall accompany you now," he said.

From Gamina Erland heard, *James said something important must have occurred. He urges you to remain quiet until we know what is happening.*

Erland remained silent as they left the guest wing and made their way back past the amphitheater tunnel entrance they had used, then on to the center palace. In a few minutes they were joined by many armed nobles, most looking grim and concerned.

When they entered the Empress's audience hall, the vast central chamber of the palace, the full roster of Lords and Masters was present in the upper gallery, which surrounded the Empress's dais. Court officials mobbed the floor below, leaving only a straight path to the dais. It was down this path Erland and his companions marched.

When they reached the foot of the dais, Erland and James bowed, while Gamina curtsied. Without preamble, the Empress said, "Would His Highness care to tell us why we just received word that your father is marshalling his Armies of the West in the Vale of Dreams!"

Erland felt his mouth open, then he shut it. He glanced at James, whose expression of astonishment matched his own. At last Erland said, "Majesty, I have no notion of what you are saying."

Throwing down a crumpled parchment, the woman who controlled the most important Empire in the world nearly screamed in frustration. She said, "For reasons beyond *my* wisdom to understand, your father is holding this court *personally* responsible in the matter of your brother's death. Not content to assume the role of monarch, and to negotiate some sort of indemnity, he instead takes the role of bereaved father, and orders his vassals into the field. Your uncle Martin and his garrisons from Crydee, Tulan, and Carse have just landed on the shores southeast of Shamata. Five thousand Royal Krondorian Lancers join them, and our reports tell us another ten thousand foot from the garrisons of Sarth, Questor's View, Ylith, and Yabon march south, and full three thousand Tsurani from LaMūt march with them. Elements of the garrisons at Darkmoor and Malac's Cross also are on the march. Will you please tell me what thirty thousand Isles soldiers are doing massing on our borders if this is not a prelude to invasion!"

Erland could not believe what he was hearing. James stepped forward and said, "If Your Imperial Majesty will permit—"

"I will *permit* nothing!" shouted the old woman. Her rage was fully unleashed. "The fool is mourning one son, yet apparently forgets that I hold another here as a guarantee against Arutha's good behavior."

Gaining control over her rage, the Empress said, "Get to your quarters, sirs and madam. See to those messages you need write tonight. Send them with all haste to the border and pray your father and Prince has learned to control himself. Or by the gods, he'll mourn another son should one Isleman cross into Kesh with violence toward my people in his heart. Is that clear?"

"Very clear, Your Majesty," answered Jimmy.

Half-pulling Erland along, he led him out of the court. Along the entire route from the dais to the front door, the glare of eyes upon them was near palpable, and there was nothing of kindness in anyone's stare. They were as isolated and alone as was imaginable.

At the entrance to the royal court, a company of Household Guards waited to escort them back to their own quarters. As they moved back through the gigantic palace, Erland sent his words to James via Gamina. *What are we now? Prisoners or guests?*

From James came, *We are both. We are hostages.*

As the party from Isles was escorted back to their quarters, Kafi Abu Harez and Lord Nirome joined them. Kafi said, "Highness, lord and lady, I have been given an apartment for the evening at the base of the upper city, just a few yards from one of the many entrances. I will be awaiting your call should you have any need of me."

Erland nodded absently as he tried to imagine what could possibly bring his father to this incredible decision. Even if Arutha didn't have some personal experience with Kesh, as Erland had, he read the intelligence personally, rather than simply leaving it to Gardan and James to advise him. He knew the scope of Kesh's power should she bring it to bear upon the Kingdom. The Kingdom's independence from Kesh had always rested upon one point: Kesh couldn't afford the losses she would endure to invade a nation a third her own size. And the mauling the Kingdom would inflict upon Kesh to enjoy whatever brief victory she might enjoy would make her vulnerable in turn to revolt by the Confederacy, or attack from the Eastern Kingdoms.

But never for a moment did Kesh live in fear of military adventure from the Kingdom. An occasional border clash over the lands in the rich Vale of Dreams had certainly become commonplace in the history of the two nations, but only once did Kesh seek to annex Kingdom lands, when Imperial forces attempted to occupy the narrow strip of land north of the Peaks of Tranquillity between Deep Taunton and the eastern point where the mountains met the sea. Then an army under the command of Guy du Bas-Tyra had crushed the Imperial forces at Deep Taunton, ending all Kesh's attempts to capture a port on the Kingdom Sea.

Since that time, no confrontation of major proportion had occurred. But the specter of the Kingdom invading the Empire was *never* imagined, for if the consequences of invading the Kingdom would be ruinous to Kesh, the Kingdom's consequences for invading the Empire would be even more disastrous.

Drawing his attention to the present, Erland became aware of Nirome's having said something. "Forgive me, my lord, my mind was elsewhere. What did you say?"

"I said, Highness, that you will certainly wish to send messages to your father at once. I shall have dispatch riders ready to leave at your convenience."

"Thank you," said Erland.

James said, "My lord, if you could provide me with a copy of your latest reports upon this feared invasion, I would be thankful."

"I'll see what I may do, m'lord. But Aber Bukar might consider this a sore issue. You are, after all, hostile aliens now."

James controlled his urge to say something nasty and merely smiled. "Thank you."

From Gamina Erland heard, *James says there is something terribly wrong here.*

Of course there is, replied Erland.

They reached the wing of the palace where their own quarters were and saw that the passages between the rooms given over to the Prince and his party were at least without guards between the entrances. "At least we can visit one another," observed Erland.

"Yes," answered James. "Now, the question of the moment is where is Locklear?"

With bitter humor, Erland spoke, as he accompanied James and

242

Gamina into their own quarters. "Even money says he is once again entertaining the Princess Sojiana."

Not willing to risk speaking, James sent, *I'm concerned about him. He has never reacted to a woman like he showed us today. Something in this has him worried, and he doesn't worry easily. I think we should wait until he joins us to decide what to do next.*

Erland nodded agreement, without speaking. To Gamina he sent, *Are we being watched again?*

Gamina glanced around, then said, *The magic device is upon us once again.*

They sat in the receiving room and James signaled for the servants to place some refreshments upon a nearby table and leave them in privacy. When they were gone, James poured all three of them wine.

See if you can determine who is controlling it, said James, and Erland knew that Gamina had established the odd three-way mind-link. It was something she did only when she could sit and not speak, as the strain was too great otherwise. Most of the time in public she simply relayed messages.

Gamina closed her eyes as if she had a headache, fingers pinching the bridge of her nose, then after a moment she said, *It's no one I know by thought patterns. It's difficult to say without risking being detected. I can only eavesdrop a few moments without being sensed by whoever is there.*

Where are they?

Nearby, she answered. *In a complex of rooms on the other side of the garden that opens on to your rooms is the most likely place, Erland.*

Erland nodded. "I think after a bit I'll retire. This has been a most distressing day."

"Yes," agreed James. *So what do you think of this invasion?*

Aloud, so that any eavesdroppers might hear him, he said, "This invasion is clearly nonsense."

James raised one eyebrow, but followed Erland's lead. "I think so, too, but what is your reasoning?"

"Father would never let anything, *especially* personal grief or anger, lead him to make so rash and destructive a decision."

That's my thinking, too, sent James. Aloud he said, "Then what are the alternatives?"

"Two possibilities—one, that the Empress's intelligence is false, that someone is sending fabricated reports of a massive Kingdom buildup along the border to cause just this sort of disruption. Or that father is not massing the Armies of the West to invade, but to counter a feared invasion from Kesh."

James glanced at Erland with a momentary pride in the youngster's reason, then said, "Those are the two obvious choices." Silently he said, *You realize, of course, the significance of the second choice, if that is the correct one?*

What? asked Erland.

It means our courier system, and more, our intelligence system here in Kesh, has been compromised.

Of course, said Erland, his knuckles whitening as he gripped the arm of his chair. *If the system has been compromised, then any intelligence we've gotten from any of our sources here is suspect. Nothing we have been told since before we left on this journey is trustworthy.*

James sighed aloud at that. Then to cover for those listening, he said, "Sorry, Highness. That was rude. I'm tired."

Erland said, "Think nothing of it."

But that means we are completely on our own, said James. *We can't even see if the alleged staging of soldiers is true or false.*

Gamina stretched theatrically, saying, "Perhaps we'll be a little more intelligent if we turn in."

Time to do some work on our own, said James.

Erland's look was questioning. *What do you have in mind?*

It's been years since I've had to run the roofs of the palace looking for murderers, but I've not forgotten how to climb.

Erland grinned, the first genuinely amused expression out of him for days. *Jimmy the Hand is coming out of retirement.*

Something like that. I want to see who is listening in on us, and I can best do that alone.

Standing, Erland said, "I think I shall send a note to Sharana. Perhaps she can intercede with her grandmother. She must know that we harbor no ill will toward her nation."

James nodded. "Good. I'm going to set pen to parchment and send dispatches to Shamata, to ascertain just what is occurring up there."

Erland bowed to Gamina. "My lady, I trust your headache is passed by morning."

"I'm certain it will be, Highness."

Erland quickly made his way to his own quarters and discovered he had no need to send a message for Sharana, as the Princess lay waiting upon his bed. Her court garments, the white kilt and vest, and her jewelry were piled neatly upon an ottoman at the foot of the bed. Smiling at Erland, she patted the cushion next to her, saying, "I was certain you were going to be in council with your people all night long."

Erland tried to smile, but it was a weak effort. "I appreciate your desire to spend time with me, Sharana, but can we speak about this mess?"

"As soon as you get in here," she said with a pout.

Erland motioned for the servants to wait outside and disrobed. He parted the hangings around the bed and lay down next to the Princess. She said, "I was hoping we might have this night to ourselves."

"Of course, but—"

She put her fingers upon his lips, then kissed him, long and lingeringly. "We can talk later. I don't want to be deprived of you one moment longer."

Erland knew there were important issues to be discussed, but quickly he found himself agreeing with the Princess. . . . They could be discussed more calmly later.

Chapter Sixteen
Stalking

Borric watched the fireworks.

From the open front of the inn, he, Ghuda, and Nakor had a fairly good field of view, as most of the crowd was on the other side of the plaza, which opened on the vast Imperial amphitheater. Colorful displays of fireworks filled the night sky, to the astonishment of the crowd. Ghuda was lost in his own dark thoughts and Nakor watched the show with the rapt attention and open delight of a child. Borric had to admit it was far and away the most impressive he had seen, far surpassing even the best the King's Master of Ceremonies had to offer in Rillanon.

Suli appeared and slid onto the bench next to Borric, picking up the cup of ale waiting for him. One thing the boy could do better than any of them was get information; he might be a poor thief, but Suli was an exceptional beggar, which meant he was halfway to being a rumormonger.

"There is something strange happening, master," he whispered.

At this Ghuda's attention was caught. The mercenary had been in a foul mood since the abortive attempt to gain the help of the local thieves. He was now convinced that two groups, the Imperial Guards and the thieves, were actively searching for them, and their lives would be measured in minutes, hours at best. He had resigned himself to dying without seeing a single copper of the money Borric had promised him, let alone having the opportunity to enjoy spending it.

"What's happening?" he asked.

"There are many important people coming and going in the palace tonight, beyond what is normal for even festival times. And men on horseback, wearing the badges of post riders, hasten to and from the upper city. Many guards race from one place to another, while others do nothing. It's as if something big is happening, like a war or revolt or sudden disease. But there's no hint of what it might be from the places you would hear of such a thing, the caravan drivers and boatmen, there is no talk of trouble in the inns and whorehouses. And there are the very odd comings and goings of servants in the palace."

Something struck Borric. "What do you mean by 'odd comings and goings of servants in the palace'?"

Suli shrugged. "As best as I can understand it, master, the servants who are not trueblood are gone from the palace after the evening meal, usually before midnight. But for some reason many are heading back into the palace from the Lower City. And fires can be seen in the cook-buildings, as if a great deal of food is being prepared for many hundreds of people. Those who would be cooking the morning meal would not usually undertake to do so for another seven hours."

Borric considered this in light of what he had been taught about Keshian politics, which while not extensive still contained one fact which fit in. "There are several hundred members of the Gallery of Lords and Masters in the city. Those not trueblood are being called to an emergency council. The food is to keep them from getting hungry during deliberations. With their retinue, many thousands of people are upon the plateau who normally wouldn't be there at this hour." He thought about what this might mean. "How do they enter this upper city? Up that long road?"

Suli shrugged. "I can find out." He slipped out of his seat and headed back into the plaza, which was filling up with citizens now that the festivities were over. Usually, most shops would be closed by this hour, just two hours before midnight, but the presence of the throng of celebrants had caused many of the businesses besides ale shops, wine sellers, inns, and brothels to remain open. Borric found it a little odd. The crowd was the match of anything he had ever seen in Krondor at high noon, yet it was four hours after sundown.

Ghuda said, "What insanity are you thinking of now, Madman?"

Borric said, "It depends on what Suli discovers. I'll tell you when he returns. Just keep an eye open for any of those thugs we lost in the alley last night."

Ghuda said, "Knowing the Imperial Guards, any of the people in that brothel who survived the raid are probably in cells right now while the city watch commander decides what to charge them with so he can sell them on the slave block. Imperial justice is fair: it punishes everyone equally, regardless of guilt or innocence."

Time seemed to drag for the twenty minutes Suli was gone. When he at last returned, Suli looked puzzled. "It's odd, master, but it seems every entrance to the upper city is open, so that those who need to return may do so by the quickest route."

Borric's eyes narrowed. "That many entrances? What about guards?"

Suli shrugged. "There weren't any at the four or five entrances I saw, master."

Borric rose and put on the black leather gloves that were part of his disguise. Overnight he had undergone his third metamorphosis in the last week, thanks to Nakor's bag and what was left of the money made from selling Imperial horses. Now his short white hair was once again dark, a brown with hints of red, and he wore black armor and a black cloak. At casual glance he looked like an Imperial Guard of the Inner Legion. Upon closer examination, he would be another nameless mercenary, in the city for the celebration. Suli wore the same desertman's garb and Nakor had put on a blue robe, which was slightly less faded and stained than the two he had worn before.

Ghuda had resisted any attempt to get him to change his armor and clothing, counting it as useless in the face of certain destruction. He had bought a new red tunic more to halt Borric's nagging than out of any real belief it would help them avoid eventual capture by either the thieves or the Imperial Guards looking for Borric.

When they were all standing, Borric turned and made his way across the plaza. Wending their way through the crowd, they reached the boulevard, which was still roped off and guarded to prevent the denizens of the lower city from entering the street, which would again be used the next day for the morning procession. Borric peered across the now empty boulevard and saw dozens of buildings with lights burning. Many had their doors open wide. A man hurried across the street, and a guardsman moved to intercept him. They spoke briefly and then he waved the man on. The man continued toward a door which he entered.

Suli said, "Those buildings built into the face of the plateau are actually part of the palace itself, housing the lowest of the trueblood, but still trueblood. And many of those apartments have tunnels up to the higher levels."

Borric glanced around, seeing several more guards stopping those attempting to cross the street. "There's a little too much activity around this street. Let's find another way."

As Ghuda followed the Prince he said, "Another way what?"

"You'll see," answered Borric.

"That's what I was afraid you would say," Ghuda answered.

Borric followed the edge of the boulevard as it bordered the gigantic plateau that put this quarter of the city into dusk a few hours after noon. Where another large street intersected, Borric saw what he was looking for. "There!" he said, indicating with a motion of his head.

"What?" said Ghuda.

"Over in the far corner, warrior," answered Nakor. "Can you not see?"

In the far corner, a large open passageway into the plateau could be seen, with no guards in sight but with several servants hurrying through. Borric glanced in both directions, and ducked under the rope. He hurried across the street, expecting someone to shout, but his dark armor must have convinced the other soldiers a half-block away that he was one of them. His companions were only a step behind, so it looked as if he escorted them.

Entering the large doorway, they saw a ramp leading upward into the dark, with torches spaced along the walls every hundred feet or so. Ghuda said, "Now what are we doing?"

"We are walking into the palace," answered the Prince.

"And how do we do that?" asked Ghuda.

"I feel like an idiot for not thinking of this sooner. Just follow me and whatever else you do, look as if you know exactly where we're going. One thing I know about is palaces and their servants. Servants don't want to know anything. That includes those guards put on duty throughout."

He glanced in a side passage about a story above where they entered and saw nothing. "When you are where you don't belong, you gawk about, looking this way and that, and you stand with shoulders round, and to anyone who does belong, you look out of place. If you walk with eyes forward, erect, and purposefully, servants and guards assume you know where you are going. They are not about to stop you and interrogate you, for fear of their instinct about you being correct; they don't want to be punished for interfering with someone who *is* where he is supposed to be.

"It's officers and lower-level officials you have to be cautious of. The officers are likely to halt anyone they don't recognize—though with the influx of several thousand strangers, that's unlikely. What could get us caught would be a minor official, full of himself, who is anxious to prove he's somebody important."

Ghuda said, "Sounds good, Madman. But then so did your idea about contacting the thieves."

Borric halted. "Look, I'm here, and if you're so fearful of your life, now, after all we've been through, why don't you head back?"

Ghuda seemed to think upon it for only an instant. "I've got both the Imperial Inner Legion *and* the thieves of Kesh looking to put me in a very deep hole, thanks to you, Madman. I'm as good as a walking corpse. So, I can go back and wait for someone to recognize me, or get caught here. But there's always the chance the impossible is happening and you're finally doing something right, in which case I might survive and get my money. That's why I'm still here."

Borric glanced back along the tunnel as the echo of distant footfalls came toward them. "Suli? Do you want to leave now?"

The boy was frightened, but shook his head no. "You are my master and I am your servant. I will go with you."

Borric put his hand upon the boy's shoulder a moment, then looked at Nakor. "And what about you, wizard?"

Nakor's grin widened. "Fun."

Ghuda looked heavenward and mouthed the word "fun," but said nothing aloud as Borric signaled they should continue up the passage.

Borric had never seen anything to compare with the palace of the Empress. As big as a large town, the traffic in the broad corridors was not that much less than a busy city boulevard on trading day. The hurrying stream of people down nearly every corridor they passed helped them avoid detection. So far, Borric's assertion that if they but looked the part of people who belonged there no one would challenge them had proven correct.

The problem proved to be that none of them had a hint as to where they were going. To ask directions was to risk discovery, for anyone who was there by rights would certainly know where he was bound.

They had been in the palace over an hour now. It was getting close to midnight and while the Keshian business day had ended only a couple of hours earlier, it was well past the time when most honest citizens were in bed.

Borric led them toward an area which seemed less congested, then down a side passage toward what appeared to be private quarters.

Expecting any moment to be challenged, he was relieved when they turned into a small garden, presently deserted. Ghuda knelt at the edge of a large fountain and drank. Sighing, he looked up and said, "What now?"

Borric sat down on the edge of the fountain and said, "I think I need to scout around, but not until things have quieted down a little." He removed his cloak and his leather armor, saying, "And if I'm going to move around the way I want, this is going to have to stay here." He glanced around the garden, noting a stand of deep shrubs and ferns which bordered one wall. "If you hide over there, you'll only be noticed if someone comes looking for you."

Ghuda was about to reply when a gong reverberated in the distance. "What was that?"

Within a few seconds, another sounded, then another. Suddenly gongs were ringing close by and the sound of people running down the hall could be heard. Grabbing his armor, Borric raced for the hedge and half-dove into it. Hunkering down with his companions, he said, "Damn! I wonder if they're looking for us?"

Peering through the sheltering hedge, Ghuda said, "I don't know, but if they start combing this little patch, we're found. There's only that one exit."

Borric nodded. "We'll wait."

Erland and Sharana both came awake instantly when the gongs began to ring. They hadn't really been asleep, but rather were lost in a soft, warm doze that came quickly after their lovemaking. Despite her soft appearance, the girl was young, healthy, and fit, and challenged Erland, leaving him exhausted when they were done. But it was a wonderful exhaustion and he could not imagine anything he would wish for more than to have it last for a very long time.

But her reaction to the sound of the gongs banished that mood in an instant. "What is it?" he asked.

Sharana leaped out of the bed, the servants drawing aside the curtains for her, and said, "Court dress!"

As Erland fumbled to recover his own clothing, the servants had the Princess's kilt and vest for her in moments. As she fastened the clasp which bound her kilt, she said, "It's an alarm. It's a command to seal the upper city. It means that something is very wrong."

Erland hurriedly finished dressing, and when he was done, they both left the garden and entered his quarters. A mixed company of trueblood court guards and men in the black of the Inner Legions

251

waited for her. They bowed and the officer in command said, "Your Highness. Your servants informed us you were here when we called at your quarters. The Empress commands us to bring you to her."

Sharana nodded, and as Erland moved to come with her, one of the black-armored legionaries said, "We have no orders regarding this one, Highness."

Sharana spun and almost spat as she said, *"This one!"* Pointing at Erland she said, "He is the Heir to the throne of Isles! He is royalty!" Her voice was powerful, commanding, and her face flushed with rage. She almost screamed at the man when she shouted, "You will address him as you would my uncle, for he is Awari's equal in rank! That is my *command!"*

Erland was astonished at the anger in the girl's reaction to the slight, and the ferocity with which she expressed it. He half-expected her to order the man to abase himself, but instead she simply motioned for the company to depart.

Erland noticed the officer was pale and perspiring and felt no envy for him this night. But as they rounded the corner, Sharana's voice was once again honey and wine as she said, "I suppose it may be something to do with this unfortunate business of your father's army. I doubt it could be anything really dangerous. Not in the upper city."

Erland tried to reconcile the sweet and smiling girl who walked beside him now to the shouting one who had dressed down an officer only a moment before, and he couldn't.

They entered the wing of the palace that contained the Court of Light, the formal hall of governing. Erland had not been inside it before, even when called before the Empress. Always before, they had met in the Empress's audience hall.

But now he entered the seat of Kesh's government, the place where darkness never intruded, for the hall was constructed with a thousand chandeliers, each with a score of large candles. Light bathed the room. As bright as day, the hall was almost devoid of shadows, for where sunlight came from only one direction, here light came from twenty thousand sources. Even as the business of the court continued, teams of workers lowered chandeliers and replaced guttering candles almost spent, for never was darkness allowed in the Court of Light.

Down the long entranceway they hurried, past assembled court officials and Imperial Legion officers. At the foremost of the crowd stood the general staff officers of Aber Bukar's Dog Legions. Upon a throne leafed over in gold sat the Empress, resting on cushions made from material of woven gold thread.

Around her on rising seats, tier after tier climbing upward in a semicircle, sat the assembled rulers of Kesh in their Gallery of Lords and Masters. And even as Erland approached the throne, more were entering the hall, hurrying to their places.

The room was humming with quiet conversation and it took no seer to sense the tone of the meeting was fearful. Something terrible had occurred and the room echoed with the most apprehensive speculation.

When Sharana and Erland reached the foot of the dais, the Empress's Master of Ceremonies struck the ground with the iron-clad butt of his giant staff. The falcon that adorned the top of the staff seemed ready to launch itself from the disc of the sun it held in its claws.

"Attend, all ye! She is come! She is come! She Who Is Kesh now sits in judgment!"

Instantly a hush fell over the room. The Empress motioned for Sharana to come up the twelve steps to the top of the dais and the girl did so, a clear look of uncertainty upon her face. This was an unprecedented act, for in the tradition of the Empire, none mounts the Imperial dais save the Empress's Master of Ceremonies, and then he remains a step below, ready to pass up to She Who Is Kesh any documents she might need to peruse. But now she hesitated at the last step, and again her grandmother beckoned Sharana to come to her. When the girl reached her grandmother, she fell to her knees. Lakeisha, Empress of Great Kesh, gathered her granddaughter into her arms and began to cry. The chamber fell to utter silence at the spectacle, as nothing like it had been witnessed by any in attendance.

At last the old woman released her confused and distressed granddaughter and stood. Breathing deeply to regain control, the Empress cried out, "Let it be known that murder has been done in my house!" Tears came to her weathered face again, but her voice remained strong. "My daughter is dead."

There was a collective gasp from the audience. Several members of the Gallery of Lords and Masters looked at one another, seeking some sign that they had not heard this. "Yes," cried the Empress, "Sojiana has been taken from me. She who was to follow after me is now taken from the light." Then Lakeisha's voice turned angry. "We have been betrayed! We have welcomed into this house one who has betrayed us, who is serving those who would seek to bring us low!"

Erland watched from the floor of the hall, and seeing the Empress's eyes fall upon him, glanced about looking for his companions. James and Gamina were standing well to the rear of the vast hall, obviously under guard. Gamina's voice came to him. *James says to remain silent no matter what. He thinks we have been made—*

Before she could finish the Empress screamed, "Erland! Prince of the House of conDoin, have you come into this nation to do naught but evil?"

Erland took a breath before speaking, and in a clear, calm voice said, "Make your meaning clear, Lakeisha."

The familiar use of her name was not lost on the Keshian nobles. Erland was asserting his rank as Heir to the Throne of Isles. He knew that whatever happened, he was assured some protection by his rank and the tradition of diplomatic immunity.

Glaring down at Erland, the Empress said, "You know my meaning clearly enough, child of woe. My daughter Sojiana, she who would have followed me in ruling Kesh, lies dead in her chamber, as you well know. Dead at the hands of your countryman."

Erland again glanced around the room, but even as he failed to find the face he looked for, he heard the Empress's voice say, "My daughter was murdered by the man you brought to our house, and if it can be shown he did so at your order, your rank and position will mean nothing."

Almost a whisper, Erland said, "Locklear."

"Yes," shouted the Empress. "Baron Locklear has fled into the night after doing his bloody work. The palace is sealed and the search begins. And when he has been brought before us, we will at last know the truth of this. Now, get you from my sight; I've had enough of the men of Isles for this life."

Erland stiffly turned and walked out of the chamber, and as he crossed the portal, James and Gamina fell into step behind him, surrounded by guards. Not a word was said until they reached the apartments given over for James and Gamina's use. Erland turned and commanded the guard Captain, "Leave us." When the man hesitated, Erland stepped forward and shouted, "Leave us, *now!*"

The Captain bowed and said, "M'lord," and ordered his men outside.

Erland turned to Gamina and silently said, *Can you find Locky?*

Gamina answered, *I can try.* She closed her eyes and was motionless for a while, then her eyes opened wide in astonishment and she said aloud, "Borric!"

Erland said, "What!"

Forcing herself to mind-speech, she said, *For a moment . . . just a moment, I thought . . .* There was a silence, then she continued, *I don't know what that was. For an instant I detected a pattern that was familiar, then just as I recognized it . . . as I thought I recognized it . . . it vanished.*

Vanished? asked James.

It must have been a magician. Only a magician could have shielded his thoughts from me that quickly and absolutely. With a note of sadness, she said, *It couldn't have been Borric, not here in the palace. I'm tired and worried. I must have just sensed something familiar in the pattern and jumped to the wrong conclusion before I was certain. I'll keep seeking for Locklear.*

The two men went to a divan and sat, watching as Gamina stood motionless, eyes closed as she sent her mind questing through the vast palace, looking for the familiar mental pattern that was Locklear's. Erland moved close to James so he could speak in confidence while leaving Gamina undisturbed. "Did you find anything earlier?" he asked, referring to James's intention to sneak out and scout around the palace.

"Nothing. There's too much ground to cover," James whispered. "It took me the better part of a month to discover most of the secret passages in your father's palace and that's one tenth the size of this one."

Erland sighed. "I thought you might . . . find something."

James shared his disappointment. "So did I."

They hardly spoke as they waited for Gamina to finish her search. After nearly a half hour, she opened her eyes. "Nothing," she said quietly.

"No sign of him," said Erland aloud.

No, she answered. *He's not in the palace. Anywhere.*

Sitting back against heavy cushions, Erland said, "I think there's nothing more we can do tonight but wait." He rose and without another word left James and Gamina.

Borric almost jumped from behind the bushes. "What—" he began, but Ghuda yanked him back down before the guards in the entrance noticed. About five minutes after the alarm bell rang, guards began passing the doorway, all hurrying in one direction. There were both the white-kilted truebloods of the Palace Guards and the black-armored members of the Inner Legion. Borric's only thought was that someone had at last grown suspicious about the odd-looking group wandering through the palace unescorted.

Ghuda said, "What are you trying to do?"

Borric whispered back, "I thought I heard someone speaking behind me for a moment."

Nakor grinned. "There was some magic."

"What?" asked Ghuda and Borric simultaneously.

"Some magic. Someone was searching the area. They reacted for a brief instant when they touched your mind."

Borric blinked in confusion. "How do you know this?"

Nakor ignored the question. "But I fixed it. They can't find you now."

Borric was about to pursue the issue when another group of guards in the black of the Inner Legion entered the garden and began methodically searching among the hedges and bushes. Ghuda slowly and methodically pulled his sword from over his shoulder, ready to leap at the first guard who parted the brush behind which they crouched. When the guards were nearly upon them, Nakor leaped up and shouted, "Ye-ah!"

The closest guard nearly fell over backwards in shock at the sight of this strange, scrawny madman leaping out at him. Then Nakor did a little dance and suddenly a dozen guards were rushing him.

Borric's eyes widened in disbelief as a repeat of the scene he had witnessed the first time he had seen the diminutive wizard was repeated, for no matter how close it seemed someone was to Nakor, the wily little man eluded his grasp. First one guard, then another, would almost close upon him, only to see the spry Isalani leap nimbly away, laughing maniacally the entire time. Twice he ducked under the encircling arms of one man, tripping another, and darting past a third, before anyone knew what was occurring. As arms sought to encircle him, he hit the ground rolling, and as guards dived to tackle him, he leaped into the air. Whenever a grasping hand sought to close upon him, it found only emptiness. And the hooting, gibbering sounds he made only drove the guards to try harder, taunting them into acting rashly.

Finally a Sergeant of the guard bellowed orders and the legionaries spread out to surround Nakor. The little man reached into his rucksack and pulled out a small object, about the size of a walnut. As the guardsmen rushed him, he threw it at the ground.

When the device struck the ground, a blinding white light burst forth for an instant, followed by a cloud of white smoke, accompanied by the same nasty sulphur smell Borric had experienced in the jail at Jeeloge. Blinking, confused guardsmen stood around a moment, then discovered that Nakor wasn't in the center of the circle anymore. A wicked laugh caused them to turn as one and there stood the Isalani before the hallway door. Whistling shrilly, he motioned for the guardsmen to follow and ran off toward the center of the palace.

Ghuda said, "How did he do that?"

Suli whispered, "He must *truly* be a magician."

Borric stood up. "They'll be back when that Sergeant remembers there were others and they hadn't finished searching this garden. We have to find another place to hide and quickly. Come on."

Ghuda snorted in derision. "One place is much the same as another to die, Madman."

Borric looked back at the mercenary for a long moment, then coolly said, "The object of the exercise is *not* to die, Ghuda."

Ghuda shrugged. "I can't argue that. Where now?"

Borric glanced into the hall door and said, "In the opposite direction from where all those guards were heading. If we can circle behind into the area they've already searched, we can buy some time."

He didn't wait for further comment but simply walked into the hall calmly, as if he knew exactly what he was doing. Silently, he wished he did.

Erland sat alone brooding. Nothing was making sense. The events of the past two days were so improbable that he couldn't for a moment believe the Empress actually thought he had come into her palace to cause this havoc. There was no motive, no reason, and no explanation, save the obvious one. Whoever had tried to ferment war between the Kingdom and the Empire was actively attempting it again and seemed bent on speeding things along. The only suggestion that offered itself was that whoever the architect of this plot was, he wished to provoke the confrontation while every possible suspect in the Empire was in the city for the Jubilee.

Erland wished he knew more intimately the names of those who would wish this madness on two nations, for he would gladly have delivered him—or her, he amended; the women in court were as dangerous as the men—trussed like a game bird to the Empress. He considered trying to get a note to Sharana, reassuring her that he had absolutely nothing to do with this violence against her mother.

Then he thought better of it. Even if he had plunged in the knife or put poison in Sojiana's cup himself, he would proclaim his innocence. Then a thought struck him: how was the Princess Sojiana murdered? And if Locklear was under suspicion, where was he? It was not as if he was a thief in the night; he was a peer of the Kingdom, a Baron of the Prince of Krondor's court. Even should some conflict arise, some argument—even the most heated—Locklear would not harm a woman.

Erland knew Locklear was being made the scapegoat, but how to prove it?

Lady Miya entered the quarters and bowed slightly. "Erland," she said softly, "the Empress has ordered that you be confined to these quarters."

Erland sat upright, anger suffusing him. "How dare she! Even she would not jeopardize the tradition of diplomatic immunity."

Miya came to sit next to the Prince. "She's lost her daughter. Her advisors are cautioning her that if she harms you or any of your party without leave of your King, she risks reprisals, and no Ambassador will dare enter the borders of Kesh again." The woman sighed and put her arm around Erland's shoulders. "She'll change her mind in a day or two, I'm certain. Until then, you're free to visit your friends in the other part of this wing, but you can't leave this area without guards and then only to return to the Empress's court should she desire to see you again."

Erland said, "How was the Princess murdered?"

Miya's eyes brimmed but she kept from crying as she said, "Her neck was broken."

Erland's eyes narrowed. "Broken? In a fall of some sort?"

The woman shook her head. "No. There were bruises around her throat. Someone snapped her neck."

Erland said, "Miya, this is important. Locklear couldn't have killed your cousin."

Miya studied the Prince's face for a moment, then said, "How can you be certain?"

"Locklear's not the kind of man who would harm a woman, even if he had cause, save to defend himself. But look, even if something . . ." Erland fumbled for words. "Even if something caused him to act . . . unlike himself . . . he wouldn't have throttled Sojiana. He's a bladesman, and he'd have used his sword or dagger. He's a skilled fighting man but lacks the brute strength to break a neck. The Princess was not a petite woman. And if she's like her daughter, there's strength under that soft skin."

Miya nodded. "Sojiana was stronger than she looked. All . . . all of my relatives from the Empress's side of the family are like that. They look soft, but they're not." She was quiet for a moment, then said, "But if Locklear didn't kill her, who did? And why isn't Locklear here?"

Erland said, "Those two answers are the same, I fear. And if I'm correct about what has happened, then Locklear is in danger . . . if he isn't already dead."

Miya said, "I think I know someone who can help."

"Who?"

"Lord Nirome. He's always willing to listen to reason. And with Sojiana dead, the strain in the Gallery of Lords and Masters will be even greater, for while most would have accepted Sojiana as the next Empress, many of those will not accept someone as young as Sharana. Nirome will be anxious to reduce the strain in the court, and finding the Princess's murderer will more than likely do that faster than anything else."

"I wonder . . ." said Erland, as he considered something. "Who stands with Awari?"

"Lord Ravi and the others who fear the matriarchy. But many who were supporters of Sojiana simply because she was eldest will now flock to Awari's cause. I can't think of any reason he would not inherit."

Erland said, "See if you can get Nirome to call. We must halt this madness before it spills over into more bloodshed."

The girl ran off and Erland sat back. Closing his eyes, he tried to picture Gamina's face and he attempted to send his thoughts to her. After a minute, her voice came into his mind. *Yes, Erland, what is it?*

Would you and James please come to my quarters. I think I was premature in planning on sleep. There are some things we need to discuss.

There was a moment of silence, then Gamina said, *We're on our way.*

Chapter Seventeen
Traps

Borric glanced around the corner.

Seeing no movement in the shadows, he motioned for his companions to follow after him. For the better part of an hour they'd been hiding from various companies of guards intent on finding the intruders. Of Nakor they had seen nothing since he led the first party of Inner Legionaries away. A half-dozen times since then they had barely managed to avoid search parties.

Ghuda put his hand on Borric's shoulder. "We're getting nowhere fast," he whispered. "I think we've got to grab a servant and find out where these friends of yours are housed. We can tie the man up—it'll just leave him uncomfortable for a while—then send someone to turn him loose when you've cleared up this bloody mess we're in. What do you think?"

Borric said, "I can't think of a better idea, so we might as well." He glanced about. "We could all do with a short rest."

Ghuda said, "I could use a few minutes off my feet, that's for certain."

"Well, these rooms all seem to be empty." Pointing to the nearest door, he said, "Let's check inside this one."

Borric opened the door as quietly as he could; it was an ornate thing of cane and ivory, and creaked loudly as he pushed on it. After it opened a few inches, he said, "Maybe we should go back to those doors with only curtains?"

Suddenly Ghuda pushed hard on the door, so that it made a single, surprisingly modest creak, then he shoved the other two through, swinging the door closed behind him.

Borric almost lost his balance and as he turned, the old fighter put his finger to his lips, indicating the need for silence. Borric had his rapier out and Suli his shortsword, and Ghuda stepped back, unlimbering his large hand-and-a-half sword. He stepped clear of the other two, so he would have room to swing. Borric glanced around the deserted room, making sure there was nothing to trip him up if he had to fight. Not that it mattered: if he was forced to fight, there would be an unlimited supply of guards as far as the three of them were concerned. His only hope would be to keep from getting killed long enough to convince someone that he really was the other son of Arutha.

Tired, they all sat upon the floor, stretching muscles sore from tension and being on their feet for hours. Ghuda said, "You know, Madman, this sneaking around in the palace gives a man an appetite. I wish I had one of Nakor's oranges right now."

Borric was about to reply when a muffled sound caught his attention. Voices, indistinct but coming closer, caused him to jump to his feet and move to the door. Suli crouched down below Borric's chin, so he might see. Borric was about to shoo the boy away, but the sound of someone approaching silenced him.

Two men came into view as they moved past the door. One was stout, with a staff of office clutched in his hand. The other was dressed in a black cloak, hiding him from view, but as they passed he turned and Borric caught a glimpse of his face. Both men were intent in conversation and Borric overheard the stout one saying, ". . . tonight. We can't wait any longer. If the Empress's temper fades, she may seek a more reasonable solution. I convinced her to send Awari north in preparation for trouble there, but that ruse will not last long. And there's this business of some maniac running loose in the palace that the guards can't seem to catch. I don't know what that means, but it must be presumed to be trouble. . . ." The voice faded as the men turned another corner.

Suli turned and pulled emphatically on Borric's sleeve. "Master!"

"What?" said Borric, trying to sort out a rush of images.

"That man, the thin one in the black cloak. He's the same man I saw at the Governor's house in Durbin—the one who wore the golden torque. The one who worked for Lord Fire."

Borric leaned back against the door, and nodded. "That makes evil sense."

Ghuda put up his sword and whispered, "What's this, then?"

"I know why trouble's been nipping at our heels since Durbin," muttered Borric.

"What?"

"I'll tell you later. I hope you both had a nice rest. It's over. Right now, we've got to find that servant."

Borric yanked open the door, rendering the squeaky hinge nearly inaudible. He moved out into the hall before Ghuda could question him further. Borric hesitated an instant, while the others moved through the door and closed it. He motioned for Ghuda and Suli to hug the wall.

At the next corner, the corridor turned, allowing for only one choice, so Borric followed the turn. No lights were burning in this wing of the palace and Borric doubted it was usual for Keshian nobles to stumble around in the darkness, so there was likely no one about.

As they reached the far end of that hall, Borric turned and whispered, "Someone's coming." He motioned for Ghuda and Suli to move back against the wall, while he moved to the opposite side of the hall.

A lone woman hurried around the corner and Ghuda stepped out to block her progress. "What—" she began, then Borric seized her from behind. The woman was lithe and athletic, but Borric easily kept her under control as he dragged her into the first door in the hall.

Light from a room across from a window gave a faint illumination to the scene. The woman was kept under control as Borric whispered into her ear, "Make an outcry and you'll be hurt. Remain silent and no harm will come to you. Do you understand?"

The woman gave him a single nod and he released her. Turning suddenly, she said, "How dare you—" Then she saw who had seized her. "Erland? What has gotten into—" Her eyes widened as she saw the fashion of dress and the short-cropped dark hair. "Borric! How did you get here?"

All Borric's life, James had been telling stories about his days as a thief in Krondor, and one common characteristic of James's far-fetched tales was his reference to his "bump of trouble." When something was wrong, James somehow sensed it. And for the first time in his life, Borric understood what James had been talking about. Something inside of him screamed that there was trouble standing directly before him.

Taking his sword out, he leveled it at the woman. Ghuda said, "Madman, that's not necessary. The woman—"

"Quiet, Ghuda. Woman, what's your name?"

"Miya. I'm a friend of your brother's. He will be so thrilled to discover you still live. What are you doing—" She laughed, and Borric knew it was as forced as it was artful, for it sounded genuine and spontaneous. "I prattle. It must be the shock of—"

"Seeing me in the palace," Borric finished.

" 'Alive,' I was about to say," said Miya.

Borric said, "I don't think so. When you first saw me, you thought I was my brother. Then you quickly understood I wasn't. Anyone who thought I was dead would not have made that guess so quickly. And you didn't say, 'You're alive,' you said, 'How did you get here?' That's because you knew I was alive and in the city below."

The woman fell silent, and Borric said to Ghuda and Suli, "This is one of those who has been involved in trying to get me killed every step of the way from Krondor to Kesh. She works for Lord Fire."

Miya's eyes widened an instant at the mention of that name, but she gave no other sign of recognition. She said, "If I scream loudly enough, a dozen guards will come here in a moment."

Borric shook his head no. "This wing has already been searched. We slipped behind the lines of those going room to room. Besides, they're looking for one man."

The woman's eyes flashed as she stepped away, her glance measuring the distance to the door. "Don't think of it," said Borric. "It would be a close thing, but I'm faster than I look and I have four feet of reach you lack," he said, pointing at her with the sword.

"You won't get out of here alive; you know that? Things are already beyond quick and easy explanations. Blood has been spilled and soldiers march. Your father marshals the Armies of the West in the Vale of Dreams, ready to invade."

"Your father?" said Ghuda. "And just who might he be when he's to home?"

Borric said, "My father's Prince Arutha of Krondor."

Ghuda blinked like an owl caught in the light. "The Prince of Krondor?"

Suli said, "And I am his servant, and will be his servant when he is King of the Isles."

Ghuda stood quietly for a long moment, then said, "Madman . . . Borric . . . Prince, whatever I'm to call you, when this is over remind me I need to knock you down again."

"If we get out of this mess, I'll be happy to stand still while you do it." To Miya he said, "My father is many things, but no fool. He'd no sooner march an army into Kesh than I'd run into a bog of quicksand carrying an anvil."

Ghuda said, "Well, from what I've seen you just might."

Borric said, "She's lying. And we need to get to my brother." To Miya he said, "You're going to guide us there."

"No."

Borric stepped forward, putting his sword against the woman's throat. When Miya didn't flinch, he said, "So, you have no fear of dying?"

"You're no murderer," spat Miya.

Rough hands moved Borric aside. Ghuda said, "He might not be, bitch." Huge hands gripped the woman's shoulders as he jerked her toward him, and from the expression of discomfort on Miya's face in the gloom, Borric could imagine they were not gentle. Bringing her face scant inches from his own, he whispered, "But I'm a different stripe of cat. I have no use for you truebloods and your superior ways. I'd just as soon pet a snake as touch your soft skin. You could be on fire and I wouldn't cross the street to piss on you. I'll kill you slowly and painfully, girl, if you don't tell us what we must know. And I will do it so you can't even scream."

The calm menace of the mercenary must have been convincing, for Miya could barely speak as she said, "I'll take you."

Ghuda released her, and Borric saw tears of terror running down the girl's cheeks. He sheathed his rapier, then pulled his dagger from his belt. Showing her the short blade, Borric then gave her a shove toward the door and said, "Remember, you can't get away. I can throw my dagger faster than you can run."

Miya opened the door and they followed after. As they walked along, Ghuda said, "What tumbled you to her act?"

"My bump of trouble."

"You could have convinced me you didn't have one, for certain," said the mercenary. "I'm glad it finally woke up."

"Me, too."

"But you were already tumbled to something," he said. "What made you alert to her?"

"She was heading in the same direction where I saw those two men heading, and one of them tipped me off."

"What about him?"

"He's been stalking me since we left Krondor. And he's one of the few in Kesh who would recognize me on sight."

"Who is he?" asked Ghuda, as they rounded a corner into a better-lighted corridor.

As the first pair of sentries standing before doors came into view, Borric moved a step closer to the girl in case she decided to bolt or call for help. To the mercenary he said, "The man was Lord Toren Sie, Kesh's Ambassador to my father's court."

The mercenary shook his head. "He's royal. Some very important people want you dead, Madman."

"And some very important people want the truth," answered Borric. "That's what's going to keep us alive a little longer."

"Gods, I hope you're right," said the mercenary. Miya led them through the palace, past a series of guards standing before doors. If they thought it odd a member of the Empress's household should escort three oddly dressed men past them, they hid it well. Miya turned down a large corridor, past another half-dozen unguarded doors.

At the far end of the hall, Miya moved to a large closed door and said, "Your brother is in there."

Borric gave her a shove. "Open it and go through first."

The woman put her hand on the latch and moved it, pushing open the door. She entered and moved the door open wider for Borric. He followed, ahead of Ghuda and Suli.

She led them through a short reception room to another door, where the opening procedure was repeated, but this time, once Suli passed through, she slammed the door behind him, and yelled, "It's Borric of Krondor! Kill him!"

Armed men in the trueblood guard uniform sat around the room and at Miya's words they were on their feet, weapons slipping from scabbards.

The servant announced Lord Nirome and Erland bid him enter. The stout noble hurried in and bowed before the Prince. "Highness, Lady Miya said you had something you urgently wished to discuss with me." Then Nirome noticed James and Gamina, who were sitting opposite Erland, just out of sight of Nirome when he entered. "My lord, my lady. I didn't see you at first. My apologies."

He's anxious to speak to you alone, Gamina sent to Erland. *In fact, he's very upset we are here.*

"Have you any word regarding Baron Locklear?"

Nirome shrugged. "Had we, you would have been advised at once. I must make you understand that most of us who sit in council with Her Majesty are not so personally outraged. We lost a cousin at most, while She Who Is Kesh lost a daughter. While mother and daughter were often at odds over court matters, nevertheless the feelings they felt were strong. And as you have no doubt repeated to yourself a hundred times over, there is no logic in any of this."

"That's what I was hoping you'd say," said Erland.

"I am a pragmatic man, Highness. My role throughout my time in the Gallery of Lords and Masters has often been that of a conciliator, for as you have no doubt seen, we have many diverse people in our Empire. Kesh is a pluralistic nation, with a very different history than your own Kingdom. You were a common people in ancient days. You have only two major subject people within your borders, those of Yabon and our former countrymen in your own Crydee, while Kesh is a nation of a thousand languages and customs."

He's stalling for time, James sent via Gamina.

Why?

Gamina answered, *He wants to speak with you alone . . . no, he wants to get you alone . . . his mind is racing . . . he's not focusing the way you do when you speak to me . . . he's thinking about . . .* Suddenly Gamina's face went white and a second later James almost leaped to his feet, his sword in hand. The stout noble sensed something from Erland's expression or from the sound of James's standing, but he turned quickly, his staff of office brought before him in a protective gesture.

"What is this?" said Erland.

Gamina said, "Borric is alive. He's somewhere here in the city. Nirome wants to take you somewhere in the palace where friends of his can kill you."

Erland couldn't take it all in for a moment. "What?"

Nirome's face went ashen. "What . . . is the lady saying?"

James said, "My wife has certain talents, my lord. And among those is sensing falsehood. Now, what part have you been playing in the murder done this night?"

Nirome edged toward the door and James moved to cut him off. Erland had his sword out and said, "Where is my brother?"

Nirome sought an exit, and when none was available to him, seemed to visibly wilt. "Mercy, my lord Prince, mercy. I will confess, but you must promise to intercede with the Empress. I did only a minor bit, to further the ambitions of Awari. It was he who plotted his sister's death and is planning on killing you and marrying Sharana."

"His own niece?" said Erland.

James waved his sword a bit. "It's been done before in the earlier dynasties of the Empire. If a succession was seen as weak, claimants married a cousin or even a sister or brother to bolster the claim on the throne. And with so many related to the Empress, a great many truebloods are cousins."

Nirome said, "Just so. But if we are to save your friend, we must hurry. He's imprisoned in a lower level of the palace and injured."

James glanced at Gamina and she said, *I can't tell.*

What? asked Erland.

He's very clever and his mind is very agile. He may not know I can read his surface thoughts, but he suspects some magic is at play and keeps his mind repeating what he has told us. There are hints of other images and some feelings . . . he's lying about the scope of his role, but I can't tell how much. You must be wary of him.

Erland said, "Now, what about Borric being alive?"

Nirome said, "It's thought to be true. A slave escaped within days after being brought to Durbin by desert raiders. It is thought he killed the wife of the Governor of Durbin to mask his escape. He matches the description of your brother."

He's . . . hiding more. But that's more or less true.

Erland said, "We have to find someone whom we can trust."

A servant arrived at the doorway and Erland's attention was drawn away for a moment. Nirome struck out with his staff of office, and far more quickly than his weight promised, he dodged James's blow. Shouting "Get the guards!" to the girl, Nirome swung widely with his staff.

The girl hesitated only an instant, then ran screaming for the guards through the doorway. James grabbed at Nirome's arm and got struck with the staff on the shoulder. Erland jumped forward and grabbed the staff, forcing the heavy courtier back. As the Prince brought his sword up to menace the court officer, guards entered the room.

Instantly swords and spears were leveled at James and Erland and a guard Captain, in the white kilt of a trueblood, cried, "Surrender your weapons or die!"

Erland thought about resistance for only an instant, then gave his sword to a guard. "I need send word to the Empress at once. There's been a vile betrayal."

Guards took James and Erland by the arms and the Captain said, "Shall we kill them?"

Nirome said, "Not just yet. Take them to the empty wing and for the sake of our lives don't let anyone see you doing it! I have to find Miya and Toren Sie and we'll join you."

Suddenly Erland realized that this stout man of obsequious manner had stationed men loyal to Prince Awari around this wing of the palace—which was how he was able to murder the Princess Sojiana and cast the blame on Locklear.

"You killed Sojiana," Erland said. "And Locklear."

Nirome's manner changed and he became, instead of the fawning sycophant, a grim-faced man of determination and purpose. Picking up a walnut from the table, he crushed it with his bare hand before Erland's face. "You silly boy. You've blundered into matters so far beyond your understanding. . . ." He studied the Prince. "Had your brother the grace to die in Krondor, and your father to send threatening notes to the Empress, none of this would have been necessary. If you cooperate and don't cause a fuss, I'll happily send you back to your father in one still-living piece. I have no wish to deal with an angry Kingdom, and once the Empress accedes to our plan, we have no further need of you."

To the guard captain he said, "Take them now, and watch the witch woman. She's from Stardock and has some sort of power to know what you're thinking if you're not careful." He glanced at her and said, "We may have to keep her. That would prove a useful talent. But if any of them causes you *any* difficulty, kill them."

The soldiers obeyed without hesitation and in a moment were taking the three from the apartment, making sure there was no chance of escape.

The armed men hesitated a moment, startled by Miya's unexpected alarm. Borric took no time to think; he reacted. He threw his dirk at the first man to rise, taking him in the chest. Another went down from a vaulting lunge that cleared five feet, and three men withdrew in haste as they brought up their own weapons.

A coughing scream and a sickening crack told Borric without looking that Ghuda had silenced the woman who had lured them here with a quickly crushed neck. Then the mercenary said, "Make room, Madman."

Borric knew Ghuda was unlimbering his bastardsword and needed more room for it than the rapier or shortsword that Suli carried.

Borric was concerned for the boy, but could not spare any attention for him. There were three angry guardsmen trying to kill him at the moment.

Borric parried a thrust from one man with his dirk, and took another in the throat with his rapier, ducking under a thrust by the third. A solid crash behind and a scream cut off suddenly and Borric knew that Ghuda had taken out another man. Four quickly down and still no attempt to organize. Borric pressed his attack. He slashed wickedly at a man's head, taking off an ear. The man fell, crying in pain and unable to defend himself, and Borric killed him with his dirk while slashing at the remaining man.

Borric heard the solid noise of steel cleaving meat and bone and judged Ghuda had killed or disabled the fifth. The Prince parried a blow toward his own head by the last man he faced and ran him through.

Borric turned quickly to discover Ghuda kicking one man in the groin while trying to free his hand-and-a-half sword from the man he had just impaled. Suli was backed into a corner, frantically waving his shortsword, keeping two men at bay. But a third was moving to come at him on his left side, and Borric leaped atop a table, sprang, and came down in time to kill the man from behind. He then struck out and wounded one of the two remaining men attacking Suli. But as that man went down, the other thrust with his longsword and the boy screamed.

Borric hacked with the edge of his blade, cutting at least three inches into the neck of the man who had wounded Suli. The man made a pitiful noise, much like a mouse's squeak, and collapsed to the floor. Then it was quiet.

Borric pulled off one dead man who lay atop Suli and knelt beside the boy, who was covered in blood and vainly attempting to hold together a gaping wound in his stomach. Borric had seen such wounds in the field before and knew Suli's life would be over in minutes.

Feeling a cold certainty unlike anything he had known before, Borric took the boy's hand. Suli's breathing came in shallow gulps and his eyes were beginning to glaze over. His face had a waxy cast to it and he tried to speak. Finally he said, "Master?"

Gripping Suli's hand, Borric said, "Here, Suli."

"I was your servant?" the boy asked quietly.

Borric gripped Suli's hand hard and said, "You were a fine servant."

"Then it will be written in the Book of Life that Suli Abul was the servant of a great man, the servant of a Prince."

Limp fingers slipped from the Prince's hand. "Yes, little beggar. You died the servant of a Prince." Borric had seen death before, but not in one so young. Impotence at being able to protect the boy overwhelmed him. For fully a minute he knelt, certain that if he could but think of something, the proper thing to do or say, somehow Suli wouldn't be dead.

Ghuda's voice said, "We can't linger. There are twelve corpses littering the floor. As soon as someone walks in here, there'll be hell to pay. Let's go!"

Borric was up and moving. He knew that he had to reach his brother or the Empress within the next few minutes. Hostile forces moved within the palace of Kesh, and no one could be trusted.

They hurried back the way they had come until they reached the hall with the sentries. Borric motioned with his head and walked calmly past one pair into another dark hall. Then, halfway down the length of the dark hallway, he heard muffled voices approaching. As one, Borric and Ghuda ducked into the recesses of a doorway, just as another pair of men hurried past.

The voice of the stout man Borric had seen a few minutes earlier said, "Damn. This is starting to unravel. Awari was not supposed to hear of his sister's death this soon. Find out who sent him word and kill the man or woman responsible. He was to be halfway to Arutha's mythical invading army when he finally found out." Borric's eyes widened. Princess Sojiana was dead! Perhaps that was what all the madness in the palace was about, not a search for four nameless vagabonds who stumbled into the palace, but a search for the Princess's murderer. Borric signaled to Ghuda to follow and they hung back a little, then darted across the intersecting hallway, getting back within earshot of the two men once more. The stout one continued his complaint. "Awari's a stiff-necked idiot. He will certainly return to the city within the day and if he marches into the Empress's chambers and demands any sort of recognition of his claim while she's this angry over Sojiana's death, we'll have open rebellion to deal with; he must be made to lead the army north. The Isleman must be made to look guilty. Where do you have him?"

A voice, one familiar to Borric, replied, "In a grain shed, near the servants' lodgings on the lower levels," said Toren Sie.

"Move him to one of the empty servant's quarters and then let the guards find him. Have the Captain report the man was found and killed resisting arrest and let it circulate among the Gallery that he was killed to keep him silent. Then have the guard Captain who finds him die mysteriously. I will denounce the plot in the Gallery. By being the first to raise suspicion, we'll divert it from ourselves for the time being. By the time anyone begins to question things, it will be too late."

"But won't that exonerate Isles?"

"No," replied the stout Keshian, "but it will again make everyone wonder who knew, who took a hand, and how high up the conspiracy went. Every rival in the Gallery will be convinced his adversary is in league with Isles. All I need for the next two days is confusion and uncertainty. I have to have the time to ensure that those supporting Sharana and Awari are equally vocal in the Gallery."

The two men reached the door of the room Erland and Ghuda had vacated and continued on to a room at the far end of the hall. "And where is Miya?" asked the stout man as he turned to open the door. He must have glimpsed the two figures following after, for he called, "Who is that?"

Borric walked up, out of the gloom, and saw the two men before the door. The thinner of the two said, "You!"

Borric smiled a grim smile as he leveled his sword and said, "Ghuda, I have the honor of presenting Lord Toren Sie, Ambassador of Her Majesty, the Empress of Kesh, to the Prince's court in Krondor."

The second man turned as if to bolt into the room, and Ghuda moved to cut him off. "And that," said Borric, "is one who is unknown to me, but his clothing is unmistakably that of another member of the Royal House of Kesh."

Toren Sie said, "If I shout, a dozen guards will be here in seconds."

Borric said, "Shout, and you'll be very dead when they get here."

Toren Sie glared. "What do you expect to gain?"

Moving so that his sword point was leveled at the Ambassador's throat, Borric answered, "An audience with the Empress."

"Impossible."

Borric motioned with the point of his blade, making a dramatic whooshing sound right below Toren Sie's chin. "I don't know everything that is going on here," he said, "but I do know enough that should we live to reach the Empress you are most likely a dead man. If you have any hope for avoiding that fate, you had best begin by telling me what I need to know."

The stout man said, "We will tell you what you wish to know. But we can do it better inside this door. We can sit like civilized beings."

Without waiting for a response, the stout man opened the door and only Ghuda's quick reaction kept it from being slammed in their faces. The large mercenary shoved hard against the door, forcing it open, then suddenly the resistance ceased and he almost fell through. Borric grabbed Toren Sie by his gold torque, twisting the woven gold collar so that it constricted the man's breathing. Dragging him through the door after Ghuda, Borric entered in time to see the stout man running with unusual swiftness for the door on the other side of the reception chamber of the complex. Ghuda was at the door when the man sprung through shouting, "Kill them!"

Borric didn't hesitate, but struck the Ambassador hard in the side of the head with the hilt of his sword. The man slumped to the floor, unconscious, as Borric sprinted toward the next door.

When he got there, he found Ghuda standing in open amazement, and the stout man dangling a foot off the ground. Around the room a full dozen guardsmen in the uniform of the Inner Legion and a few of the trueblood lay stunned on the floor. Also unconscious were Earl James, Lady Gamina, and Erland.

Sitting atop a large round table was Nakor, grimacing strangely and making odd noises as he pointed two fingers at the floating man. Seeing Ghuda and Borric, he stopped his grunting and said, "Borric! Ghuda!" Instantly the stout Keshian fell to the floor with a harsh thud, and Ghuda reached out to grip the man by the neck.

Borric crossed to where his friends lay and said, "Nakor, what have you done?"

"I was having fun with the guards, playing a merry game of 'catch-me,' and they got lost. So I went looking for them. I saw you, or so I thought, being led away by guards and thought to inquire how you managed to find such splendid clothing, and where you had lost my friends Ghuda and Suli. Where is Suli?"

Ghuda glanced at Borric, who said, "Suli is dead."

"That is sad," said the little man. "He was a good-hearted boy and would have been a good man. He most likely will be when next he travels the Wheel. Is this your brother?" he asked, indicating Erland.

"Yes," said Borric. "What did you do to them?"

"Oh, I came into the room and everyone got very excited. Some of them were not very pleased to see me, and I was growing tired of the game, so I stunned everyone. I assumed you would come along, sooner or later. See? I was right."

Suddenly the tension erupted in Borric and Ghuda and they laughed. "Yes, you were right." They found they couldn't stop as the grinning little man seemed to enjoy the merriment as much as they. At last, with tears running down their faces, Borric said, "You stunned everyone? How did you manage that?"

Nakor shrugged. "It's a trick."

Borric laughed again. "What now?"

Nakor reached into his rucksack and said, "Want an orange?"

"I never thought I'd say this to you," said Erland, "but I have missed you."

Borric nodded. "Same here. Now, what are we going to do about this mess?"

James was shaking off the effects of Nakor's stun while Gamina was still barely conscious. Ghuda stood watch over the reviving guards and looked convincingly ready to cut in half anyone who moved, so they sat quietly and gave no trouble.

Erland had been the first to revive, something to do with being the youngest, according to Nakor. The brothers had spoken about what each knew and had come to the conclusion that many double dealings had taken place.

James said, "Perhaps if we get word directly to the Empress herself . . . ?"

"How?" asked Borric.

"Gamina," answered Erland.

Borric looked uncomprehending and Erland said, "She can do mind-speech, remember?"

Borric nodded, then his face reddened. "I could have 'called' for help with my mind when I first got in the palace and she would have heard."

"Why didn't you?" asked James as Gamina began to rouse.

Borric's grin was sheepish. "I didn't think of it."

"And," said James, "how did you escape her mind touch when she stumbled across you earlier today?"

Borric hiked a thumb at Nakor. "He sensed it and somehow blocked her out."

James said, "You're a magician?"

Nakor made an unpleasant face. "No. Isalani. Magicians are somber men who work in caves and do terrible and serious things. They do great magic. People don't like magicians. I just do a few tricks that make people laugh. That is all."

As Gamina fully roused, James said, "From the look of the guards and our fat friend over there, yours are no mean tricks, and not always funny."

Nakor's grin widened and he said, "Thank you. I'm pretty good at what I do, and *I* thought this was pretty funny."

Gamina caught sight of Borric and said, "You're alive!"

"Apparently," answered Borric with a laugh.

Gamina gave him a hug and said, "How, then, couldn't I find you in the desert?"

Borric's look showed he didn't understand, then comprehension registered. "Of course. That bloody robe I won before we left. The slavers took me for a magician and clapped some manacles on me that somehow prevent magicians from using their powers."

"Bah!" said Nakor. "That couldn't happen if those magicians knew what they were doing."

James said, "Perhaps. In any event, the next question is: how do we get from here to the Empress?"

"It should be easy," said Nakor. "You just follow me. And bring these fellows along."

Ghuda had disarmed the twelve guards and dragged the stunned Toren Sie into the room. With four armed guards, Borric, Erland, James, and Ghuda, the fourteen captives didn't seem inclined to start any trouble. Nirome warned, "As soon as we see another company of guards, you'll be prisoners. Men loyal to Awari control this entire sector of the palace."

Nakor grinned. "Maybe."

When they reached the occupied hallway, where they would begin to pass dozens of guards, Nakor reached into his rucksack and pulled something out of it. Borric and Ghuda were almost blasé about the sack at this point, but everyone else was astonished. For as the little Isalani brought his hand up, perched upon it was the red- and golden-speckled falcon, the royal bird of Kesh, and most revered and holy symbol of the Empress's power. It was a bird thought to be almost extinct—three females were all that remained in the Imperial mews. The falcon shrieked and spread his wings, but remained upon the little man's wrist as he moved down the hall.

The guards they passed simply gaped at the splendid bird. Nakor said to each sentry he passed, "Please, come with us. We go to see the Empress."

No matter what Nirome or Toren Sie said, the guards seemed mesmerized by the sight of the falcon. They joined in behind the

274

Islemen and their captive band and soon a procession of two hundred guards followed Nakor and his companions as they entered the hall of the Empress.

The Master of Ceremonies said, "What is this?"

Borric and Erland both came forward and Erland said, "The Princes Borric and Erland of Isles wish an immediate audience with Her Majesty. We wish to discuss a small matter of treason."

The entire Gallery of Lords and Masters was in extraordinary session when the odd procession entered the hall, Nakor leading the band with the falcon perched boldly upon his arm. When at last they reached the dais, they bowed, and Lakeisha half-rose from her throne. "What insanity is this?" Her eyes swept the party below her and suddenly she became aware that Borric stood beside his brother. "You—unless I'm sadly mistaken—are supposed to be dead."

Nirome attempted to speak, "Majesty, these criminals—"

Ghuda rested his blade on the stout man's shoulder, saying, "It's not polite to speak until you're given permission." To the Empress he said, "Sorry, mum. Continue if you please."

Lakeisha seemed to sense some mysteries were about to be unraveled and chose not to take offense. "Thank you," she said drily. To Nakor she said, "Let's begin with you, little man. You know that to possess the royal falcon is a sentence of death."

Nakor grinned. "Yes, Empress. But I do not possess this bird. I am merely providing the falcon transport to your august self. I'm just bringing you a birthday present." Without waiting for permission, the audacious little Isalani mounted the dais and crossed to the throne. The two black-clad Izmali bodyguards moved to block his approach, but he veered past the throne. Behind the throne was the empty sun symbol. He set the bird atop it and the falcon flapped his wings.

The Empress said, "Only a male can perch upon the royal sun, Isalani."

"Nakor understand, Empress. This one is a boy. He will father many falcon hatchlings for you. I caught him last spring in the mountains west of Tao Zi. There are a few more up there, too. If you send your Imperial falconer, he can bring them to the mews. The line will be revived."

Since the death of her daughter, the Empress had not smiled. Now she smiled. Something in the little man's words touched her, and she knew he was speaking not only of the rare birds, but of the Royal House as well. "This is a gift of stunning splendor."

Stopping next to the throne before descending the steps to the floor below, Nakor leaned down and said, "It would be a very wise thing if you were to believe the twin boys, for those two over there" —he indicated Nirome and Toren Sie—"are very bad men."

The Empress studied the tableau below then at last said, "Prince Erland, why don't you begin and we can start to sort out this mess."

Erland and Borric held the undivided attention of everyone in the chamber as they wove together their separate accounts, attempting to make sense of all that had transpired since the desert raid. They spoke without interruption for nearly a quarter-hour. As Erland concluded his account of the events leading up to their arrival in the chamber, he said, "And the last thing that convinced me Nirome was responsible for Sojiana's death was his crushing a nut with his bare hand. Sojiana's neck was broken—only someone with powerful hands could accomplish the feat. Locklear is a master swordsman, but he lacked the strength." Pointing at Nirome, he said, "There is the murderer. There is the mysterious Lord Fire!"

The Empress rose and said, "My lord Nirome—"

But from the door came a cry, "Mother!"

Prince Awari entered, with a dozen officers of the army at his back, including Lords Ravi and Jaka. Coming to stand before the throne, he bowed, then said, "What is this terrible news about Sojiana?"

The Empress studied her son's face a moment, then said, "We are about to determine just that. Stay and be quiet a while. This concerns your future, as well." Returning her gaze to Nirome, she said, "I was about to ask, my lord Nirome, what you had to say regarding these charges."

The stout courtier said, "Mother of Us All—"

"Please," interrupted the Empress, "I despise that title most. Especially now."

"Most Majestic Ruler, have mercy. I did but what I thought was best for the Empire, which was to bring your son to primacy. But it was never my wish to see anyone harmed. The attempts upon Prince Borric were but a ruse, to keep the Islemen from reaching the city. We only wished to keep Sojiana's followers' attention to the north— which is why we falsified the reports of Isles' gathering to invade. But the murder of your daughter was *none* of my doing! It was Awari who sought to remove his rival."

Prince Awari went livid at that point and had his sword halfway out of its sheath before Lord Jaka put a restraining hand upon him. The Empress shouted, "Enough!" Glancing around the room, she said, "Is there any path to truth in this?" To the twins she said, "Your arguments are convincing, but where is the proof?"

She looked down at Gamina. "You can read thoughts, you say?"

Gamina nodded, but Nirome shouted, "She's the wife of an outlander, Majesty! She would lie to serve her husband and his cause is Isles!"

Gamina seemed about to respond, but the Empress said, "I doubt you would lie, my dear." She gestured around her, indicating the now full gallery above her. "But I doubt others here would be so kindly disposed to believe you. If it's not come to your notice, this is a rather tense situation."

A guard Captain in the armor of the Inner Legion hurried into the room and whispered into the ear of the Master of Ceremonies. He, in turn, made a gesture requesting permission to approach the Empress. She gave permission and he hurried up the dais.

When he was finished passing on the Captain's report, the Empress sat back. "Well, then, there you have it. We have reports now that two companies of the Household Guard are barricaded in one wing of the palace, in open defiance of orders to put down their arms, and throughout the city armed companies of men are moving.

"Now," she said, rising from her throne, "we are faced with armed rebellion in our own city! The Imperial Seal of Peace is upon Kesh, and the man who draws sword first, or whose retainer draws sword first, that man, be he base born or most noble lord, is under death sentence. Do I make myself clear?" The last was directed at Lord Ravi, who stood motionless.

The Empress sat again and said, "Again I am faced with betrayal and disloyalty, but have no means of discerning the truth."

Nakor cleared his throat pointedly.

"Yes?" said Lakeisha. "What is it?"

"Empress, there is an ancient Isalani means of determining the truth of a thing."

"I would be pleased to know what it is."

Grinning, Nakor said to Ghuda, "Bring the fat lord out here, before the dais." As the mercenary did so, Nakor put his rucksack on the ground and began rummaging in it. After a moment of searching, he said, "Ah!" and pulled something out.

All near to him reflexively stepped back, for in his hands he held a cobra of stunning beauty and impossible proportions. The snake was easily six feet in length and as thick as a man's forearm. The back scales were the gold of beaten metal, and the inside of the hood and throat were the green of the darkest and most vivid emerald. Eyes like fire opals, blue-black with red flame dancing in them regarded the crowd, which muttered with astonishment. A blood-red tongue flicked in and out of its mouth. Then it opened its mouth with a loud and ominous hiss, revealing two terrible-looking fangs of ivory. It writhed and hissed again as Nakor set it down on the floor in front of Nirome. The courtier shrank back against the steps of the dais as Nakor said, "This is the Truth Snake of Sha-shú. To lie before him is to embrace death." With a cheery note to Nirome, he added, "It's very painful."

The serpent slithered to Nirome's feet then raised itself up, so that it appeared to look the stout trueblood lord in the eyes. The broad hood flared out and silver sparkles danced on its golden back.

Nakor said, "The snake will not strike so long as you speak truth. One falsehood and you die. There is no warning. It is infallible."

Nirome could barely move, he was so mesmerized by the swaying serpent that rose up before him. Then when it was but a foot away, he said, "Enough! I will tell all! I planned this from the beginning."

Several members of the Gallery spoke in hushed whispers. The Empress said, "What was Awari's part in this?"

His fear turning to anger, Nirome turned to face his Empress. "Awari! A strutting peacock and a fool. He thought I was but seeking to bolster his claim. I was going to place blame upon Awari for Sojiana's death, or at least cast enough suspicion that no one would accept him as heir to the throne."

"So," said the Empress sitting back in her throne, "you would put Sharana in my place. But why?"

Nirome said, "Because Ravi and his allies would never accept another Empress. The southern nations are ready to rebel once more and with the Brothers of the Horse holding the pass through the Girdle of Kesh, Lesser Kesh would be lost for all times. And Lord Jaka and the other truebloods would never accept a nontrueblood consort. So there was only one solution."

Lakeisha nodded. "Obviously. Marry Sharana to one who is heir. Make her husband Emperor upon my death." She sighed. "And who better but the Great Conciliator, Lord Nirome. The only member of the Gallery without enemies? The one man able to speak to trueblood and nontrueblood alike?"

The Empress covered her face with her hands, and for a moment it appeared as if she might be weeping. When she at last removed her hands, her eyes were indeed red-rimmed, but no sign of tears could be seen. "How have we come to this, that our best plot for their own aggrandizement, and not for the well-being of the Empire." She sighed loudly and said, "My lord Ravi. Would this plan have worked?"

The Master of the Brothers of the Horse bowed. "Mistress, I fear the traitor was correct. Until this evening, we believed the Prince, your son, to have been the one responsible for Sojiana's death. We would not have accepted Sharana as our mistress, but we would not have allowed one who has spilled royal blood to command us. Nirome would have been the logical compromise."

The Empress seemed to lose her strength, so far back into the throne did she slump. "Ai-eee!" she half-screamed. "All is tumbling toward the pit! All trembles on the brink of chaos, but for the kind fortune that sent these two boys to our court!"

Erland said, "Majesty! If I may ask a boon?"

Lakeisha said, "You have been as wronged as any here, it seems, Prince Erland. What is your wish?"

"A question of Nirome." To the trembling lord he said, "Locklear has been branded with the murder of Sojiana. I told you that only a man with powerful arms and hands could have broken her neck in such a fashion. Did you kill her and cast the blame upon my friend?"

Nirome gazed at the hovering serpent and barely whispered, "Yes."

James said, "Where is Locklear?"

Attempting to sink even farther back into the stone steps, Nirome said, "He is dead. His body is hidden in a grain room in the lower levels."

Gamina's eyes began to brim with tears and James and the twins all looked stricken at the news. They had known against all hope that Locklear was most likely murdered, but until they had actually heard the news they had held out hope. Borric was the first to speak. "Majesty, I know that Kesh had no part in the death of one of our Ambassadors. The Kingdom of the Isles will demand no reparation." He spoke calmly, but everyone close to him could see the tears that were gathering in his eyes.

Rising, the Empress turned to look at the assembled Gallery. "Hear my judgment!" Pointing at Nirome, she said, "This man, by his own words, has condemned himself." Turning to stare at the traitor, she said, "Nirome, lord no longer, by your own words you have confessed your evil and for this you shall die."

The stout man stiffened and said, "I demand my right to die at my own hands!"

"You shall demand nothing!" spat the Empress. "You are not of the blood from this moment forward. There will be no sweet death as you drift into intoxicated oblivion from a gentle poison, no lightly cut wrists in a hot bath as you drift away into eternal sleep.

"In ancient times a punishment was decreed for those who betrayed their kings and queens. It has not been pronounced in centuries, but it shall be now. Nirome, this is to be your fate: you are to remain in a cell this night, to dwell upon your wrongdoing and your coming death, and at every beating of the quarter-hour, a guard shall repeat this sentence aloud to you, so you may have no rest. Then at dawn, you are to be taken to the temple, and there shall the guard read your sentence to the High Priest of Guis-wa, so that the Red-Jawed Hunter will hear that you are not worthy of a place in the Eternal Hunt. Then you shall be taken to the base of the plateau and stripped naked. Then shall a dozen guards of the trueblood whip you and run you through the city. Should you fall, they shall apply hot coals to your buttocks, until you rise and run again. At the gates of the city you will be hung in a cage, and your sentence will be read aloud by guards upon the hour, so that all passing may hear of your crimes. Even the lowest shall be offered sticks of bamboo with which to torment you, so you may feel the wrath of those you betrayed, yet you shall endure and no one shall grant you merciful death. When you are near unto death from exposure, you shall be taken from the cage and revived with water made bitter with vinegar and bread covered with salt. You shall be driven by lash and hot coals to the edge of the Overn Deep, to the marshes where the first Kings of the trueblood hunted. There you shall be made to drink the bitter wine of betrayal and eat the rotten meat of treason. Then shall your manhood be cut from your body. You shall then be bound and thrown into the marsh, where the crocodiles of the Overn shall devour your flesh.

"In every royal decree and record of your time among us, your name shall be stricken so that no one shall ever speak it again. In its place will be written 'one who betrayed his nation,' and the name Nirome will be forbidden to children of the trueblood from this day forward. In time, even the gods will not know who you were. And in the black void of the nameless and forgotten will your soul endure eternal confinement, alone.

"This, then, is my decree!"

The Master of Ceremonies called out, "She Who Is Kesh has spoken! Now, let it be done!"

Guards hurried forward and hesitated as they reached the cobra. Nakor motioned that the snake wouldn't touch them, and the guards seized the terrified Nirome. "No!" he screamed as they dragged him from the court, and his cries echoed through the halls.

The Empress said to Toren Sie, "You, my onetime friend, shall name every accomplice in this plot and perhaps I shall be kind to you: a quick death or perhaps even mere banishment. Otherwise you shall follow your friend in humiliation and pain."

Lord Toren Sie bowed and said, "Your Majesty is merciful. I shall reveal all."

As he was led away, the Empress motioned to Nakor. "Do something with that."

The grinning wizard hurried over and said, "This, Empress?" He reached down and grabbed the cobra around the middle, and when he stood, there was only a long strand of cord in his hands. "This is just a piece of rope."

He coiled the line and put it back in his rucksack. Erland's eyes were wide, but Borric said, "It's only a trick."

Chapter Eighteen
Triumph

The servant bowed.

Borric, Erland, and their companions entered a small garden, and the servant bade them sit upon soft cushions surrounding a wondrous table, with all manner of delicacies and a choice of fine wines. A cold pitcher of lager and a warm pitcher of ale were the choices of Ghuda and Nakor respectively, and the guests began without their hostess.

When the Empress entered, carried in a sedan chair, all began to rise. She gestured for them to remain where they were. "There are so few occasions I can manage a little informality, I relish those times. Sit, sit." The servants who carried the chair placed it at the head of the low table and removed the long poles that they used to carry it.

Sharana entered a moment later, and came to sit between her grandmother and Erland. She smiled at Borric, who looked her over with open and frank appraisal. Borric now wore his own clothing, from among those bags not stolen by the raiders in the desert. His hair was its own natural color, the dye having been washed out with some foul-smelling lotion that Nakor provided. Ghuda and the little wizard wore fine robes provided for the occasion by the Empress's staff.

"I wanted a little informal chat before we return to this miserable business of the Jubilee. I can't believe we'll have to endure another four-and-a-half weeks of it."

Erland said, "I was somewhat surprised that you ordered it continued, Majesty."

The old woman smiled. "Nirome's plotting would be nothing

compared to the troubles I'd start if I tried to cancel the festivities, Erland. The Lords and Masters might wish land or power, but the common man of the Empire merely wants his fun. If we tried to take it away from him, we'd have blood in the streets. You've the look of a common enough fellow, Ghuda Bulé. Isn't that true?"

Ghuda, uncomfortable at being this close to such powerful and important people, said, "This is true, Majesty. Most men won't give you much trouble if they get food to eat, a roof over their head, a good woman now and again, and some fun along the way. Too much bother, otherwise."

The Empress laughed. "A philosopher. And a serious one." To the others she said, "Didn't even notice I was having fun with him." She sighed. "I think I may have lost the knack of fun."

Looking at Ghuda, she said, "So then, what is your reward to be for helping save our Empire?"

Now Ghuda looked terribly embarrassed, and Borric said, "He was promised ten thousand golden ecu, by me, Majesty."

"Done," she said. "And again that much from our treasury. How would you like to stay on and help run my Inner Legion, Ghuda? I have many openings for officers, and more to come as Toren Sie confesses."

Ghuda smiled weakly, uncomfortable to be refusing such an offer, but he said, "I am sorry, Your Majesty, but I think I'm going to take the money and open an inn, in Jandowae maybe. The weather's nice there, and there's not much trouble. I'll get a couple of pretty serving girls and maybe even marry one of them and have some sons. I'm getting too old for travel and adventure."

The Empress smiled warmly and said, "I envy you your modest ambitions, warrior. You'll do well telling your stories around the taproom in the evening. But you have my debt and should you ever need an ear at court, send word and I'll listen."

Ghuda inclined his head and said, "Your Majesty."

"What about you, little man?" she said to Nakor. "What can we do to thank you for your part in this?"

The Isalani wiped foam from his mouth with the back of his sleeve and said, "Could I have a horse? A large black horse maybe? And a fine blue robe to wear when I ride her?"

The Empress laughed and said, "A thousand horses if that is what you want."

Nakor grinned. "No, just one will do, thank you, Empress. It's difficult to ride more than one at a time. But one beautiful black horse and a grand blue robe would once again make me Nakor the Blue Rider. That would be a fine thing."

"Anything else? Gold? A court appointment?"

Reaching into his rucksack, Nakor pulled out a deck of playing cards. Riffling them, he said, "As long as I have my cards, I don't need gold. And if I take an appointment at court, I won't have time to ride my black horse. Thank you, Empress, but no."

The Empress regarded the two men and said, "The two most refreshingly original characters to walk into the palace in my life and I can't keep either of you around. Very well," she said, with a hint of humor. "But if I were Sharana's age still, I'd find a way to keep you here."

Everyone laughed at that. The Empress said, "Lord James, I'm sorry to turn the conversation to more serious matters, but we've located the body of your companion. Baron Locklear will be made ready to return to Krondor and a guard of honor shall escort him to his father's estates at Land's End. The Empire stands ready to make any reparation your King may ask. He was a noble of the Kingdom and our guest; his safety was in our hands and we let him come to harm."

James said, "I think Prince Arutha and the King will both understand." He looked thoughtful for a moment. "We knew coming down here there would be risks. It's the price we pay for our privileges."

The Empress regarded him with a penetrating look. "You Islemen are a strange lot. You take very seriously your concept of the obligations of the nobility and the Great Freedom."

James shrugged. "The Great Freedom gives even the most lowborn rights the nobles cannot abridge. Even the King is not above the law."

"Brrr," said the Empress with a mock shiver. "That gives me a chill. The idea of not being able to command what I wish is . . . alien."

Borric smiled. "We are different. Erland and I, each in our own way, have learned many things by coming here, being among 'aliens.'" Regarding the lovely Princess, whose thin robe hid none of her physical beauty, Borric drily added, "Though by most any measure, I suspect my brother's lessons were by far the more pleasant."

Erland said, "What is to happen now? I mean with you and your son?"

The Empress said, "Awari has always been a strong-headed boy. That's the reason he is not the man to guide Kesh when I am dead."

James looked at Sharana. "So the Princess will be named your heir?"

"No," said the Empress. "As much as I love her, Sharana does not have the temper to govern. Perhaps if I lived another twenty years, she might learn enough, but I doubt I'll survive half that." Sharana began to protest that she would, and the Empress waved her off. "Enough. I'm seventy-five years old and I'm tired. You have no idea what tired can be until you've had the weight of over five million people on your shoulders every day for forty-seven years. I took the throne when I was younger than your mother, may the gods give her peace. Twenty-eight years when my mother's weak heart gave out." There was a bitter note in the air as the Empress paused. "No, it's no gift I give when I name my heir." Looking at Borric, Erland, and James, she said, "If I had one of you here, then I would not fear half so much my people's future." Pointing at Erland, she said, "If I could I'd keep you here, boy, and name you my successor and marry you off to Sharana. Now wouldn't that be a fine mess." She laughed, but Erland's face showed he didn't think the subject was comic.

Seeing Erland's distress, Lakeisha said, "Girl, take him away and talk to him. You're going to be spending some more weeks together and you need have an understanding. Get along."

Sharana and Erland rose and departed, and the Empress said, "Sharana can't marry anyone but a trueblood, or we'd have a revolution here upon the plateau, and Awari would be our next Emperor. We'll barely have enough support as it is."

James considered what he knew of the court, then said, "So you're going to marry her to Diigaí?"

The Empress's eyes went round in obvious pleasure. "Oh, you are a clever one. I do wish I could keep you here, but I'm sure your King would object." Looking at Gamina, she added, "With a lady at your side who can read the thoughts of those you negotiate with . . . what a treasure you would be, my lord James. I must remember to have you banned for life from the Empire. You're too dangerous to allow back here."

James couldn't tell if she was joking. "Yes," she continued. "I'm going to marry her to Lord Jaka's eldest. No trueblood, save Awari and perhaps a handful of his most ardent followers, will object to Diigaí being the next to sit upon the Throne of Light. And with his father's sage council, he will grow to rule wisely."

Looking off to where Erland and Sharana had disappeared, the Empress said, "All ends well, I think." To Borric she said, "I know that when you become ruler in Isles, you'll have at your side a brother who will always remember this court with some affection. And in Diigaí, Kesh will have a ruler who will feel obligation to your house." Borric inclined his head in acknowledgment. James had told him of Diigaí and the lion and Erland's part in that.

Borric said, "I hope, that as long as I rule in Isles, Kesh will count us her friendly neighbor to the north."

Tapping her fingers upon the arm of her sedan chair, Lakeisha said, "I hope that is so. I fear we shall have trouble with our more fractious subjects south of the Girdle. Lesser Kesh wears its yoke poorly."

"If I may suggest," said James, "remove the yoke, Majesty. There are many able men who would serve you with their life's blood if needs be, but because they are not trueblood they are denied the highest ranks in court. There was never a more vigorous servant and brilliant mind in Kesh's employ than your late Ambassador Hazara-Khan, and the man who has been our guide lately, Lord Abu Harez, puts me much in mind of him. To limit such a man from serving you because of his ancestry . . . seems a waste."

The Empress said, "It may be you're right. But there are limits, my lord. Old ways die hard and there are men in my service, blood kin, who would die rather than see such changes. And our position is not, at this moment, what I would call the best. I have no idea how much my son was in league with Nirome, but if he truly was ignorant of what Nirome was apparently doing on his behalf, it was because he chose to be blind, deaf, and mute.

"No, revolutionary changes cannot be considered."

James said, "Be warned, then. I fear that revolution is the only alternative."

The Empress was silent for a long time, then at last said, "I will think on this. I'm not dead yet. There might still be time."

All fell silent around the table; each hoped that would be the case.

Erland held the girl's hand tightly as he said, "What does your grandmother mean, 'need have an understanding'?"

Sharana said, "She knows how much I enjoy having you in bed with me. But I need to spend less time with you in public."

"Why?"

"I'm going to wed Lord Jaka's son, Diigaí. Grandmother's decided that. The rebellious lords will get their male ruler and the trueblood will get their trueblood Emperor. He's a cousin, you know, so it's still in the family."

Erland looked away for a moment. "I knew it was impossible for us to remain together . . . yet somehow . . ."

"What?"

"I love you, Sharana. I shall always love you."

The girl pulled Erland around and kissed him passionately. "I am very fond of you, Erland. It will be good to know you are so close to the throne of Isles when I sit at the Emperor's side."

Erland felt disappointed his statement hadn't provoked a more enthusiastic response. "I said I love you."

"Yes," said Sharana, with wide eyes fixed upon him. "I heard you."

"Doesn't that mean anything to you?"

"Of course it does. It's very nice. I just said so. What else did you have in mind?"

"Nice?" Erland turned around from her for a moment, feeling icy pains in his stomach. "Nothing, I guess."

She pulled him back around and said, "Stop this. You're being very strange. You said you love me. I said I'm fond of you. That's all very nice. You act as if something is wrong between us."

Erland laughed and said, "Nothing is wrong. Just the woman I love is going to marry another man."

Sharana said, "You say 'woman I love' as if you will not love anyone else again."

"That's the way I feel."

"That's a silly way to feel, Erland." The girl took his hand and put it upon her breast. "Feel my heart. Can you feel the beat?"

He nodded, feeling heat rise in his body at the softness of her under his hand. "I have much room in there for many people. I love my grandmother, and my mother and father when they lived. I even love my uncle, though he is a strange man at times. I've loved other boys before you and I will love others as well. Loving one takes nothing away from the others. Can you see?"

Erland shook his head. "I guess our ways are too different. You're going to marry another, yet you talk of other loves."

"Why not? I'll be Empress and will love anyone I find worthy. It will be the same with Diigaí. Many trueblood women will want to sleep with him. To have an Emperor's child is a very special thing."

Erland laughed. "I guess I just don't understand you. Anyway, I won't cause any difficulty with you and Diigaí."

She looked puzzled. "Difficulty? I don't know what you mean. I shall have to spend a few nights with him, so he gets used to the idea of being husband to the Empress's granddaughter. And if he is to be named heir I must spend most of my public time with him. But I will have most of my nights for you while you're with us. If you still wish to come to me."

Erland felt more conflict than he could remember ever having. Then he laughed and said, "I don't know. But I think I would have trouble staying away."

Moving sensuously under his hand, she rubbed against him and gripped him tightly to her. "I thought you might." She kissed him and said, "Tell me, are you and your brother very much alike?"

He stepped back from her, then laughed aloud. "In most ways. But there are some things we just *will not* share!"

Sharana pouted. "Pity. It could have provided some interesting possibilities."

At the city gates of Kesh the mounted escorts were ready. Borric, Erland, and their party rode down the last boulevard to the edge of the town. Near the city gate, the metal cage that had held Nirome swung empty, a grim reminder of the fate of traitors. The former trueblood noble had hung there for almost two days, enduring the taunts and prodding of anyone who passed by and chose to stop and add to his torment. And there were many who relished the idea of seeing a trueblood noble brought low.

Nearly a thousand people had lined the streets as he had been taken from the cage, forced to eat salted bread and drink vinegar mixed with water, then was whipped like a beast out to the marshes on the edge of the great Overn Deep. There he was mutilated and cast to the crocodiles, while hundreds of citizens cheered. Erland and Borric had declined the invitation to watch the spectacle. Prince Awari had watched, and no one was certain if it was to witness justice or to hear if Nirome would implicate more of Awari's followers. There was a strong feeling that somehow the stout noble had died still holding secrets within.

At the gate, the newly named Prince Diigaí waited in his chariot, with Sharana at his side. She now wore the short kilt and golden torque of her rank, and waited formally next to her future husband. Behind, ranks of Keshian nobles waited to bid farewell to their royal guests.

Lord Jaka came forward and reined in his chariot next to his son's. Erland halted and said, "Good day, my lords, Prince and Princess."

Sharana smiled warmly at Erland. "Good day, Your Highness."

Borric said, "We are pleased you felt moved to come see us upon our way."

Diigaí said, "Your Highness, we are much in your debt. If we can ever repay you, you have but to ask."

Borric bowed. "You are gracious, Highness. We hope the friendship we have begun here shall endure."

Sharana said, "I shall miss you, Erland."

Feeling himself coloring a little, he replied, "I shall miss you as well, Princess."

Then Sharana said, "And while we have known each other only briefly, I shall miss you as well, Borric."

Erland's eyes narrowed as he turned to look at his brother. "What—"

Borric said, "Good-bye, dear friends," and spurred his horse forward. Instantly the dozen Krondorian Palace Guards moved out and Erland was left sitting behind.

"Wait a minute!" shouted Erland, spurring his horse on after his brother's. "I want to talk to you!"

As the company moved out, James turned and found Nakor moving up to ride beside him. As they left the city gate and entered the road to Khattara, James said, "Nakor, you're coming with us?"

The little man smiled. "For a while. I fear things will become dull in Kesh when Borric and his brother leave. Already Ghuda is bound for Jandowae and the inn he will build. It is lonely when you don't know people."

James nodded at that. "What about Stardock? Have you thought of going there?"

"Bah! An island of magicians? Who could have fun there?"

"Perhaps they need someone to teach them fun?"

"Maybe. But I think that someone is someone other than Nakor the Blue Rider."

James laughed. "Why don't you come with us until Stardock, spend a little time there, and decide later."

"Maybe. But I don't think I'm going to like it."

James thought for a while, and became certain of something. "Do you know of Pug the Magician?"

"Pug is famous. He is a very powerful magician. He works arts like none since Macros the Black. I am a very poor man who knows some simple tricks. See, I would not like it there."

James smiled. "He said something. He said that if I ever needed speak for him, on his behalf, then I should say this thing."

"Something you think will make me want to go to Stardock?" said the little man with a grin. "This must be something very wondrous."

"I am convinced he somehow knew I would meet you, or someone like you, someone who would bring a different perspective to magic than anyone else at Stardock, and he felt that it was important. I think that is why he had me remember these words: there is no magic."

Nakor laughed. He seemed genuinely amused. "Pug the Magician said that?"

"Yes."

"Then," said Nakor, "he is a very smart man for a magician."

"You'll go to Stardock?"

Nakor nodded. "Yes. I think you are right. Pug wanted me to go there and knew you would need to tell me this thing to make me go."

Gamina had been riding silently beside her husband and at last she said, "Father often knew things before others. I think he knew that if left to their own devices, the Academy of Magicians would grow introspective and isolated."

"Magicians like caves," agreed Nakor.

James said, "Then do me one courtesy."

"What?"

"Tell me what 'there is no magic' means."

Nakor's face screwed up in concentration. "Stop," he said. James, Gamina, and Nakor moved their horses out of line and halted by the roadside, just beyond the boundary of the city. Nakor reached into his rucksack and pulled out three oranges. "Can you juggle?"

"A little," said James.

Nakor tossed the three oranges to him. "Juggle."

James, who had always had dexterity bordering on the supernatural, caught the three oranges and propelled them upward, and quickly was juggling them while holding his horse steady: no mean feat. Then Nakor said, "Can you do it with your eyes closed?"

James tried to get it into a rhythm as even as possible and closed his eyes. He had to force himself not to open his eyes and yet every instant he felt as if the next orange would not land in the palm of his left hand.

"Now, do it with one hand."

James's eyes opened and the oranges fell to the ground. "What?"

"I said you were to juggle with one hand."

"Why?"

"It's a trick. Do you see?"

290

James said, "I'm not sure."

"Juggling is a trick. It is not magic. But if you don't know how to do it, it looks like magic. That is why people toss coins to jugglers at the fair. When you can do it with one hand, you're learning something." Then he spurred his horse on and said, "And when you can do it without using your hands, you'll understand what Pug meant."

Arutha and Anita stood before their thrones as their sons marched into the court in Krondor. In the four months since the boys had left their court, the Prince and Princess of Krondor had felt pain and joy at news of Borric's loss and his return. And they felt an empty place within that matched the empty place in court where Baron Locklear should have been.

The twins came to stand before their parents and both bowed formally. Arutha couldn't put his finger on it, but something in them was different. He had sent boys south to deal with Kesh and young men had returned. They were now confident where they had been brash, decisive where they had been impulsive, and in their eyes was an echo of loss, of seeing the results of vicious and hateful acts. Arutha had read the reports that hard-riding dispatch riders had carried ahead of the returning Princes, but now he understood them.

So that all could hear, he said, "It pleases us that our sons have returned. The Princess and I welcome them back to our court."

Then he stepped down from the dais and embraced Borric, then Erland. Anita came behind and hugged both fiercely, lingering a bit when she held Borric's cheek next to her own. Then Elena and Nicholas were there to greet them, and Borric held his sister close to him, saying, "After those Keshian noblewomen, you are a simple and rare treasure."

"Simple!" she said, pushing him away. "I like that!" Grinning at Erland, she said, "You must tell me about the ladies of the Keshian court. Everything. What did they wear?"

Borric and Erland exchanged glances and started to laugh. Borric said, "I don't think you'll be starting any fashions here, little sister. Keshian ladies wear almost no clothing at all. While Erland and I found it very attractive, I think Father would take one look at you in Keshian court regalia and have you locked away in your room forever."

Elena blushed. "Well, tell me everything anyway. We're going to have a wedding celebration for Baron James and I'll want something different."

Nicholas had been quietly waiting next to his father, and Borric and Erland as one noticed him. "Hello, little brother," said Borric. He bent down hands on knees so he could look Nicholas in the eyes. "Have you been well?"

Nicholas threw his arms around Borric's neck and began to cry. "They said you were dead. I knew you couldn't be, but they said you were. I was so scared."

Erland felt tears come unbidden to his own eyes and he uncharacteristically reached out and pulled Elena into his arms, hugging her again. Anita wept for joy, as did Elena, and even Arutha was hard-pressed to keep a dry eye.

After a moment, Borric picked up the boy and said, "That's enough, Nicky. We're both just fine."

Erland said, "Yes, we are. And we missed you."

Nicholas wiped away his tears and said, "You did?"

"Yes, we did," answered Borric. "I met a boy in Kesh who was only a few years older than you. He made me understand just how much I did miss my little brother."

Nicholas said, "What's his name?"

"His name was Suli Abul," said Borric with a tear running down his face.

"That's a strange name," said Nicholas. "What happened to him?"

"I'll tell you about him."

"When?" said Nicholas with the impatience of most seven-year-old boys.

Borric put the boy down. "Maybe in a day or two, we'll take a boat out of the harbor and go fishing. Would you like that?"

Nicholas nodded his head emphatically, and Erland tousled his hair.

Arutha motioned for James to come away from the others and then when they were off a little way, Duke Gardan joined them.

Arutha said, "First of all, I'll want to talk to you at length tomorrow. But from your reports, I think we owe you thanks."

James said, "It was something that needed to be done. Really, the boys deserve most of the credit. If Borric had returned to Krondor rather than risk his life trying to catch up with us, or had Erland not been so quick to see through some very clever ruses . . . who knows what harm could have come of it?"

Arutha put his hand on James's shoulder. "It's become something of a joke between us about you being named Duke of Krondor someday, hasn't it?"

James smiled. "Yes, but I still want the job."

Gardan, his seamed face showing disbelief, said, "After all you've just been through, you still want to sit at the right hand of power?"

James glanced at the happy faces in the court and said, "There's nowhere else I'd rather be."

Arutha said, "Good. Because I have something to tell you. Gardan is finally retiring."

James's eyes widened. "Then . . ."

"No," said Arutha. "I'm offering the post of Duke of Krondor to Earl Geoffery of Ravenswood, who's serving in Rillanon with Lyam's First Advisor."

James's eyes narrowed. "What are you saying, Arutha?"

The Prince smiled his crooked smile and James felt his stomach turn cold. "When the festivities of your wedding celebration are over, my dear Jimmy," said Arutha, "you and your lady are bound for Rillanon. You are to take Geoffery's place as second in command to Duke Guy of Rillanon." He grinned, one of the rare occasions James had ever seen him do that. "And who knows, when Borric is at last King, he may make you Duke of Rillanon."

Motioning for his wife to come to his side, James slipped his arm around her waist and with a dry note said, "Amos Trask is right about you, you know. You do take the fun out of life."